THE FIREBRAND

PRAISE FOR THE FIREBRAND

"The tale of King Arthur has been told by so many authors, and in so many ways, that it might seem difficult to do anything new with it. Yet Debra Kemp has succeeded. She confronts a question that isn't often considered. Why is so little said about Arthur's children? In *The House of Pendragon* we meet one that we haven't met before-his daughter, Lin. We follow her strange career from slavery to possible succession as Arthur's heir. This well-told and very original story adds a fascinating newcomer to the legend's immortal company."

—Geoffrey Ashe

"Throughout the year I get asked on many occasions to revue either film scripts or forthcoming books that deal with the subject of King Arthur and The Holy Grail, some are good, many are dire, few are excellent. When I started reading *The House Of Pendragon* I felt that perhaps this was going to fit into the latter category, I was not disappointed. Ms. Kemp deals with the subject of Arthurian Britain in a style normally adopted for modern issues, it is refreshing to read what I can only describe as a 'Warts and all' account of life in the period we call The Dark Ages. This book does not give us the heavily romanced tales that many do, thank heavens, instead it gives us a gritty and definitely adult view of the struggles in Britain at the time of Arthur, 'The Bear.' Only too often we are served with over-sentimental offerings that scarcely hide plagiarism from Thomas Mallory or 'New Age' books that borrow heavily from the superb work of Marion Bradley. Here at last we have a fresh approach, a glimpse of struggles and realism so often denied us and yet, still written with a modern audience in mind. Highly readable, highly enjoyable and highly recommended."

—Prof. Dr. Roland Rotherham

"Debra Kemp has created a lively, compelling expansion to the tales of King Arthur and Camelot in her debut novel, *The House of Pendragon I: The Firebrand.* Here she introduces the spirited and stubborn Lin, an unknown daughter of Arthur's. Ignorant of her birthright, Lin becomes an unwitting link in the vengeful plotting of her father's enemies, Queen Morgause and her son Modred. Though only wishing to maintain simple dignity amidst hatred, injustice and cruelty, Lin proves that her remarkable heritage is truly a part of her. With finely crafted characters and originality, Kemp skillfully blends history, legend and fiction in a story that illuminates one of the darkest corners of the Arthurian legend."

—Kathleen Cunningham Guler,
Author of *In the Shadow of Dragons*

THE HOUSE OF PENDRAGON
BOOK I

THE FIREBRAND

BY

DEBRA A. KEMP

AMBER QUILL PRESS, LLC
http://www.amberquill.com

THE FIREBRAND
AN AMBER QUILL PRESS BOOK

This book is a work of fiction. All names, characters, locations, and incidents are products of the author's imagination, or have been used fictitiously. Any resemblance to actual persons living or dead, locales, or events is entirely coincidental.

Amber Quill Press, LLC
http://www.amberquill.com

ISBN 1-59279-883-7

Layout and Formatting provided by: ElementalAlchemy.com

PUBLISHED IN THE UNITED STATES OF AMERICA

To Bill, David and Missy,
who put up with so much. And to my little "Honey,"
our Once and Future Queen Bee.

Thanks to the gang, especially LP and DH.
This humble scribe could not have
done it without you.

Thanks to the Black Hills Writers group
and my faithful critiquers.
I love you guys.

Last, I need to extend a very special
"thank you" to Bill. You have always believed in me,
even when I doubted. And you
never let me give up.

CHAPTER 1

I had no idea what hour it was. The sun had set a lifetime ago and thick clouds obscured any moonlight. Battle weary and with heavy hearts, we picked our way from the river in the dark, our joyless task compleated. My four companions formed an escort around me. They knew what I thought of protocol, but I fell in step with the men simply because I was of no heart to argue. The only sounds were the lapping water behind us and our boots crunching the earth.

Odd, such stillness after the mayhem of battle.

When we reached the supply wagons and cooking fires, Dafydd hurried ahead without a word and disappeared into the crowd of soldiers and servants awaiting our return. I noticed immediately that an unnatural hush hung over the entire encampment, like a pall. I saw none of the usual camaraderie or back-slapping, heard none of the light-hearted banter normally present after victory. But my father's men were a special breed, cut from finer fabric. To a man, they snapped smartly to the instant I appeared. I acknowledged their salute with an "at ease" and hurried on my way.

Camlann a victory? Camlann was nothing short of internecine. Not Britanni against Saxon this time. We had all been part of the same army mere months ago. Yet this morning we had faced each other in the twilight mist, astride our battle steeds, in full armour, lances couched, anxious for the signals to be given, the battle cries to be sung, and have at each other. Men who had once been friends met as mortal enemies and slaughtered everything that moved in their paths. Who are the victors in civil strife?

Wfft. What had made us so bloodthirsty?

I saw a different question in the eyes of the men through the smoky firelight as we swept past; the man they had expected to see, the one their eyes sought, the one they had waited for, was not among us. We had lost our king as well as the Round Table. Modred, my half-brother, had driven a pike through Britain's heart. And as my father's heir, the duty fell on me to tell them. But not now. Instead, I announced to my companions that I would meet with everyone for reports after I had changed.

Bedwyr barked out orders and the place seemed to come back to life. Of a sort. I trusted him and the others to know what must be done, and do it, as my father had. *He* would have addressed the men first most likely, but my father was the Pendragon, and I never would come close to being his equal.

I was not the least surprised to see Dafydd lighting the last of my lanterns when I lifted my tent's flap a moment later. He even had water ready so I could wash.

He offered to undo the laces of my armour, but I declined.

"At least let me help you with this." Dafydd grasped the shield still hanging from my shoulder.

Why had I bothered to retrieve it?

I accepted his assistance without a word.

Dafydd regarded me. Impossible to hide my emotions from him. He knew my heart was shattered. I knew he wanted to offer comfort. But if I allowed myself his embrace now, I would crumble.

"Later, Dafydd," I said.

"You do not bear this alone, Noble One."

"I know. Thank you."

After he left, I stared into the steaming basin. Tor must have had the kettles over the fire hours ago.

I felt dirty far beyond the filth covering me from crown to toe. I needed purifying to my soul and I doubted there was enough water in the Irish Sea for that. Even so, I would not have turned down the opportunity for a prolonged soak in the Great Bath of Aquae Sulis had it been offered. Anything to avoid the grim duty hovering just beyond the walls of my tent.

My muscles screamed in protest as I peeled away layers of armour and clothing. Through years of habit, I inspected woollen and leather tunics, then my *lorica*, and last the wide belt lined and padded with fleece as each came off. All stiff with dried blood and mud. Most were beyond repair.

Naked to the waist, I noticed a small wound just beneath my left collar-bone. No wonder it pained me. As I dabbed at the area, I recalled the arrow burrowing in. I must have shorn off the shaft with my shield so it would not be in my way as I slashed and hacked in the battle frenzy. When had I pushed it through?

But other than that, and an assortment of minor cuts and bruises, I was not seriously damaged. I was in much better shape, in fact, than my clothing attested.

Then I saw my feet and a wave of nausea rolled my guts. By the gods. What had I done? I had no desire to touch my boots. Had no wish to touch what remained of the men who had fallen beneath my sword. *My* sword. Drawn without thought to kill an adder slithering towards my horse. I had meant no more harm than that. I sank to my cot and waited for my stomach to settle. Waited for my hands to stop shaking so I could finish undressing. What I would have given for a stiff drink. Wine, ale, *uisge beatha* Anything.

Ballocks. Why can Bedwyr not address the men? He would know what to say. True. But what made me believe that his pain and grief were any less than mine? Addressing the soldiers was my duty now. I could no more walk away from it without so much as a by-your-leave than I could bring my father back. They had a right to expect my father's heir, not the weakling I had become, too much the coward to face them. Yet I had no idea what I should say. That Arthur, the Pendragon, was gone? Unthinkable. Once the Saxons caught wind of the day's disaster, they would be on us like a pack of starving wolves on an unsuspecting doe. And if not the Saxons, then all our fickle allies would descend like carrion crows, with Camelot as the feast.

If my father could not depend on the aid of his fellow countrymen as the Pendragon, what chance in *Annwn* did I have?

Between the Saxons and Britain's own people, Camelot would be torn to shreds. And it would take far more than the meagre remnants of the Round Table and my father's army to prevent such calamity. What could I possibly hope to achieve in my father's wake?

I tossed the damp cloth I had been using to bathe with into the basin and filthy water splashed over the sides onto the table.

My bath finished, I had exhausted my excuses for procrastination. I dressed in the clothes Dafydd had set out for me. The softness of the clean wool gave me pause as I slipped into trews and tunic. Such lovely comfort. Warmth had even returned to my toes and fingers.

Right then. What to say? A lie was right out, but neither could I give the entire truth. I needed to buy Britain time and I could purchase that with hope. Quite simple, really, now that I saw it.

Resolved.

I tugged at the stiff leather of my dress boots. I wanted nothing more to do with the old pair. Those I would have Dafydd burn along with the discarded tunics.

With my wounded shoulder, my hair would prove a challenge. Easier to leave it in what was left of the braid I had woven this morning.

Is it still the same day? Year?

Finally, I wrapped a cloak around myself and reached down. Silly pillock. I had left my *fibula* in the grove. Laid it on the ground when I had removed my wrap for Father to use as an extra layer of warmth. Went off leaving it in the muck. Dolt. Well, there was nothing for that now. It was gone forever, like so much else in my life. As I had no spare with me, I draped the cloak over my shoulders, and went out.

Gaheris awaited to escort me. My kinsman held a small object in his hand that glittered as it caught the light of a nearby torch.

"Funny," he said, "what people leave laying around in the mud, wouldn't you say?"

"I was only just thinking this was lost for good, Ris. Thank you." I clasped the gold dragon, symbol of my rank, into the deep green cloth, in its place above my right breast. "Where is Dafydd?"

"With the others. Are you ready, Highness?"

"No. But I might as well have it done."

I found my trust well placed. Gaheris and the others had been busy and thorough. Everyone still able now stood in formation outside of my father's tent. The Pendragon standard, blood red silk emblazoned with the brilliant gold dragon, flew high on its pole, as it should, snapping in the brisk breeze. Obviously Bedwyr's work. I caught his gaze with a grateful smile. He gave the Latin command and all came to attention.

There were more men assembled than I imagined possible after what I had witnessed on the battlefield that afternoon. Gaheris had counted one hundred and thirty-five infantry, plus a few dozens more in the makeshift infirmary. But no further members of the Round Table had survived. Not so very long ago the *equites* of the Table had been one hundred and fifty strong. A single battle had reduced us to five.

I gazed upon that sea of faces. The last of the men loyal to my father and his dream to unite our people. I drew my courage from them and began.

"Modred is defeated. He is dead. Once again the day belongs to Arthur, the Pendragon." There was no cheering; I expected none. "You have done a faithful service to your king, fighting bravely and well today, and he sends his gratitude."

He should be here doing this. Damn you, Modred.

I thrust my emotions back down, hoping my struggle was not obvious.

"My father was wounded and has been taken to a place where he can rest and be healed." I had heard Brother Lucan speak of Heaven as such a place. A fragile truth, at best, laced with hope. Let them make of that what they will.

"Has he named you regent until he returns, Highness?" some faceless voice asked from the dark. Did these honest men even realise that the glint of steel that had sparked the battle had come from my blade? How can I dare face them?

"No," I said, my trembling hands hidden inside my cloak. "Lord Constantine remains at Camelot serving in that capacity."

"Well said," my Orkney kinsman whispered. "Bedwyr, Lancelot, and I will see to the rest. Say the same to the wounded. Take Davy and his harp with you."

I nodded.

The infirmary was better lit and I feared my emotions would betray me. I managed by keeping my words brief. This was no time for eloquence. Fancy words are for bards, not warriors. When I finished, I visited a few moments with each man individually as my father always had done, acknowledging their bravery and skills. Sharing a jest. And answering enquiries of fallen comrades. As I moved through the tent, Dafydd strummed his harp, evoking soothing chords that travelled straight to the heart.

Only after I had seen the last man did I have a physician tend to my own wounds. He poked and mashed around at the one in my shoulder, sending fresh waves of pain through my arm.

"The arrow's barb is still within you and naught of the shaft is left to push it through. Your Highness, I am afraid I shall have to cut it out."

"Never mind the apologies, man. Do it."

Wiping his hands on a cloth already stained crimson with blood, the leech turned to prepare his instruments and called for an assistant.

My mind reeled with the massive responsibility ahead of me. Bedwyr and Lancelot might have more experience, but I now held the highest rank. I tried to remember everything that Cai and Bedwyr and my father had taught me over the years. I'd had the best teachers. Why did I feel so ill-prepared?

I declined the elixir offered to dull the pain. I required a clear head. Besides, others had a greater need for that mercy.

"Dafydd?" I raised my voice so he could hear me from behind the screen that had been set up for my privacy.

"Highness?" Not so much as a pause in his chords. His public deference still rubbed me in spite of the years.

"Has anyone taken account of the horses?" Good, basics first.

"Sir Lancelot, Highness. He will make his report when you are ready."

"And what of provisions?"

I grimaced as the physician probed deeper into the wound. Pride kept me from crying my agony. Pride and everything I had learned from Modred during my years in Orkney.

The physician paused. His assistant mopped my brow.

"What are you waiting for, man? Finish."

"My apologies, your Highness."

I regretted snapping at the poor man.

"That will be Sir Gaheris," Dafydd said in answer to my earlier question.

"Lugh's cullions." I cursed more in aggravation at my own stupidity over having allowed the wound, as the leech withdrew the arrow's head.

The worst over, I began once again, "Dafydd, has—"

"Your Highness." He cut me off almost curtly. It bordered on insubordination. Anyone else—"Lord Bedwyr has been arranging things."

I should have known.

After the physician secured a bandage in place and cleansed the gash on my cheek, I thanked him as I slipped my tunic back over my head. I sat up a bit too quickly, for it brought on a wave of dizziness. When the tent stopped spinning, I stood and made my way to the tent's entrance. Halfway there, I turned back.

Dashing sweat from my brow, I said, "Dafydd? I will meet with all of you later to get your reports. My tent."

"I shall make sure the others are there, Highness."

I took the remaining steps, calling over my shoulder, "And find me something to eat. I'm famished."

"Getting more like your father by the hour," I heard him say as the tent's flap dropped behind me. The men laughed, and I smiled in spite of myself, unsure whether he paid me curse or compliment.

* * *

Naturally Bedwyr stood sentry at his usual post outside my father's tent. Bedwyr was always on duty. The man could be summed in a single word—stalworth. He was at my father's side from the beginning. He and Cai both. Along with my father, they comprised what I had dubbed "the Holy Trinity of Camelot". The three were together long before the idea of a united kingdom of Britain began to take shape.

"Everything is done then," I asked as I approached.

"What can be until morning. There is still you to look after."

"Me? I am right as rain."

Bedwyr frowned.

"I know you have not eaten yet. Shall I send for something?"

"I just asked Dafydd to."

He peered at me, an eyebrow arched.

"What? I swear, you are as bad as Dafydd. I am having food sent 'round to my tent. That is where I go after I finish here. I even had the leech bind a wound." I pointed to my shoulder.

"Had your shield down again, did you? Will you ever learn, *tiro*?" He demonstrated the proper position once more for my benefit.

Chastised yet again by my first and best teacher.

"It does not seem likely, does it? A reflection on the poor quality of the student, not you, sir." With imaginary shield, I assumed the correct stance for a moment of inspection.

My thin smile quickly faded as I stood in the chill night air, listening to the wind snap the silk above my head. I relaxed my arm. He knew my mission and the reason I hesitated.

If I looked up at him now I would see the understanding in his warm eyes, see the caring. And the pain. No one loved my father more than the man standing beside me. No one. Not the Queen. Not Lancelot. Not even myself.

"I shall be here if you have need of me."

Very comforting, that.

"My father was most fortunate to have had such a friend as you, Bedwyr."

"Thank you. It has been my honour just to have known him." He raised the tent flap for me.

The lanterns had been lit as if *his* return was expected at any moment. The tent itself was unremarkable, much like my own, though larger and with the trappings of a military leader—a table strewn with war maps and papers, a few chairs, his cot. Rather spartan for the Pendragon.

I felt quite the intruder. I did not belong in the Pendragon's tent alone. But he was my father and he had commanded a duty of me. Disobeying was out of the question. I had protested the necessity of this duty. Protested the necessity of the key in my purse. He had such an uncanny way of being right nearly all the time, so that even in grief I could curse it.

With two steps, I was at his cot and lifted a small oaken chest from beneath. For several heartbeats, I stared at the box in my lap.

"Remember. You will only hold this for him until he returns," I whispered aloud to encourage myself. I slid the key into the lock. It opened without a sound. My breath caught as the flickering lantern light brought the gleaming red-gold dragon ring to life where it lay in its soft bed of purple. The king's ring, the seal of Camelot. Whoever possessed this, possessed the power of Britain.

I could take the ring back to Camelot and declare what was mine by birth. Could show it immediately.

How like Modred.

No. I slammed my fist against the wood frame of the cot. There was no Camelot to return to, the tides of Britain had turned. The Round Table and the Pendragon were no more; those had been destroyed on the battlefield of Camlann. The mere thought of the vile creature with whom I shared a father made me realise I must take that seal, as my father had commanded. But not to wield. The main difference between Modred and me was his insatiable craving for power. All I had ever wanted was my own identity. What a strange fate that I still emerged with everything Modred had tried so hard to keep from me. According to my father's wishes, I was now Pendragon.

I would trade title and ring just to have my father back.

"May your next life be as a leper, Modred. Shunned by all, Maggot-feed." I spat to wherever his spirit might be dwelling.

I snatched up the ring and used the leather cord I had brought with me to fashion a pendant. The gold was heavy; the weight of an entire nation hung at my breast. I hid it under my tunic next to my heart, where I vowed to keep it the rest of my days.

There, you have done it and the world is still here.

I replaced the chest then crossed to the table. I gathered everything, maps and papers alike, stuffing them into a leather satchel, slung it over my shoulder and left.

"So. It is finished then? What you needed to do?"

I heard Bedwyr ask his questions through my haze of emotions.

"It is done." Focusing on the now once more, I noticed Gaheris had joined Bedwyr.

"Ah, Ris," I said.

"Highness. All is ready for the morrow," he said.

"Well done, Ris," I said.

By reason of my rank, my tent had been pitched near to those of the men I had led into battle. Clear on the opposite side of the camp. Bedwyr, Ris, and I wended through the maze of tents, cooking fires, carts, and piles of supplies and weapons. There is always a faster, shorter, route than the *via principalis* and *via praetoria* and other main thoroughfares. On the way, I declined countless bowls of stew, crusts of bread, cups of ale, despite their aromas causing my mouth to water. I greeted the men as civilly as my frayed emotions would allow as I hurried for the privacy of my tent.

A fire burned briskly in the pit a few paces from my tent. More of Dafydd's work. But I saw no sign of my brother. Foster-brother in truth. But brother of my heart. Did we not survive the horrors of Dunn na Carraice together?

Lancelot stood on the fringe of light. I ignored his bow.

"So," Ris said. "What are your plans for the morrow? Where will we go?"

I felt Dafydd beside me before he ever spoke.

"We could go to the Continent, disappear in Armorica until things settle here." Dafydd placed a steaming bowl into my cold hands. The warmth felt exquisite. And the aroma…

"Dafydd, you are a darling man. See, Bedwyr? I did not lie." I attacked the thick venison stew, barely tasting my meal. I soaked up the last of the gravy with a bit of bread. My hunger appeased, I handed the empty bowl back to him.

"My thanks," I said.

He produced an ale jug that met with enthusiastic approval.

Exhausted, I sank onto the log serving as my chair. I threw the folds of my cloak off my shoulders and drew my warmth from the blaze. I gestured for the others to join me.

"Aye," I said finally in answer to Dafydd's suggestion. "Aye, I could go off to Armorica, like the Roman gentry who fled when things got too difficult for their cultured sensibilities. And only spend the rest of my days in a foreign land. A Pendragon in exile. It will be a long while in future, my friends, before things settle here. A very long while."

It seemed unnatural, using the title for myself.

"My family would gladly grant you well come and aid you in any way they could, your Highness." Lancelot spoke to me for the first time since our return to camp.

"I want nothing from you, Lancelot. Or your kin. I tolerate you now because I must." Why he had not accompanied the Queen to the stake was beyond my ken. "Then with your permission, Highness, I shall take my leave." He started to rise, but Bedwyr stopped him.

Both men regarded me.

Bedwyr was correct. For the benefit of the men beyond our circle, I had to maintain an air of normalcy. Any outburst now might raise suspicions that something was amiss.

"No law states I must like you, Lancelot. But I have always respected your skills as a warrior. And my father forgave you. Stay. I will hear your counsel."

Lancelot rubbed his hands over his face, his head bowed.

"I hope someday you will forgive me as well, Highness. Gareth's death was an accident."

I shot him an icy stare to signify I would not.

"Gareth stood guard at my mother's stake, unarmed and unwilling."

"I—" The shoulders of the mighty Lancelot drooped. "Any choice you make cannot be easy for you, Highness," he said softly. "You cannot depend upon Constantine relinquishing the power of regency to you."

I had expected the obvious and suffered no disappointment in Camelot's foremost warrior. The Queen's champion.

"Who else is most likely to oppose me?"

Bedwyr scratched at his chin. It needed a shave. He and the others ticked off the names of the chieftains and princes who had been absent from the battlefield of Camlann. They had remained in their homelands and awaited the outcome in order to pledge loyalties to the victor.

The same men who had opposed my place in the army, and my appointment to the Round Table.

"You haven't much time to deliberate," Bedwyr said. "You can leave at first light, saying you go to join your father. It will be only a short while before today's terrible truth leaks out. The sooner you are away from here, the better. If that is what you truly wish."

What I truly wished was to turn back time by a few years and have another go at it, to avoid the events we had just lived through.

"What is the use? The mighty Arthur, Subduer of the Saxon Horde, could not control his own wife or his closest friend. Could not depend on the loyalty of his *equites*" I glared at Lancelot until he averted his eyes. "Why should I even bother trying to salvage this cock-up?"

I rubbed my aching brow, remembering our last encounter with the barbarian Saxons. The now famous Battle of Baedd hen Dunn. My first command. Myself and a mere eighty men held off the onslaught for three days until my father led reinforcements from Camelot to help turn the tide. And for what?

I shook my head and thought aloud, "All that work we did, the blood spilt, the lives spent. For what? For today? What a waste. What a waste." I scooped up a handful of damp earth, held it out to my companions. "For this? Did he really think this cares a fig about who lives on it? So many of our own people did not give a damn one way or the other." I tossed the dirt down in disgust. "Well, I say, the Saxons are well come to it, if they want."

I saw the consternation on my companions' faces, and they had the right. We each bore the scars of the hard-won peace we had wrested from that lot.

No one spoke.

"Maybe they would take better care of this land than we did." My last words tangled in my throat for it pained me to see my father's dream in ruins, like a tattered tapestry.

Would this day never end? I closed my eyes and pressed the heels of my hands hard against my forehead in a vain attempt to cancel out the throbbing in my head and the pounding echo of the war drums. The screams of the dying.

Leave me be!

The wind gusted and I shivered with the chill. I wrapped myself into the folds of my cloak, while my companions stared. I felt their gazes burn through my skin, directly to my soul, as keenly as I had felt the glowing iron brand searing into my left wrist those many years before. I rubbed at the silver wristband covering the scar. Can they not leave me in peace? What did they expect of me? I am not the person my father was. I was a fool for believing I could even try.

"What are you staring at?" I flailed my arms at my companions.

"We only wish to help." Dafydd's touch on my sleeve brought part of my senses back. "We are all exhausted and in need of rest."

"Aye. High time to end this. I cannot take the throne. You know there is no throne for me to take. I have a worthless title. Modred made bloody sure that if he could not have Camelot, then neither would I. All my work to be accepted into the Round Table and earn my place at my father's side was wasted. It is over. Gareth and Cai and the others, they are gone. Who is left to support my claim? Let the mad dogs scramble for the non-existent prize. I shall be gone as well. We leave at dawn. Dafydd. Ris. North is as good a direction as any. Happy now?"

* * *

"We could have sold that sword you know," Dafydd said, wiping his mouth with the back of his hand. It was the first any of us had spoken since Bedwyr and Lancelot retired for the night quite some time ago.

The jug of ale came back to me once more. I took my turn with it before answering.

"Really? I cannot imagine anyone paying real silver for that worthless bit of… of steel."

"But why? Why did you do it? To just chuck it away?"

I could not bring myself to answer or face him. I was not ready to confront the truth behind his innocent question.

"Have you gone mad?"

There was an excellent question to ponder. I had already begun to doubt my reason. I offered the ale to Gaheris.

"I have had my share, cousin," he said.

In truth, I'd had more than my share. *Wfft*. Why was I not yet sotted? I should have been ages ago, with all the ale I had consumed. That, plus the wine from this afternoon with my father before he… I raised the jug. But Dafydd clutched my wrist and held my arm.

"Are you mad?"

I wrenched my arm free and drank.

"Perhaps," I said finally. "Perhaps I am. And who among us was not a little unsound today? Bedwyr? My father? We allowed Modred control of our destinies. Modred. Can either of you blame me for anything I did today?"

Ris shook his head. He knew better than to get into this. Dafydd should have as well. In fact, he knew me best. The ale emboldened him; he was unused to so much libation. In no mood for talk, I wanted to drop the whole thing.

But Dafydd spoke again. "No, I do not blame you at all. I am sorry you believed that."

I accepted his apology with silence. But he deserved an explanation at least.

"I suppose throwing that sword into the river was my tribute to those who did not survive the battle. A mad act to crown the madness. And to say once and for good, my warrior days are over."

I finished the last of the ale in a long quaff. I preferred *uisge* for my purpose. *Uisge beatha*, the Water of Life. What better for drowning your sorrows? I wanted the oblivion of potation. And ale was a poor substitute.

"But really, Dafydd. If my having a sword means so much to you, you can fetch me another before we leave. Surely there are plenty and to spare around here. It should not be difficult for you to find one, especially as you are such a master of procurement."

"You know well it is not the sword alone I am meaning. Why are you walking away from your birthright? Do you not feel a duty to stay and try? Why did you throw away who you really are?"

His words cut directly to my heart. Why did he not simply plunge his dagger there instead?

"That, brother, I did not do," I said, curling a fist. A hurt for a hurt. "How could you think that of me? Throw away who I am? Am I not my father's daughter? Never think I would deny that, Dafydd. Never."

Dafydd stared at my raised fist; his blue-grey eyes, wide with surprise.

"I am sorry, Lin. I…" He dragged slender fingers through his sandy hair. "Nothing we did today made sense."

No, it made no whit of sense. Modred's hatred and ambition had driven us beyond the point of reasoning. Yet it was far too simple to lay the entire blame on him, my own feelings aside. The tapestry of Camelot had begun to unravel long before Modred arrived with his schemes and those of his mother. It had never been tightly woven. Modred only plucked the threads out one by one. When that did not achieve his purpose fast enough, he set the tapestry ablaze. The rotted material burned quickly. Modred's sole mistake was that he did not get out of the way in time, for he was consumed as well.

Wfft. We had all played our parts in destroying Camelot. My father. Morgause. My mother. Lancelot. Modred. Me. Not one of us any more—or less—culpable than the others. Our destinies had been set before my father's birth.

I felt wretched. I always did after an argument with Dafydd. The thought of how close I had come to blows with him frightened me. I touched his sleeve.

"Would you rather be alone, Lin?" He accepted my unspoken apology.

I shook my head. He knew how much I hated being alone.

Dafydd took up his harp. It was never far from his reach. He cradled it in his lap as a mother does her infant. His fingers touched a string here and there to test its pitch. He adjusted a few then played in earnest. Music is the one salve for a rent soul and tattered heart. It may not cure but it certainly is a soothing balm. The effect on me was immediate. I was grateful for the darkness, to hide my tears. To hide my weakness. Damn my gender.

The bards make war seem glorious, even romantic. They lie. Trust me. They are paid to lie. Oh, there are times when war can be justified; at least we had a purpose at Baedd hen Dunn. But Camlann? I guess we needed the Saxons to keep ourselves out of trouble. There was no reason for the blood-bath we had been through today. I had been nothing more than a butcher in the midst of a gory slaughter, no better than the others. No better than Modred. We had been to Hell. How could everyone else be so calm? How could they sleep?

My eyelids closed and the scene of carnage played out before me.

By Toutatis. Thick blood surrounded me. I felt it spill hot onto my sword hand, saw it splatter my shield and clothes, drip from my sword. Mangled bodies, devoid of life, and pieces of humanity littered the field. I slipped and nearly fell and realized I trod upon the entrails of a dying man. Grisly? Ghastly? Most assuredly. But that is the truth of war.

I wiped my hands on my cloak, but they remained sticky. I could not recall soiling them recently. It must have been the remnants of that clot of dirt. But when I held them out to the fire for inspection, the sight horrified me. My hands dripped with fresh blood. It flowed down my fingers and wrists in thick rivulets, hissing as it hit the ground before me. Struck dumb, I stared while both my pulse and breathing quickened.

Surely this was a sign. I had never been meant for the warrior's life. Many had accused me of going against nature fighting in my father's army.

A female warrior? How daft. Even Bedwyr had questioned my

father's sanity at first.

I ran trembling hands over my clothes and dragged them across the grass in a futile attempt to remove the stuff of life.

"Dafydd, I have blood on my hands and I cannot wash it off. I was nothing more than a butcher today. And here is the proof." I thrust my arms towards him.

His own fingers froze on the harp's strings, in rare discordance. A deep red drop splattered onto the frame and quickly soaked into the wood. Dafydd seemed unconcerned at the defiling of the beloved instrument, his most precious possession.

"Can you not see it?"

By the puzzled look in his eyes, I knew that he did not. Nor did Ris.

I grasped my brother's ivory tunic and stained the fabric scarlet.

"Have I gone mad? Is this my penance for killing that adder this morning? Father told me to go to the parley unarmed. Am I to blame for starting the battle of Camlann?"

CHAPTER 2

"Lin. Lin."

I heard him call me from where he stood on the far bank of the expansive, racing river of crimson. What gave the water such a hue? The sunset? Needing to cross, I waded out to my ankles. Much too thick for water. And too warm. The truth made me cringe, but I continued because I saw neither bridge nor boat. I had to reach my betrothed on the opposite side. My Gareth.

Now waist-deep, I swam. I dared not open my mouth to cry for help, lest the viscous fluid fill my stomach and lungs and consume me. I struggled to keep my head clear. The current caught me despite my efforts, and I sank beneath the surface for several terror-stricken moments. My mind now screamed for my love to save me.

The torrent carried me farther from Gareth. He ran along the shore to keep apace.

Ahead, I saw a bridge. I reached for its stones, but gained no purchase.

"Swim, *cumal*. Swim."

Modred's battle-begrimed and decaying head, fixed to my spear, towered overhead. Mocking laughter spewed from its mouth.

"Gareth, help me."

"Lin?"

I became aware of a gentle shaking.

"Lin, wake up."

I felt firm ground beneath me. Gareth must have pulled me free of the blood river. My chest heaved from the recent exertion. Still damp, I clung to my saviour. His strong arms enfolded me. Protected me.

"Gareth, my love."

"You were having that nightmare again, Lin."

The Irish lilt was right, but…

"You're safe now."

Nightmare? *The gods*. Did the groan come from my throat?

I opened my eyes. Full daylight greeted my gaze. Ris, my husband, held me, not Gareth. *Stupid get*. Of course it could not possibly be Gareth. He has been dead these dozen years and more.

And Modred.

I pulled myself from the embrace and wiped my hands on the grass. Then I straightened my tunic to cover my bare knees.

How long had I been without my guard raised? How much had Ris seen and heard?

"Why did you not wake me earlier, Ris? You know I did not wish to arouse the villagers' curiosity."

"You've avoided Camelot for twelve years. Another hour or two makes little difference." He stoked the campfire. "It seems as though your nightmares have worsened."

"They usually do this time of year, Ris. Beltane is but a few days from now."

"I mean worse than that."

"I am well enough," I lied. The nightmare left me shaken every time. Rare was the night without it. Modred always seemed to laugh loudest around Beltane. Near my natal day.

But a Round Table *eques* never displayed weakness. Or fear. Especially over a childish nightmare.

"Where are the children?" I said, combing my fingers through my tangled hair.

"They followed your brother to the Cam. No doubt he is filling their heads with tales of whimsy."

Better than frightening them by the sight of their mother in the throes of nightmare.

"You know how they love his stories, Ris. Melora even seems to have some of his talent."

"Aye. Her fingers never faltered once on the harp's strings last night while she practised. It is good of Davy to teach her. He would make a fine father. He really should have children of his own."

"Indeed. In the meanwhile, he spoils ours."

"That is *nae* such a bad thing. Are you certain you want to go up there?"

I realised we both stared at the hill rising from the plain before us. It was crowned by an imposing fortress of wood and stone. Camelot humbled the other hills in the near distance. Proud. Defiant. A worthy lair for the Pendragon. Once it had been my home.

I had vowed never to see it again. Yet, yestereve we had pitched our encampment practically in its shadow. What was Camelot's power, that it could pull me back in spite of myself?

"Yes, Ris. I must," I said, groping behind my back.

"Searching for this?" A small pouch of black leather dangled from his fingers.

"Is there hot water?"

"When is there not?"

I found my cup where I had left it the night before. I emptied its contents onto the ground, then took a pinch of the herbs from the pouch. Ris was closer to the kettle, so he poured out for me. I nodded my thanks.

"You cried out his name in your sleep again."

Was it in my mind, or did Ris set the kettle back in its place more heavily than required?

I cried out many names in my sleep; principally Modred and Gareth. One in hatred. The other…

"I—"

"Ach. You were asleep and could not help yourself. I should not have brought it up. Here, you need something to break your fast." He handed me a barley bannock. "Eat. If not for me and Davy, you'd waste away."

I nibbled on the cake, watching my husband fix his own cup. Why had he mentioned Gareth, only to dismiss him so quickly? It certainly must hurt a man to hear his wife speak his brother's name in her sleep. Odd. I called Ris husband. Friend. Kinsman. But I could not fathom his thoughts at the moment.

Well, what could I do if he refused to discuss it?

I felt a tiny flutter in my belly and gasped.

"What is it, Lin? Something wrong?" Concern changed his entire demeanour.

I smiled to reassure him. The stirring was undeniable.

"Ris, the babe quickened."

"Truly?" His smile lit his face as though we had never shared this moment before. He placed his sword-calloused hand gently, protectively, on my slightly swollen abdomen just as our fourth child kicked once more. "A bonny boy, if ever I felt one, Lin."

"And just how many besides Bear have you felt?"

"Mark me. You're carrying a warrior within your womb, my wife."

"Aye. A warrior to follow in *her* mother's footsteps."

"I yield," he said with a chuckle. His hands rose above his head, fingers splayed. "Finish your tea, the bairn needs the strength."

I drained my cup, then suggested we join our family.

Ris pushed himself to his feet, turned and extended a hand to assist me. Side by side, we passed through a sparse fringe of trees and emerged on the bank of the River Cam.

"Mummy." Our youngest daughter squealed when she saw us. She ran to me and hugged my knees. "Are we going to that old fortress today?"

"Yes, Gernie." I reached down and smoothed her unruly auburn tresses. They needed combing.

"Bear says it's haunted. With ghosts."

"Indeed?" I must have a word with Dafydd if he was the source of such nonsense from his story telling.

Our five-year-old nodded, then dashed from my side to hug her father. He swung her high into the air, bringing on a wave of giggles.

He made a good father as well. I could have done worse, I suppose.

"And what are you about, Melora?" I stepped to where Gernie's elder sister sat, hunched over the damp earth. She clutched a stick like a stylus.

Raven curls swung from the studious seven-year-old's face. "Practising the letters you taught me last night, Mother."

I glanced over her shoulder.

"Nicely done."

She returned to her task.

I stepped into the frigid water and stooped to bathe my hands and arms. These were the times I dearly missed the luxuries of Camelot—the hot baths. As I washed, I felt my brother studying me from where he stood thigh-deep in the river. My son strained as he wrestled with his uncle. Dafydd knew I had slept poorly, but I wanted to show him I had recovered.

I gave him a smile in greeting. "Careful, Dafydd, else Bear bests you and you end up in the river."

"What? You mean this wriggling braggart?" He grasped Bear

around the waist and in a single twist had my son off his feet and in the water. "I think not."

Bear bobbed up doused and laughing, but undaunted. He renewed his assault on Dafydd, growling.

I had named my son Arthur, but I do not recall any of us using it. From the moment he was born, he was my "Bear Cub". And at ten, he showed the signs of both size and strength his grandfather would be proud of, and living up to his nickname.

I sat on the bank beside my husband, enjoying the peace of watching my family. Bear's wet frolic with Dafydd. Gernie copying her sister's actions. Would that life could always be so sweet.

Dafydd effortlessly pulled free of his nephew and joined us. "I hear the Saxons call this place Cadbury," he said and stretched out on the bank.

"Ach, bloody *Sassenach*." Ris' Irish accent always grew more pronounced when provoked or agitated in some way.

"They are so pretentious," I added. "They seem to rename everything in their ghastly tongue. And they have the cheek to call us '*Wealh*'—foreigners. Us."

"Are we Saxon, Mother?"

"What?"

My son towered over me, his arms folded across his chest. With a bare foot tapping the smooth rock beneath it, even drenched he looked like a miniature version of his grandfather.

"Are we Saxon?" He repeated the words slowly, as if I were incapable of understanding.

"Whyever do you ask that?"

"You always talk about heritage, and yet you hardly ever speak of ours. I mean we speak the language." He tossed his pale, wet hair from his face, spraying his father and I. "So?"

"We speak the language. When necessary. *Britanni sumus*."

Ris and Dafydd shot me questioning stares at my choice of words. When had we last thought ourselves in such a patriotic vein? Why dredge up what I had forsaken so long ago?

"Even Father? I thought you were Irish, sir."

"My father was indeed Irish, Bear. And I am proud of that. But my mother was British. Once I moved from my father's lands I did not return, save for one time only. A time I regret. I have lived in British land so long, I consider myself a native."

I noticed Dafydd's slender fingers stroking his throat at the mention of Ris' mother, Morgause. An old, all too familiar gesture. Would either of us ever be totally free of that woman? My own fingers rubbed at my silver wristband, recollecting—

"Mummy? Why do you look so sad?"

I thrust the memories of my childhood aside, refusing to acknowledge them.

Instead, I gave my youngest a smile and took her into my lap. "I was just recalling an unhappy time, Gernie. But it was a long time ago. Come. Let us return to the camp so I can comb and plait your hair. And your sister's. We must look our best when we go to Camelot."

As I walked back, the children chattered amongst themselves about the day of adventure they faced. Ris engaged my brother in a conversation which left me alone to reflect on our son's motive for his recent enquiry. He had mentioned heritage. It was merely a matter of time before he reached the pith. It might appear as though he had forgotten the matter, but I knew better. I had been expecting this for quite awhile.

Nigh time for the truth. I shivered and told myself it was naught but the breeze.

* * *

The morning was still young when we finally entered the village. I could not bring myself to call it Cadbury. Everything was as neat and trim as ever, only quieter. Less bustle without the endless parade of *equites*, warriors, servants and visitors, as when my father had been in residence.

We cut across the Green, past the well, and headed for the village hall at the very base of the hill. Behind the building of grey stone and thatch lay our goal—"The Wash", the track up to the north-east gate. *Eques* and common soldier had dubbed it so, because one felt the notion it might be easier to swim up it in the rain rather than climb. The slightest drizzle turned it into a nightmare of ankle-deep mud. I could have wept at the derelict condition of the path and the earthen ramparts. Ris, Dafydd and I had served numerous times on the detail to keep the tracks and defences clear of bush, hedges and weeds—any sort of growth that might provide cover or toe-hold to an enemy. No warrior was ever exempt from the duty. I had always considered it a labour of love. Bramble and brush now reclaimed what only treachery had been able to breach.

The children dashed ahead, eager for their quest. Ris and I walked abreast, but there was no room for Dafydd. He brought up the rear.

The weather had been fair for several days, so the ground was firm and dry beneath our boots. But I was glad I had remembered the old centurion's vine-stick I used when walking. I leaned on the *vitus* appreciatively.

"What will you tell Bear?"

I glanced at my husband.

"About his question. He shall be on it again, you know."

"And too soon, Ris. I think he is ready for the truth of who, and what we are. Yet I have held the secret for so long. Am I ready?"

"You doubt? You have never been known to lack confidence, Lin."

Have I not? How little he truly knew me. How well I had concealed my nature.

I paused to catch my breath. "Well, I shall let Bear set the pace. I suppose when the time is right, the words will be there. Just like when I addressed the soldiers after Camlann."

"And a grand job you did, too. The people still await your father's return."

"Desperate people will believe anything. Besides, I had help from Dafydd. Was it not brilliant when he added Avalon and the Lady of the Lake?"

My brother grinned and inclined his head, saying, "I am honoured my humble efforts please, Noble One."

"Hardly humble," I said.

Before we reached the first earthen defence, Gernie needed to be carried. Her father scooped her into his arms.

"Come, little dove," he said.

She nestled against his breast.

Halfway up, Melora asked to rest. She was too big a girl for any of us to carry. I, myself, leaned rather heavily on the gnarled and twisted piece of wood, but my pride refused to allow me to stop. In my selfishness, I did not wish Bear to have his first sight of Camelot alone, nor with any one save me. He and I continued at a steady pace while the others stayed behind to catch us up later.

At the summit we paused in the shadow of the guard tower. No sentry questioned our presence. The wood and stone stood mute. Despite of the pang in my heart, I took a deep breath and pushed one of the massive doors. Its hinges squeaked. No one had remained behind to bar the gates from within.

I stepped inside and touched a fist to my breast in the familiar salute, and gave a silent "*ave*".

"Glory," my son whispered in reverence. Even empty and silent, Camelot could stagger one's wits with its size. "I never thought it possible. Camelot is exactly as you described it, Mother. Exactly. How did you know?"

I watched as his gaze darted from one side of the compound to the other, taking in everything—the stables, the barracks, the craftsman's stalls, the practice field as I pointed them out. I knew he was storing every detail for future inquisitions.

"Later, Bear. I shall tell you everything later." *And there is much, my son.* "Go on, have a look 'round. Just be careful. Things might not be quite as solid as they appear on the surface."

He dashed off in a twinkling, directly towards the stables. My son. Arthur's grandson.

My own feelings wavered. The place had an unnatural air about it. What had once been vibrant with noise of every sort now stood desolate. Had I been mistaken in returning?

I found myself clawing at my neck in an old habit. The same gesture as Dafydd had made earlier. The shadow of a painful memory constricted and choked me.

No. I refuse to think of that. I forced my hand back to my side.

I wandered about the compound, aimless. Taking my time. Weeds had encroached everywhere, and the buildings stood in a general state of disrepair but, surprisingly, seemed fairly intact. Little had been carted away for use elsewhere. It would not take much to restore Camelot to her former glory. Why had she been abandoned? Why did my kinsman, Constantine, not stay?

"Why did you not return after Camlann?"

Sod off, Modred. You are dead.

The cries of delight from my daughters, as they had their first sight of Camelot broke my musings. And none too soon.

Without thought, I had made my way to one of my own favourite parts of Camelot—the stables. Bear had wandered off already, no doubt intent on exploring the whole of Camelot at once. The familiar odour of horses and leather remained—or was it my imagination?—mingled with the mustiness of time. I walked down a double row of stalls, counting as I went, although I could have found my way blindfolded. Straight to number six, left-hand side. Rhyddid's stall. My war stallion, a magnificent gift from my father. His name meant freedom. He had been slain from under me at Camlann. Rhyddid and I had been as close a team as Dafydd and me.

I stepped into the empty stall. Dust covered the floor, but someone had mucked out the place before Constantine moved headquarters. I heard a rustling in the corner and peered into the dimness. A mouse scurried across the boards. I half-expected one of the cats to be close behind, ready to pounce.

What had I hoped to find here after a dozen years? What answers could an empty fortress possibly contain? I would show the children around. Perhaps give them a peek at the Round Table Hall. Then we would move on. There was nothing for me here any more. Having forsaken Camelot after Camlann, I had no claim to it. I had no right to even be here. How did I dare criticise Constantine for moving his headquarters?

I am sorry, Father.

I heard footsteps and looked up to find Ris approaching.

"I knew you would be here, where the heart of Camelot beat."

I agreed.

"Those were grand times. The world may never see the like again."

"What do you feel about being here, Ris?"

"What I feel does not matter." He joined me in the stall.

"Yes it does. It matters to me."

Ris leaned against the wooden slats, gazing into the empty expanse, deep in his memories. In twelve years of living and travelling together, neither of us could say we knew each other in the slightest.

"A hundred years could not have made me ready to return."

"Why did you then? You could have stayed at the camp."

My husband stepped towards me and bowed deeply at the waist. "Where you go, I go. That simple. Before you were ever my wife, you were and always shall be, my Queen." Ris straightened. "Why do you feel it so necessary to come here again, reopening old wounds?"

"I wish I could say. But I cannot. I only know it has been tugging on me for some time now, like a hand gripping the cord around my neck with my father's ring and pulling me. I had hoped to find the answers in here."

"Have you?"

"I have come all this way, and all I got were bits of memories. I see no reason for us to stay very long. Just enough for the children to explore a little. I thought we could show them—"

A loud whoop pierced the quiet. It came from outside, in the direction of the practice field.

"Come," Ris said. "Let us see what Bear has discovered."

I tucked my vine-stick under my arm and we walked out.

Our son had found the armoury, and a sword nearly as tall as he. He brandished it two-fisted. I froze in my tracks. My son was magnificent.

"My word. He is a natural," I whispered.

"You expected less," his father asked.

I shook my head, for I had not expected anything. Had not wanted to think of the possibility.

"Arthur would be proud of this one." Dafydd leaned against the door-frame of the stable.

"Wouldn't he just? I guess it's nigh time to start his lessons." Ris had a greedy look on his face, much like men do when they learn their woman has new been delivered of a son, claiming the glory for the woman's labours. As though a son was a spoil of war.

Playfully, Bear attacked his sisters. They scattered, shrieking at the game.

"Arthur!" I summoned the command from somewhere deep within me. Drew it up from where I had allowed that aspect of me to sleep for a dozen years.

My son halted immediately, as if stunned by the sheer force of his name. He turned, wearing a bewildered expression. The sword dangled in his hands.

I covered the distance between us in five or six long paces, and grasped the sword by the rusty blade. He released it without a sound. My gaze held firm as the weapon passed into my hand. He had seen his father's sword many times. Had watched it being sharpened. And Dafydd had his as well, of course. Thus, I was disappointed that our son had so little sense in a sword's use.

"This is not for play. Nor is it ours. It belongs to the Pendragon."

I strode off, swinging the sword at my side, to replace it in the armoury, wishing my son could have lived his life without his hand ever knowing how cold and heavy iron truly feels.

CHAPTER 3

"Why did you take the sword from me, Mother?" Bear's words echoed in the expanse of the empty armoury.

Sliding my hand along the once highly polished wooden rack dissecting the main room, I pushed aside years of dust. I thought he might follow.

"You have been here before," he said.

"Aye."

"You have had a sword in your hand before, as well."

"Yes."

"And you know how to use it."

So. The time has come.

I compleated my task. The blade looked forlorn without its hundreds of brothers standing hilt to hilt.

I faced my son.

"Again, yes. And you want to know how, and why your mother would know such things."

He nodded.

"Fair enough. Sit down, Bear." I pointed to a bench that stretched along the length of the outer wall. I had spent many a morning sitting there, hour after hour, surrounded by my friends, my brothers-in-arms, polishing weapons, swapping lies, laughing a great deal. In my mind, I could conjure them all and fill the room to its capacity.

"I am going to start at the beginning. My own. Before I knew about swords and shields and armour and war. Many years before I came here."

I paused a long time, staring at the past. I needed courage for what I had to say.

"When I was a child… I was a slave." I had never before admitted that to anyone.

Bear's blue eyes widened for an instant, but he made no sound. A chill ran through me and visions of Camelot vanished.

"Dafydd and I lived far away from here then. Far to the north, in the small island kingdom of Orkney, within the fortress of Queen Morgause."

"You mean King Arthur's sister?"

"Half-sister. We were considered her property."

Bear sucked his breath through his teeth.

Dafydd told stories of Camelot to my children nightly. My son knew well the Pendragon's line, including Morgause's five sons. What Bear did not know was that Gawain, Agravain, Gareth and Modred were his father's brothers. He did not know Prince Gaheris of Orkney, son of Morgause, was his father.

This would not be easy for either of us. I constantly grappled with that portion of my history. The pain. The bitterness. The fear. Over the years, I had suppressed and hidden it from my husband and children. I intended only to answer my son's questions and move on to my father, and my time and position in Camelot. A much happier life. Then we would return to camp.

"Where exactly is Orkney, Mother?"

"Here. Easier to show you." I drew a map on the dust-covered floor with my finger as Bear watched. "This is the wall built during the time Britain was a Roman province." I indicated with a line. "This wild territory north of it, we know very little about."

"That is Pictish land Father has spoken of."

"Yes. Even the Romans had no interest in that part of the country, except to build the wall to contain the Picts. And the Romans are generally an efficient lot, making the most of whatever they conquer.

"Orkney," I continued, "is a group of small islands, just off the northern-most coast of Britain's mainland. Here."

My thumbprint served to represent the main island where I had lived a twelve-year nightmare.

"I must admit, I do not know much about it. Slaves were not allowed to venture much beyond the fortress walls. Just to the stream and the fields."

Bear hovered over the map, studying it.

"Then we must be—" He paused as he considered our location without benefit of any landmarks. "Here." He placed his finger in a spot not far off the mark.

I nodded with a smile. How proud my father would be of this one, indeed. The son he should have had. Instead, my father had been cursed with me—and Modred.

"Orkney is awfully far north, Mother?"

"To be sure. I never felt warm. Nor dry. The place was every bit as harsh and cold as those who would have been my masters."

"Would have been?" Bear looked up from the map.

"Morgause and Modred tried very hard to break my spirit, to dominate me with their will, but—"

"Lin?"

I had to twist in my place to see the door and my brother standing just inside, wineskin in hand.

"I knocked," Dafydd said. "But you must not have heard. I thought you might want this." He held the skin out by its leather strap. "Story-telling is a thirsty business."

"You would know. Come in."

He crossed the familiar room and set the wineskin within my reach. Then he sat on the floor facing us.

"Mother? Was Father a…"

"No, Bear. Your father was never a slave." I spared him the word and his face relaxed. I was glad to have that small bit of happy news to offer him. But just what would the lad think when he learned the whole truth?

My son fidgeted as he pondered the recent information. Mayhap I had misread him. I tended to overlook his youth during his interrogations. I would need to hold tight rein on my answers from now on.

After a time, Bear levelled his gaze at me. It took a physical effort not to gasp. Another man had possessed eyes the same shade of blue as those of my son and father. Never before had the similarity hit me so hard as in that moment. I had known it since his birth. How could I not? I simply had kept Modred and thoughts of him buried deep. For if I had not, I think I would have gone mad, consumed by the hatred I continued to harbour for my other brother.

Hidden in the folds of my tunic, my fists clenched.

"I am the son of a slave woman, then."

The simple statement stabbed my heart. Everything I had planned to calmly and rationally tell my son fled my mind. Only the raw memories remained. Of the whip. The blood. The chains. Modred. Every detail of our slavery battled to be released first. My son must understand that before I could tell him of his grandfather.

Dafydd placed a comforting hand on my knee.

"You find that shameful, Bear?" My brother asked what I could not. "Your mother is a slave no longer. Nor was she at the time of your birth."

Bear's cheeks coloured and he lowered his head.

"I… I meant no disrespect, sir. Mother."

Dafydd regarded my son a moment. "Of course not, Bear. Still, I suggest you listen to her story before you judge."

"It would be an honour to hear, if she will tell it."

Dafydd and I had no need for words. Especially when it came to Orkney. He rose.

"I had not intended to stay so long, Lin. I think I shall go help Ris with Melora and Gernie. That little one is very much like her mummy and can be quite a handful." Despite the lightness of his words, his voice lacked the usual merry spark it held whenever he spoke of my children. He bent to kiss my brow.

"You can do this, Noble One," he whispered. "You must. I shall see that you are not disturbed."

I watched him leave and called out a weak "thank you."

"What did happen on Orkney, Mother?" Bear asked when the door closed behind Dafydd.

My son wanted to know. Then by the gods, he shall.

I took a quaff from the wineskin as I recalled a stormy winter night many years and thousands of miles ago.

My earliest memory.

"I saw little beauty in the island kingdom of Orkney, Bear. Sheer crags, scored by relentless waves rose to dizzy heights straight from the North Sea. Perched on the summit of the headland which overlooked the Sound of Hoy and Cairston Harbour stood Dunn na Carraice. "Fortress of the Rock." Home of the banished Queen Morgause.

"The place was aptly named. My eyes met grey stone at every turn. The ramparts and all the buildings within the fortress might have been carved from the bedrock from which it arose. Even the sky was invariably grey much of the time, heavy with storm clouds blown in from the sea.

"Largest and most prominent of the dunn's buildings was the Queen's palace. It housed the Queen and the five princes, whenever they were in residence and not at Camelot, as well as visitors, warriors of rank, and the house servants. Smaller buildings which functioned as stables, barracks, storage and our quarters flanked the palace. Towering stone walls enclosed all. To keep enemies out. And me and Dafydd within.

"Slaves are less than human, Bear. Slaves do not share living-space with the free-born, except when working. The oblong building allotted us enclosed a single room as home for some thirty people at any one time. It had a thick sod roof with a hole cut in the centre for smoke from the fire-pit.

"It was always cold, damp and draughty. And ugly."

* * *

I was five the year of the Samhain blizzard; Dafydd had recently turned seven. The storm swept in before cockcrow. By noon the sky had disappeared in the swirling white and we realised the bonfires for the new year's festival would be impossible. At eventide everyone prayed for the gods to understand the omission while huddled around our indoor hearth fire. We prayed we would not awake at dawn buried alive.

Because of Samhain, Queen Morgause provided our quarters with a small cask of ale and extra blocks of peat as fuel for our fire. Our feast consisted of the same fare as any other day—a stew of fish and turnips, thickened with barley, and a portion of bread. One of the men said that if winter continued so harsh, we would all be eating seaweed before spring, even the Queen. Men and women agreed, their faces ruddy with the glow from the blaze.

Several children, Dafydd included, launched into a familiar tune extolling the virtues of seaweed, clapping in rhythm to accompany themselves. When they finished, the room rang with the adults' laughter and applause for the comical song. Gossip and complaints ceased then, and we turned to stories and music to pass the night.

Dafydd loved this portion of the evening. Each night he listened to every word uttered by the story-tellers and singers. He committed every word to memory. I liked that time as well, when the yarns concerned heroes and brave deeds. But Samhain called for darker tales of the Otherworld and of Faerie. Stories to raise the hair, each more strange than the last.

I pressed myself deeper into Mummy's lap, reluctant to leave her safety. She hugged me and called for Dafydd to come to bed. In the midst of a narration.

"Why so early, Mother? The stories are not finished yet," Dafydd said.

"Because they are frightening Linnie," our mother answered.

"She is such a baby. They are only stories."

"Dafydd, she is too young to know the difference."

"Why not just put her to bed then, and let me stay up a little longer? I am not even tired." He yawned.

"I am not scared," I said, trying to spare him.

"You are so," he said and turned his back. "It's unfair. I have to go to bed because she is scared."

"Just lie down and hush, Dafydd. You, too, Linnie."

I slipped from her lap.

"Son? Please?"

A moment later, my brother laid down in an angry huff and jerked the blanket over himself.

"Share the blanket with your sister, please, Dafydd."

"I do not mind him having it, Mummy," I murmured. "I am no warmer with it than I am without."

"My darlings." She kissed my cheek, then Dafydd's before lying down herself. I used the crook of her arm as a pillow. She had none. Very soon I felt her relax.

Sleep came less easily for me. Bogies might well be lurking in the shadowy corners beyond the firelight's reach. Besides, I could not block out the story-teller's voice. Then, when the last story finally ended, conversations were slow to wane while the ale lasted.

Darkness enfolded me. Closer to the fire, a woman giggled above a man's grunting. Snoring came from every side. Occasionally, the entrapped smoke would overwhelm someone into a fit of coughing, myself included.

The wind rose and whistled through cracks between the stones of our dwelling. We had no tapestries to help block it like the Queen did within her palace. Even latched, the window shutters rattled. Snow blew in wherever it found a breach.

I shivered and inched closer to Mummy. She did not move in response. Odd. Her skin felt cold against my cheek. Maybe Dafydd would know what to do. At least he should share the blanket.

"Dafydd?"

The straw rustled beneath him.

"I am trying to sleep. Leave me be."

He was still cross with me.

But I had to tell him about Mummy. I spoke his name again, a bit more urgently.

"Oh, do stop your whining, Linnie. Why must you always be impossible? You follow me all day. Can I not have a moment's peace?" He shifted his weight and hugged the thin blanket tighter. And I got no further response from him.

"Sorry, Dafydd," I whispered, defeated.

I snuggled closer to Mummy to give her what warmth I could, secure in the knowledge that Dafydd would regret his selfishness come the dawn.

And for the rest of his life.

Although determined not to, I eventually cried myself to sleep, trying to draw comfort from my thumb. A cold and lonely comfort.

I awoke not by cockcrow, but by the door of our quarters banging against the wall. The overseer barged in, tailed by his assistant. I sat up and stared around me. Mummy had not moved.

"The overseer is here, Dafydd. Wake up." I nudged his shoulder.

He muttered something I could not understand and rolled over.

I turned to warn Mummy. Too late. The assistant towered over us. He prodded her with the toe of his boot.

"Come on. Wake up, you lazy creature," he said, shaking loose the cords of his whip.

"Please, Mummy. Wake up so he does not hurt you." I tugged on her sleeve.

"Out of my way or I'll do you next." He had his arm drawn to strike.

I shrank back.

"No sense beating a dead horse," someone nearby said.

"What?" My mother's assailant paused. His whip hand hovered, frozen at the height of its arc.

"Can't you see? This one's long cold, man. Been dead all night from the looks of her."

"Dead?" Dafydd, fully awake now, grabbed me by the shoulders and shook. "All night? Did you not know?" He shouted at me.

I stared. The storm in my brother's blue-grey eyes, normally so warm and kind, frightened me more than stories of Faerie and the *Sith* ever could. More than the overseer's whip. But I would face them, every each, if it would calm my brother.

"How could I know? Dafydd, please do not be cross. I am sorry." I cringed from the stranger he had become, desperate to stay his anger. "I tried to tell you last night something was wrong, but you kept pushing me away."

"Stop that. You are not a baby any more." He jerked my hand from my face and slapped my fingers. His anger stung worse than the blow.

His innocent words would haunt me for a very long time.

Two men lifted Mummy, and none too gently either. They wore leather collars around their necks, same as Mummy. That meant they belonged in our quarters. They half-dragged, half-carried her out. Were they not even going to give her a blanket? It was so bitter cold out there, she would need one. The dead deserved at least that, even a slave.

"I warned you last night, 'twas the screaming o' the *Bean Sith*."

Hands fluttered as people made the horned sign to ward off evil at the old woman's words. Everyone knows the *Bean Sith* are heralds of death. Christians crossed themselves. It did not hurt to invoke as many gods as possible in matters of the Otherworld. Everyone cast furtive glances about the room, afraid of who else might be found in a similar state. Death, like all things in life, comes in triads.

I found no comfort in the honour of the *Bean Sith*.

"These two are old enough to start earning their keep around here." The overseer's words sliced into my thoughts. Earn our keep? "You, there. Take this one with you to the kitchen. Find some pots for her to clean." He shoved me forward.

After the morning meal of tasteless porridge, which I swallowed from habit only, I followed an older girl to a part of the dunn I had never been before. In the kitchen, I found no shortage of filthy pots that required scouring. The aroma of roasting haunches of beef and venison, the bubbling kettles of stew, knotted my stomach with hunger, but at least it was warmer than in the slaves' hall and Dafydd no longer had to put up with my constant questions nor did I have to face his wrath.

Wrapped in my loss, scared and confused, I obeyed whatever was commanded of me. Alone in a sea of strangers.

The hours dragged. I missed my brother and—

"You. Prince Agravain needs more wood."

A woman pointed at me. She had been giving orders most of the morning to everyone working in the kitchen. Before I could move, she turned away and to her next task.

I set down the bowl I had been scrubbing and dried my hands on my skirt.

Mummy had always taught Dafydd and me to be polite, especially to our betters in the dunn.

"If you please," I said. "I do not know where the wood pile is or the prince's chamber."

The clatter and chatter of the bustling kitchen ceased. The tall, slender woman without a collar glared at me through narrowed eyes.

What had I done? I stared at my bare feet.

"Why do I get the stupid ones?" she said. "The wood is in the bin. The royal chambers, above."

A snap of her fingers and work resumed.

I found the woodbin by the door and gathered up as many of the split logs as I could. How would I ever find my way in the palace?

"I am sorry about your mother, Linnie."

The girl who spoke was the same one who had led me from our quarters. Her small kindness caused me to blink back tears. I would not let them spill. I was not a baby.

"Thank you."

She glanced around, then gave me directions to the prince's chambers. "You had better hurry, Linnie. First you will have Brisen's anger on you, then the prince's. Neither are pleasant."

The door to Prince Agravain's chamber stood open when I arrived. Laden as I was, knocking was impossible. Not knowing what else to do, I stopped just outside.

Two youths lounged at a table covered with the remains of a hearty meal. The elder of the pair held a scrap of meat to the dog at his feet.

My stomach gurgled and I licked my lips as the animal gnawed.

The young man scratched the dog's ears a moment before finally speaking to me.

"What are you waiting for, girl?" he said. "Put it next to the brazier."

"Yes, my lord," I murmured.

"How about a bit of sport, Agravain?" I heard the younger boy say as I drew close to the table and the nearby iron brazier. There was already a stack of wood beside it, plenty to last the night, I was certain.

"Sport? In this weather? Are you daft, Modred?"

"Not outside, brother. We need not even leave the warmth. Watch."

The youth with the short-cropped black hair chose that moment to stretch in his chair, extending his legs in my path.

I landed on my knees with an "Oh." The wood scattered across the floor. Boyish laughter filled my ears as I rubbed my bruises.

"Clumsy. Pick that mess up." The older prince raised his hand to strike me.

I cringed, raising my own arms in self-protection.

"How dare you hide yourself from me? Slaves take what they're given."

My arms were no match for his warrior's skills. His sword-calloused hand connected with my cheek. Then he hauled me to my feet by my hair.

"Pick it up."

I scurried to obey, wanting nothing more than to quit the royal presence and return to the kitchen.

* * *

By eventide I stumbled into our quarters along with the others. I collapsed near the fire and stared straight ahead, seeing nothing. A bowl of pottage appeared without warning in my hands. I glanced up and saw Dafydd. Still wounded by his rough treatment of that morning, I immediately redirected my attention to the bowl. It was kinder. At least it gave a little bit of warmth, and it did not shout at me or strike me.

When the bowl cooled, I set it down. Wishing for privacy, I walked to our usual sleeping place. I wanted no part of the stories or songs or gossip. Or anyone. I sat with my back to the fire and the others, facing the wall and hugged my knees to my chest. My throat ached with tears, but I refused to let them flow lest the others see me weep. Babies cry, and Dafydd had told me I was no longer a baby. I held them in my heart.

"Please eat something, Linnie." The voice sounded more like the Dafydd I was familiar with than it had that morning.

"I am not hungry," I said to my knees.

He knelt in front of me and set the bowl within my reach.

"Linnie, you have a bruise." He reached out as if to touch my face.

"Stop." I swiped his hand away. "So what if I have a bruise? So what if one of the princes beat me for being clumsy and slow this afternoon? Can you change it?"

Dafydd had no answers. He stared, obviously wishing he could do something.

Before he offered pity, I pointed to the bowl. "Take that away. I told you I am not hungry. Eat it yourself for all I care."

He removed it immediately, leaving me alone. It felt good to command someone after receiving so many commands myself throughout the day. And being obeyed was sweet indeed.

Still hugging my sore knees, I slumped to the floor. My mind echoed the keening I wanted so desperately to release. I must show him, show everyone, I was not a baby.

At some point Dafydd silently slipped to my side. I let him tuck the thin blanket around me without complaint.

"Lin, Lin." He repeated the grown-up name over and over, as his hand smoothed my hair. "Lin? I'll take care of you. I promise. I'll do better. You'll see."

CHAPTER 4

Dafydd and I settled into the new routine of our life. Having been given little chance to adjust to our loss, we tried our best to ease the holes left within each other's hearts. But Dafydd was merely two years my elder. I often heard him crying while the others in our quarters slept. Those nights were by far the worst.

The dunn had no need to resort to eating seaweed that winter. Supplies held until the weather broke and I entered my sixth summer.

Among my many chores, Brisen often sent me to fill the pigs' food trough with kitchen scraps. And I did not mind the task because the pigs were penned across from the dunn's small practice yard. While I emptied the buckets of slops, I could watch the warriors practice their hand-to-hand drills. The intricate steps of their deadly dance fascinated me.

One sunny morning, I saw three of the princes enter the fenced area. The boys ranged in age from twelve to fifteen, with Prince Agravain the eldest still at home. I must say, they looked quite smart in their polished battle-gear. It promised to be a good show even if I could not tarry long.

"Hurry up, Modred," Prince Gaheris shouted. Queen Morgause's middle son, he had her dark hair.

Orkney's youngest prince emerged from the armoury and trotted past me on the path. He also had the look of their mother. Unlike his brothers, Prince Modred wore no armour. But he was laden with weapons, which did not seem fair to me.

"Do you want me to drop everything?" he said. He was eleven that summer.

The older boys had begun a series of exercises, stretching their arms and legs.

"You wanted this," Prince Gareth said. No other Orkney prince had inherited the golden hair of their grandmother, Queen Igraine.

"I did not ask to be your bloody slave," Prince Modred said.

"Grumbling is unseemly in a shield-bearer, little brother."

I lost track of who spoke, having my own work. I emptied the first bucket amidst the squeals and grunts of the swine.

The boys had armed themselves by the time I could watch them again. Prince Modred brandished a sword, jabbing the air with its point.

"When do I get to learn something besides how heavy this stuff is?"

"Give me that," Prince Agravain said. "I'll teach you when I think you're ready, boy." He reached for the blade.

But Prince Modred leapt backwards. Smaller and more lithe, he escaped his elder brother's lunge, laughing.

I grinned.

Prince Agravain growled. He shared their father's ruddy colouring with their eldest brother, Prince Gawain. He also often displayed the temperament for which redheads were infamous. I had learned to avoid his path.

As for Prince Gawain, the eldest Orkney prince and rightful lord of Dunn na Carraice, he was in Camelot at present. It was whispered that he served as a hostage for some reason, perhaps in connection with Queen Morgause's banishment to Orkney.

"Ach," Prince Modred was saying. "I wager I could take the lot of you on. Now. Without any lessons." He squared his stance.

"I am game to teach the braggart a few things. You, Ris?" Prince Gareth said. He leaned towards the brother he addressed. The gold of his hair shimmered in the morning sun.

I suppose each was handsome in his unique way. There were favourites among the girls with whom I shared quarters. Mine? What did I know of those things at six? But I must admit, Prince Modred's blue eyes were striking, the few times I got close enough to see them, that is.

He stared his brothers out, his sword level.

"So. The Golden Child will be first, huh?" he said.

Prince Gareth drew his sword. "I shall have you to know, Modred, I am twelve and not a child."

The youngest prince did not flinch. Instead, he bit the thumb of his shield hand at them.

"All right, piss-ant. Arm yourself." Prince Agravain spoke, bringing his blade over his head to strike.

Prince Modred snatched up a shield and blocked the blow in the nick of time.

It was a slaughter, three to one. I pitied the dark-haired youth as his brothers pummelled him. He gave such a brave try, swinging the shield in defence. I admired how he held his own against the odds. In spite of our class difference, I felt a bond with the youngest prince. He seemed to have as little control over his life as I had of mine. Mayhap it had been an accident when he tripped me. I hoped he would triumph in the end.

The sight of the unfair beating Prince Modred's brothers gave him was too painful to watch any longer. And I was glad it seemed to be over by the time I finished my chore and began the return journey to the kitchen.

"Do you yield?" Prince Agravain shouted over his brother's prone form. They had cornered the poor boy near the gate.

"The smeg-head doesn't even know when he has lost," Prince Gaheris said.

Prince Modred sat up. "I yield," he said slowly, dabbing blood from his chin. But his blue eyes had not lost their defiance.

Perhaps I should offer to fetch water so the prince could bathe his face. It seemed the thing to do. Dafydd always helped me when I was hurt.

"What are you staring at, pig-girl?" Prince Modred shouted.

His brothers joined him in his laughter.

"I only thought—"

"Thought? Did you hear that, lads? The *cumal* thought."

Their taunts rang in my ears as I ran back to the kitchen.

* * *

"What is wrong with your mother, Meg?"

"She says it's the babe, Dafydd. But I am sore afraid."

Enid had been in distress all evening, rubbing her swollen belly, sweating, groaning a great deal. At the moment, two women supported her as the trio walked around our quarters. It looked cruel. Should they not allow her to rest?

"I am certain she will be well," my brother said, hugging our friend.

"May it be so." She leaned against my brother's shoulder.

"Sometimes I still fear going to sleep at night, that I might wake and find her…"

I drew my knees to my chest. I knew what she feared.

"Please, Meg. Weep not." Dafydd wiped a tear from her cheek with his fingers. He was doing his best to offer comfort.

More than half a year had passed since Samhain. It never took much to send my memories hurtling back to that night. That morning. Aching for my mother, I stared at the wall opposite where we sat. Dafydd had enough worries at the moment, caring for our friend. He did not need a baby for a sister. I held tight rein of my tears.

The women finally helped Enid to the floor. They hovered over her. One commanded her to push.

How odd. Push what?

"I… Oh, Blessed Mother."

"Maybe I should go to her," Meg said, kneeling.

"Push, Enid. The bairn's nearly here. I can see the head."

"They will only send you back here," I said.

"Lin is right, Meg. The midwife has helped other babies into the world."

Enid screamed.

Would she die?

My brother squeezed his eyes shut. He was as frightened as Meg. She sobbed into his breast. He smoothed her hair.

"Good girl, Enid. One more like that."

How long could we endure the poor woman's suffering? I wanted to flee.

Then a different cry pierced our cramped hovel. A baby's. It was answered by a cheer. Another slave had been born. The noise drowned out the words of the midwife.

The babe had cried, but what of Enid? She had fallen silent. We still had to wait.

"Meg?" Custennin, Enid's husband, stood beside us. He spoke softly.

"Yes, sir?"

"Come meet your new sister." Custennin offered his hand to his adopted daughter. For a man who had seen battle, he had a gentle smile. "Dafydd and Lin, you are well come too, if you like."

"What of Mother?"

"Tired. She wishes to see you."

Our friend scrambled to her feet. Dafydd and I were not long after.

The women surrounding Enid made way for us. Custennin knelt and kissed his wife's sweaty brow. Enid's eyes fluttered open.

"Meg," she whispered. "Greet Olwen."

Our friend gasped in delight when her sister's tiny fist curled around her own finger.

"My sister," she said, wearing a grin.

As for Dafydd and I, we merely stared in silent wonder as Olwen suckled at the breast for the first time.

* * *

"Open this door. Agravain! Ris! Gareth! You bleeding bastards. Let me out. Mother will have your hides for this." The shouting, accompanied by pounding came from inside the privy. A board had been wedged against the door so that it could not be opened from inside. No mistaking the angry voice of Prince Modred. His brothers were nowhere in sight. Nor was anyone else.

It sounded like the prince threw his entire weight against the door.

"Do you hear me, you pus-bags?"

I knew I could be punished if I took over-long at my duties. But what would Dafydd think if I ignored someone in need? He said everyone deserved kindness, no matter what they might have done in the past.

The board had been jammed tightly into the ground and it took several moments for me to work it loose. As the freed wood fell to the side, the door burst open and the prince slammed into me.

Amidst his barrage of curses, I hit the mud on my back.

"Bastard," he screamed, his fingers at my throat. "I shall kill you for that. And Mother will—"

Kill me? For helping him? Oh, he must think—

Struggling beneath the prince, I said, "Your Highness, I—"

It took another moment before he relaxed his grip and stared down at me, his blue eyes cold with rage.

Somewhere behind us, I heard a boy giggle as Prince Modred realised I was not one of his brothers.

"See that, Ris? Modred the Brave, fending off his mortal enemy. A slave-girl."

Orkney's youngest prince glared at me a moment longer, then rose to his feet, straightening his tunic.

"Did the fierce *cumal* ambush you?"

"Shut your gob, Gareth," Prince Modred said, but not before he released his anger by kicking my side.

I clutched my ribs and guarded my breathing for it lessened my pain.

He joined his brothers, saying, "You had no right to block that door."

"Run to Mother, then. Like you always do."

Run? If I tarried any longer, I would suffer worse than a bruised rib. Confused by the prince's angry reaction to my kindness, I returned to my duties questioning my brother's advice for the first time.

CHAPTER 5

Nothing truly momentous happened in the next four years. We woke. We ate. We worked. Pain bred work. My bruises faded only to be replaced by fresh on a regular basis. Dafydd had his share as well. Work bred pain.

I avoided the young princes whenever possible and even managed to succeed, most times. Their realm—comprised of horses and swords and spears—rarely overlapped with mine. The royals only wanted our labour anyway. But occasionally a duty sent me to Prince Modred's path. As the youngest prince grew older, his demeanour towards me never changed. In fact, I think he took even more delight in my misfortune after I freed him. I never left his presence without a physical reminder of the encounter. I became the catch dog for his vexations.

Betters? Dafydd was wrong. Cruelty does not deserve kindness.

Every day I added another stone to the inner rampart I had begun building around my heart that snowy Samhain when Mummy had passed over.

Each night I heard tales of life far removed from my own. Stories of the Queen's famous half-brother and his elite cavalry in Camelot. And thoughts of heroes and brave deeds crowded my head. But they were simply stories, told for our amusement.

Or were they?

My wall of protection cracked wide open one morning in late summer of the year I turned ten.

*   *   *

The cock crew and rudely interrupted my sleep.

"Can a bloke not have a dream even?" Dafydd said within a yawn. He had wound himself compleatly into the threadbare material we called a blanket, head to foot, like a shroud. Around us, the others stirred.

"I see you slept well, Dafydd."

He nodded and rubbed his eyes. "You?"

"Enough, I suppose."

"Nights are too short in summer. Shall I fetch our porridge?"

Dafydd did not wait for my answer. He pushed himself to his feet and padded to the fire-pit, answering friendly greetings on the way. He returned, balancing two bowls and two crusts of brown bread.

I took one of each.

Dafydd tucked into his meal immediately, scooping out the boiled barley with his bread. I had less enthusiasm for my food and ate more slowly.

I was not half-finished when the door at the far end of the hovel crashed open. If the overseer had a name, I never knew it. He bellowed a command to leave off the laziness.

"Lazy. He can be such a jester," my brother said.

I nodded, my mouth filled with porridge.

"What did you dream of, Lin?"

That was our ritual every morning, trading dreams. Every morning that I could remember. Whatever my brother's dream had been, I would carry it through the dreariness of the dozens of mindless chores I would have to do. Dafydd's dreams made the work a little easier, more tolerable. The blows endurable. I never believed my dreams to be worth much, especially to Dafydd, but he always asked first.

"Some place warm, where it is summer all the time and I do not need a blanket."

He grinned and said, "Sorry Lin." Then after the briefest pause, he continued on in an excited rush. "But there is such a place. It is called the Summer Country, ever so far from this dreary place, in ancient Logres. That is the old name for Britain," he added with authority. "The Pendragon lives there with his beautiful queen, Gwenhwyfar. The Round Table is there as well."

"Camelot?"

"Camelot," he answered. My brother's wealth of knowledge amazed me.

"What was your dream, Dafydd?"

I never learned it because a commotion arose not far from where we sat and interrupted him in mid-thought. I remembered the current phase of the moon with a familiar sinking of my stomach. Time for collarings.

A collar, an insipid thing really, harmless to look at on its own. Made of stiff leather, about the width of two thumbs' breadths, and long enough to wrap around a neck snugly. Our coming of age gift from the Queen. It served as a constant reminder of our place, as if the incessant verbal taunts and jeers of everyone in the dunn were insufficient to keep us informed of our lowly lot in life.

Yet on that summer morning, I was still innocent and believed that it could never happen to me, or any one I knew and cared about. Casually, I glanced towards the source of the noise.

When my stomach stopped its wild descent it formed itself into a tight knot.

"Dafydd," I whispered. "Meg is getting…" I turned to see my brother's face had gone ashen. His blue-grey eyes had lost their lustre and his jaw hung slack. He knew. We both knew what was coming.

In the next instant, the overseer jerked Dafydd to his feet.

"Your turn, boy."

What gave them the right? I could not allow it, not to my brother. I had to help him.

"No," I shouted, rushing forward. I swung at the man who would dare violate my beloved Dafydd with the obscene strip of brown leather. The overseer swept me away with one heavily muscled arm. The blow sent me sprawling. As though on a quest, I sprang to my feet again, screaming the gods know what.

Before I reached the overseer a second time, his assistant caught me by the hair, yanked me back and held me fast. I watched helplessly.

My brother blinked once, otherwise he did not move. How could he be so silent? How could he accept that thing so peacefully, like a lamb with no idea it is about to be slaughtered?

The appalling scene ended swiftly, and the overseer turned to me.

"So. You would protect your brother from his fate, hmm?"

The man holding me by the hair snickered.

My defiance dissolved as the overseer towered over my head. Eye-level with his waist, I got a close-up view of his badge of office, the whip dangling from his belt. He did not reach for it. Instead, he nodded to his aide behind me who unloosed my hair.

The burning across my back came from nowhere a moment later.

The force of the blow sent me flat and winded. Before I could catch my breath, a second stroke landed between my shoulders. I was still gasping for air when a fist gripped my hair again and hauled me to my feet.

"You, I'll be watching," the overseer said, then released me.

My wobbly legs collapsed immediately and I landed on my knees. I heard satisfaction in the overseer's chuckle.

"Entertainment is over. To work." He and his aide strode out. Several of our companions filed after.

Dafydd rushed to my side, followed closely by Meg, both ready to lend me aid.

"Leave me be. I can do this myself. I do not need your help. I do not want it."

My brother dropped his hands at my outburst. Meg backed away. Everyone else stared mutely as I composed myself. The whip had inflicted more than pain. The overseer had achieved humiliation. It smouldered within me. I *had* to stand up on my own. Or—I did not understand what drove me, I just knew that I must.

The effort to heave myself to my feet taxed me greatly. Each movement ignited my fresh wounds and I stumbled as though besotted.

No one had moved, although I know Dafydd wanted to. His eyes displayed his thoughts clearly.

"What are you staring at?" I said.

That infused some life into the crowd and more people shuffled out. Our duties awaited. And who would risk a beating for me, the heartless one who had not wept for her mother's passing?

"Lin—"

"We have to go, Dafydd," I said and walked away.

The day was impossible, having to carry on as if nothing had happened. But something dreadful had occurred to my brother and me. Dafydd's collar ground the reality of our condition into me. Until that morning, we had been simply children who worked long and gruelling hours for the comfort of others, and reaping none of the benefits of our sweat.

Now the world would know at a glance what Dafydd was. Not who, but what.

I found strength from Dafydd, even though I did not see him until evenfall. I remembered how silent and dignified he had been throughout his ordeal. Maybe if I tried harder, I could be more like him.

* * *

"Lie down, Lin." Dafydd set a basin of water and a cloth on the floor beside my half-eaten meal. In spite of the day's labour, I did not have much of an appetite. I was too tired and in a great deal of pain.

Throughout our quarters the adults gossiped. No word was spoken of the morning's events within our dwelling. Collarings never were. They were merely accepted and tolerated.

Why? The question seared deep within me, leaving a scar on my heart like the ones the lash had laid open across my back.

"Why?" I said.

"Because someone must see to your back. Now lie down." My brother misunderstood my question. "Enid gave me some herbs to cleanse your wounds."

Meg's mother had some knowledge of herb-lore and was the closest we would ever have to a healer. She had also been trying to mother Dafydd and me ever since our own had died. Dafydd relished the attention. Me, I was getting along fine. I had all the family I needed with my brother.

I eased myself onto my belly, hiking my gown up so that my back was exposed for Dafydd to work.

He draped our blanket over my legs.

"Only one of the blows actually broke your skin," he said. It had also torn my clothing. "The other is bad enough though. A long, angry, red stripe. I shall try to be gentle."

In spite of his soft touch, every contact the damp cloth made with my torn flesh brought another flash of pain. This was worse than the actual wounding. I burrowed my face in my arms and bit the insides of my mouth to keep from crying out. I could not let Dafydd see how badly it hurt. As it was, I heard him sniffing every now and again throughout the slow process.

"I hurt you, Lin. Sorry," he said when he had finished.

"It was not so bad," I said, keeping my face hidden from his sight. I knew he did not believe my lie.

Several moments passed. The burning slowly dulled to a more tolerable throb that enabled me to relax my strained muscles. I sat up.

Was it only because I knew it was there that my gaze fell straight on the collar? His neck had been perfect just this morning—slender, graceful, the skin a warm brown from the constant exposure to the summer sun. I would never look at him in the same way again. I knew, deep inside, he was still Dafydd. The same boy who fed me songs and dreams as when we awoke at cockcrow. And yet, he was not. With one swift, deft movement, the overseer had taken my brother from me, and replaced him with a slave. A slave. Collars were for slaves. I had never considered either of us in that way, in spite of the many times we were told otherwise. He had always been Dafydd, my brother. Nothing less. Ever.

Because I did not want to see the truth of our life around his throat, I had to force myself not to turn my gaze from my brother. I struggled to focus my attention to the boy beneath it. A caring, kind boy, who did not deserve this.

"Thank you, Dafydd." I managed to quell the raging emotions within me. For the moment.

"Why, Lin? What on earth possessed you to do something so mad? Have you lost your reason?" My brother's eyes were red and his fair features drawn tight. Because of me.

"I had to try. I thought of what Arthur, the Pendragon, might have done."

"What? Scream like a *Bean Sith*? It was stupid, Lin."

I was aware of that. Still, his anger stung.

"I must have made it worse for you, Dafydd. Drawing everyone's attention the way I did. It must have been horrible."

He drew out a long sigh. "I paid no mind to the others, or even to you for that matter. I could not, not with the surge of shame coursing through me at that moment. It was not until afterwards that I became aware of your—of your scene."

Dafydd pressed long slender fingers to his collar. "It does not hurt, Lin," he said. "It is simply a nuisance. I suppose one gets used to it after a time. It is only leather. Custennin says the Saxons use iron on their slaves."

"What makes leather any better than iron? Comfort? Are you already resigned to that vile thing? I pray you are not."

Dafydd looked weary.

Collared or not, I would never accept my brother as a slave.

"You cannot change things, Lin. Thank you for your effort, but I wish you had not. The overseers really hurt you, although you refuse to show it, stubborn girl that you are. You did not so much as gasp, let alone scream this morning. The pain must be unbearable. How could you remain silent?"

"Everyone was staring at me, Dafydd. What would they think if I cried like a baby in front of them?"

"You stubborn, impossible girl." Dafydd sighed again, shaking his head. "Each lash they laid on your back ripped my heart open. I cannot bear to see you suffer."

"I felt lost, Dafydd. The assault came so suddenly, it sent my mind into a panic. I did not know what to do. I was scared."

I shuddered at my confession. I reached for my brother, hugged him fiercely, and he very gently returned the embrace. The motion inflamed my tortured back, but I did not care. I needed the tenderness. I needed my brother. I held him tighter.

"Lin, you know I shall always help you find your way."

"Always, until you are taken from me," I whispered.

Dafydd stiffened, but said nothing.

I had the time to cry then and did. I pressed my face to his bare chest as hot tears spilled onto his heart, and I listened to its steady beat. After a time, he began to hum a soft, sweet tune from our distant past. A gentle soothing lullaby our mother had sung for us.

We no longer exchanged dreams after that day. Dafydd still told me his, but I had no more to share. It is hard to dream when you do not sleep, except through exhaustion alone. Then the dreams change to nightmares.

CHAPTER 6

"Did you not even want to fight him putting that thing on you, Dafydd?"

The question had been with me a full sennight. I had come no closer to acceptance of my brother's collar in the time.

He drank his water. How did it feel to swallow now?

Dafydd set his cup on the floor. "There was a time when I thought I might. A year or so ago. I guess I was about your age. But I have seen how they quell rebels. I had no desire to be whipped. This is much easier."

"Is it?"

My brother fidgeted under my stare. I knew his discomfort. I wanted an answer.

He pushed my bowl towards me.

"Honestly, Lin, I do wish you would eat."

I shoved the bowl away with my foot, upsetting it.

"Lin." He set it a-right before everything spilled out.

"You have not answered me, Dafydd. Is the collar easier?"

Dafydd stretched his neck and used his fingers to readjust the band at his throat. He sighed, his face turned from mine. The leather did bother him, more than he would admit.

"I thought not," I whispered, not vindicated in the slightest.

"It makes me feel like a dog, Lin. But we have no choice. You have time before you get yours. I hope you will be wise." This time he placed my bowl in my hand. "Please eat."

Would my brother still be in Dunn na Carraice when my time arrived?

"For me?"

No matter what the future held for us, at least he was with me now. I tried my best to see beyond his collar.

He smiled as I raised the bowl to my lips and gulped the now cold pottage, using my fingers for the larger chunks of fish and turnips.

Not long after I finished, Meg joined us, as usual.

Dafydd shifted closer to me.

"My mother found an extra needle for you, Lin," she said, handing me a sharp piece if bone.

"You certainly are in a happy mood," I said, pulling a thread from the hem of my shift. Dark stains of my blood still discoloured the material, even though I had scrubbed hard in a vain attempt to wash it out.

"Have you not heard?" She had brought her younger sister's gown and began to work tiny, even stitches into its hem. My needlework was never so neat. "The entire dunn is buzzing with it. A ship arrived in the harbour this morning."

Ships always stirred conversations throughout Dunn na Carraice. Of course I had heard. Ships meant news of the outside world beyond the sea. But I saw little reason for Meg's excitement.

"Prince Gawain and Prince Agravain were on it, I heard," Dafydd said.

"Well, now. Is that not jolly lovely?" I said.

Dafydd shrugged. He knew well about my encounter that afternoon.

Meg peered around my brother at me.

"I was in the wrong place at the wrong time. My misfortune to be working in the Great Hall when all five brothers gathered there. Had Prince Agravain not demanded wine—"

"You served the princes, Lin?" Meg said.

"Are you impressed," I asked, my sewing now forgotten.

"Lin, I am sorry," Meg said. "Is that how you got that bruise near your eye?"

"I am never fast enough for him."

"Who?" Meg said.

"Prince Modred." I tugged at my shift, wanting to shred it.

Dafydd pried my fingers loose and set the garment aside.

"Meg, do you think your mother has anything that would help my sister?"

"I am certain she does, Dafydd. We can ask."

"That is kind, Meg."

I'd had a glimmer of hope for compassion during those moments with royalty when Prince Gareth had questioned his younger brother if hitting me had been necessary. To which Prince Modred replied that slaves needed constant discipline. Prince Gareth's next words crushed all thought of humanity from that lot.

"But so hard, Modred? She is just a girl."

Foolish me. I thought he had been concerned about my being beaten.

"Lin?" Dafydd shook my shoulder.

It took another moment of staring at my brother before my mind returned to the now.

"Would you rather talk of something else?" he said.

What else was there?

"No. I am fine. I am sorry if I ruined your mood, Meg. What news do you have?"

"You mean the princes did not speak of Prince Gawain's bride?"

Bride. That was news. But if they had spoke of it, I was not listening.

I shook my head.

Meg seemed disappointed I had squandered an opportunity to glean gossip. She turned to my brother.

"What of you?"

"I heard a little. The Princess Rioghnach is Pictish. Your da says Prince Gawain is probably forming an alliance for the Pendragon that will serve as a buffer beyond the Wall. He also said it was too bad the Pendragon's daughter had died so young. Her marriage to Prince Gawain would have forged a strong dynasty."

"That is if he ever had a daughter, Dafydd," I said. "I have never believed it. The Pendragon would never have a daughter. He would have a son. Nay. Not one, but many sons. More than his sister, Queen Morgause."

Not even Dafydd could speak ill of my hero. To my ears, this was the basest of insults. King Arthur with a daughter? Whatever would he do with a daughter? The very idea was absurd. And I told my brother so.

"You are impossible. I say he did have a daughter. Why is that so difficult for you, stubborn girl?"

"Because the Pendragon is a great warrior. And great warriors have sons."

"What? Not only impossible, but mad as well. I honestly do not know why I bother." Dafydd folded his arms across his breast and watched me.

I could see the amusement in his blue-grey eyes at my utter nonsense.

I smiled and shrugged.

"May I finish now?"

Meg and I nodded.

"I, too, have my doubts, Lin. I doubt the Princess is dead."

And he called me mad. Just where was the line dividing his story-telling and my madness?

"Why do you say that, Dafydd?" Meg said.

"Enemies of the Pendragon would be hers as well. They might even wish her dead. I think news of her death was a lie to stop enemies from hurting her."

Even I had to agree he made sense. More than I had a moment ago.

"Where do you think she might be, then?" Meg said.

"The one place no one would ever dream of looking, most like. She might even be here."

"Nobody would willingly send their child to Queen Morgause." My voice rose. "Certainly not King Arthur. He is not daft. It is common knowledge that she was in league with her husband and his treason against the Pendragon, her own brother. That is why she and her sons were banished here. And why Prince Gawain had served as a hostage."

"Shh. Not so loudly. You might be heard." Dafydd was wise for his youth, and far more cautious than I would ever be. Common knowledge or no, those were dangerous words, for anyone in Orkney, slave or free, to utter. Worse, in fact for a slave, for we were beaten simply for showing the slightest sign we might have a thought of our own within our heads.

"Well," I said more quietly. "I still say, better for the princess if she is dead, than alive here."

I shivered as I spoke, and yet I had no obvious reason. The night was calm, the fire warm. I had no explanation for the cold. Had someone trod on my grave? My companions seemed unaffected. I crept closer to my brother. He draped an arm across my shoulders and the chill vanished.

Meg hunched over her sewing. Her four-year-old sister tugged at the elder girl's sleeve. Meg ignored Olwen.

"Come, little one," my brother said, holding his arms out.

She settled into his lap.

"Now. Where is that pretty girl named Olwen? I cannot see her with these fingers hiding her face." With boundless patience, which he had lacked five years before with his own sister, he pulled the two fingers she had in her mouth away from her face.

"There she is," he said, and the two smiled. "I was very worried that she was gone from me. Please, do not hide your pretty face like that ever again, for it will make me quite sad. Will you promise Dafydd that you will not?"

Olwen's brown curls bounced as her head bobbed. The boon of my brother's attention was so great, she was never seen with her fingers in her mouth after that.

"She is probably in Little Britain," I said. I finished my seam with a knot, then bit off the leftover thread.

"Who," Dafydd asked, busy wiping Olwen's nose with the hem of his tunic.

"Why the Princess, of course."

"Do you mean in Armorica, Lin?" Meg asked.

"With Sir Lancelot's family. Quite simple actually. Who else but the Pendragon's best warrior could possibly have such an honour?"

"Lin, that is far too obvious," Dafydd said.

"Which is why no one would think of searching there for her. The obvious is perfect." I believed the Pendragon brilliant for having thought of the plan. "I say, she is there. Assuming, naturally, that you are right and she exists at all." I dug, playfully contrary.

"Impossible One," Dafydd muttered. "No matter where she went, it is a mystery. Just like when King Arthur himself was born, and was whisked away as a baby. Nobody knew until he became Pendragon that it was Sir Ector who had raised him. Even Sir Ector was surprised to learn of his foster son's true identity."

"You and your stories, Dafydd. Do you never stop?" I asked.

"Only by royal command."

Meg's shoulders shook as she joined our laughter.

"Mummy," Olwen announced quite unexpectedly.

"What about Mummy?" Meg said, glancing up.

Olwen said nothing further.

Meg set her sewing aside. "Here, Dafydd. I can relieve you of my sister now. Thank you for minding her."

"Dafydd," Olwen said, clinging to his neck.

"Let her be, Meg. You know I do not mind."

Our friend looked grateful. "Now. Olwen, you must tell me, what about Mummy?"

"Wants you."

"Oh, why did you not say so sooner? Dafydd, Lin is not impossible, as you say. That one is." She stood and pointed to her sister, who was now busy inspecting the leather around Dafydd's neck. Olwen gripped it with chubby fingers and tugged.

My brother grimaced, but said nothing.

"Olwen, you must stop. You are hurting him. You are hurting Dafydd." She scolded as she bent and pried the tiny fist loose and slapped it.

Dafydd flinched at the smack. The small one in his lap made no noise. Neither did she shed a tear. She simply nestled closer to the sole source of comfort that she, her sister, and I shared.

"Never mind, Meg," he said softly, as he rested a cheek on the tiny head at his chest. "Please, do not strike her. She is just a baby. She does not understand. We have far too much violence here as it is." He rubbed his neck as he glanced around the room, never focusing on any one person, and avoiding me. He could be as stubborn as me at times, and now he was determined to show me that the collar could be accepted with grace, or at least with a minimum of harm.

My skin crawled with his honesty. Every person in our quarters had some form of bruises or scars upon them. We were naught but slaves. Jackstraws.

"Go see about your mother, Meg," I whispered, my mouth dry of a sudden. "Olwen will be well with us."

When she was gone, I faced Dafydd. "I do not understand anymore than Olwen does, and I am not a baby."

I reached out, and for the first, and only time, touched his collar. I pressed my fingers to the leather. The thing did not burn them. Just ordinary cowhide, of fair quality. The fine boots, saddles and bridles of the princes were far better, I was certain. Yet I jerked my hand away as though it scorched. Why did it repulse me so? I had seen it on scores of people, since my earliest memories. Even our own mother had been disfigured by one.

"I do not understand, and it shames me to say how difficult it is for me to simply look at you now because of a small strip of leather. It tears my heart to gaze upon my own brother. Dafydd, I am sorry that I must say such a thing." On the verge of tears, I buried my face in my hands.

"Please do not weep, Lin. I know how hard it is. You think it easy for me to see Meg now?"

I had not thought of that.

"What gives the Queen of Orkney the right to do this to you? To us?" I asked my hands.

"Custennin says that inside the palace the Queen has a locked cabinet, in which are sheaves of sheepskin, stretched thin and dried. He says they have marks and symbols on them, telling only those who know how to decipher them, a list of all the Queen's property. Maybe they are magic symbols."

Custennin had once been a hired warrior for an ally of the Pendragon. He had been taken by a Saxon during a battle, and spent several seasons as a slave of the barbarians before being sold to the man who brought him north to Orkney and Dunn na Carraice. Once here, he met Meg's mother, sired Olwen, and even though Meg was not his true daughter, he treated her kindly. They had become a family.

"If those symbols contain that much power, the power to possess the body and soul of another, they must be very magical, indeed. I would very much like to learn that sort of magic."

"Not I. Power of that sort is dangerous, Lin." My brother made the horned sign with his fingers, in case there was evil simply in speaking about such magic.

But power of any kind to me was inviting. I held firm to my desire to learn some day.

"Does Custennin know how to decipher them, Dafydd?"

"He says he can, but only if they are Roman letters."

"You mean there are other kinds?"

"I suppose."

Dafydd shrugged, as I pondered the magic of writing.

"You know," he said, after a time. "I should not be at all surprised if Orkney loses another prince to Camelot when Gawain and Agravain leave this time."

"Oh? What do you mean?"

"Prince Gaheris. The stable-hands say he is of age now, and quite skilled at arms."

"Good riddance to him when he goes," I said, envious of the young man who had such an opportunity.

""Why so uncharitable? Has he hurt you as well as the others?"

"He has no need. He was born of Queen Morgause and that is

enough for me. What charity has any of them given us? He will not be going too soon. Neither will the others."

"Every lad here I know of dreams of going to Camelot to join the Pendragon's army. It seems all anyone ever speaks about."

"Even you?" I could not envision sweet, gentle Dafydd, the youth with the sleeping child cradled in his arms, clad in armour, with sword in hand.

"An *eques*? Me?" He laughed. My brother could dream many things, but never that. "No. That is not for me. I want to be Camelot's bard." The smile lingered in his eyes.

"Now, there is a grand dream. Camelot's bard. Well, and why not? You have the voice for it."

"No," he said. "I just enjoy singing. I know that dream will never come true." He sighed and seemed to regret sharing it with me. "Lin? If you could go to Camelot, what would you wish to do?"

I often thought of going to Camelot; of what it would be like, the Round Table, the Pendragon, and his queen. Oh, how grand it must be. But I never gave a thought to what I would do with the chance. And no one had bothered to ask.

"If I could go to Camelot? I would be Lin, Dafydd. I want nothing more."

"What do you mean? Of course you are Lin."

"Only to you and precious few others. I hate being called 'girl' and 'slave.' Surely even servants have names in Camelot and surely those names get used. I often want to scream my name aloud from the ramparts."

Meg returned then, and lifted her sleeping sister from Dafydd.

He stretched his long legs out before him.

I could see in his eyes that he understood what I had just said and that he was trying to answer.

"*Croch suas e*, Davy." A man spoke in Irish above the crowd.

"Yes, a song," several others agreed in chorus.

Dafydd's talents were already famous at our evening gatherings. Rare was the night that his voice did not rise pure and clear to enchant us with stories of far away.

"It seems as though your 'Camelot' is demanding its bard, Dafydd," I said. Perhaps more than any one else in our quarters, I needed my brother's skills most.

"Davy the Bard," Meg said, clapping.

He blushed yet again, but was quite keen for this game. He rose and bowed with a flourish.

"What be your pleasure then, this night, my lords and ladies? A tale of heroes and adventure? Love perhaps?"

I saw him as the suggestions were tossed about, not in the usual tattered and dirty rags, but in fine, brightly coloured linen and wool. Round his neck a gold torc glittered in place of the crude leather. I am not taken with visions very often, so I shall never forget that one.

A performer above all else. It was what he breathed for.

* * *

The next day began in much the same manner as all the others in my life ever had. A dream from Dafydd to garnish the barley porridge. A quick word with Meg, and then we were off in dozens of directions to our various duties. The brilliant, unseasonably warm late summer sun gave no warning whatsoever as to how black the afternoon would become. It should have hidden its face in shame for Orkney's vile deeds.

By sunset, I was numb from what I had witnessed at mid-day. I had chanced upon the scene, the people gathered around the platform in the dunn's courtyard. A different task and I would have been elsewhere. It took several moments to understand why Meg was up there. By then, she was being led away in chains. Too late for my feeble protests.

Who else had been knocked down?

I managed to learn that Dafydd had been seen within the fortress since the auction by more than one person. That heartened me some.

But Meg. And the others.

Confusion filled our quarters that evening as we sought out loved ones. Dafydd pushed his way to me and nearly fell into my arms.

"Lin, I was worried I might have lost you."

"Me too, Dafydd."

He released me and glanced around the room. "Have you seen Meg?"

He had not heard. How could I tell him what I had witnessed?

"Lin? What is wrong?"

I could not hold back the tear that slid down my cheek.

"No," my brother said and sank to the floor.

Heartsick, I picked up our bowls and filled them from the kettle on the hearth, unable to think of anything better to do at the moment.

"You need to eat, Dafydd." I set his bowl near him and sat.

He continued to stare at the stone floor for what felt like an eternity.

"Were you there , Lin?"

Relief washed over me to hear him speak once more.

"Yes. And right glad I am that you were not." I would have given anything to protect my brother from that horror.

"Did you… Did you see her?" His whisper was choked with the tears he fought to contain. A battle he was not destined to win.

I gave no reply.

"Tell me. Did you see her? Did you see Meg?"

"Yes." I drew the word out in a long hiss. Why could I not just lie? Say "no" and have done with it? Would it not be better that my brother did not know how frightened our friend had been? How her eyes had searched the crowd for a last glimpse of the face belonging to the boy who loved her? How she sought out Dafydd's comfort while on display, sought and never found? Would it not be kinder to him to say nothing?

I had searched for him, too. Searched and hoped I would not find him among those who were up for sale.

"How did she look?"

Why did he not allow me to spare him? Pale and frightened, Meg was, exposed to the world. Turned this way and that. Her strong back extolled. But her selling quality—the feature which closed the deal—she was female and would be breeding soon.

"Please, Lin." Dafydd's hand gripped my arm. "I must know. Tell me."

How could I not tell him? I would expect as much.

"Alone. Dafydd, she looked alone. One solitary shred of dignity in that seething sea of profanity. And I could do nothing to stop it. Nothing I said did a whit of good."

"But you did something, and that's far more than anyone else. You got a fresh bruise for your effort."

I shrugged.

"Did they—did they whip you?"

I shook my head. "No wounds for you to tend tonight," I said.

"Good. Oh, Lin. I was not even there for her when she needed me most. I was not there. I never told her that I love her. Never. And now… She shall never know."

I coaxed his sandy curls to rest upon my shoulder. I wanted more than anything to ease his hurt as he had eased mine so many times before.

"She knew. You had no need to tell her, because she was shown every day. Everyone who knows you cannot help but come away feeling loved." The words sounded useless as they passed my lips.

I felt his tears soak through my gown and my shift, straight through my skin and directly to my soul.

What good were the ideals of Camelot to us?

My brother did not sing that night.

"One must have a heart to sing," he told me. "Mine has gone."

CHAPTER 7

Dafydd eventually recovered his heart and resumed his story-telling. He even created new works of his own besides reciting the familiar ones he had memorised over the years. Loss and pain seemed to inspire my brother. Tales, both wondrous and magical, burst forth and delighted everyone in our quarters.

As for me, I did not fully understand the force that drove me to defiance that fateful morning of my brother's collaring. I still do not, to be honest. I only knew the rightness of my words and deeds of the moment. I felt it in my gut. And I could not stem the flood I had released. At the very least, I viewed our condition differently from then on.

For two years, I waited. What happened to Dafydd would happen to me in the end. Knowing one's destiny does not make things any easier.

Knowing is not acceptance.

*   *   *

As the day I dreaded most encroached upon me, Dafydd sensed my agitation and voiced his concern, but did not press when I answered him in terse words. He understood their source. I swallowed the food he brought me twice a day only to comfort my brother. I had to force each mouthful into my knotted stomach, where it settled in an uneasy lump. He did a gallant job of soothing me and coaxing me to rest at night.

How long would they hold off? How long could I wait?

I awoke Beltane, my natal day, and wondered. Will it be today?

After a dream and a bowl of gruel, I walked to the kitchen, lagging behind the other girls. They chattered and giggled over nonsense. One tried to include me by asking my opinion about the newest youth in our quarters. Was his name Padrig? I merely shrugged. After a moment they left me to my thoughts.

Today. Surely it will come today. I would be ready.

The kitchen stood apart from the palace as a separate building. Brisen barked out orders like battle plans as soon as we arrived. It took countless loaves of bread to feed everyone within Dunn na Carraice. Three days a week were set aside for baking. The dunn's housekeeper needed an army of her own those days.

Inside, the oven fires had already been lit. Some of my companions were assigned to stand sentry and keep the flames fed. I took my appointed post at one of the waist-high tables and bent over a quern fixed into it, turning the wooden handle to grind my allotment of grain into flour. At other tables, women mixed and kneaded the dough, then cut it into loaves. Soon the mouth-watering aroma of the fresh bread none of us would ever taste teased our mouths and noses.

The hours dragged. To pass the time, the women around me gossiped. But I could ill-afford distraction by such trifles as to what warrior had gotten which of the Queen's maids with child.

"You there. Fill those from the well and no dawdling." Brisen pointed to two wooden pails near the doorway. My lot to be closest, I suppose.

I stretched the aching muscles of my back and shoulders. My sweat-soaked gown clung to my skin and my hair had worked free of its plait. I pushed damp strands from my face and snatched up the pails before stepping into the noontide sun. I had to shield my eyes a moment in the sudden brightness. I shivered as a cool, salty breeze swirled over me. A well come respite from the ovens.

I followed the cobbled path through the kitchen yard, swatting at the flies swarming the middens heap, and then past the herb garden to the gate opening onto the main courtyard.

It seemed as though everyone from the dunn had turned out to enjoy the pleasant weather. I caught snips of conversations on my way.

"Weather this mild cannot last long."

"'Tis a sign. The rest of the summer'll be hard, mark me..."

"Try smearing some sheep's fat on your breasts after giving

suck…"

"The Pendragon routed…"

I wanted to linger over that one, but a finely dressed man jostled me. He glowered as though it were my fault.

I murmured an apology because it was expected and made my life easier.

I finally reached my destination, mounted the well's steps and drew up the bucket.

"There she is, our firebrand!" The overseer's voice carried above the din of the crowd.

I did not pause in my work, but kept pulling steadily. I nearly had the full bucket to the top when my hands were torn from the rope, and it went plunging back to the bottom. All my labour in vain.

The men laughed. A pox on them.

"Look what I have for you, Defiant One." The overseer presented the leather I so despised, dangling it in front of my face. His calloused fingers brushed the collar against my cheek, caressing me with it.

Today. My soul cringed.

"I think I shall enjoy this even more than striping your back."

Not the relative privacy of our quarters. The entire dunn would partake of the spectacle.

Strong arms pinioned me from behind. But when the overseer's hand came close and nearly had the thing around my neck, I bit him. Bit him hard enough to draw blood. He snatched his hand away, cursing, and I had my extremely brief moment of triumph, for in the next instant, the same hand struck my jaw. Was it the salt of his blood or my own I tasted?

"Little bitch. Your mother surely must have lain with a dragon, to conceive the likes of you. I swear, you could breathe fire if you had the mind to."

"Wrong." The new voice held a frosty edge in its tone.

Everyone nearby bowed immediately. My heart sank as I realised who spoke. Prince Modred. Well I remembered the times I was cause for his sport. His cruel jests of my plainness, my lack of grace. No longer a boy, the prince was now a grown man of seventeen. What did his presence mean?

"It was not a dragon, but the very devil himself who put his get into her mum. That hellion has the flames of Hell coursing through her veins." The prince silenced the overseer's snicker with a narrow-eyed glare. He pointed to the leather strap clutched in the older man's fist.

"Do it."

It eventually took two fully grown men to hold me long enough for the overseer's bloodied hand to snap the collar around my neck, and test its security by pulling taut from the side. The gesture choked me. And strands of my hair had been caught in the lock. For all my struggle, they had still won. The accursed band strangled me anyway. Every breath I took, every time I swallowed, I would be reminded of its presence. I bucked against the men restraining me, screaming. *Treat me like an animal, I shall act like one.* A dragon seemed best. Better than bleating like a lamb.

Was I braver than Dafydd and his peaceful acceptance? Or simply foolhardy and headstrong?

The men released me and I sank to my knees. Laughter rang in my ears from every side as I clawed at my neck.

Prince Modred hauled me to my feet by the collar. He stared at me for several long moments. Even though he frightened me, I was not about to let him see it. I squared my shoulders and glared back, as he had faced his brothers in the practice yard. 'Twas what I had always admired in Orkney's youngest prince. He never yielded against them. Nor would I now.

He shoved me in the direction of the overseer.

"Take care of her. A taste of the lash ought to quell her spirit."

"My pleasure, your Highness."

Did the prince not remember how I had once helped him? Or did he not recognise me? But I had no more time to ponder. The overseer seized my arm and pulled me across the courtyard to its centre and the scourging post. The crowd cleared a path for us. My heart thudded in my chest as I felt the cold iron close around my wrists. I took a firm grip of the chains and steeled myself for the pain to come. Rough hands tore the thin material of my gown and drew it clear of my back. I had witnessed this violence often. I knew the bite of the whip. I focused on keeping the rhythm of my breathing steady. A stiff breeze blew in from the sea and nipped my bare skin, raising goose flesh. My hair was pushed aside. The last of the caught strands ripped free from the collar's lock. I set my jaw, determined not to show weakness.

Somewhere behind me the prince kept a steady count. I do not know at what number I fainted. One or one hundred lashes makes little difference as far as pain is concerned.

*   *   *

When I regained my wits, Dafydd hovered over me, his face wet with tears. We were in the cool shade of our quarters and alone. He risked much to be with me. I could not imagine that he had received permission to leave his duties. I would only be allowed the remainder of the day to recover from my wounds. A token. And that, grudgingly.

"Lin," he said, when he realised I was awake. He wiped his face with his sleeve. "Can you move?"

"A little, I think."

"Here. Drink this. It might help." He held out a cracked piece of pottery. It served for his cup.

Already lying on my side, I tried to raise myself up on an elbow, but my strength had deserted me.

"Dafydd, I… Help? Please?" I sounded as weak as I felt. The pleading in my voice shamed me.

He lifted my head gently and held the cup to my dried lips.

Determined to hide how much agony the movement caused me, I clenched my muscles, averting my gaze from my brother.

"Why such a show for me, Lin? You need your strength. Do not waste it for your foolish pride."

I sipped. The potion burned my throat, and it felt as though flames ran rampant through my veins just as Prince Modred had said.

"What is that?" I asked, coughing.

"*Uisge*."

"Where did you get *uisge*?" The potent drink was reserved for the royal family of Dunn na Carraice—the Queen, her sons, and their personal guests, as it was very costly to distill. It certainly was not for slaves. The consequences of our having the stuff would be dire indeed, if we were found out.

"Never mind. I have my ways. Drink."

He helped me sip the remainder with care so as not to lose a precious drop, wiping my lips after with the sleeve of his tunic. The potion did ease my suffering somewhat. At least I had that other fire to concentrate upon.

The effort taxed me though. Dafydd helped me to lie on my side once more. He slipped our folded blanket under my head as a pillow.

If I did not move, the pain eased. Slightly. But I had to breath. And that simple task racked me.

A long time passed before either of us spoke again.

"They made sure I was close to the front, and that I witnessed every mark placed on your back. He beat you so hard, I was scared. So scared. I feared…I feared…he would…kill you." The youth who never had trouble with words stammered, and tripped over them now, and had to force them out.

"How many?" I said.

"What does the number matter? Your back is a mass of blood and welts, Lin. The more your blood flowed, the greater the prince's pleasure. How can anyone enjoy watching another's pain?" My brother burrowed his face into his hands and sobbed. "The collar is our life. There is nothing we can do to change it. Nothing. Why must you fight it so? Why?"

"Why have you given in so easily?" I said. "It is wrong. You know this is wrong. They treat their horses and dogs better than they treat us. Why? What makes the royals special? Put the lash across any of their backs and they would bleed just as quickly. I saw Prince Gareth one day, he was riding back from the hunt with others. A sleeve of his tunic was torn and stained bright red. His blood was no different from mine."

I clutched Dafydd's leg. He had lowered his hands to study me. "Why are they special? Do you never wonder about that? I know you are not stupid, Dafydd."

"I wonder about it all the time," he said, barely above a whisper. "But I do not think it worth the flogging to say it aloud."

"Well, I do. Someone must. This is not fair." I touched my collar.

"Maybe life is not supposed to be fair, Lin."

"It should be."

"I know," Dafydd said with a sigh. "I just wish… Oh, Lin. The way your body… I never want to witness such a horror again."

It took some effort for me to raise my arm so I could smooth his hair from his face.

"You asked why," I said. "I do not know. Something inside me snaps when the unfairness is shoved at me. And I must release my anger."

My brother nodded and several more moments of silence passed.

"You were very brave. Everyone said so."

"People thought me brave because they probably did not know I had swooned."

"Nobody in the dunn has ever seen anyone walk so calmly to the post as you did today."

My heart had been numbed by then.

"I thought the prince might have… Part of me hoped he would have repaid a kindness I had shown him a few years ago." My brother knew about the privy incident. "But… It hurt far more than I was prepared to withstand," I whispered, reluctant to admit it. "After the first few strokes, Dafydd, I begged the King of the Dead to take me, to free my body, as well as my spirit. You call that brave?"

My brother gasped. "Don't say it, Lin."

"I would rather the overseer had killed me today, than end up like… Perhaps the next world will be better."

To think, we used to trade childish dreams in that very spot but two years before. Now I was talking about my death wish.

Meaning well, my brother swabbed the raw skin where my wrists had borne my weight in the chains after I had fainted.

"Ow! Do not touch me." I jerked my hand free. Pain coursed through me. Tears stung my eyes.

Dafydd sat back on his heels.

"Do you have any idea how it hurts to see you this way, Lin?"

"No. I do not have near the experience you do. You are such a good, obedient slave. Slave." The word screeched out of my throat, sounding jagged and far more cruel than I intended. And seeing the injury reflected in my brother's eyes did nothing to silence me.

"As long as you believe it, Dafydd, that is what you are. A slave. Is that what you want?"

I regretted the entire speech immediately. Would have given anything to snatch it all away again.

"Lin."

There now, I managed to inflict a deep wound this time, with words as sharp as the lash, spoken hastily. My rage and pain had brought them on, and they were what kept me from saying more. When would my anger hold my tongue before I caused damage?

He waited several moments in the silence, while I seethed. After a heavy sigh, Dafydd rose without a word, and left me with misery as my sole companion. 'Twas everything I deserved really, after being so thoughtless. I did not want him to go, but my defiance had a firm grip of my tongue and would not let it loose. It kept me from calling him back. Would he have returned if I had? Or had I finally gone too far and driven him away forever?

Dolt. When would I learn? He was the only person in the world I had to care about, who care about me. And how did I repay him?

The rank smell of the stale straw sickened my stomach, but I was too weak to push free of it. And the effects of the *uisge* had long since faded.

"I am sorry, Dafydd. Please, come back. Don't leave me alone."

I tried to console myself that Dafydd would indeed return, as he always did. And he would forgive me, refusing to hear my apology. But just what if he does not come back? What if they have already taken him and put him on the block? What if he has been sold?

A racking shudder took hold of my body, which I could not stop, as I envisioned that horror. It was a feeling worse than the dread of the collar.

I gave in to my tears at the thought.

The door of our quarters opened and closed quietly. I heard footfalls muffled by the straw, crossing the empty room.

I knew my brother could not stay away long. He cared too deeply. But my pride did not want him to see me too anxious, so, I dried my eyes and waited. Only when he was near would I cry out that my harsh words had been wrong and ask him to forgive me.

CHAPTER 8

I learned it was not Dafydd as soon as I saw the highly polished black boots, and the fine, clean trews woven in the colours of clan mac Lot before my eyes. Dafydd's feet were always bare like my own. And our filthy rags—

"So your precious brother has left you to suffer alone. About time the lazy idler got back to his duties. I should have him at the post, too, for wasting so much time."

Prince Modred. Again.

"How dare you look at me? Have you no manners? Do you not know who I am?" He jabbed my ribs with the toe of his boot.

"I know you, prince," I said.

Why must I avert my eyes? Rumour had it, he was not even King Lot's son. Nobody knew who had sired this one, although opinions abounded. The Queen had birthed a bastard. Why should I defer to a bastard?

"Why do you not address me properly? Are you not afraid of me?"

"Should I be?"

"I am your master. I can have you beaten for your insolence. I can have you flogged simply because I desire to see you bleed."

"Is my blood so special then, that a prince desires to see it?"

"Silence. You gave us quite a show today. Much better than I expected, really," he said.

As he paced a circle around me, the prince stirred the foul odours of the floor coverings. His face twisted in distaste and he pressed a hand over his nose. He muttered an oath in Irish.

What more could he want of me? Had not the sport of seeing my back lashed to ribbons been enough?

He stopped pacing, bent over and hooked his fingers around my collar, pulling it across my throat. He used it to lift me to my feet, and continued to hold firmly. My toes brushed the floor and our faces were close enough for our breath to mingle. Could he smell the *uisge*? I struggled to hold up my torn garment, crossing my arms over my breasts, so that it did not slip and expose them to the blue eyes scrutinising me with such cold passion.

He grinned at my attempted modesty.

"You are mine now, did you know? Mother gave you to me, as a gift, just this morning."

Gift? I glared into his eyes. *Wfft*, but they were ice.

"You are still too proud." He backhanded my cheek with his free hand. "The overseer did not beat you nearly hard enough today. I should have handled the whip myself. Next time, I think I shall. Perhaps then you will finally learn what a proper beating feels like. It is the only thing slaves understand. You are too stupid for anything else."

His spittle flew into my face as he spoke.

"I can do whatever I like with you now," he continued. "Do you realise that?"

I held my tongue.

"Answer me." The fist clutching my collar shook.

Could there be life without pain?

He wanted to see me suffer. I saw the cruelty in his eyes. I bit the insides of my mouth to keep from crying aloud. I would not satisfy his desire.

"Answer me, *cumal*."

I knew quite well the despised Irish word for slave-girl.

"Yes." I hissed through clenched teeth.

He struck my face again, harder than the first time. His heavy gold ring caught my cheekbone below my eye.

"Yes what?"

"Yes, prince."

"Still so very proud. No matter. I shall break you of that soon enough. You shall learn to address me properly. I wanted your dear brother as well, you know."

"Leave Dafydd alone."

The prince regarded me a moment before he laughed.

I saw no mirth in his eyes.

"I can do as I please with him. And you. Never forget that. The next time you dare command me, I might not be so easily amused. Put your arms down."

But I would be unable to hold up my gown then. I did not respond.

He gave my collar a twist.

"Are you deaf as well as stupid? I gave an order, slave."

Slowly, after adjusting the rent material as best I could upon my shoulders, I lowered my arms. Held them stiffly at my sides. My breathing sounded as ragged as the dress.

Prince Modred did not allow it to stay. Never loosening his grip on my collar, his other hand jerked the garment down. The entire rag fluttered to the floor. Nothing remained between Prince Modred and me except a small band of brown leather.

By age, I was no longer a child either. But my body spoke otherwise.

What next?

"I can do what ever I please with you," he said again. "I think I shall have you as my personal whore, starting now."

The word meant naught to me, but his smile caused my flesh to crawl.

He flung me to the ground in much the same manner that he would cast off his boots, then pressed his weight upon me, and forced my legs apart. The straw and stone burned against the raw skin of my torn back. 'Twas a struggle not to cry out, crushed as I was, like herbs between mortar and pestle. I had no way of fighting him. There were no weapons of any sort in our quarters, and the prince had sense enough to come in unarmed. He did not even have his meat knife. Any struggle was futile.

I had only my hands.

Hands.

With nails.

I slashed at the prince's face while he was occupied with the string of his trews, gashing his cheek from eye to jaw. He recoiled and a bejewelled hand flew to his wounded face.

I wriggled free.

My eyes searched the room for a weapon. Anything. The water bucket?

Dowse him with its contents.

Then what? Run? To where?

Fling it at his head.

I would gladly pay the price of murdering a prince.

Giving in would be easier, Lin.

No!

The bucket was too far anyway. If I could but find a loose stone near the fire pit.

I continued to creep backwards, each motion a fresh agony to my own wounds.

I never reached my destination. The prince caught my ankle and pulled me towards him. He locked both my wrists into one of his hands. How easily he could have crushed my slight bones. He had warrior skills and four older brothers. What hope did I really have against him?

Without loosening his hold of me, he rolled me onto my stomach. He sat on my legs while he tied my hands behind me with what turned out to be my gown. Then he flipped me back over and glanced about him. He snatched up a square of neatly folded brown homespun and stuffed a corner of it into my mouth.

Dafydd's tunic.

"Lest you get the notion to bite."

Sitting on my stomach, he surveyed his handiwork.

"Much better. Shall we start again?"

Trussed, all I could do was lie there as he pried my legs apart, and shoved into me. His hipbones ground against mine. All I could do was lie there as he stabbed me again and again whilst the cries of my soul clawed the inside of my head bloody.

Time stopped until I felt his final spasm. Heard his last grunt. As if from a distance, I watched him pull away to tower over me once more. I followed his gaze to the blood streaked on my thighs.

Had he pierced my entrails?

"You were still virgin. How absolutely delicious." He giggled, sounding triumphant. "Well, now you are a whore, just like your mother. I could sell you this very moment, you know," he said as he tucked his tunic into his trews.

"I will not though. Not yet, anyway, because I want the pleasure of seeing your pride finally broken to be mine. Be assured, I will do it, and I will enjoy it. I want your *brother* to be there when you call me master. For that, slave, I am. You will not have a moment to forget it."

He jerked the cloth from my mouth.

I gasped for air.

He strode from our quarters, wiping his hands on his trews, as if they had soiled from touching me.

"Bastard," I whispered hoarsely to his back. Why did I not leave him locked in the privy?

Weakness and exhaustion had a toe hold on me. But my hands were still tied beneath me. And I could no longer feel them. It would be hours before Dafydd returned. Besides, how could I let him see me thus, bound and naked? And violated. I had to try and free myself somehow.

I managed to twist to one side but only after a great deal of effort and pain. I strained against the bonds. I had to use care so as not to tighten the knot rather than loosen it. Fortunately, the material was too thick for a secure binding in the first place. My hands slipped free. Several moments passed before they were of any use to me though.

I had neither the strength nor the will to stand and walk to the water bucket, or even crawl. I used my gown to wipe away what remained of the prince from between my legs. The sticky fluid, mixed with the blood from my maidenhead, had already hardened. Not that mere water could ever wash the stain left upon me by Prince Modred.

Nausea rolled my stomach. When it subsided, I slipped my thin shift over my head and my hand touched leather. The reason for my defiance. The reason for my pain.

I clutched Dafydd's tunic, burrowed my face into it and wept until exhaustion overcame me.

CHAPTER 9

I slept until the noise of the others returning to our quarters roused me.

I hurt everywhere. My battered face. My arms. My torn back. The hip I had landed on when the prince had thrown me to the floor. My… Dwelling on it brought me no ease, however. I shut my mind to the agony and sat up to watch for Dafydd.

A handful of girls entered first with our supper of bread and stew. None glanced in my direction. They continued their discussion as though I was not there. No one cared about my collar. I had failed to avert that event in my life. I was just another slave amidst the countless others. Why bother resisting any longer?

I tried to adjust the strangling band, but nothing I did relieved the pressure on my throat. The edges chafed and itched. How has Dafydd tolerated it for two years, with never a word of complaint? And the others? Every one endured in silence, save me. The leather band served no useful purpose. It was simply a leash, a tether for Prince Modred to wrap his fingers around and pull in restraint. Like a horse's bit.

Familiar laughter drifted through the doorway and I looked up in time to see Dafydd enter with Custennin and Enid. Thank the gods he had not been sold as I had feared earlier. Or beaten as the prince had threatened. But what of how we had parted last? In the midst of his conversation my brother directed his gaze towards me and smiled. I felt his forgiveness instantly and my mood softened.

Dafydd crossed the room, exchanging brief pleasantries as he walked. How could I have called him a slave? I felt so unworthy to be his sister.

He knelt beside me moments later, a cup in his hand. He frowned.

"You should be resting, Lin. I brought you water."

I took the cup he offered with thanks. I was thirsty.

"Lin, your face. That bruise beneath your eye was not there when I left."

I finished the water, then shook my head.

"Shall I fetch more?" Dafydd reached for the cup.

I wanted more, but I told him no. His closeness was dearer to me at the moment.

"Enid has an elixir that will ease your pain. And she is preparing herbs for me to tend your wounds. I can do it after we eat."

That would mean removing my shift and exposure before the men and women in our quarters. And Dafydd. Surely he would see…

I shivered with a memory of the way the prince had stared at my body.

"Do not bother, Dafydd."

"What? Lin, we must take care of those gashes on your back. You could die."

I wrapped my arms across my chest. The movement reopened some of the wounds. I clamped my jaws shut, locking in the moan from the pain.

"I do not want you to die."

Dafydd's loving plea melted part of my resolve. But I had to keep the truth of my reluctance from him.

"I do not deserve it after what I said to you this afternoon."

"Never mind that. I know you could never mean it. You are acting so strange tonight." He glanced at his rumpled tunic still in my lap, then back at me. "What happened after I left?"

How could I tell my gentle brother the violent truth? I had been sullied. And there was naught Dafydd could do to cleanse me. No matter the price, I would spare him my shame.

Besides, I was afraid to unloose the rage within me. A single word and it all would get hurled to the wrong person. Because Dafydd was near, he would take the full force of my hatred. Hatred meant for the prince. I had to contain it.

But I had to tell him something.

"Prince Modred came in not long after you left."

"I saw."

"He said his mother gave me to him as a gift. A gift. He called me his…"

A shadow fell across us.

"How's it feel to be a new initiate?" A brawny lad, about Dafydd's age, interrupted me. He flicked his fingers at my collar.

"Shut up, Rhys." I slapped his hand away.

"How's it feel for the Queen of Slaves to learn she's no different from the rest of us? Because of your rebellion, they watch us closer, beat us harder. Maybe now that you've had a good taste of leather, you'll see you're no better than any one in this room."

"I never…"

I wanted to leap to my feet and face my opponent. In reality, the effort to stand taxed my tortured body. Yet I managed, fists balled at my sides.

"How dare you?" I said, my teeth clenched in a mixture of agony and anger.

In the next instant, the door crashed into the wall. Heads turned in its direction. The overseer had come to account for the Queen's property, as he did every night.

He surveyed the scene a moment, then strode across the room to stand in front of me.

I had grown since Dafydd's collaring. My eyes were now level with the overseer's chest. I raised my head to meet his gaze.

"I see your scratches have healed. You'll work tomorrow."

"Aye. You laid naught more on my back. I thought your weapon capable of worse, but I was wrong."

He grabbed my collar and pain shot through me as he jerked me closer to his body.

"You want worse? I'd be happy to oblige."

A shadow crossed my soul as I caught my brother's expression. He did not need any more suffering today.

"Perhaps another time."

"Insolence," the overseer shouted. The back of his hand clipped my jaw. "Anyone else?"

The others shrank from him, casting their gazes to the rotting straw at their feet.

The overseer dismissed me by turning away. He pointed to a handful of young women and girls, commanding them to follow. They would not return until cockcrow. Some would have swollen and bruised faces, much like mine. Those still virgin would be no longer. They had been chose for the honour of serving the Queen's warriors in their barracks.

The door closed behind them, enclosing our silence.

Rhys had fled before the overseer had reached me.

"Coward." I flung the insult in his direction, rubbing my sore jaw.

"Leave it, Lin." Dafydd touched my arm.

The remainder of our companions had already returned to their own affairs.

"Does everyone think the same of me, Dafydd? Do they all agree with Rhys?"

"Of course not. Those are just words. Don't swallow his lies, Lin. Please, sit."

I shuddered, feeling exhausted and overwhelmed by the day's events. I let my brother help me to the floor.

Dafydd seemed to sense my need for solitude. He fetched our meal and we ate in silence.

No beating had ever pierced more than my shell. Wounds close and bruises fade. I felt I had been well armed to withstand any assault life could throw at me. Until this afternoon. Prince Modred had torn every one of my defences to shreds, as easily as the gown the overseer had ripped down the back before my lashing. I had never felt more defenceless than when the remnants of my garment slipped to the floor, and all I was left with was the leather collar around my neck. With no regard whatsoever, the prince stole my last bit of innocence and dignity.

He had reduced me to nothing. Less. A pound of smoke was more substantial.

The pain from the invasion had not lasted long. But its ghost would continue to haunt my memory. Always.

May your manhood rot from a pox and fall off, Prince.

"I'll do these tonight." Dafydd picked up our empty bowls and went to wash them in the water-barrel outside our quarters.

"Dafydd?" I waited until he had settled beside me again. "What is love? Is that just a word too?"

"What?"

"Love. You said it about Meg. And Mummy used the word when we were children, remember? Do you think she took all the love with her when she died?"

Dafydd sighed.

"Can love exist amidst so much hatred and suffering? Is there love anywhere?"

"I love you. You do know that, don't you?"

My brother's gentle blue-grey eyes never lied. At the moment, they displayed his feelings quite plainly.

I nodded. Why did I find it impossible to say I loved him too? Easier for me to vent my vexations at him.

"But why is there such a place as cruel and as hard as this place of stone? Why did she have to die, Dafydd? Why did Mummy have to die and leave us alone?"

I buried my face in his shoulder and gave in to the tears.

"My sweet sister." He laid his cheek on the top of my head. I felt his body tremble and I knew he wept, too.

Why her, now? Can I never keep my mouth shut and not hurt my brother? I pulled from his embrace, wiping at my eyes.

"What is it, Lin?" His eyes were red. He dragged a sleeve across his nose. "What brought this on?"

His question matched my thoughts. And the reason reared within me.

The prince. He had called her a whore. He had called our mother a whore. I had heard the word before. Knew it was hurtful. The prince had showed me what it meant. My mother was pure and clean, a lady of worth. She was not cheap or common. She could not have been anything so filthy as I was now.

"It is just…"

I felt my lower lip quiver. For the first time in many years, I wanted to suck my thumb. I sat on my hand so as not to act on the urge.

I needed our mother. I needed her comfort and it was gone. All I had was my brother and he could not help.

"We never got to say farewell, Dafydd. We never knew where they took her."

"Aye."

"You are crying, Dafydd. I am sorry I reopened those wounds."

"Don't be. Will you let me tend your wounds now, Lin?" Dafydd used the back of his hand to dry his face.

"Yes."

It was a long process, because Dafydd first had to soak the dried blood that had crusted on my shift and had bonded to the wounds. I refused the brew he offered to ease the pain because Enid warned it might induce sleep.

"Might that not be best?"

I shrugged. “I promise, I’ll drink it later.”

After he finished, I could not find the words of thanks I wanted to say. They seemed too feeble for his tender, diligent care.

I gave him a smile, which I hoped conveyed the message from my heart. He squeezed my hand and returned the smile.

“Wait until you hear my new story.”

Dafydd rose and faced the others, calling for attention. Within moments, our companions fell silent, their eyes focused on my brother.

Dafydd never simply told a story, he brought it to life.

The tale was a pure flight of fancy, compleat with a sorcerer and a magic sword held fast in a stone, and only the rightful man, the man destined for it and to be Pendragon, could draw it out.

Miming the young Arthur, my brother approached the fire-pit reverently, as if it was the magical sword jutting from a massive stone. His face glowed in the firelight. With eyes closed, he was caught up in the spell he wove. He placed his right foot firmly on the ledge of the fire-pit. Then, in all solemnity, Dafydd grasped the imaginary sword-hilt in both hands and pulled.

He held it aloft, high and victorious, and proclaimed, “And then, the entire assemblage of chieftains and clansmen and holy men gathered within the Sanctuary let out a cry as with one voice, ‘Hail to Arthur! Hail our Pendragon!’”

The room, so silent but moments before, resounded with cheering that surely must have matched those noblemen who had witnessed the making of our Pendragon.

There had once been a time when I believed every one of the tales my brother spun of the Pendragon and of Camelot. Believed that an unknown lad could appear from nowhere and draw a magical sword from a stone to become the High King over Britain. Believed that even the lowest scullions working at Camelot were treated with dignity as humans and received adequate board in exchange for honest labours. But that had been before my brother had been replaced by a slave. Before we had lost our friend to the highest bidder. Before the dreams had been lashed to ribbons along with the skin of my back.

CHAPTER 10

"*Cumal*."

I recognised the voice behind me and my skin crawled despite the warm air, as though the speaker trod on my very grave. I hoped his command was meant for some other unfortunate passing into the courtyard of his mother's fortress along with me.

One of the gate guards hailed a greeting, which Prince Modred did not answer. Instead, the prince repeated the despicable word, with increased venom. My companions stopped and gave the arrogant bastard obeisance before scurrying into the dunn, abandoning me to my fate.

I shifted the weight of the basket filled with damp clothes on my hip, and clenched my teeth with the flair of pain across my back. I knew it was dangerous to ignore him. What did I have to lose? My life? What was that worth? I kept walking, my back straight.

"Thick as a plank, and thrice as dull-witted," the prince shouted.

The guards guffawed.

I heard the jangle of reins and bridle as a horse approached me from behind. Soon I felt the heat from the animal's recent exertion.

Before I took another step, the prince placed his booted foot squarely on my back, and ground it into the wounds from the lash, undoing all of Dafydd's careful ministrations.

I clamped my teeth together.

"I speak to you, pig-girl." His foot emphasised his final word.

The force pushed me forward, and with the heavy basket set on my hip as it was, I lost my balance. The basket tumbled from my grasp, and spilled its contents onto the road. As my knees and palms slammed into the cobblestones, tears stung my eyes with the body-jarring pain.

Prince Modred was not alone when he laughed. My misfortune caused much mirth for the passers-by.

My cheeks burned.

"Still as clumsy as ever, I see. If it is not firewood you are scattering across my brother's chamber, 'tis our clothes in the road," he said, dismounting. He stepped around his horse, kicking piles of laundry out of his way, and stood in front of me.

I noticed that my nails had caused more damage than I had thought. The three scratches on his cheek were not deep, but I could tell I had drawn blood.

I wiped my filthy hands on my gown, and rose to my knees, intending to stand. Before I was firmly balanced, the prince backhanded my face. I swayed under its force.

"I never gave you permission to rise. I told you, your place is the dirt, wallowing like the pigs in the filth, pig-girl."

He began to mimic a swine's grunt, which drew more snickering from the guards on duty.

The prince I had once admired.

He towered over me, his loins near my face. Too near. All the horror returned. Especially the feeling of being ripped in half while he acted as if I was not there, as if he were pumping himself into a clay jar instead of into a girl. Into me. And I knew he could do it again whenever, however, wherever he so pleased. The gashes on his face were too small a vengeance. Oh, for a knife, to repay him in kind. My fingers closed around the hilt I so desperately wished was in my hand.

"By the powers." Diverted from the taunting, he picked up a brightly dyed bit of cloth from beneath his boots. A scowl wrinkled the fair features of his face.

I hoped the motion pained him.

"This is mine." He held up the muck-splattered *leine*, inspecting it. "You call this clean?" He shoved it under my nose.

It stunk.

How funny, the high one's clothes were covered in dung, just like mine. Just like I was. He really was no different from me after all. I wanted to laugh aloud at the joke. At the absurdity of life. But I dared not. The prince could snuff my life there and then, with no effort whatsoever. For my brother, I had to live. I had not realised how much we depended upon each other until last night, when we wept for our mother. Dafydd's pain was as great as mine. I had been selfish to lean on him so heavily. I had to help him as he always helped me.

"Do it again. Rightly this time." Prince Modred draped his reins over an arm and strode through the gates, kicking more laundry as he went. What he did not kick, his horse trampled.

Wfft. I surveyed the ruins of my labours, strewn in every direction. I was hopelessly late in getting to the kitchen yard now. Brisen would send someone in search of me soon. That needless torment would be the cause of the punishment I was bound to receive for tardiness. And the prince would be on hand gleefully watching. No use to try and explain what happened. There were no excuses in Dunn na Carraice. Dung got more respect.

I tossed heavy, damp, filthy tunics, shifts, and trews back into the basket. Everything was much worse than before I had done them the first time.

I growled in frustration.

"Lin, there you are. Brisen is very angry you aren't back yet." Olwen stopped short. "Oh my. Did you fall?"

"I was pushed."

"Are you hurt? Here, let me help." She scrambled to the farthest strewn items.

"Just scraped up a bit. I shall mend."

We placed the last of the clothes in the basket.

I struggled to my feet, grimacing.

As the pain ebbed, I said, "Thank you, Olwen." I smiled to allay the concern in her young face. Young. I was merely twice her age. "I shall be fine. Tell Brisen you found me. Say that I stumbled up the hill and had to return to the stream."

The one quality of my brother's I felt capable of emulating was his honesty. Now I had broken that because of a man I despised.

Olwen nodded. "Maybe she will let me come back and help."

"Maybe." But I did not believe in that remote possibility. "Hurry now. They will have reason for beating us both."

Mine would be enough.

She dashed through the gateway and was swallowed by its shadow.

I felt the stares of the guards boring into my back as I trudged down the hill once more. They made me uneasy, even though I knew they could not leave their posts in order to torment me. I increased my pace to reach the footpath leading to the stream, and be out of their view.

I promised myself a washing before I even started with the royals' things.

I was nearly at my destination when I noticed two men on horseback riding up the road from the town. In curiosity, I stopped and watched them advance, clutching the heavy basket against me. The sun was too high in the sky for any more merchants to be coming to the dunn. They brought their wares early. The man in the lead was clearly not dressed as a merchant. His clothes were too rich, and he had a sword buckled to his side. Perhaps he was a prince of one of Orkney's smaller islands here to pay tribute to the Queen, accompanied by his servant. If that were the case, I had better stay out of his way.

"You, there. Lass?" Can you tell me, is this the road to the Dunn na Carraice?" He spoke the Irish words tainted with a British accent. He was not of Orkney.

"I speak British, lord."

His features relaxed and he smiled at hearing a language he was obviously more familiar with.

I could not help but notice he was quite handsome, and I became painfully aware of my wretched condition. My dirty bare feet and filth-splattered gown, my tangled and matted hair, the bruises on my face. I wanted to hide from this stranger. But I was rooted to where I stood and he spoke again.

"You are the first soul I have met since landing on this island who does not speak that damned Irish."

"I know both, lord. But I prefer British as my mother was British."

"Was she now?" He sat so comfortably and casually on his horse. He made me very much at ease with his pleasant manner. He seemed to really want to know.

I nodded.

"Tell me now, lass, for I fear my Irish is not very good and I might have misunderstood the directions I was given. Is this the correct road to reach Queen Morgause's fortress?"

"Yes, lord. This road will take you straight to the gates. With the exception of the footpath here, there is no other."

"I thank you kindly. It is most pleasant to hear a friendly British voice in the midst of all the Irish. I did not expect to find anyone besides Queen Morgause who spoke my tongue so far north. Are you a servant of the Queen?"

Perhaps he did not realise what my leather collar signified. Or maybe he simply ignored it out of kindness.

"No, lord. Nothing as lofty as that."

His brow furrowed at my words.

I touched my collar, hating the thought of admitting that truth to anyone. Saying the word would make it so.

However, his servant whispered a few words to his master before I could draw breath.

"Slave? She dares to keep slaves when the Pendragon has forbidden slavery in his realm?"

The Pendragon?

"That is not for me to speak of, lord." I thought it wiser to be relatively humble with a stranger. It seemed as though the nobility was not quite as predictable as I had once thought.

I had come to believe all were like Prince Modred and his brother Agravain, nothing but harsh words and heavy hands.

"Indeed. At least allow me to commend your faithful service. What is your name so that I might speak well in your favour."

"No." The last thing I wanted was more recognition from the royals. "I mean, that is not necessary, lord."

I simply do as I am bid. Like any dumb sheep ought.

"Is there naught I can do to repay your trouble?"

He wanted to pay me in some way. What of that? I thought a long moment.

"If you please, lord, may I ask a question?"

"Rather small payment, I should think."

"From where I stand, lord, it is large beyond measure."

"Very well, ask your question, lass."

"Are you from Camelot?"

His reaction was curious. He threw his head back and laughed. But his laughter was quite different from Prince Modred's. It was not the least stinging, rather it was gay and musical. Much more like Dafydd's. I liked the sound.

"That is all you wish to know?" he said when his laughter finally subsided. "Aye, that I am, lass. Lamorak by name." He gave a slight bow.

How charming he was. I felt even more embarrassed by my appearance. But I liked this man from Camelot.

"Truly, lord. This is a high honour you have given me, allowing me to speak so freely with you. I shall remember it always. Is there aught else I might assist you with?"

"I fear I have kept you over-long from your duties as it is. Pinel, help the lass with her burden to her destination."

"Gladly." His servant dismounted.

"Oh, this not necessary, lord. Truly, I manage this all the time."

"I insist, lass." Sir Lamorak nodded and the servant took my basket.

"I… I… Thank you, lord." I dropped a curtsey. "It isn't far," I said to the servant. "The stream is just a little way down this path." I led the way.

Hope surged within me once more. I could not wait to share the adventure with Dafydd.

* * *

"Well. So the proud one sees fit to return. I set a simple chore. Since when does laundry take half a day?" Brisen began chiding as soon as I set foot in the kitchen yard. Nothing I could say in defence would make a thread of difference. She would have me for lying were I to speak of my encounter with Sir Lamorak. She would have me for lying were I to speak on how Prince Modred had pushed me. Better to keep silent and conserve my energies for encountering the punishment.

She stood in the doorway of the kitchen, fists on her narrow hips.

My brief encounter with humanity was over so swiftly.

"You sorry creature. If anyone in this household deserved a flogging, 'tis you. But you would be of no use to me bound to the post. With that visitor here, all unexpected from Camelot, I need every available hand. Mind you, that is the only reason your back is being spared. Instead, there will be no supper for you tonight. The Queen's generosity does not extend to laggards.

"Now get those things hung on the line to dry before they wrinkle beyond repair. When you've finished, get to cleaning the Hall with the rest. A feast to prepare, and here it is nearing mid-day. Why I end up with the laziest of the lot, I shall never know. Brigit!"

A muffled female voice, from deep within the kitchen, answered.

"Brigit, get out here. There's chickens what need plucking." Brisen began to sit on the stoop, then cast her gaze at me again.

I had only had time to lift my basket.

"What are you gawking at? Get busy, girl." Brisen was not a large woman, rather scrawny. Thin and wiry. But appearances are sometimes deceiving. Her small frame belied her true strength. She clouted me on the ear, hard enough to make me dizzy. "Off with you."

The weight of the leather around my neck grew heavier.

I set to my task.

"Did you get a glance at that young lord from Camelot?" Brigit said, feathers in her hair. "He certainly is a fair one."

"Oh, he's pretty enough," Brisen said. "The Queen certainly displayed her charms in making him well come to Orkney and Dunn na Carraice."

"I should say. He'll no doubt be warming her bed tonight."

"Mind your cheek, Brigit. I'll not have my staff speaking such dishonour of the Queen or her family."

What did either of those two know of honour? What did anyone on Orkney know of honour? The word was spoken often enough, but there was no honour amongst the royal family of Orkney. I met honour on the road that morning, in the form of Lamorak of Camelot. Brisen and Brigit would not have recognized it if it had snapped at their noses.

* * *

The rest of the afternoon was a mad flurry of work. The feast hall was given a thorough cleaning. Tapestries were brought down for airing, and to have the dust beaten out of them, then were rehung. The stale rushes were swept out and burned. The stone floor was scrubbed. Clean rushes were laid. Wood and brass furnishings were polished until they gleamed. It took many pairs of hands, knees, feet. Many backs. And throughout, Brisen seemed to be everywhere at once, directing and chastising, and always quick with a reproach or a buffet to an ear.

Lazy, she called us. But at last, even she had to admit nothing was left for us to do. Besides, the Queen and her guest would be coming down soon. And it would never do for the nobility to lay eyes upon our shabbiness, our dirt. The servants took over, bustling in with linen cloths and a flower garland for the high table. Others set trenchers and goblets on the trestle boards. A maid scattered a mixture of sweet-smelling herbs amidst the floor coverings.

We were dismissed and allowed to return to our quarters for the night.

While the others crowded around the fire occupied with their meal, I sat on the step of our quarters, and denied the gnawing emptiness of my stomach.

"It is wrong to deprive a meal to anyone," Dafydd said from behind me.

"Oh," I sighed. "I do not mind."

"Yes, you do. At least you should. And I most certainly do." He sighed, too. "No one said a word though about you not having water." He handed me a cup and sat down beside me on the step.

I smiled at him before I drank.

"I do not deserve you, Dafydd."

"I know." He glanced over his shoulder, slipped his hand under his tunic and fished around a moment.

"What are you doing?"

"Shh," he whispered. "Ah. Here." He passed a lump of bread into the folds of my gown.

"Dafydd, is it not enough for me to be punished for nothing? If anyone sees you helping me like this…" I could not bear the thought of my brother in pain like I endured.

"Eat, you stubborn girl. Why must you always be so impossible? I promise you, I will not leave you in peace until you do."

I ate the dry bread.

Laughter and the sound of the Queen's piper playing a lively jig floated to us from the palace. The sun never seemed to set during the summer months. Even though the hour was late, the sky more closely resembled early twilight.

"Davy? Are you keen for giving us a song or two?" The question came from within our quarters.

Proud of my talented brother, I rarely minded the disruption to our conversations. But tonight, I hoped…

"Not tonight, my friends. My sister and I have much to discuss. You must entertain yourselves for one night."

The crowd voiced its displeasure.

"You needed me last night," my brother said softly. "You needed me, and I had no help to give except to clean your wounds. I am sorry."

"I managed."

"You always manage. Sometimes it isn't enough to manage. What did you do this time to bring on Brisen's wrath, anyway?"

"Do?" I asked, my mouth full of the last remnants of the bread. I washed it down with the final swallow of water. The food had done little to appease the hungry knot in my stomach. But the kindness mattered more.

"It was Prince Modred. I was already late with the load of clean laundry I had done. He pushed me."

"His Highness is making your life miserable, isn't he?"

"What? Your life is paradise without him? How blind I have been."

"Lin." Dafydd shook his head. "You know what I mean."

"Truce?" I offered.

"Truce."

Our relationship was of war and peace. I cried out sharp words. He forgave me.

The Queen's piper played another jig.

"That man from Camelot, feasting with the Queen? I saw him this morning." I was unable to contain the news any longer. Usually it was my brother who had the adventures, had the news to share, the latest gossip of the dunn.

"You didn't. How?"

"On the road, on the way back to the stream. After Prince Modred. He asked if he was on the right road. He was most courteous. He neither raised his hand nor his voice to me the whole time. His servant even carried my basket down to the stream for me."

"Truly?" He was quite clearly impressed.

"He even told me his name. Oh, he was so…so noble. Just like your stories."

"You must tell me everything you can remember about him. What did he look like?"

Dafydd pressed me for every last detail, and when I thought we had exhausted my memory, my brother pried even more from me. Finally, though I had nothing else to give, and we sat quiet for a while.

"Is that not the loveliest sound ever to land upon your ears, Lin?" Dafydd closed his eyes as he listened to the Queen's harper. The music from his instrument drifted out to where we sat. It was pretty, but my brother's voice was far superior in my judgement.

"I know, it's madness, my dream of Camelot and bards. But—"

"Promise me you will never stop your dreaming, Dafydd. That you will always share your dreams with those who are around you. We need them so very badly. Promise me?"

"Then you must promise me something."

"Name it," I said.

He took a long time to make his request.

"Please be careful, Lin."

"About what?"

"With Prince Modred. I know how strong-willed you are."

I pulled away from my brother. "Do you think I provoked him this morning? I did nothing, Dafydd."

He patted my arm and I relaxed.

"I know, Lin. But you could not see his face yesterday during your beating. There was something about his pleasure at your suffering. You will have no need to provoke, I think." Dafydd pushed strands of hair behind his ears. "He is dangerous."

"What do you want of me? To accept this?" I jabbed at my collar. "I cannot do that."

"Just be careful, Lin. That is all I can ask of you."

I certainly did not relish the thought of future beatings.

"I can try my best, Dafydd."

His smile was sad.

"Good. And I promise you the same."

CHAPTER 11

I never learned Sir Lamorak's business with the Queen. Dafydd was usually good at gleaning gossip within the dunn, but not this time. Nearly a sennight passed before we even got the news the man from Camelot brought with him of the latest Saxon advances, and of the Pendragon's current campaign to push them back. Custennin, having experienced battle first-hand, gave us details that were most likely—explaining the savage way the Saxon's fought. He demonstrated their fearsome battle-cries and gave vivid details of the berserkers, men who went mad in the frenzy of battle, wielding terrifying axes and who were virtually unstoppable killing machines.

"'Tis enough to chill my blood," Dafydd said after Custennin had finished.

"Aye. But more exciting than the titbits we usually get from visitors. Who cares about the High Queen's wardrobe? How grand it must be for men to have such a noble purpose."

"What is noble about war, Lin?"

I tucked my feet under my skirt and rested my chin on my knees, staring dreamily into the fire.

Dafydd nudged my shoulder and pointed to my bowl.

My food had gone cold, but I finished it anyway. Soon the clamouring would begin for my brother's talents. I smiled at the thought. To be a warrior, or a bard. Men were indeed fortunate to have choices.

In the lull, a girl named Julia got to her feet and proudly announced she was with child.

"Is she not worried? I certainly would be concerned. I mean, look at what that child will have to face. All this suffering. And a collar."

"'Tis a baby, Lin. Pure and sweet."

"And that purity will be stained before its first year is over. Nay. It will be tainted with its first breath of this foul air which surrounds us, of slavery."

"Oh, Lin. 'Tis love. I realise that concept is unknown to you. But it does happen. The gods know, it might even happen to you, although I doubt you would recognise it. How I wish I could help you understand, make you see. A baby, a new life, means hope."

"Hope for what?"

"By the stars, I wish I could sweeten your bitterness and give you a better life than what we have. If I could do only one thing in my life, it would be that. I would exchange my tongue for it."

What was he saying? I was unworthy of such a sacrifice.

Dafydd brushed breadcrumbs from the front of his tunic.

"We have so little to be happy for here, Lin. I find a baby reason enough to rejoice."

A baby. The days since my coming of age had been busier than usual. With the visitor from Camelot, I had not had time to consider the consequences of what Prince Modred had…

The thought struck me as hard as his hand across my cheek. What if the prince's seed had gotten me with child? A prince getting a bastard on a slave. Hardly a new occurrence in the world. Doubtless he would find the news amusing, and would laugh his mockery and his scorn into my soul. Any babe sired by that monster would be better off never seeing the sun.

And just what sort of monster had sired the prince?

Not meaning to, I groaned aloud.

"Lin? Are you ill?"

Indeed I was. The smoke-filled room had become close and I felt weak and dizzy. However, I shrugged my brother and his concern away as I struggled to my feet. I had to get out of there. Had to get away from the happiness, away from Dafydd's caring.

"Lin?" I heard him call as I staggered to the door.

Once outside, I did not care that it was raining heavily. I wanted the rain to wash away my doubts, my fears, my despair. I clung to the damp stones of our hut, demanding them to support me. But they refused their aid. My legs weakened under me and I slid to the ground.

I did not want to have the prince's bastard. I hugged my knees and gave in to my tears.

"I will ask again. And this time, I shall not let you run away. Are you ill?"

"Let me alone, Dafydd." I wiped at my eyes. Could he not understand? I did not want him to see me weak. I wanted to be miserable by myself.

"Still buried in your pride." He sat on the step. "I have seen you cry before. Now, what is wrong?"

I shook my head, too distraught to form words. Dafydd could not remove the stain of rape from my soul.

"Nothing," I said at last. "I felt a bit dizzy from the smoke. I needed some air."

I sensed his displeasure with my lie.

"Ho, there. What do you out here at this hour?" An armour-clad guard challenged us.

"My sister was ill, Master. We shall return indoors when she is recovered."

Dafydd sounded so humble.

"See that you do."

"Yes, Master."

The guard moved on and we were alone again.

"How smooth it comes from your lips, Dafydd."

"I do what I must, as you do. You think I like it any more than you? But I want to survive. I want us to survive."

We studied each other for a long time while the rain soaked into our hair and our clothes.

"You are my sister, and yet there are moments I swear I do not even know you. Like now, when your whole bearing changes. It frightens me."

"I—"

"You missed the rest of the excitement. Julia and Rhys exchanged vows."

"Rhys? That obnoxious ass?"

"Now, Lin. He might make the odd harsh comment, but I doubt he is mean-hearted and cruel."

"Who knows what any of us are capable of until we are pressed to it? I have not been given reason to like him. So I missed a wedding? I promise you, I shall wish them both well."

"Good."

"At least their baby was happily conceived."

"Are you still on about that?"

"I cannot help it. How can a woman allow a child, one she carries within her womb for months, be born to a life so uncertain? A life where it might be snatched away at any time, and sold for a few coins. No child should have to live in fear of losing its mother for the profit of some heartless shrew. That is blood money, Dafydd. Money for flesh and blood. That child will end up like Meg."

Wfft, but I did it again, and it was too late to pull the words back.

"Dafydd, I did not mean to be so cruel."

"Never mind." He always forgave me, although he sounded pained this time.

If I was not careful, some day his forgiveness was going to run dry.

"I am sorry."

"I said never mind. Lin? Do you think Mother abandoned us, the way you said?"

"I..." Tears renewed, I shook my head. Had I truly implied that? "I hate this life, Dafydd. Most times I wish I had never been born."

"Please, Lin. Stop talking nonsense. My life would be unbearable without you. Do you want to come inside now? Or do you plan to stay out in the rain all night?" He had risen and extended his graceful, slender-fingered hand to me. "Come on, Impossible One. You really will be ill."

I took his hand. His grip was firm and warm. Reassuring. Forgiving. He helped me to my feet. I did not deserve him.

"Come on," he urged again. He put his arm around my shoulders and pulled me to him. His daily care of my back over the past sennight had been diligent. I could now embrace my brother with little discomfort to the wounds inflicted at the scourging post.

"I know something is troubling you. Your pain is my pain. And I would help you, if you would only allow it."

"There is nothing that can be done, Dafydd."

"Whatever is gnawing on your soul, I know you will manage to find the strength and courage needed to get through, as always."

"My collar troubles me. Your collar troubles me. Our existence troubles me. How can you help that? You made such a grand offer earlier. Self-less and beyond any price. But I am not worth it."

"You are. But we shan't get into that at this moment."

We went back inside. The room bustled with merriment from the recent vows. The women fussed over the new bride. The men greeted

Dafydd with enthusiasm as he shook off the rain. I always faded to the background when I was with my talented brother. The party could begin in earnest.

"Lin, do you mind if I—"

"Of course not. You have a gift that must not be squandered by a selfish sister."

He smoothed water from his hair, tucking the damp strands behind his ears.

"Don't be so melancholy. Enjoy the party while we have it."

I would have preferred to remain outside, raining or not.

"Julia? Rhys?" Dafydd turned his attention to his task. "Where is the happy couple? I have the perfect song."

Withdrawn from the joy, I sat and stared at the fire. A child? Me? Was it possible? I knew it was. I'd been bleeding on a monthly basis for some time. The doubt would consume me.

* * *

Sir Lamorak stayed for more than a fortnight. His servant, Pinel, turned out to be his kinsman. An odd twist, I thought. A nobleman had willingly taken a slave's burden.

I was in the kitchen on the afternoon they left Dunn na Carraice, scrubbing the floor. I would have liked to have seen Lamorak one last time. But perhaps it was best I did not witness the embodiment of my hopes ride through the fortress gates, leaving me behind.

Hope. I had no time for such fancy. I shoved the thoughts from my mind with the same strength I used for the scrub-brush I worked over the stones. Hope was fleeting. Work, now there was a constant I could rely on.

"Come with me," the overseer growled and hauled me to my feet. "The prince wants his slave."

My respite from the prince had not lasted long enough.

The overseer indicated I was to follow. In no hurry to have my back reopened, I did not hesitate.

Without a word of explanation, he led me across the courtyard to the entrance of the stables. I had never been allowed in there before. The nobles' horses were quite easily their most valuable possessions. Slaves rarely had reason to go near them. So thinking he had other business here first, I paused at the threshold.

"What do you wait for, stupid cow? Hurry." He grabbed my wrist and yanked me into the forbidden realm.

Row upon row of stalls stretched back into the gloom. Some were empty, but many more had fine beasts in their confines. Busy grooms and stable-hands paid us no heed as we went back and back to the farthest, darkest corner. The air hung still, pungent from horses, hay and manure.

The overseer halted outside the last stall. Very little of the sunlight reached this far into the building, but I knew the prince was there. I heard him speak softly in Irish. I could not make out the words, but he nearly sounded kind. They were not for me.

I had time for my eyes to adjust to the darkness and make out some of my surroundings. Not far from the prince's reach stood a coal brazier, its contents glowed blood red. It gave off plenty of heat and enough light to see the prince's skin glistening with his sweat as he brushed the horse within the stall. I could even discern the colour of the beast's coat—as pale as the thin heather ale we were sometimes given with an evening meal. The prince was unconcerned about the lack of dignity, continuing to work diligently, lovingly with the animal in his care.

It was many minutes more before he acknowledged the overseer, and me.

"High time." He reverted to British. He had spoken what he considered the more noble language to his horse.

"Apologies, Highness. This is a hard one to get to take even the simplest orders."

The lying dung heap.

Prince Modred wiped his hands on some straw.

"As you might have noticed, I have been rather busy of late. Mother had me occupying that incredibly dull Lamorak of Camelot. At least he had an interest in horses. You probably thought I had forgotten you entirely."

Actually, I had not. Although—

"To show you I have not forgotten, I have something for you. I had it made during the past fortnight. You see, we have a way of marking our special property here to show how we value it."

He had taken hold of one of the handles protruding from the brazier, and drew a glowing iron from amidst the coals. He spoke to the horse again, stroked it gently, and then touched the brand to the animal's rump. The poor beast whinnied and the tang of burnt flesh stung my nose.

My soul recoiled in horror as I realised what he planned to do.

Custennin had told me once that a warrior must never display fear to an enemy. It was the deadliest of mistakes.

I pulled myself to my full height. Drops of sweat slid down my back.

The prince wanted to see my fear. I intended to leave him disappointed. Let someone else cower at his feet.

Prince Modred gave a slight nod, and the overseer forced me to the wall, pushing the sleeve of my gown up. My arm prepared, he held it out straight and firmly against the stones.

The prince took a lifetime to replace the first iron with the second.

I could not give in to the scream. I bit the insides of my mouth and drew blood. But I could not give in to the scream echoing in my mind as the iron came closer to my wrist.

"Afraid, *cumal*?"

My breath had become ragged, shallow panting. Every fibre of my body strained to bolt free. The iron hovered over my skin now. Yes, I was afraid, of the pain as much as of losing the contest of wills with the prince.

I gulped what air I could and kept my gaze fixed on my tormentor.

"No," I said.

The prince clutched my collar and sank the iron into my flesh in one quick motion. My body went rigid the instant contact was made. I fought to remain conscious. I could not give in to the scream, for if I did, the daemon would have won not only the battle, but the war as well. The prince would have what he wanted—a slave. He would own me, body and soul. I could not give in to the scream.

And did not. I know not how I managed, but I did not.

The time the prince held the iron to my wrist crept like years. When he finally removed it, the overseer had no more reason to hold me. He released my wounded arm and it crashed into my side.

A gasp escaped my lips.

Prince Modred smirked, still supporting me by the band of leather around my neck.

"Now you are doubly marked. You have your leash," he said, giving the collar a twist before relaxing his grip.

I crumbled like a rag.

"And like all our animals, you now have our family's mark of ownership as well. So see, I did not forget. By the time I am finished with you, *cumal*, you will be pleading, begging me to end your sorry existence."

As though to drive his point into me, he raped me, as the overseer held me down.

CHAPTER 12

"Touch my property and you are a dead man."

At the prince's words, the overseer's hand dropped from the string of his trews. He fairly leapt away, bowing as the prince left.

When we were alone, the overseer glowered at me. His chest heaved, certainly not from the exertion of holding me against the wall. Any female wearing the leather collar was open sport to the men of the dunn, and everyone knew it. But now I had been marked and claimed as the property of Prince Modred. No one would dare touch me in that way. The thought did not make me feel special.

The overseer growled a command to return to my duties. He did not wait for me to obey, but left me lying in the filthy straw with my skirt bunched around my waist. Using the one hand of use to me, I worked it down to my knees.

Why did the prince not kill me and have done with it?

Many moments slipped by while I remained curled in a ball. A huddled mass of pain.

"What's this?"

I wiped sweat from my face and tried to stand. I needed the strength of the wall for that and only made it to my knees.

"What do you here, *cumal*? And by whose leave?" The stable-hand jabbed the wooden handle of his pitchfork into my side.

That lackey was no more my master than the Queen of the Island herself was my mistress. I would have none of his abuse. I staggered to my feet. I might have been swaying, but I did not cringe and cower for the prince, or any other man.

"I am here on orders of Prince Modred."

"And what would His Highness be wanting with the likes o' you in here?"

"Whatever he bloody well pleased, you stupid git."

The stable-hand stood there, his jaw hanging, and his tool poised to strike me. But it never fell. His hesitation bought me time to walk away.

I put an air of purpose and haughtiness in my step as I strode past the rows of horses, past the other men who had paused from their tasks to watch, and left them staring. I went out with my head high and my wounded arm cradled against my body.

* * *

"What is wrong with your hand, Lin?"

In spite of my efforts, Dafydd had noticed me guarding my wound.

"Nothing."

"You do not lie very well, you know. Especially to me. Now, let me have a look. Please?"

"No. I do not want you, or anyone, to see what the prince did."

"Him again? Can you not stay out of his way for one day?"

"Do you think I seek him out, and ask? Dafydd, he is of the mind that I belong to him and that alone gives him the right to do whatever he fucking pleases with me. I cannot avoid him."

"Where did you learn such a word?"

"Rhys. The princes." I plucked at my skirt. "Others."

"Rhys has a filthy mouth. And it is even more unpleasant from you. It…it is debasing."

"What? You mean to forbid me to use it, Sir Dafydd of the Clean Tongue?"

"How could I forbid you doing anything? But that word is unworthy of you, a discredit to everything you have done since Mother died. Everything you have fought for. Coming from your lips, it brings you down to the mire, exactly where Prince Modred wants you. I am simply disappointed that you would even consider using it. You are not dirt, Lin. Do not make yourself sound like you are. Do you even know what it means?"

"Do you?" I cast my usual angry response, but it did nothing to relieve the burning in my cheeks. Disappointment from Dafydd was equal to failure. It went against my grain to do anything that might displease my only companion.

His crimson cheeks told me we both knew what the word meant.

"Whores do it for money, in case you don't know, Dafydd." Rhys stepped between Dafydd and I, inviting himself into our discussion. He squatted directly in front of my brother. "It's how I put that baby into Julia, you know." He gave me a wink that turned my stomach.

"Then why do you not go busy yourself and put another one into her, since she is so pleased about the first."

"A woman can only have one baby at a time by a single man. If she births more than one in her confinement, 'tis a sure sign she's been whoring around on her man. Then it's his right and duty to beat her, so as she learns her lesson."

Dafydd paled.

Poor Julia, wedded to this beast.

"Do you want me to put one in you too, Lin?"

"You arrogant ass. Nobody asked your opinions. You are not well come here. So sod off." My right hand balled to a fist. "Besides, you could not afford my fee." I might as well act the part the prince had given me.

Rhys thrust a hand deep into his tunic and scratched.

"Suit yourself," he said, flicking a flea into the fire. "Dafydd could do it as easily as me, I guess. Come to think of it, you'd rather whore with your brother anyway, I suspect."

My brother's fist came swiftly from nowhere, smashing into Rhys' teeth. We were, all three of us, stunned to silence while Dafydd slowly withdrew his arm, prepared it for a second blow if necessary. Blood smeared across his knuckles and Rhys' face.

"Lin asked you to leave. Do you understand what *that* means? Or do you only understand my fist?"

Rhys left, a hand pressed at his bruised lips, no apology offered. My reputation went with him.

I gaped at my brother while he wiped the blood from his hand on his trews.

"You hit him, Dafydd."

"He insulted you."

"He did you as well."

Dafydd shrugged. Violence from the last bastion of peace in that brutal place. I could scarce believe it.

"I recall asking about your hand before we were so rudely interrupted." He was busy inspecting his hand, flexing it, moving the fingers stiffly.

Minor damage I was certain.

"Why will you not share what happened between you and Prince Modred today? I have seen some awful things. What can be worse than watching as they flog you?"

"This." Reluctantly, I extended my arm towards him.

My brother's hand flew to his mouth, but was not swift enough to stifle his gasp. And not in time to mask the horror in his eyes or stay his tears. He stared at the brand, then at my face.

"You think me ugly now." I drew my arm back to where it had been supported in my lap before he had asked. "I do not want your pity, Dafydd. You can take it elsewhere."

"I shall do no such thing. I have never thought you ugly, nor do I now. How can you think that of me? What has come over you since…" Dafydd touched his collar, but he meant mine. "Lin, you are beautiful. I wish you would not belittle yourself so. Come with me, please." He helped me to my feet before I could protest.

Nobody had ever told me I was even pretty. And here my brother had said he thought me beautiful. Why did he always do that to me? Say kind things? It always made me ill-at-ease, made me feel inadequate. I never knew how to answer, except with the usual angry, often cruel, words. For once, I was even out of those.

"Come along," he coaxed. "That wound must be tended, lest the wound-rot sets in. Enid should know what can be done."

"Good heavens," she exclaimed at first sight of the brand.

"Can you help, Enid?" Dafydd said.

"I can make no promises, but I'll do what I can, Dafydd," she said, then went in search of her medicines.

I sat beside Custennin, who had Olwen nestled in his lap.

Dafydd answered the girl's wave with a wink.

"Do you know what the symbol means, Custennin?" I said.

"It seems to be a Roman letter. Probably for *servus*. *Cumal* Slave. Every language has a word for us. I had heard that the Romans used to mark their property in that fashion, with a brand. Even their soldiers. A practical and efficient means of identification, for unlike a leather or iron collar, it can never be removed."

Dafydd gasped.

Gall burned my throat.

"Have you eaten, Lin?" Enid had returned. She swabbed the wound with a damp cloth.

I clutched tightly at my clothes and clenched my jaw so as not to wince or cry out.

"No, she has not, though I tried to get her to take a few bites." Dafydd spoke as though I had not a tongue to speak for myself.

"Well, don't worry over that, Davy-*bach*. I'll take care of it. I held back my portion of bread tonight. Lin, I want you to eat it."

"I am not hungry."

"Did I ask if you were, child? There's a medicine I am mixing for you, to help you rest. It isn't wise to take it on an empty stomach. Olwen, fetch that crust for me, love."

"Yes, Mummy."

"No need to say who was responsible for this," Custennin said. He held the bowl of water for his wife. "Did Davy not warn you to have a care with the young master, lass?"

"Why is it always assumed to be my fault?" I said and jerked my hand from Enid's grasp in the midst of her ministrations "Thank you kindly for your concern. But I can look after myself." I rose to walk away from the cosy family only to find Dafydd blocking my path, arms folded across his chest.

"Do you want to lose your arm, Lin?"

A one-armed slave would be useless to the dunn. I would be turned out to beg in the streets, most likely. Swift mercy was out of the question with the mac Lot. It would serve the prince right for bringing it about. I liked the thought of his mother's displeasure.

"If it would hasten my death and release me from this hell, then yes I do." I side stepped my brother.

He grasped my shoulders.

"You cannot mean that."

"I can and most certainly do." I strained against my brother, as I struggled with my inner daemons. I could not allow the truth to escape. Dafydd called me beautiful, but the prince gave me a different, stronger, message. "I hate seeing you in a collar, Dafydd. I hate watching as our friends are led away in chains. Death would be better than this life."

Dafydd shook his head.

"To think," I said. "I was kind to him once. And he treats me like dirt in return. I can handle the prince's abuse. But not yours."

My brother's hands dropped from my shoulders.

"Abuse?"

"I know every one here thinks I provoked the prince and merely got what I deserved. What do you think of the Queen of Slaves now, Rhys?

I am branded property of a prince. Should I feel superior?"

He did not meet my gaze. And Dafydd looked stricken. He always took things to heart.

"No one deserves to be branded, lass," Custennin said, quietly.

Reliving those moments in the stable, my arm clutched my belly. No one deserves to be raped either and yet it happened.

"Linnie?"

How long before my brother whispered that name from our childhood to break into the horror I relived in my mind? How long before I heard him and Prince Modred's face finally vanished? How long would I continue to feel the prince's weight?

Surely he must have branded the word whore upon my soul for the world to see.

Everyone knew. That was why they stared at me. They saw me as the prince had labelled me.

"Linnie?" Dafydd whispered. He took my face between his hands. Despite their callouses, they were kind, loving.

"Dafydd? What is happening to me?"

"I do not know, Lin. I want to help you. But… Please, tell me what you are hiding."

But like the coward I was, and still am, I could not.

Weary, I did not resist as Dafydd helped me to sit. I did not protest when Enid dabbed a salve over my wound.

Still, I would show them. I did not need their pity. I contained my countenance despite the agony.

When Enid finished, I swallowed the sweet potion she gave me then bedded down beside my brother for the night. The elixir's effects were swift. I had just enough time to wonder whether the prince's seed had taken root within my womb before slipping into a dreamless sleep.

CHAPTER 13

The clanging of the porridge pot as someone settled it into place at the hearth jolted me awake. Morning noises filled our hovel—mothers roused children from dreams, the ladle clattered against the sides of dozens of clay bowls. Men snorted, clearing their throats, spat into the straw and rightly grumbled that the fare was unfit for dogs, and the portions too small to boot.

I yawned and stretched joints and muscles stiff and sore from sleeping on unyielding stone.

"Good morrow, sister." The gentleness of my brother's soft-spoken greeting amidst the chaos caused me to jump. "I did not mean to startle you, Lin. Will you eat this morning?"

I took the proffered bowl. The barley porridge was a sickly white in colour. It more closely resembled wash-water than food. But it was warm, and staved off the early morning chill. And I was hungry.

"Whatever was in that potion Enid gave me last night worked too well. My head aches. I did not even hear the cock crow."

"I know. I cannot recall the last time you slept so soundly, and the entire night through besides. No nightmares?"

I shook my head.

"Good. Eat your bread, Lin. We haven't much time."

"Do this, Lin. Do that, Lin." I folded my arms across my breast and peered at my brother. "You are such an old woman, Dafydd."

"I am—" Dafydd then saw my smile and what I meant and laughed.

"I guess I try too hard to take over for Mother," he said.

"Only a little. I do not want you to stop entirely."

"I am glad to see you in such a gay mood, Lin. It has been overlong since you smiled."

"It must be because my sleep was untortured last night."

I dipped the brown bread into the porridge to soften it.

"Mayhap we should have Enid mix that potion for you more often. How is your arm?" Dafydd glanced at the bandage on my wrist.

"It still burns," I said, knowing better than to lie about that. "I must have sounded mad last night, ranting the way I did. Why 'Linnie'?"

"It worked, did it not?"

Having finished his meal, my brother used a second cup of water to wash his face and hands. He smoothed his tunic to dry them. As the last of his morning ritual, he tied back his hair with a length of string.

"You gave me such a fright," he said. "Your face… Whatever caused it, your terror was quite real. You saw daemons that no one else could. Enid tried to reassure me, that you were reacting to your pain. That, and anger at the prince for marking you."

I noticed a crack in the base of the hearth. Why had I never seen it until now?

"But it is more than that, is it not, Lin?"

To avoid answering, I raised my bowl.

"That's right, swill your gruel. And don't dawdle over it. This isn't a feast at Camelot." The overseer spoke into my ear from behind.

I had not heard him enter.

He was close enough for me to smell his unwashed skin. My appetite fled.

I felt his whip's handle jab between the shoulders. It reminded me of Prince Modred's…

I leaned forward until I no longer felt the stiff leather in my spine.

"Drunken, highborn sots in the palace swill. I do not," I said without turning.

Dafydd stared, disbelief all but branded into his eyes. He laid a hand on my leg, pressed it, pleaded silently for me to have a care.

"Grand words, for a slave. Seems you have yet to learn your place."

"My place? My place is beside my brother. How difficult is that?"

The overseer brayed. "Indeed?"

Our quarters fell silent and expectant.

My brother's face turned as white as the uneaten porridge in my bowl.

With the flick of the overseer's wrist, the lash landed once, and then again, on the arm that had not been branded, just above my wrist. I watched as the lines the whip left behind filled red. It was only blood. A very cheap and common ware in the Kingdom of Orkney. I clutched my bowl in that hand, did not spill a drop of the porridge.

"Your place, *cumal*, is on your knees. Groveling thanks for the master who provides your keep in spite of your insolence."

The gods know, Dafydd tried to stop me. His fingers dug into my arm. Not a warrior in Camelot, not even the mighty Sir Lancelot, was strong enough to hold me in check. There was no turning back for me, no stopping what I had begun when my brother had his collar. I leapt to my feet and faced the overseer. Dafydd, I would have to face later.

"This is what I think of the keep Orkney provides." I poured the remaining gruel onto the floor at the overseer's feet.

"No," Dafydd whispered. His hands rose to his face.

The overseer's dark eyes glistened with anticipation of seeing more of my pain so soon. He motioned to one of his assistants, who trotted to his side immediately. An obedient cur.

"Go tell the young master that his property is requiring more discipline. We'll await His Highness in the courtyard."

The lackey dashed off towards the palace on his mission. And I was dragged by the collar, like a cow to market, to the shadow of the scourging post. My brother, and the others, were herded out in our wake. Everyone would benefit from my example.

* * *

It was not long before I saw the prince emerge from the palace, simply and hastily dressed. I recognised the saffron yellow *leine* as the one that had tumbled onto the road on wash day. An *eques* of Camelot had spoken to me as an equal that same morning. It felt a lifetime ago. The prince had not bothered to belt his shirt. It swung around his thighs as he strode across the yard to climb the platform and stand over me in judgement for my crime.

His coal-black locks were uncombed. Rare to see the normally well groomed youth so dishevelled. He had been jostled from his sleep on my behalf. I, a slave and born of a slave, was of enough importance to disturb a prince's dreams.

We stared at each other, two warriors met for battle, while the world below us waited. I had plenty of time and nothing to lose.

"Kneel." The overseer curled his fingers around my collar and jerked. His silent command for me to heel, like a dog. The leather cut off my air.

Never breaking from the frigid regard of the prince, I moved my head to ease the pressure on my throat.

"You were given an order. Obey." The prince's hand smashed into my face.

Ordinarily, his hand would have been bedecked with gold and jewelled rings. But since he had been hurriedly summoned, his fingers were naked. The lack of jewels meant little to my cheek. It would be bruised with or without them.

The overseer shoved me to my knees.

"Ingrate. You dare repay my mother's generosity with impudence?"

Was his mother watching? It would be like her. Someone had told me he had seen Queen Morgause at a palace window the morning I was collared. He also said she had laughed as my limp body twitched under the lash in my swoon.

I wanted her to hear me.

"Generosity? That pittance?"

"Silence," the prince said, allowing the word to hiss.

"Your hounds are wise enough not to touch your mother's generosity."

"Did you not hear me? I commanded you to be silent."

"I heard you, prince. I am not deaf. The truth is hard, is it not, prince?" I spoke as if the young man towering over me were of no more consequence to me than Rhys. Driven by events I had no control over—did not fully comprehend—I reacted on pure instinct.

The prince's fingers curled into tight fists at his sides. His body quaked.

"Shall I give the wench a lesson in proper manners, my lord?" The overseer's voice lilted with the prospect of sport. The very manly sport of tethering a defenceless soul to a chain, and striking a naked back with a whip until it resembled a raw beefsteak rather than human flesh. The sport of watching as the poor wretch writhed and danced under the lash. For a sense of place.

I held firm under the prince's cold scrutiny. I might be on my knees, but I did not cringe.

"Yes," he said at last. "Yes. Fix her to the post."

I was hauled to my feet by my hair.

"Where is the other one," the prince asked. "I promised that her brother would be on hand as a witness. And a prince of Orkney does not break his word."

"A plague take the princes of Orkney. Every last bloody one of you.

And the whore that birthed you," I shouted as my gown was ripped down my back. The material fell from my shoulders. Only the length of rope which served as my belt kept it from falling to the ground all together. It no longer mattered to me whether the whole world saw me so exposed.

I watched as my brother was shoved to the fore of the crowd. The scent of blood was in the air, and the folk of Dunn na Carraice were attracted to it like birds of carrion. A flogging was diversion, a way to pass the time. Noble, servant, slave, they all gathered close. Entertainment. My brother stared at me in anguish, a hand at his collar. His lips formed a single word, why.

How to make him understand?

Indeed. First I had to understand.

My hands were secured in the shackles. The iron rubbed against my wrists and rekindled the fire under the bandage.

"What is this?" Prince Modred flicked at the cloth. "Hiding the pretty mark I gave you?"

My skin crawled. Why did he not just have done with his work?

"Give me your whip," the prince said to the overseer. He intended to fulfil his vow compleatly.

Dafydd had been positioned where I could see him, where we could watch each other's pain. He closed his eyes before the first blow landed.

It took my breath away.

"Well placed, my lord."

The man who had pushed Dafydd through the crowd was the same lackey that had gone to fetch the prince from his sleep. He had remained at my brother's side. The man's lips moved. The familiar, loving eyes opened but he kept them cast downwards.

Others might have called my brother weak for that. Not me. Our unity ran deep, I had no need of an outward show of his support or comfort.

Prince Modred took a lifetime between each stroke. And each stroke came far too soon. Every blow was given with muscles trained and strengthened by the sword.

I used all of my will and concentration, each muscle tensed and strained to the limit, simply to keep my lips pressed tightly together. I was determined that I would not be entertainment for the prince, or his mother.

Dafydd did nothing to hide his tears. Would his cheeks ever be dry?

No one bothered to keep count of the blows. The prince struck again and again, his viciousness increasing as the lash burned line after line into my back.

Let me die.

But the gods would not even cheat the bastard wielding the whip by allowing me to faint.

The fire seared hatred of the haughty young royal into my soul.

"Now that is beginning to look like a properly scored back," he said without a catch in his breath, without a pause in his work, the rhythm steady as a *bodhran* "I think you have gone soft in your age. No wonder she was not getting the message."

Lugh's cullions. How much more can I endure before my screams begin? I…

What? The blows had stopped. When? For how long? Long enough to replace the blood saturated leather cord with a fresh weapon?

"Bitch," the prince screamed.

An unusual slip of his cool reserve.

He stepped close to me. I could feel his rigid phallus against my side. He was bound not to waste the chance. Another rape surely awaited me when he had got his fill of the sight of my blood, perhaps this time in full view of the whole dunn. For Dafydd to see.

He grabbed my collar, with a handful of my hair besides, and jerked my head back so that my face was tilted towards his. Both of our chests heaved, both of us were drenched in sweat from our exertion.

A slave sweating like a prince. How rich.

"Address me, slave." His order came through clenched teeth.

I heard his command, but knew that if I were to relax my lips even a little, all that would come out would be a moan.

Hold firm. I must.

My silence denied him what he craved. In front of countless witnesses, I defied Prince Modred, the pampered and favoured youngest son of the Queen. Rare for anyone to dare such insolence in the first place; for it to continue after such a savage scourging was beyond the collective imagination of everyone on the entire island.

"I ordered you to address me, slave." His contorted face flushed red.

Still, I held my tongue.

"Why do you not scream? You should be writhing from what I have given you. Why do you not scream? Address me."

Finally, I found the self-control I needed to form a single word, instead of piteous whimpering cries.

"Prince." I flung it at him with my own scorn, wishing my mouth was not so dry. A spray of spittle into his eye would have been sweet.

A gasp arose from the crowd.

"Dog's meat!" He released my collar and dealt a few more lashes to my back for extra measure, then tossed the whip down behind me. It clattered on the wood planks. He muttered an unintelligible Irish oath under his breath.

"If a decent flogging does her no good, then perhaps time in contemplation will. A night or two in the guard room seems to be in order to deliver the lesson home to her stupid, dull-witted mind. Let this be a lesson to anyone who would follow in our recalcitrant's footsteps. Impertinence will not be tolerated. This is not finished, *cumal*."

His last words were meant for me alone. He pressed himself closer and used the Irish word I despised. "I have not done with you yet. By the powers, you will know your place. You will know I am your master, and you will acknowledge it loudly, in public."

The overseer released the locks of the manacles. Sheer will power kept my legs from buckling under me when I no longer had the aid of the chains. I gathered the ragged folds of my gown up, each stiff movement igniting my fresh wounds, and crossed my arms over my breasts.

"Keep binding me to your wooden phallus, prince," I said. "It is but an extension of your own. Flay the skin from my back. It will change nothing. You are going to have to kill me. In the end, you are going to have to kill me."

"I know, *cumal*." His smile was smug and self-assured.

"But will you be man enough when the time comes?"

I saw his confidence drop. I was reminded of a young boy of eleven summers, the butt of endless taunts and pranks by four older brothers. The boy who had masked his wounded pride by calling me pig-girl.

"Ach. Lock the creature up in the guard room. I grow weary of her." He leapt from the platform and sprinted to the palace.

I followed the overseer, forcing my legs to move, telling myself there was no pain, praying that I would not collapse. I feared glimpsing my brother. If I had seen his sorrow, my resolve would have vanished and I would have crumbled.

Another man, someone I had not seen before, trailed after me. He had a sword at his hip. A soldier. I suppose they feared that I might bolt, when I could barely set one foot in front of the other.

We stopped before a doorway, set deep into the stone wall. The overseer unlocked it using one of the many keys from the ring he kept hooked to his belt. The hinges squeaked as the thick door swung open.

Pure blackness greeted us.

The overseer reached inside and drew out a pair of torches. With flint from his pouch, he lit them and handed one to his companion. He entered.

I knew I was meant to as well. But, like the stables, slaves were never given cause to venture to this part of the dunn—the storerooms wherein were kept the kegs of ale, wine, and *uisge* And the darkness before us was absolute. I had expected the flogging. I had not bargained for this. My courage rapidly drained from me. I hesitated.

"So. The rebel slave is daunted by a wee bit o' darkness," the soldier said.

I drew myself up as best I could, and stared directly at the overseer.

"I am not afraid of anything Orkney could throw at me." Never show fear to the enemy, Lin. I stepped over the threshold, and the blackness pressed upon my shoulders, saying, "Lead on."

The overseer was kind and struck me but once.

"Insolence. She'll be cured o' that soon enough though, I'll wager. We shall have a compleatly new slave when his Highness decides to let her out."

I had heard of the changes men had gone through from time spent in the guard room. They would emerge simpering, cringing, pitiful creatures. Although I had never seen it myself. I had also heard the tales of men who had gone in, and were forgotten, were left to die and then rot. Alone. I believed them stories to frighten children into behaving. I began to wonder as we drew closer.

The overseer had started forward again, and this time I did not pause, but followed down the straight, steep, and very narrow stairwell. At the bottom, and without cause, the soldier shoved me forward. I lost my balance and fell to my hands and knees.

He brayed, then swore in Irish. "Clumsy. By the gods, where did His Highness get this one?"

"She was born here. Her mother was not but a British whore, Niall. And the Horned One himself was her father," the overseer said.

If I did not stand soon, he was going to grab me by the collar and drag me the rest of the way.

"Worthless, if you ask me," Niall said.

"Aye. Indeed, a waste o' the prince's time and trouble. He should sell her off, take the loss, and have done with the wench. But does my experience count for anything? At least her brother is not so bothersome, although he can be as lazy as the rest at times."

I forced myself to my feet.

"Liar. Dafydd is never lazy. And Mother was not a whore."

"Enough. Silence, collar meat," the overseer shouted.

Niall guffawed and slapped his companion's back.

At least I was standing when the overseer gripped my collar and jerked me to his side. In that way, we made the last steps through the passageway until we stood before a second door. The overseer fixed his torch to a wall sconce across from the door, before he chose a key to unlock it, never loosening his grip of my collar.

"Ugh," the soldier cried out when the door swung slowly open. "How long has it been since we used this?"

The sick-sweet stink of decay wafting from the blackness made my gorge rise. And they planned to leave me in it?

"That Saxon, Prince Agravain brought with the intent to enslave, remember? I could have told him the *Sassenach* do not make good slaves. "

"That was two years ago."

Had a man died in there? Were they going to make me stay in there with a dead man?

"I'll need you and your torch in here, Niall."

Niall nodded and lit the way into the tiny cell. The men had to duck in order to enter.

I searched for signs of a skeleton as I was pulled inside, but my view was mainly blocked by the men. The overseer shoved me against the opposite wall. The raw skin of my back ground into the rough stone.

"Sit. I've a present for you, slave." The overseer forced me down. "A pretty, matched pair of bracelets." He attached shackles to my wrists. "And I even have a set o' bangles for your ankles."

The warrior snickered.

"Now that she's dressed up with her fancy baubles, maybe we can have a bit o' sport, eh," Niall asked. He pulled my gown away from my breasts once more, then held his torch so he could have a good look. He squatted on his haunches in front of me and pawed at my chest with his free hand.

Inside, I recoiled under his touch. Instinct told me to draw back and press against the wall. I fought my instinct and remained still.

"Do you suppose she has the kip skills o' her mum?"

"Whore's whelp, she's no doubt the same."

No.

"Let's have a go at her and find out." Niall covered my mouth with his. His breath tasted as foul as the air within the cell.

I gagged, then retched when he finally withdrew.

The overseer chuckled before saying, "His Highness gave strict orders. No one's to touch his special property."

"His Highness doesn't have to know, does he? How would he find out?" Niall fumbled with the front of his trews.

"I would tell him," I whispered. "His wishes were quite explicit. On pain of death."

Niall stumbled backwards and fell on his rump. Such a brave warrior. I could not help my own laugh at his fear of his young master. I did have some small bit of power of my own.

"What find you so amusing, slave?" The overseer pointed to the door. "Go, tell Prince Modred. We'll wait here." He tugged at the chain binding my ankle to the ring embedded in the floor.

Despite his warning to Niall, the overseer could not resist tweaking my breast either. Even bolder than his companion, he pushed the skirt of my gown out of his way and shoved his hand between my legs and I felt his fingers stab deep into me. I tried to ignore the violation, to close my mind to the weeping of my soul at the shame. A feeble effort, when every uninvited touch caused me to feel unclean and worthless.

Niall looked away nervously, saying, "Come on, we've taken far too long with this task. We've our own skin to mind."

"Aye." The overseer withdrew his hand. "Still, there's naught like a young girl's honey pot to stir the loins, eh, Niall? Ah, to be a prince. He has his choice of women, whatever he wants, and he sets his sights on this ungrateful slut. Come on, then."

They took the torch with them.

CHAPTER 14

How can darkness weigh so much? The chains binding my wrists and ankles were like feathers compared to the blackness of my gaol cell. My tomb. All consuming, I felt it crushing me. Breathing it into myself, it enshrouded my vitals.

What on this earth caused me to commit such folly? What had gone on inside my head to make me spill that bowl of porridge? What sort of daemons possessed me to undertake any of this madness? What made me think I could win against Prince Modred and his mother the Witch Queen of Orkney? I had nothing except my strength of will with which to fight. They had the real power, wealth. Wealth to buy whatever—nay!—whomever they desired. Why did I continue despite the odds? For a delusion of justice? Aye. A delusion. Naught more. There was no justice on Orkney.

Why did I waste the effort?

Something large and furry scurried over my bare foot. I stuffed my fist into my mouth to stifle the scream, not that anyone would have heard, and drew my feet under the folds of my gown. The chains rattled with the movement.

It is but a mouse.

Or a rat…

Stop it, Lin. Stop it this instant. You have only been here a few moments. Who knows how long you shall have to remain. If you are to survive intact, you will need all your wits. Do not lose them so soon. So what if it is a rat? What is a rat after everything the prince has done to you in the past weeks?

"Do your worst, prince. I am not afraid." I felt no better for speaking the words aloud.

Wfft, but I was cold. I worked the threadbare material of my gown back to my shoulders, trying to cover as much of my exposed flesh as I could. It did nothing to stave off my shiver. With the movement came pain. No sense checking my tears in such a forsaken place. Who would see? Who would care? I let them spill.

Dafydd would care.

Aye.

But he might as well be in Camelot at the moment, for all the use he was to me in my present condition. Chained. Caged. Like a beast.

And alone.

Ever since Mummy died, I had been gripped by frightful nightmares of losing Dafydd as well. I could not bear the thought of never again hearing his sweet, clear voice raised in song, giving me encouragement to carry on another day. He lived to sing. I lived to hear him sing. The idea of that silence was more than I could endure. I often spent entire nights without sleep, wondering if my brother would be alive come the dawn. Then two years ago, a new fear was added to torment me. After Dafydd's collaring I became tortured by visions of my brother on the auction block, and often awoke drenched in cold sweat.

I had been blessed with one night without the nightmares. To what purpose? To be shut away from him? For how long? Anything could happen to him in the meanwhile, and I would not know.

Please don't let them sell my brother.

Who was I to ask such a favour? My head drooped to rest on my knees and Dafydd's tear-stained face rose in my mind.

Oh, Dafydd. I am sorry. I do try to control myself. It would be a great deal easier if they would leave me be. If the prince and the overseer did not goad me, I just might be successful. A person can only take so much. How is it you can accept this fate when I cannot?

I adjusted my collar. Again.

Well, Dafydd was right about one thing. The leather was not really painful. What hurt was one plain fact—I could not do a bloody thing about it. No amount of protests was going to remove that strap from my neck. Nothing I did could ever relieve its pressure from my throat. The collar's very existence gnawed at me, chafing my soul as well as my neck.

That was the thing. No matter how humble and contrite I might be when the prince finally allowed my release, I would still be collared. I would still have the brand. I would still be considered slave, *cumal*, by the rest of the world. Less than a beast of burden, but a creature none the less.

It galled me to think I existed according to the whims of one man.

"I shall not be your slave, prince. Or anyone's."

The straw rustled. I had stirred up the other occupants of the gaol cell. They were most likely hungry, and probably would very soon consider me as their next meal. My stomach lurched, and I hugged my knees tighter, my body pulsing with pain. The prince had said, "a night or two". How could I possibly carry on that long in these conditions?

At least the privy had a window for light.

Why had I dredged up that? I could hear the prince throwing himself against the blocked door, screaming at his brothers. Now I was trapped as he had been. Except I was engulfed by darkness. I had rats for companions. And I needed to relieve myself, but there was not even a bucket.

Did Prince Modred remember?

Why should a prince bother with such a trifle?

I shivered with my next thought. I had been his saviour and now I was at his mercy.

My earlier bravado was a lie.

*   *   *

Having no way to mark time, I quickly lost sense of it. What does one do whilst chained and in utter darkness? I spent my anger in short order. I must have slept, for surely I spoke to the rats in a nightmare. They did not seem impressed by my interpretation of Dafydd's stories. Well, my brother was the bard, not me.

My anger renewed itself in cycles. I eventually resorted to cursing our mother for dying and deserting Dafydd and me, to my shame. At one point I even promised to cease rebelling, if I only I could be with my brother once again.

And I wept a great deal.

Mercifully, I was not weeping when I heard the rattle outside the door. My mind was so muddled by that time, I did not recognise it as the bolt being unlocked at first. Then the door creaked open and blazing brightness filled the cell. My hands rose to my eyes in self-defence of the light.

A shape hovered. Too large for the prince. The overseer. The shackles fell from my ankles. Unseen hands released the chains from my wrists.

"Get up." The light receded.

I would have no time for my eyes to adjust to the abrupt change from the darkness. I used the chains to pull myself to my feet and stood on shaky legs for a moment. I had no notion as to whether it was day or night. Or even the same year.

I staggered behind the overseer, clinging to the wall. He did not spare me a glance. I tripped once, coming up the stairs. I stumbled forward and bumped into his back. I had to clutch a handful of his tunic to regain my balance, and I felt my cheeks flame with the humiliation of having to rely on someone for assistance. Someone other than my brother. That it was also a man I despised, deepened the shame.

He cursed me, and pulled away.

When we emerged into the courtyard, there was not a cloud in the heavens to help dull the brilliance of the sun. The torchlight had been but a candle-flame by comparison. I sank to my knees.

"Up, worthless baggage. You're to report to Brisen in the kitchen. She's a special task for you." He shouted at me as though the sunlight had affected my hearing instead of my sight. I felt his hand tugging at my gown. "Put something decent on first though, shameless little whore."

I tried to obey before his foot connected with my midsection, but wasn't fast enough. His kick sent me flat on my face in the mire.

"Lin!" The voice was music to my heart. He had not been sold.

"Dafydd?" I rose to my knees and turned towards the voice.

"This business is none of your concern, boy. Get back to your duties," the overseer said.

"Please, Master."

I stiffened to hear my brother say it so smoothly.

"She is my sister, Master. Please allow me to help her, at least to our quarters."

"She can crawl for all I care."

"By the stars, what does it take?" I heard my brother whisper. Then aloud, "With my assistance, Master, she shall be able to get to her work that much more swiftly."

"Perhaps I do grow soft. Very well. But see that you're quick about it. And mind you, there'll be twice the work, boy, when you return to your duties to make up for the lost time."

"Thank you, Master. And Master?"

"Bloody hell. Now what?"

"Master, might I please give my sister a drink of water? She has been dreadfully long without."

"By the Horned One! Next you'll be wanting to sit at meat with the Queen. Ach, one ladle-full and not a drop more. Understood?"

"Yes, Master. Thank you, Master."

I wanted to weep for the joy of my brother's presence, yet the joy was tainted with the bitterness I felt at how perfect a slave he was. Did he not feel the slightest shame at having to beg a cup of water?

"The brute is gone," Dafydd whispered. "I am sorry, Lin. But I had to do that. I had to say that in order to help you. You do understand, I hope." He did not wait for an answer. He knew what it would be. He just slipped an arm around my shoulders.

I groaned. "Dafydd, please. Please, don't come too near me. That place stank fiercely. The stench was horrid. Surely I must have it all over me. And I… There was no… I had to…"

I tried to pull away from him, to spare him my filth, but he held me firm.

"Hush, Lin. I do not care a grain of sand about that. We can wash your clothes. And you. I was worried to tears over you. Here, lean on me. We shall go slowly."

Dafydd practically carried me to our quarters, I clung to him so tightly. He soothed my fears and patiently coaxed my legs forward with gentle words.

"You can do this, Lin. I will not let you fall."

"But I can't see, Dafydd. The sun—"

"I know. That will not last forever. Here we are, up the one step. Only a little farther now." He helped me to sit on the ledge of the cold fire-pit. "I shall be gone but a moment."

I could hear him moving about on the far side of the room. Heard water splashing. It was not long before I felt him at my side once more. He began to bathe my face with a damp cloth. After the long horrors of the guard room, his simple kindness was too much for me to bear. I leaned against my brother and sobbed.

"He did not sell you, Dafydd." Weeping, I flung my arms around him and held him as tightly as I could. "He did not sell you. I wondered and worried the whole time whether he would. I never dared to hope…"

Dafydd returned the embrace with equal vigour. "No, he did not sell me, Lin. I am still here. Someone has to make sure you eat." He spoke a few more soothing words of comfort before gently pulling away.

"Now hush, Lin. It is over. We are together once more. You have beaten the prince again. But we haven't much time. We must be getting to our duties."

"Yours will be trebled, I fear."

"There is nothing I can do for that. I do not mind, though. You are much more important than anything they can do to me. Here, I saved this for you." He placed a small, hard object into my hand and moved away again. At first, I wondered why my brother would give me a stone, then realised—

"Your bread?"

"From this morning. I was hoping you would be released today." He was across the room already. "I guess the gods heard my prayers. Go on, eat."

"But what about you? I cannot take what little you have."

"You are not the only one here who can manage without a meal once in a while. Eat."

"Thank you." How small the words sounded, compared to the oceans of gratitude I felt for the gift.

"Here's water. Can you manage?" He pressed a cup into my hands. They shook, but I told him yes anyway. A full racking shiver took hold of me when I tried to raise the cup, and I felt water spill onto my fingers.

"You have spilt half of it," he scolded gently and took back the cup. "I'll get more."

When he returned, he sat beside me. "I shall help you this time." He held the cup to my lips, and I drank, feeling like an infant. It was surely more than twice a ladle-full. He was not content until I had swallowed every drop.

"Thank you again, Dafydd."

"Never mind."

I tested my eyes again and the light was less painful. I still needed to squint and Dafydd was blurry, but it was my brother who was my first true sight after the long hours of darkness and I was glad of that.

"How long was I in there, Dafydd?"

"Since yestermorn. To me, it felt like years. I cannot begin to imagine how it must have been for you. We can talk of this later, though. I have to be going. And you do, too."

"The bastard told me to put something decent on. How am I to do that? I do not have anything decent. Nothing besides this rag. I cannot see well enough to repair it, and even if I could, they will not spare me the time."

"No need, Lin. Enid gave me this for you, last night. She said it was once Meg's, that it should fit you." He placed a bundle in my lap.

I did not have to unfold it to know that it was a gown—clean, well repaired. It had never been ripped down the back like mine had been. I swallowed a large lump, stroking the soft cloth.

"Enid is too kind to give me this."

"Are your eyes any better? Can you see well enough to change?"

"I will be all right. You really should be going, Dafydd."

"I am loath to leave you. I wish I had time to tend your back from the lashing yesterday. I shall first thing after supper, I promise. You are sure you can manage?"

I nodded.

He kissed my brow, then started to leave.

But I called him back. I had not yet had my fill of seeing him, being with him. Having recently experienced the separation, I was reluctant to have it again, so quickly following the first.

"Yes?" He gazed at me in concern.

"Nothing really," I blurted to allay his worry. "It's just... I..."

My words failed me. I wanted to tell my brother how much I appreciated him. All the wounds he had tended, the meals he had coaxed into me, the tears he had shed on my behalf. Everything he had ever done for me. And I wanted him to know how much I cared about him in return. But the words refused to surface.

"Dafydd? I am glad you are my brother."

Not enough against the sacrifices he always made. Yet it was all I had to offer, and I did mean it with every drop of my blood.

He tightened the string holding back his hair, and grinned. Dunn na Carraice and the prince were endurable for it alone.

"And I am glad that you are my sister. But please, do hurry. My heart could not bear to witness you being beaten again, so close after the last time."

I did not see my brother again until much later that evening. I was obedient and dutiful at my chores, in fulfilment of the vow made in the guard room. Nearly a model slave, keeping my mouth shut. Dafydd would have been proud of my patience, had he been there to see it. Of course, it helped that Prince Modred had not come around to check the effectiveness of my time spent in confinement. I thought it strange that he was not eager to see whether I was yet tamed. I watched for him, but never once saw or even heard mention of the young prince.

*　　*　　*

Released from duty hours later, I returned to our quarters several moments before Dafydd. As I waited, I promised myself to improve as a sister. I would give my brother fewer causes for heartache. I even knew how I would begin.

I usually knew when he entered. He was always well greeted by his friends. So I was surprised when he sank to his knees beside me without warning.

"I'm too tired to even think," he said.

Preoccupied with my plans, I rose and went to fetch his supper for him. He did it for me often enough. I nearly dropped the bowls when I turned back and got my first full sight of him in the firelight.

His face! No wonder the others had been silent when he came in.

"Dafydd, who beat you?"

"Does it matter?" He took the bowl I handed him, staring into the steam rising from it. "If you really must know, it was his Highness."

My body tensed. I wanted to break something. I wanted to hit something. Someone.

"Oh, he is good," I whispered. I wanted to watch the prince's life drain from him, just as he was draining the spirit from me. My vow to stop rebelling forgotten, I envisioned Prince Modred's blood pooling at my feet.

"What was that, Lin?"

"The bastard is good. A worthy adversary. He knew precisely where to strike. Where it would hurt most. That is why I did not see him today. Oh, for a bard's curse."

"Lin, leave it. You cannot win against him."

"Ah, but I will. Just you watch me, Dafydd. So help me, I shall win." I heaved my bowl across the room towards the palace. Its contents flew in every direction, and people in its path ducked their heads to avoid being hit by the missile. "This is between you and me, prince. Attack me all you want, but leave my brother out of it."

CHAPTER 15

Now it was indeed personal. But why? Why my brother?

It should have been me.

Silence followed my outburst. The prince's assault upon my brother touched every heart beating in our quarters. He had sent a powerful message to us.

And to me.

"Maybe you should ask Enid—" I began, but choked on my words. "I will clean up my mess."

The others continued to watch me. I hoped no one had been hurt.

"I am sorry," I said to them and my brother, unable to stop trembling. "Sorry."

I crossed to where the bowl had smashed into the wall. Fortunately, no one had been sitting there. The boy who usually did was already gathering shards.

"You need not do this, Padrig," I said, kneeling near him.

He smiled, but kept working.

"I think we'll be finding bits of this for a month," he said.

I nodded and we finished the task in silence.

When I sat by the fire once more, my brother was still with Enid. He seemed deep in conversation with her and Custennin. Dafydd would be better off staying with them, rather than returning to a sister who only caused heartache. Who had no doubt cost him a beating.

I hated myself for that, as much as I did the prince.

Why had I been singled out to be his slave?

I busied myself by taking up my gown and plucking a thread from its hem so I could stitch a new seam up its back.

My hands were again occupied, but my mind was still free to torment me. It would be all that I merited if Dafydd did stay with Enid's family. I supposed Olwen would be a far better sister than I ever was. Sweet-tempered, like her elder sister. Dafydd adored the little girl. Besides, he deserved a mother and father to care for him. And Custennin most likely wanted a son. Men usually did. The arrangement would be perfect for everyone. Save me.

By the time Dafydd rejoined me, I had finished my sewing. I also had myself convinced he was there to gather his few belongings and take his leave of me. I decided to offer him the blanket as I hardened myself for his announcement.

Without a word, he folded his long legs beneath him and sat.

"Do you hate me? I shall not blame you if you do," I said, unable to contain my fears.

"Hate you? I can never do that. Will you never learn, you impossible girl?"

My fingers fidgeted with the bandage on my wrist. The wound beneath the filthy rag throbbed.

"But your beating was my fault," I said.

"Don't be daft, Lin. I have had my share of beatings before."

He sounded resigned over the terrible truth. Beatings were a fact of life for slaves, but—

"But never so severely. Never by him."

Guessing my intent, Dafydd unwrapped my branded wrist. The mark had been irritated red by the iron manacles.

"You should have Enid put some more of her salve on this," he said. He dipped a corner of his tunic into his water cup, and swabbed at the wound.

"I have no intention of doing any such thing, Dafydd. I am unworthy of kindness. And I least deserve yours."

He settled my arm back in my lap.

"Lin. Look at me. Please?"

"I cannot. I now know what you endure whenever I… Oh, Dafydd. I am sorry. If only I were not your sister."

"If you were not my sister? How could you possibly suggest such an utterly absurd notion? Not my sister? Who would I have to mind then?"

I felt him studying me and I risked raising my gaze to meet his eyes.

"Yourself perhaps?" I said. "Everything was simple until today, when it was only me getting knocked about for daring to give voice that I might actually be a person beneath the collar and the scars. The purpose was right, I felt it in my gut. It has gone sour. I am not sure what to do any more. Now that the prince has brought you into our war, I do not know what to do."

"Follow your soul."

"My soul screams, *'fight the collar,'* while my heart whispers, *'remember your brother.'* If I follow my heart, I betray my soul. If I follow my soul, you and I shall pay dearly. Are you truly prepared for that? The prince will use you, like he did today. And he has given you but a taste of what he can do."

"I know what he is capable of."

"He might even sell you. I cannot risk that."

"He could sell me anyway. With or without your so-called assistance. I would still be his slave if you were not my sister. Nothing would change.

"Lin, I have begged you for years to leave things be. To stop throwing yourself at an unyielding stone wall. And I have watched your struggle to try and do what you thought would please me. What I thought would please me. I realise that it would be the same thing were you to ask me to stop singing. Because I love you, I would try. But the trying would tear me apart. I have been wrong to ask you to change your nature. I have been very selfish. Can you ever forgive me?"

"Why do you always turn things around to bear the guilt? Let me be responsible for my deeds."

"We are all responsible for our deeds. Even the prince. He was the one who threw his fists at me, not you."

"He should not have drawn you into the fray, Dafydd. Using you to weaken me is unfair. It is my fault he beat you, don't you see?"

"That is only what he wants you to believe."

For once my brother was wrong. The prince had coldly calculated and timed beating my brother.

I closed my eyes and I was back in the guard room.

"They chained me to the wall, Dafydd. Like a beast. The place was pitch black after they locked me in. They took the torch. I felt as though I had been sealed alive in my own tomb."

I rested my head on Dafydd's shoulder, leeching his warmth to ease my chills.

"It was so cold. And damp. And dark. There were rats." My voice had gone raspy.

"It is over now, Lin. You are safe. I am here."

"Until the next bout," I said. "The entire time I spent in that hole I kept seeing your face, wet with tears, as the prince flogged me. I would have given anything to replace your sorrow with the smile I am so fond of. I realised that your tears were not only for me, but because of me. I have the power to ease your suffering. It will take but one word. And I was prepared to offer it this afternoon. Had I seen the prince—"

"No." Dafydd's alarm startled me. "No, I cannot let you do that. You have earned far too many battle scars to let the prince and his mother win now. I could never forgive myself if I were the cause of your soul's betrayal."

"There is my dilemma. You tell me to carry on fighting, when I am so consumed with guilt over your beating all I want to do is lay my soul at the prince's feet so he can crush it under his boots and finish it off. The guard room humbled me, Dafydd, as the prince wanted. If he were to walk in here this moment, he would know I have changed. Tell me. What happened? When you met him."

A spark from the fire landed close to my feet. In a motion, graceful and fluid, Dafydd swept it away. His fingers skimmed over the red scratches left by the rats on the top of my foot.

"You are so brave, Lin. And I am such a coward. My pain is nothing compared to what you have suffered in this last month. It is beyond my ken how a person can be so consumed by the hatred of another, but hate you he does. I saw it in his eyes. Heard it in his voice. It was not me his blows were aimed at, I simply happened to be there. Any one of us would have suited him as well as the next because he was really hitting you. Through me, he was actually beating you. Neither do I mind, having spared you one.

"It was some while after I had left you here to change. I was still wrapped in the happy glow from your release back into the world. Rhys and a few other lads were with me, working on that stretch of the defence wall that needs mending. Prince Modred came riding up the road from town. Aloof and haughty. Daring somebody, anybody, to stand in his way.

"'You,' he said from his horse. 'You are the one called Dafydd.' The prince did not ask it like a question. I thought silence would be best. I cast my eyes at his boot, and hoped it was humble enough for him and he would be satisfied. He fairly screamed for me to answer. But before I could even draw breath, he struck me with his riding whip."

The blow had landed dangerously close to his eye. I would have Enid teach me how to tend it properly.

"Lin, if that is anything like the pain you must feel under the lash, I know not how you do not cry out. I am sure the prince did not use a quarter of his strength in that single blow. I think he used his full strength flogging you. It took a long moment for me to catch my breath. When I did, I gave him the most humble, 'yes, Master,' I have ever uttered.

"Then he said, 'You are *her* brother, are you not?' No mortal could have put more contempt into such a simple word as *her*. I spoke my second 'yes, Master,' quicker than the first, which seemed to please him. He dismounted, and stood before me. I am glad you were not there to see any of it. I could not stop myself, Lin. He is a prince."

I kept my eyes fixed on the shape-shifting flames. They were kinder to my heart than the damage the prince had done to the fair features of my peaceable brother. I knew what Dafydd did next. I wished I had not asked. I felt his hand resting lightly on my knee, and heard his long exhale.

"His mother is queen, Lin. His kinsman is the Pendragon. We are—I am—nothing. He stood before me, steeped in his own importance and glared. Without a word spoken by either of us, I…" He squeezed my leg. "I sank to my knees. I had to, Lin. I am not like you. I am not as strong, not as brave. He frightens me."

Dafydd hung his head.

"Lin, I am sorry I shamed you so. Surely you must think me contemptible."

Fie on the prince. On the house of Lot. My own brother was the pinnacle of subservience. They had turned my brother into a slave and possessed him.

"I could never think such a thing, Dafydd," I whispered hoarsely.

"Very smugly, the prince said, 'At least you have been trained with some small degree of success. You know your place is on your knees. Why can she not be trained?' I had no answer. Most times you are more like him than you are me. In the next moment, he was screaming at me, saying the most dreadful things. His fists kept coming at me again and again. I was so stunned at first, I did not realise that his gibes were about you. He used the ugliest names a woman can be called, both in British and in Irish. No man should ever say such things about another man's sister. I know they were lies, Lin. But…"

My brother paused. I know he battled his tears.

"Finally, he delivered a last blow, saying, *'She cannot be trained because she is nothing but a stupid whore. A whore has only the capacity to take a man between her thighs.'* I wanted to kill him for calling you such filth. I wanted to end your torment by him once and for good. But I could not. I feel so worthless, Lin. So useless. I could not defend my sister, whom I love dearly. I could not even move my lips to tell him to leave off with his lies."

"Perhaps they were not all lies, Dafydd." My whisper sounded ragged.

"He said you liked it, that you begged for his… What am I to believe, Lin?"

My throat felt dry as sand. It was worse than I had thought. Even Dafydd wavered. Did he consider me unclean, too? Despite the pain it brought, I hugged myself, unable to speak in my defence.

"Why did you not tell me that he raped you?"

"He told you?"

"He said enough for me to know. How could you discount me so? Have I been so terrible a brother?"

No, never that. And why did I not say those words when I opened my mouth? Instead, I heard myself saying, "And just what would you have done? Weep for me?"

My hand flew to my mouth in a futile effort to catch the words and pull them back. Why could I not be stupid and dull-witted like the prince said I was?

"Dafydd, I am sorry. Truly. I… You know I would take that back if I could."

"Never mind," he said quietly. But it was clear the cruel words and my lack of trust had wounded him deeply. He removed his hand from my leg. But he made no move to leave.

I waited.

"Are you not afraid of him?" he said.

"Not at first. He was just a boy, Dafydd. With four older brothers who constantly tormented him. I felt sorry for him because he had to endure their pranks and teasing. He seemed powerless, like me. Whenever he taunted me, I told myself 'twas but a show he had to put on for his brothers."

"But his brothers are no longer here, Lin. Rape is a far cry from name-calling."

"Aye. He is cock of the roost now. He must be reeling from his new-gained power. Did he gloat?"

"Please, Lin. You need say no more. It was selfish of me to feel betrayed."

"I suppose I should have told you though. Honesty has always been important between us."

Dafydd managed a grin. "I have taught you something."

"You have taught me many things, Dafydd. Mother would be proud."

"How can I help you now though? Is there anything?"

I shook my head.

"You cannot change that it happened. You cannot prevent it happening again. And you cannot…"

My true fear renewed itself.

"What?" Dafydd said.

"You cannot remove the pain. I can manage that on my own."

"But how long do you think you can keep up your mask of pretence? Nobody can do that forever, not even you."

"I can do it for however bleeding long it is necessary, because it does not bother me any more."

"Yes, it does. What of the honesty you just spoke of?"

"I do not lie, Dafydd. The physical pain is naught compared to the possibility of bearing his child."

My brother gasped. His fingers curled into a fist, then relaxed.

"I feel so helpless, Lin. You have so much to endure. I would avenge you, if I could. Perhaps Enid knows of a way—"

"Dafydd, I swear, I only thought to spare you this extra heartache over me. I cause you enough grief as it is. More than is right. I can never think you a terrible brother. I am the worthless one. Can you forgive me yet again?"

He did not answer my outburst right away, as he normally did.

I shifted about in my place.

"You have run out of forgiveness. I knew it was bound to happen."

"What are you on about? I have not run out of forgiveness. You can be so daft, Impossible One." Dafydd's blue-grey eyes smiled. They told me he was teasing.

My heart sang.

"I need to believe your bounty of forgiveness will last forever. Thank you for being my brother, Dafydd. For being my friend. We do not deserve each other."

"I know. Now. 'Tis past time I tended to the wounds you received yestermorn. I dread the thought of how they must look, after the filth you were surrounded by. Enid should have that poultice ready now. I shan't be long."

CHAPTER 16

I did not see Prince Modred the next day either. Strange. Still, I spent the time listening for the voice that could freeze my blood. I could ill-afford to drop my guard. My nerves were frayed raw by eventide of the end of the second day without a sign of Prince Modred.

Dafydd and I ate our meal in silence. He seemed to sense my mood and did not press. And I felt grateful. After, he left me alone and went to talk with Custennin and some other friends.

Their laughter drifted to me as I twisted the hem of my gown into a knot. How many days since my last bleeding time? Before my collar? After? I could not remember.

"Lin?"

I started at my name. It was not often used, except by Dafydd. The solitude I craved was short-lived.

"May I sit with you for a time, and warm myself nearer to the fire?" Padrig said.

Fairly new to Dunn na Carraice, he most likely did not understand my habits as the others did. But to deny access to the fire would have been rude.

I shrugged and hoped he would take his leave quickly.

The presumptuous fellow settled himself directly in my brother's place, totally oblivious to what I considered a grave sacrilege.

I stiffened at the intrusion, but said nothing.

"I say, the air seems more chill than usual for a summer night." Padrig spoke cheerily, holding his broad hands out towards the warmth before us, rubbing them briskly together.

"I suppose," I said.

"Ah. There. 'Tis colder than the Queen's own heart back in the drafts by the doorway."

"Aye."

"Summers are glorious where I come from, the nights are so mild, one hardly needs a blanket, let alone a fire."

Moved to curiosity, I said, "Where did you come from, Padrig? Were you born in slavery, too?"

We both fingered our collars. My companion was about a year, perhaps two, older than my brother. He was much larger in all respects. Taller, broader at the shoulders. His size belied his quiet nature. Other girls had been giggling over him since he arrived in Dunn na Carraice. Each hopeful he would cast his attention her way.

"Nobody except Davy has bothered to ask me that since I got here. My father was a simple farmer. He owned a few cattle, enough for our family. And a small plot of grazing land, a tiny homestead in the southern part of Dumnonia."

"Where is that? Dumnonia?"

"It takes many days to journey there from here, even by ship. Ah. The grass of my home is thick and soft under bare feet, not like this hard stone of Orkney." Padrig slapped his palm on the floor. "How I miss that sweet smell. My father might not have owned much, but he was a free man."

"What is it like? To live without the weight of a collar? I have spent all of my life here. I saw my mother with a collar, witnessed countless girls and boys receive theirs. Dafydd's was most difficult. Worse than my own. What is it like to live without that shadow of fear? That some day, you would have one too?"

"It is a feeling worth more cattle and gold than the Queen of Orkney possesses."

I ran out of words to say to the young man beside me. I preferred my usual isolation for this very reason.

"'Twas a brave thing you did, Lin. Pouring your porridge at the overseer's feet."

"To hear Rhys talk, everyone here believes me a fool, and worse."

"I don't know a soul who believes that. How do you think of those things to defy our masters?"

"It simply happens, Padrig."

"Your gesture spoke for everyone here and I silently cheered you."

The young man laid a hand on my knee, in much the same manner as my brother might. Yet it certainly did not affect me in the same way. My pulse raced as I recalled the grunting of the prince as he thrust into me.

My breath caught and I shuddered.

“Cold?” My companion sounded concerned.

I nodded. I preferred to lie rather than speak the truth to a stranger. I breathed easier when he finally removed his hand. I was also angered by my lack of action. I had not wanted Padrig touching me, but I froze. I had not even demanded that he leave. What was wrong with me?

“Is the guard room really as horrible a place as everyone makes it out to be? You don’t seem damaged by the experience.”

“Worse, Padrig.” I answered, unwilling to reveal how I had been nearly quelled in that tomb.

“Davy was distraught the whole time.”

“To be sure.”

“We sorely missed his story-telling. I am glad he is at it again.”

My Dafydd? Not before an audience?

“You mean—”

“Not even a note of a song, Lin. He was quite beside himself, worried he would never see you again. Can’t say as I blame him, though. If you were my sister, I would have been worried, too. I’m not saying I wasn’t concerned over you. I mean, we’re all in the same fix, right? And it’s plain how cruel the prince can be.” Padrig ducked his head, grinning. “I didn’t say that very well, did I?”

Another, longer, silence passed between us. I had no idea how to answer him. The fire cracked. I studied my hands and again wished Padrig would leave.

“Is it true you did not scream when the prince set the branding iron to you, Lin?”

“How did you hear of that?”

“Davy wanted you to be remembered as a hero if… May I see it?”

With some reluctance, I showed him the mark on my arm.

“Coo! And you did not scream?”

“My brother spoke true.”

“Coo.” Padrig scratched his head. “I heard you called him a stupid git.”

“I am not that crazed, Padrig. ’Twas a mere Irish stable-hand I called the stupid git. After the prince had left.”

“Still, an Irishman. And he did not hit you or anything?”

"Too stupid to think on what to do or say. I spoke only truth."

Word had travelled quickly. I had gone from "Queen of Slaves" to hero, with the mark of a hot iron.

"What do you plan to do next time your path crosses with Prince Modred?"

Plan? I fussed with my gown, smoothing it over my knees and around my ankles.

"Did you get a new gown, Lin?"

"What a strange question. Why do you ask?"

"I don't remember seeing it before."

"I never get anything new. None of us do," I said, more bitter than angry.

"I meant no harm." He spread his hands as a sign of truce. "Well, even if it is not fresh from the loom, it's new on you, and the colour suits you. The brown sets very nicely with your hair."

"What are you on about, Padrig? This colour is no different from my other garment, or anything else I have ever worn."

"Are you giving my friend a hard time? That isn't very polite, Lin. Little wonder people rarely come to speak to us." Dafydd teased as he sat down, cross-legged in front of me. "I did not interrupt anything, did I?"

"I was telling your sister how well the colour of her gown suits her."

"Indeed." Dafydd seemed more interested in the fire's shadows as he spoke.

"And I think it a daft notion," I said.

"Indeed," my brother repeated.

"What? What has happened, Dafydd? Have you used up all your words in your story-telling?" I said.

He returned my smile.

"I was thinking. Can a man no longer do that?"

Padrig shifted his weight and cleared his throat.

"Well," he said, pushing himself to his feet. "I've said my piece. Thank you, Lin, for sharing a bit of the fire with me. I enjoyed passing the time with you. I hope I might join you again in future." His stiff, clumsy bow from the waist was rather sweet. He was just as uncomfortable as I. And I realised the meaning of his sudden interest in my wardrobe. Dafydd had used words like those with Meg. Padrig had attempted to woo me. I felt my cheeks flush.

"Perhaps." I forced the word from my lips. The gods, my mouth had gone dry.

My brother's gaze darted between us. He could not have missed seeing my distress.

"Good, Lin," Dafydd whispered.

"Sleep well, Davy."

"And you Padrig."

I watched my brother's friend wend back to the far corner of our quarters, greeting friends as he went, to the place he shared with no one.

At least I had my brother.

"It did my heart glad to see you just now, talking with Padrig." Dafydd had slid back to his customary place at my right. "He's a good bloke. I like him."

"Likeable enough, I suppose. He certainly seems to have taken a liking to me, did you know?"

"He has mentioned it once or twice. He is not the first to express an interest in you, either."

"What?" I shot a side-ways glance at my brother.

"If you would come from your isolation every now and again, you might notice these things."

"Who besides Padrig?"

Dafydd rubbed the back of his neck, grimacing.

"Here, Dafydd, let me." I knelt behind my brother, brushing his hands away so I could knead the knots from his muscles.

"Kevyn. Manus. A few others. They think you are pretty."

"And the prince thinks the world owes him obeisance because of his royal mother. Does that make him right?"

"You find it surprising that boys should take an interest in you? In a kinder vein than the prince?"

"Yes, I do. And they will want nothing further to do with me once they have found out how the prince has used me. No man will. I am nothing but used, damaged goods."

"Please, do not speak so. You mustn't believe that of yourself. What the prince did to you was the worst of violations. I cannot begin to fathom your pain. But it was not of your making. It was not your fault. Any man with a heart will understand. Padrig has a good heart. Give him a chance to show you. If I did not trust him, I would not allow him near you, you know."

"Tell him to set his sights on some other girl. Someone safe."

Someone pure.

"You cannot distance yourself from the entire world."

"I can try. I must. More than ever, I have to distance myself from everyone here."

Dafydd twisted to face me.

"Even me?"

The cuts and bruises on my brother's face, but days old, had not had time to heal yet. My hands fell from his shoulders.

"Perhaps especially you. I cannot let him know he can hurt me through you."

"Lin, he already knows. You are wasting your efforts."

I had nothing to throw. Nothing to tear. And I could not very well hit my own brother.

"*Wfft*. The *equites* of the Pendragon are not powerless, Dafydd. That is what I would seek in Camelot. I never want to be as helpless and as powerless as I am here and now."

My brother stared at me.

"An *eques*? You cannot be an *eques*, you're a girl."

"You cannot be a bard, you are a slave," I lashed out. This time I would not apologise. I know he was waiting for it.

We sat in silence for a long time, before I spoke again.

"It is no more daft a notion than your being a bard."

"I never said it was. I was only just trying to envision you in armour, with a spear in your hands, and a sword at your hip. If you had those things, and power, would you want and seek revenge on the Queen and the prince?"

"Revenge? No. Justice? Yes. I would very much like to see justice served on the Queen and her bastard. I would enjoy doing it myself."

"Sometimes those two can be confused, Lin. Revenge and justice. I have heard even wise men have trouble distinguishing them."

We did not say much else after that. We settled down for the night together. As always, he fell asleep first, quickly and easily. I listened to his even, relaxed breathing.

The moon had yet to go through a compleat cycle of its phases since I had first been collared. The prince never knew how close he had gotten to victory the day I was released from the guard room, I am quite certain. Otherwise he would have charged in for the final blow. But I knew, and understood that I had to be extremely careful. I would not be allowed another such slip without his notice. Were I ever to falter again, the prince would seize his spoils.

In the stillness of the night, my woman's blood began to flow. I wept tears of relief into Dafydd's shirt. I had been spared a bastard. This time. Dafydd stirred and without a question, took me into his arms.

CHAPTER 17

"Up from your nap, lazy whore's melt. To work."

I was doubled over with a cramp in my belly, which felt as though a fist, gloved in iron, had shoved its way deep within my bowels, seizing my guts in order to squeeze the life from them. I suffered this every time the moon went through a cycle for the first day or two of my flux.

"Move. Brisen says this passageway is to be clean today."

"Then why does Brisen not simply do it herself?" I muttered, loud enough for the overseer to hear.

I felt the sting of the lash across my shoulders. A warning stroke, meant to wheal, not cut. I was glad I had decided not to wear Meg's gown during the day though. I did not wish it to end up like my others had.

Refusing to acknowledge the petty presence of the man looming over me, I resumed scrubbing the stone floor. He was naught but one of Queen Morgause's many pawns. I needed to reserve my efforts for my true enemy. I was determined to be ready for the confrontation.

The overseer glowered at me a moment longer, then realised he could do nothing more to intimidate me.

When he was gone, I assessed my progress. Nearly finished.

Dafydd had shared my relief at cockcrow when I whispered to him I was not with child. He did not press the issue of Padrig or the other boys' interest in me as a woman. Why would any of them notice me? Other girls were much prettier. My hair was straight and ordinary. My face always seemed to have a bruise or two. What was there to catch their attention?

I had more important things to consider than boys anyway. I had not seen the prince since he had sent me to the guard room. Where was he?

Would any sort of vengeance for Dafydd's beating be possible? How sweet it would be to smash one of the hanging oil lamps over Prince Modred's head. And watch his hair burn. Lost in the daydream, I paid no heed to my task and carelessly sloshed the scrub-water around me.

"Ach. Worthless. Clumsy." The contempt in the young man's voice felt like an icy mid-winter rain falling onto my head. I recognised the water-soaked boots. I had seen them before. I knew the black leather, teamed them with voice and words. There was no doubt to my conclusion.

Wfft.

"Do you realise the value of my boots? Ach, why do I bother wasting the question on such a stupid creature? The boots are worth a great deal more than the likes of you. You have ruined them. You shall pay dearly for this."

And just how was it my fault? Could he not have stepped around me? No. Easier to let the slave take the dross. That was why there were so many of us.

I slammed the scrub-brush into the bucket, splashing even more of the filthy water onto us.

My action brought a wave of epithets. In the next breath, he snatched up the wooden bucket and held it aloft, ready to dash it over my head.

"What are you waiting for, Prince? Afraid?" I would not die a cringing slave.

"Your temper, my son." A woman spoke gently, in Irish from the shadowy doorway at the near end of the corridor.

"Mother?" Prince Modred sounded like a frightened child, having just been caught at being very naughty. Gone was the self-assured, calculated arrogance. Gone was the reserve of superiority. The proud, young Irish prince, in the water-sodden boots was naught but a boy, afraid of his mummy.

How rich.

He must have realised how foolish he looked with the bucket poised as it was, for he began to lower his burden. A sneer curved his lips upwards as he hesitated. Then he tipped the bucket over, spilling its contents over my head. The scrub-brush tumbled out and hit my shoulder. I shivered, and heard a woman's high-pitched giggle that seemed too frivolous to belong to the Queen of Orkney.

The prince heaved the bucket the length of the corridor. It crashed in the distance. If it was broken, I would be required to make restitution for that as well as the boots. My debts were rising rapidly.

"Mother," the prince repeated, his composure returned. He tugged at the hem of his tunic to straighten it.

My enemy had weakened first. A glorious feeling, unquenchable by the foul water dripping from me.

"Bring the slave closer," the Queen of Orkney commanded her son, still in Irish.

He obeyed by grasping my collar and jerking me to my feet. I was shoved forward to where his mother awaited.

"Kneel before your queen, pig-girl." His command to me was in British.

"Break my knees, prince."

I felt his muscles tense as his fist tightened around my collar.

"Damn your defiance."

"Let her stand, Modred."

"Why is it, Mother, that you have given me such a sorry excuse for a slave?" He reverted to Irish.

"You are not pleased with my gift?"

"Never that, my dear lady."

A touching response from a loving son. They might as well have been discussing a new tunic, dyed the wrong colour.

My fists balled at my sides.

"But as you were just witness to, my lady, the wench cannot even respond to a command in plain, simple British."

"Indeed." The Queen stepped from the shadows.

We took a long measure of each other.

I could see why men considered her beautiful. In spite of having five grown sons, she had the body of a much younger woman. A maiden, rather. Her creamy complexion was flawless, unwrinkled by her years. She had jet black hair, untouched by the frost of time, like her youngest. It hung in a single, thick braid down her back to her waist. The gown she wore was of the faerie colour, grass green. The material shimmered in the flickering light of the lamps. It looked very soft, but not very warm or strong, as though it might tear easily.

I had heard the whispers about the Queen. How she was of the faerie folk, and knew their magic ways. Behind my back, I made the horned sign with my fingers, to be safe.

She began to take a step closer, but halted. The fair features of her face twisted into a prim, dainty grimace of distaste.

"That stench wrinkling your nose is but your own offal. It comes of your own household. The dirt you hide so well from visitors," I said.

The prince quaked.

"Hold your tongue, slave. You were not given leave to speak," he said.

His mother showed no reaction to my impertinence.

"Is this the one, sister?" A second, younger woman spoke in British as she joined the Queen. She must have giggled at my dowsing.

"*Antaidh* Morgan." The prince exclaimed the Irish word of kinship, then switched to British, for it would seem that his mother's sister knew not the Irish tongue. "When did you arrive in Dunn na Carraice?" He released my collar before sweeping his kinswoman into an embrace.

"This very morning, Modred. My word. You have changed since last I saw you." She held him at arms-length. He was a good deal taller than his mother's sister. "You were a mere boy then."

"I've grown," he said, grinning like a child starved for attention.

"So you have."

I was in the presence of the infamous daughters of Queen Igraine. The scheming siblings of the Pendragon. They bore a strong resemblance to each other, although Lady Morgan's hair was burnished gold rather than black. I wondered which of the two favoured their half-brother.

The Queen of Orkney's eyes never left me during the family greetings. Their colour matched her gown. Her delicate fingers played with the thick gold collar at her throat as she studied me. The *torc* looked too heavy for her slender neck.

I wanted to mirror her gesture, for it heightened my awareness of my own constricting leather. But I held my hands rigidly at my sides, and tried to stand straighter and taller than I already was.

Her sister, now finished with the pleasantries, turned her gaze on me as well. The Lady Morgan, squinting in the dimness, inspected my drenched and ragged appearance as though I were a curiosity she had never before seen.

What did they want from me? I put on my best scowl and glowered at the royals.

"This is the one?" she said again.

Her sister nodded.

"She is as you say, Morgause. They are very much alike."

"You doubted my word?"

"Certainly not, Morgause."

Orkney's queen was a powerful woman, accustomed to unquestioned obedience. Even her sister wavered.

My own curiosity certainly was piqued by the oblique exchange. If, as they seemed to imply, they referred to me, whom or what did I resemble?

"The creature does not look as dangerous as you say. How can anything so emaciated be strong enough to withstand a summer breeze? Quite stupid, though, Morgause," Lady Morgan said, turning to her sister, dismissing my presence. "A slave who has not even the sense to bow to a queen. And with prompting. The slave cannot be worth the trouble you are going through."

"Her training amuses Modred. Now his brothers have left, there is little for him to do here."

Training?

"I wish to sell her, Mother."

"Why, my dear?"

"She has ruined my boots. The ones Agravain sent me. May I sell my slave for the price of them?"

The Queen peered at her son's boots. "Modred," she said with a smile. "Her sale would not raise the replacement cost of those boots. They came from the mainland."

"Tell me, how many slaves would it take to purchase another pair of boots from the mainland?" I reminded the royal trio of my existence.

"What? Oh, Morgause. If that were my slave, I would have her whipped so that she could not stand for a week. How do you tolerate such impertinence?"

"I do not. The slave belongs to Modred now. He branded her to seal it legally. He shall know how to deal with the affair. Amuse yourself, my son. I am quite certain you shall extract satisfactory payment from our rebellious little dragon without selling her." She patted her son's sleeve as she strolled past him. "Come along, sister."

"I shall see you tonight at supper, Modred?"

"With pleasure, *antaidh*."

"Branding. You wicked boy." She smiled at him, as though she approved. She no doubt did.

"And Modred?"

"Yes, Mother?"

"When you have finished here, Agravain wishes a word with you. He said he was heading for the stables."

The prince bowed as the ladies departed.

I remained erect.

As soon as the door closed behind them, he whirled on me.

"How dare you embarrass me in front of my mother? That last flogging I gave you should have done you more good than the ill manners you just displayed," he screamed, while at the same time his fist landed on my left cheek.

I staggered back a step.

"Maybe a decent fisting is what you need. It seemed to work on your dear brother." His hand flew at my face again, open this time. It landed on the side of my head. "By the powers, I shall soon leave you as colourful as him."

No whip this time. No chains. No post. Dafydd had taken the blows because he had no choice. Resistance of that sort was not in my brother's nature.

I was not my brother. My hands were free. When Prince Modred's hand came at me once more, with a strength I did not realise I possessed, my own hand caught his wrist before he could strike again.

The blue eyes glaring at me widened with surprise.

"How careless of you, prince."

Our arms strained against each other. I knew my strength could not outlast his. I needed to act decisively, for this was my sole opportunity. My action would have to be worth the painful consequences to follow.

My knee went for the one vulnerable place I knew he had.

"I am not my brother," I screamed, grinding my knee deeper. "Nor am I your slave."

The prince doubled over.

"And this—" I aimed my knee once more and it smashed into the side of his head. "That was for Dafydd."

I stood over the prince's bent form, panting.

Still hunched and gulping air himself, the prince raised his head.

My gaze met eyes cold as the grave. I had tempted the fates for the last time.

I was too frightened to move. Perhaps in his anger, he would be swift—break my neck and be done.

He gripped my collar.

Strangling took time.

I felt a warmth trickle between my legs and heard water splash at my feet. I had…

An icy chuckle filled the passage. His hatred had naught to do with wet boots, or spilled porridge or insolence.

"You seem to have forgotten your place, *cumal*. Time you were reminded."

He nearly dragged me down the corridor and outside.

People scurried out of the way.

I assumed he had another flogging planned for me, but we passed the scourging post and crossed the courtyard to the stables.

He shouted for one of the men to follow. At the entrance to the stall where I had been branded, he released my collar before entering.

I clutched a wood support beam.

"Your Highness?" The stable-hand had caught up to us. He did not spare me a glance.

"I have another assistant for you," the prince said without looking up from untying his horse's halter.

"My lord?"

"This stall needs a good mucking out. See that she does it right. With her hands."

We glared at each other as he led his horse past where I still leaned against the post.

"Beat her if she gives you trouble."

"Indeed, my lord." The man's cruel smile conveyed his intention to obey the command regardless of my behaviour.

"Is my brother here?"

"He just left for the practice field, my lord. Shall I have your mount saddled for you, sir?"

"Aye. "The prince tossed the rope to the servant. "Get to work, girl." He shoved me into the foul straw. "And be grateful I did not give you to them for their pleasure." He gestured to the men who had gathered outside the stall to watch the sport.

He left amidst their guffaws.

CHAPTER 18

I should be dead, but I was not. Cold sweat dribbled down my back. Would the prince sell Dafydd, then, to pay for his boots? Was that the reason he had spared my life? Because the prince could devise a far worse punishment for me?

A vision of my brother stepping onto the auction block replaced the murky stable.

I wanted to curl up in a corner and weep. Instead, I knelt in the centre of the stall, hugging myself until the stinging laughter of the stable-hands and the rain of filthy straw reminded me of reality.

"Enough lads. To your own work."

I presumed the man was the stable-master to have such authority when they obeyed.

I was left in peace and set to chucking straw and manure by the handful into the aisle where it could be swept out.

'Twas twilight when I finished the job and emerged from the stable. Several of my companions were already filing into our quarters as I crossed the courtyard. Dafydd was not among the small group milling near the water barrel.

No cause for panic.

Yet.

I pushed my way through to plunge my arms into the rain-water to wash away the mire.

"Just how long are you going to keep taking his shit before you really fight back, Lin?"

"What are you on about, Rhys?" I splashed water on my face and neck. The best I could do for a bath.

"The bastard prince, Lin. What I want to know is when you plan to quit talking and do something. People here look to you. What's it going to take to piss you off? Davy on the auction block?"

I grabbed his tunic and pulled him over the barrel towards me.

"What do you mean by that? Where is Dafydd?"

Was he already gone?

I felt a hand on my shoulder.

"Lass," Custennin said. "Lass. Davy's already within."

I released Rhys and spun to face the former warrior.

"Truly?"

Custennin nodded.

I shook water from my arms and dashed inside.

Padrig hailed a cheerful greeting as I entered. I acknowledged him with a nod, but did not stop. I would not be satisfied until—

I saw my brother's sand-coloured hair amidst a group of youths near the fire-pit, his back to me. Custennin had spoken true. I vowed to thank the man later.

I now noticed the light-hearted conversations, accompanied by a great deal more laughter than usual. The reason was a tapped cask of ale set up near our drinking water.

The overseer passed me on his way out, grumbling about our unworthiness for any kindness.

No punishment for my absence from the rest of my duties while I had been in the stables?

Dafydd already had my bowl filled and was prepared to hand it to me, as I joined him. His countenance sagged as we faced each other. His good cheer disappeared before my eyes. I expected concern when he saw my latest bruises and my filthy appearance. But there was much more than concern in the beloved blue-grey eyes which studied me so intently.

My own relief in learning he had not been sold got shoved aside. I wanted to hide from his scrutiny.

We ate in tense silence. Rather, Dafydd ate. I merely swirled the contents of my bowl around more than raising any to my mouth. The pungent odour from the stables clung to my hands in spite of my efforts to rinse it off. The stench did little for my appetite. I stopped trying. And for once was not chastened.

Dafydd set his bowl aside and wiped his mouth with his fingers.

Tapered fingers suited for a life of leisure, not slavery. The fingers of a harper, not a slave.

"I am afraid to ask, you know," he said.

I did know. Only too well. I stared straight on, without focus.

"I heard Prince Modred was in a terrible rage this afternoon. Nothing in his path was safe, Lin."

I searched Dafydd's face for signs of fresh bruises. Felt relief when I discerned none. The fates had spared my brother in more ways than one.

"I am glad you did not meet up with him." I spoke to my feet.

"And I?"

With boundless care and gentleness, he curled a finger under my chin and turned my face up towards his. He had intended to be angry. The emotion had been in his initial words, but it was not in his eyes.

"And I prayed and hoped that for once it did not involve you."

Much time passed before he spoke again. When he did, there was no anger. No blame. Only truth. Only resignation. Tired resignation.

"I suppose I should have known better. Should have known that somehow you would be at the heart of his temper. Which is why I am afraid to ask. I can picture the entire scene."

"Just once, Dafydd, I had to feel justified. I knew the consequences of my actions would be grave, so I had to make it worth the beating, for once. But I gambled your life at the same time."

How could I ever forgive myself for that?

Dafydd's hand smoothed my hair. His silent presence was more valuable to me than any words of comfort.

"I will never do so again, I promise."

"I doubt that is possible, Lin. How can I not be involved? I am your brother."

"I swear, I did not provoke him first, Dafydd. It began quite innocently and spiraled from me splashing scrub-water onto his boots. Accidentally."

"How is it that the two of you set at each other's throats whenever you're together? It is like you are a different person in his presence. A person who frightens me, because I do not know that Lin. I cannot understand her rage or from whence it comes. Where is the sweet-natured sister I once had before our collars? Before he came between us?"

"I am still here, Dafydd. But he gave me an opportunity I had to take."

My brother sighed and crossed his arms over his breast.

"What did you do," he asked.

"I hurt him, Dafydd. I went beyond the pale, beyond words and hurt him."

Dafydd's eyes grew wide as I described my deeds.

"You didn't," he whispered.

"Well done, I say."

I had not seen, or heard, Padrig approach. But there he stood between myself and the fire-pit. He sounded pleased with my feat.

"No wonder the prince was in such a wax," he said. "Ale?"

Concerned over my brother, I took the cup Padrig offered.

Dafydd groaned, looking ill. "By the stars, Lin, you did?"

"Here. Drink." I gave the ale to him.

His hands trembled but he managed to drain the cup.

"Better?"

"Yes, thank you. And you, Padrig. Well timed, my friend." His thin smile lacked its usual warmth.

Padrig shifted his weight from leg to leg. "I did not mean to interrupt you," he said. "I only thought you might be wanting your portions from the ale cask. Shall I leave?"

For some reason, both boys looked to me for an answer.

My brother liked Padrig. He and I could always talk later.

A nod to my brother signified his friend could stay.

Dafydd squeezed my leg. "That is not necessary, Padrig," he said.

"I am sorry. I couldn't help but overhear what you said, Lin."

"Never mind. No harm." I gestured for our friend to sit with us.

He did not accept the invitation right away.

"The dunn will be a-stir with the news, though. Lin *cumal* crushes the—" His voice rose to be heard above the conversations around us, ready to make the announcement.

"Don't Padrig. Please?"

"Why not? It makes you a hero." His disappointment was plain.

I knew what a hero was. And I was not one. Not after risking Dafydd as I had today.

"It isn't important, Padrig. I would rather forget it."

"As you want," he said. "You've not had your ale yet, Lin. I'll get us more."

"Let me help." Dafydd rose and followed his friend.

They were not gone long.

I took the cup Padrig handed me.

He faced the palace and raised his cup in salute. "To the Queen," he said. "For her generosity tonight."

"Fie on her. I saw naught in her demeanour this afternoon that showed kindness."

"You saw the queen too, Lin," Dafydd asked.

"She was with her sister, Lady Morgan."

"Coo, Lin. You do tangle with high persons."

"Not by choice. You call this generous? A spot of libation? They collar and whip us like dogs, Padrig. The Queen has a heart of stone. It was all too convenient that she and her sister chanced down that passageway when they did, with the prince poised to kill me."

My brother gasped. Padrig's brown eyes held a mix of horror and admiration.

"Queen Morgause spared the life of a lowly slave. How touching."

I had intended to wait until Dafydd and I were alone to relate my royal audience. Too late.

"Again, I fear the details," Dafydd said. "How did the prince come to be ready to kill you? Was it because—"

"'Twas before my knee made the connection. His initial anger was over his water-sodden boots. His mother's entrance was timely. 'Twas comical, really, his reaction to his mother's appearance."

"And you, Lin? How did you handle a royal audience?" Padrig said.

"I asked the Queen how many slaves it would take to replace a pair of boots from the mainland."

"Honestly, Lin. Do you fear nothing? Do you not fear anyone?"

"He wanted to sell me, Dafydd. He wanted to sell me for a pair of soggy boots. That is how close you got to not having a sister tonight. A single word and he could have sold you instead. Only the hands of the gods—or his mother—stopped him."

Surely Dafydd knew how I feared that. I would die if I were to ever lose him.

During the lull of our conversation, one of our companions began playing a reed pipe.

"We shall have dancing tonight." Olwen clapped her hands and leapt to her feet. She began to twirl to the gay tune.

Custennin was the first to join his daughter, pulling Enid with him.

Olwen led them around the room, and one by one, people joined in.

Dafydd and Padrig were willing to take part in the festivities. But my royal encounter had dampened my spirits.

"Oh, Lin. Don't be so grumpy. You are always so solemn. But not tonight. I refuse to allow it. Come on, you impossible girl. Help me, Padrig."

They each took one of my hands. I could not resist their combined strength.

"Conspirators," I said.

Padrig laughed.

Dafydd drew close and spoke in my ear. His eyes glistened, on the verge of tears.

"Enjoy this holiday. 'Tis a gift. The gods have given us this chance to heal some of our sorrows here. You and I have ample cause to celebrate." He squeezed my hand. "Forget about the prince, just this one evening. For me?"

There is a freedom of sorts in the frenzied, breathless swirling and spiraling of the dance. Linked between him and Padrig, I soon laughed along with everyone else. And for a time, I did forget the prince, his mother, my pain and bitterness, even my collar. All hardships were pushed clear of my mind.

Not a soul remained sitting. As the piper trilled faster, so too did we dance. Hands became unlinked and eventually I was separated from Dafydd. I stumbled and would have fallen but that Padrig's arm slipped around my waist for support. Out of breath, we stopped in a darkened corner.

"It is good to hear you laugh, Lin," he said. His breath warmed my neck. "In all the while I've been here, this is the first time you have. Your brother was wise, drawing you into the dance."

"It was jolly," I said, gulping air.

He still held me very close.

Our eyes met.

Padrig's smile was nothing like Prince Modred's had been as he possessed me with his body. There was a gentleness in my brother's friend, despite his strength and size. Gentleness and kindness. Two properties that the prince lacked.

"Lin." He sighed my name. "I do wish the prince would not destroy your lovely features so." His fingers stroked the curve of my chin, as he continued to proclaim my beauty.

Flustered by his closeness and the kind words, I broke from his gaze, finding it impossible to move any other part of me.

The pressure of strange lips on mine took me totally by surprise. Padrig was a man, after all, and he seemed to be wanting that same possession of me as the prince had. The thought of any man taking his pleasure with me was repulsive, and my guts churned. I pulled free of his embrace, backing deeper into the shadows, my heart racing.

Padrig stepped back at the same time.

"I…" He lowered his gaze. "Dancing is thirsty work, Lin. I'll see if there is any ale left."

I nodded, unable to speak.

Why did I become so clumsy whenever I was near him? I had no such trouble with my mortal enemy. I was never at a lack of words or deeds when faced with the dangers of the prince. And here was a youth speaking kind words to me. Dafydd trusted him, why could I not? Like my brother, I do not think Padrig was capable of harbouring a cruel thought, much less the ability to undertake such action. And all I could do was run from him like a frightened rabbit. I had not even the courage to slap him for the assault of my lips. He had called me a hero. Heroes were brave. I was no hero. I despised my cowardice.

"Cheers, Lin."

I jumped at Padrig's abrupt return.

"It would be much more comfortable if we sat down, Lin."

I sought for Dafydd. He was in the midst of the revellers, dancing with several girls at once and oblivious to my distress.

Padrig was very near and I had nowhere to hide from him. Worse, I could not think of a single word to say to him. Strange emotions surged through me. Anger and hatred do little to prepare one for gentleness.

He took my hand and we settled ourselves against the wall.

"Lin, perhaps I was wrong to be so bold just now… I meant no dishonour. It's just, I'm not very good with fine words like Davy. I wish I were. My words fall short of how I feel about you." He continued to hold my hand. "My father taught me many things, like how to till a field, but not what to say to a woman. I'm certain I am not the first bloke to take notice of you, and to admire what he sees. They have probably all tried to tell you the same thing, too. I most likely don't have even a prayer of a chance—"

"I—"

"Let me finish before I lose my nerve, please. I don't have a ring to give you, to pledge my troth, but would you accept my word? Accept me?"

What was he saying? Marriage? Me?

"Padrig, I… What about this?" My stomach knotted as I fingered my collar.

"The life we have is uncertain. But that doesn't mean we should deny ourselves happiness if given the chance. What I'm saying is, I would very much like to help you find some happiness. It would be my great honour."

Padrig scratched his throat, just below his collar.

"As you don't have a father, I suppose I'll need to ask Davy for—"

"Ask my brother for what?"

"Permission for your hand, of course."

"Indeed? I will have you to know Padrig, my hand is not Dafydd's to give. It happens to be attached to me. Were you, or was Dafydd, going to chop it off once you had permission? Good evening to you."

I rose and made my way to the door.

He called out a feeble apology, which I did not answer. Thankfully, he did not follow.

Outside, I did not mind that the night air was chilled by a stiff breeze. I could taste the sea's salt.

My hand indeed. I paced to the end of our quarters. Permission. I spun on my heel.

The cheek.

Even for marriage, I was not my own mistress, only chattel, my brother's to dispose of to whomever he chose. Even without my collar and brand, I would be no better off. I would not be free. For then, my own brother would be my master, until my husband took over. I felt the rising sting of tears. Women were merely property for fathers, brothers, and husbands. Not for the last time, I hated the world of men, and detested my womanhood.

CHAPTER 19

As usual, dawn came far too quickly to those in the slaves' quarters of Dunn na Carraice.

"Did you get any sleep last night, Lin," Dafydd asked through a yawn.

I had been awake long enough to patch a tear in my brother's tunic and mend its hem.

"Some."

He did not argue, but I was not entirely certain he believed me. After a few moments, I rose to fill our bowls.

Around us, we heard the complaints of aching heads and thick tongues. And curses to the Queen for providing the source of their discomfort.

Dafydd plucked a stalk of straw from my hair when I returned. It showed I had at least tried to sleep.

"What on earth had you so nettled last night, Lin," he asked. "One moment you were dancing and laughing, enjoying our holiday. You even talked to Padrig."

"You make it sound a miracle, Dafydd."

"Of a sort." He nodded, swallowed. "Of a sort, it is a miracle. You hardly ever talk to anyone. You need friends." He nudged my shoulder playfully.

"I do not want friends," I said, ignoring my own aches and pains. "You know what happens to friends."

Dafydd's cheerful expression vanished. "Can we please not start that this morning? I had so hoped we could make last night's merriment linger—at least until the overseer arrives."

"That revelry was naught but a dream, Dafydd. Leather is the only reality on Orkney. Leather collars and leather whips."

"What shattered the dream for you, then? What sent you storming out of here as though you had stepped in a nest of vipers? When you did finally return, you sat in a darkened corner, shunning everyone the rest of the night."

"As if you do not know," I said. "He is your friend. Not mine."

"Friend?"

"Do not play innocent with me, Dafydd. I am quite certain you and Padrig planned the entire scheme together." I watched, convinced of my self-perceived truth, as my brother raised his bowl to his lips. "You plotted to get me dizzy from dancing, only to betray me."

"Betray you?" Dafydd sputtered and coughed on his porridge.

"How fortunate for your plan that the Queen provided a cask of ale. That way you and he could get me besotted as well, and truly have my brains addled. All the easier to commit the foul deed."

Slowly, my brother wiped his lips with his fingers, staring at me throughout.

I sat, firm in my conviction that I had been wronged by my brother and his friend and stared back.

"What are you on about," he asked after a final bout of coughing. "You sound like a madwoman. What plot? What betrayal?"

I gave him silence.

"Just how much ale did you drink last night, Lin?"

When I still had not answered him, Dafydd released a long sigh.

"I cannot talk to you when you are like this. Calm yourself first, Linnie." He patted my leg.

I jerked away. "Stop patronising me."

"Then stop behaving like a child. You have not been a child since Mother died. Why start now? All I asked was a question. When did that become a crime?"

Any reference to Mother cut through my emotions immediately. I stared blankly at the space between us.

Perhaps I had been unfair.

"Now that we have finished with that nonsense, will you please tell me what happened last night? Did Padrig hurt you?"

I saw his fingers curl into a fist, and remembered how it had flown into Rhys' face the day I had been branded. He would do it for me again.

"Padrig? He could not a flea."

The fingers relaxed.

"What then?"

Encouraged by the knowledge that my brother would consider avenging my honour—where he could—I confided.

"He kissed me, Dafydd." I watched his hand, expecting the fingers to clench once again.

They did not.

"A kiss?"

I glanced up.

He was smiling.

"A kiss?" His voice held a hint of humour.

I saw nothing funny in the incident.

"A small display of affection distressed you this much?"

"My discomfort seems to amuse you, Dafydd."

"My apologies, your Highness. But most other girls would be quite pleased by a young man's attentions. Indeed, they would have worked to encourage them."

How could my brother mock me?

"I assure you, I did not. I neither encouraged nor did I invite. I did not appreciate the liberty he took with my lips. As you well know, I am not like most other girls."

"Aye." Dafydd nodded. "Well, at least you did not hit him or worse—"

"I regret that I did not."

"I wonder what you might have done had he proposed marriage."

"You were a part of it, Dafydd. You knew. How could you betray me so?"

"Stop right there, Lin. I need not explain myself to you, but I will not suffer you to accuse me of something of which I am innocent. You are wrong to believe that I could ever betray you. Never think that of me."

He took my hands in his and patiently worked my fingers loose.

I relented and let them relax from the fists I had made. But I could not disguise my hurt from the one who knew me so well. And I could see in his eyes that he was equally hurt by my accusations.

"True, Padrig mentioned his intention to me. Took me in his confidence, I might add. He merely asked me how you might react to a betrothal offer."

"You should have warned him then."

"You are impossible in your stubbornness. If you would just once open your heart, and your eyes, you would see that not all men act as violently as Prince Modred. A man can be tender."

"Tender?" I nearly screamed, rousing the curiosity of those people closest to us. I glared at them until they returned to their own business.

"You mean like the tenderness you displayed by laughing at your sister's distressed reaction to a man's uninvited advances? Or do you believe all was well simply because you were given warning?"

Dafydd's features sobered immediately. But his reply was silenced by the entrance of the overseer barking out the day's work orders.

"Here." I tossed my brother's tunic into his lap. "I mended it for you this morning, having nothing better to do with my time."

He looked remorseful, clutching the rag to his breast.

I rose and joined Enid and Olwen as they were leaving our quarters.

Padrig, I ignored compleatly, although I passed quite near him.

* * *

The Queen had entertained her sister with a feast in the Great Hall the night before. The duty of cleaning up fell to me and a few others. The place stank of unwashed bodies, both human and animal, greasy food, spilled wine, ale and *uisge*, urine and sickness. The highborn could not even go outside to relieve themselves, let alone visit the privy.

In the middle of the room, amidst the rushes, a pair of hounds wrestled over a bone. Julia tossed the remnants of a lamb's leg to the dogs and broke up the fight.

Scraps from the feast would be divided between the hounds and the pigs. I scraped a platter of leftover vegetable into a bucket.

"Such a waste," Enid said. "Where would be the harm in giving us a little? Especially for the children." She stacked empty platters so we could carry them out for washing.

"I must needs be starving to eat this refuse," another woman said. "I have no stomach for what has already been gnawed upon."

"More's the pity, I say," Julia said. "With so much to spare, the Queen could provide better for us."

We spoke in whispers because a few of the revellers still snored in their places at the boards. One man slumped in his chair on the dais, his face buried in the ample breasts of the light-haired woman sleeping in his lap. I recognised his bright head of flame-coloured hair.

"We would do well to remain clear of him," I said to no one in particular.

"Why should you worry, Lin?" Julia said. "You can slash Prince Modred's face open with your nails and drive his cullions to his nose with your knee. Why not render the same to all his brothers?"

Despite my efforts to quell that episode, others had learned of it anyway.

"Davy says your wounds are healing well, Lin," Enid said.

"Yes, Enid," I said, thankful for the diversion. "My thanks for the herbs you have been sending. What is in that poultice?"

"I use wool-fat for the salve, with green mould from old bread mixed into it. My own mother learned the trick from her mother."

"And you taught Dafydd."

"He is such a fine lad. You can do no better for a brother. I have worried about the two of you, alone in the world. Seems as though you're doing well enough together. The way Davy-*bach* fusses over you, he'd do any mother proud. And you—our little Linnie—blossoming before our very eyes. Soon Davy will be singing at your wedding."

"Padrig has certainly become bold of late, Enid," Julia burst into the conversation uninvited. "Who did not see how close he was to Lin while dancing with her last night?"

"And fetching ale for her," Seren said.

Their tones bordered on mockery.

"And to think, a few days ago, the bloke was too bashful to even speak to her. All he could do was stare at her from across the room, moon-eyed, like a love-sick puppy."

Seren imitated the expression and the girls nearest us burst into giggles.

"He'll be wanting more than a dance and a kiss next time." Julia winked at me, patting her pregnant belly.

Had the entire room witnessed that kiss? I heard more laughter as my cheeks flushed.

"Shut your gob, Julia," I said, tugging a handful of her hair.

She yelped.

"By the Christ! Can't a man sleep in his own fuckin' hall?" The roar came from the dais. Prince Agravain was on his feet. His woman, gone. He glowered at the small figure, cringing at his feet.

My hand dropped from Julia. The quarrel abandoned by all.

No one had warned Olwen to avoid working on the dais for the time. She had been eager to help.

"My baby." Enid whispered, taking a step forward.

"No, Enid," Seren said. She and another of our companions clutched Enid's arms to hold her back.

"He's going to beat my baby."

"How can you comfort your child if you're beaten, too?" the second woman said.

Somebody had to do something, though. How could we stand idle and allow that giant of a man to hurt a defenceless child? He was already unhooking his belt to use as a whip.

Olwen shrank away as the prince's first blow caught her arm.

"Mother!"

Her scream moved me to action, so that I found myself between the warrior and the child in time to receive the next blow on my own back. If the brute wanted to beat Olwen, he must needs go through me first. Perhaps by then, most of his anger would be spent, and she would not have to endure the worst of it. I had to spare her the pain I knew too well.

"Do not move, Olwen," I whispered, hovering over the girl.

She trembled, but at least her screams had stopped.

"What's this? Get out of the way. This is not your concern."

I swallowed my pride and fixed my eyes on the top of Olwen's head, my back still presented to Prince Agravain. At least his youngest brother would not witness what I was about to do.

"Please, lord. She is but a child. Truly, she meant no harm. She was only doing as she had been bidden. Please, lord, show her mercy." My flesh crawled as I begged.

"Mercy? The wretch dares demand mercy? Here's a taste of Orkney's mercy."

I already knew how Orkney's mercy tasted. Bitter.

He flailed his strap, bringing it down in rapid succession. In his fury, he lost accuracy in his aim, thus many blows simply hissed through empty air. His brother would never have been so sloppy.

"Agravain? What are you doing with my slave?"

"This sack of bones is yours, Modred? Tell me you didn't pay real silver for this ill-mannered creature."

For the time, the rain of blows ceased.

"Coins? For that? Agravain, our dung-heap has keener wits."

The man behind me brayed, while his brother crossed the length of the hall to join us on the dais.

"I paid nothing, it was a gift from Mother. Remember our pig-girl?"

It?

"Her? But why would Mother give you a slave?"

"She gave slaves to you and Gawain. She even offered one to Ris and Gareth. Why not me as well?"

"Aye. I forget you're no longer a boy, Modred."

"So did *antaidh* Morgan. My fa— Our famous kinsman, Arthur Pendragon, probably does as well."

The red-haired man behind me used my collar to jerk me up straight.

"I doubted that you would have chosen anything so scrawny. Your tastes in females runs a bit fleshier, and a wee more mature, I'd wager." He clamped my breasts in his massive hands. "And with larger teats."

Prince Modred chuckled.

"I suppose, Agravain, a slave does have a multitude of uses besides labour." He made it sound as if he had only just that moment thought of the idea of using a slave to slake his lust. "And who am I to question Mother's choice?"

"Indeed."

"You know, I believe the *quean* enjoys your caresses, brother," Prince Modred said.

"Does she now?" Prince Agravain pressed himself closer to my backside. His…

Not again.

"Then you won't mind sharing, eh Modred?"

I dared not move. I made a mask of my face to hide my shame from those witnessing the scene.

The youngest son of clan mac Lot was a long time in his response. His lips curled in a sneer as he watched my struggle to maintain a shred of dignity.

"Ach, you old sod. I can see that Camelot has not changed your taste any. The *cumal* has a brother you might fancy. He has a pretty mouth."

What did that mean?

"Hmm." The man behind me made the noise in my ear. It sounded like a growl. "Perhaps you can point him out to me later. But why waste this?" He brought a hand to my cheek.

"Careful. She bites."

The hand was abruptly withdrawn and Prince Modred laughed.

"Now who's afraid of a slave-girl?"

"Shut your gob, Modred. I could crush the two of you at once."

A boast he was quite capable of fulfilling. And the outrage would be over the prince. The slave's body would get swept away. Forgotten by the royals.

Modred danced out of his brother's reach.

"If you're still wanting a piece, I might share. But not today. At least not now. We have business to attend to for Mother."

"Ach, your insolent slave caused me to forget. You would do well, Modred, to tend to the defiance in your property. A decent, hard flogging would make a world o' difference." Prince Agravain squeezed my breasts once more, then shoved me away.

I stumbled, but righted myself.

Olwen had used my diversion to slip from the dais. She stood reunited with her mother at the opposite end of the hall, safely clutching Enid's skirt.

"Indeed. Sage advice, brother. You can trust the whip is not spared on that one's back. See the marks for yourself." Prince Modred jerked my sleeve, tearing the neck of my gown enough to expose my shoulder.

The elder prince murmured his approval.

"But come, let us see what Brisen has in the larder to break our fast," Prince Modred said.

"Aye. I'm starving. Some eggs. A rasher of bacon and a loaf of her bread, fresh from the oven would set well, would it not little brother?"

I thought I saw Prince Modred flinch at the words "little brother".

Prince Agravain glanced about the hall. Work had stopped and every pair eyes were directed the dais.

"What are you gawking at? Get to work, lazy sots, or I'll have the lot of you flogged." He threatened with his belt.

But no one moved. In fact, Enid, Julia, and the others seemed to be waiting for what I would do next.

I passed between the brothers, drawing closer to Prince Modred.

"I would be wary the next time I had need of the privy, if I were you, prince."

A powerless threat. But I achieved my purpose nonetheless. I caught a fleeting glimpse of terror in his blue eyes. I knew a weakness in my enemy.

He cursed and shoved me so that I landed on my knees. Both brothers guffawed and grunted at the pig-girl as they left the hall, shoulder to shoulder.

Before pity could be offered, I shouldered my gown and stood on trembling legs. I began clearing the high table. If no one knew how I hurt, they could not feel sorry for me.

* * *

“I never thanked you properly, Lin, for caring enough to protect Olwen this morning,” Enid said.

She and I were working side by side in the kitchen yard, our arms immersed in large tubs filled with soapy water.

“Did the brute hurt you over much?”

“It was nothing, Enid. Really. ’Twas the least I could do to repay you for everything you have done for Dafydd and me. The gown. The herbs.” I continued to scrub the tableware in the tub before me.

“Nothing? Lands, child. You sacrificed your own back to spare my daughter’s. And mere days after a beating of your own. That is far from nothing. But that is not the hurt that concerns me. Prince Agravain has the hands of a warrior, not made for gentleness of any kind. And you are so young. He might have bruised you.”

I released the platter I had been scrubbing. Truth was, my breasts still ached from the prince’s touch, but I had pushed the event from my mind. I found long ago that focusing on the labour was kinder to my heart than brooding on the pain. Now that Enid had brought the memory back, the shame nearly overwhelmed me. How Prince Modred had relished and mocked my discomfort, before so many witnesses.

The very thought of Prince Agravain ripping my clothes, and staring at my body… The thought of his massive weight crushing me beneath him… of his forcing his—

I shivered.

Without a thought of Enid and the others in the yard, I hugged my arms across my chest.

“Are you all right, Lin?”

I felt Enid’s hand on my shoulder, but simply hugged myself tighter. What could she possibly do or say to end my pain?

“You heard them, Enid. Everyone there did. They want to share me, like a cloak. I have managed Prince Modred before. But both? Prince Agravain is so very…”

I made a futile gesture, then dropped my hands. The words to describe the man eluded me.

“And I cannot stop it. No matter how hard I try, I cannot stop it. I try and try, but the prince will not kill me. I wish he would. Why does he not kill me and have done? He might as well, for what man would wish to be my husband, knowing I am naught but Prince Modred’s whore?”

My words tumbled from me in a rush before I could contain the emotions behind them.

"You poor child," Enid whispered.

I stiffened when I felt her arms enfold me. Distance. I must maintain distance, at all costs.

She did not tighten her embrace, but neither did she release me.

And I did not force her away. It was, in truth, comforting in her arms and I relaxed, giving in to the warmth and closeness of another. As I did, memories of my mother holding me to her breast, smoothing my hair, soothing my fears, poured over me.

"What man will want me?"

She held me tighter, rocking gently. She had no magical words to heal me.

I knew she would not, so I was not disappointed by her silence.

Wfft. Fool. What was I doing? I could not afford that closeness. My mother was gone. Coming to my senses, I stepped from the embrace.

"Nobody will want me," I answered my own question, wiping my eyes on my sleeve. "I am less than a drop of sea water. Why was it me the Queen chose for her son? Why was I even born? Life is pointless."

CHAPTER 20

"Enid?" The man stepped into the kitchen yard and stood inside, near the middens. "'Tis Olwen. I think you had best come."

"What of Olwen, Brynn?" Enid said, straightening from the tub she had been hunched over for the last hour. She wiped her hands on her skirt.

He shrugged. "Some accident."

Curious, the women around me stopped working. Julia cast a concern-laden glance about her. It was mirrored by the rest of us.

"Is she hurt? Who is with her?"

Brynn's hands shook and he did not meet Enid's gaze.

"Davy's with her. Enid… Ah, Jesu, but why did this fall to me?" he said, crossing himself. "I am truly sorry, Enid. Your little one, your Olwen, is dead."

I could not see Enid's face but she held her back arrow-straight as she walked from the yard with Brynn.

Dead?

Olwen?

But that cannot be.

Mere hours ago I had saved her from Prince Agravain's belt.

My companions and I followed, paying no heed to Brisen's shouted threats. Olwen was one of our own.

As we crossed the dunn's courtyard, our band was joined by curious servants and other slaves, swelling our ranks, so that by the time we merged with the on-lookers already at the well, we were a force not to be taken lightly.

The crowd parted to reveal Dafydd sitting cross-legged on the well's step, with Olwen in his arms. He rocked as though coaxing her to sleep, his eyes red and swollen. Her battered face told her painful story.

Why? What could a child of six summers have done to deserve such a cruel fate?

Without a word, Dafydd raised Olwen to the outstretched arms of her mother.

"What rot is this?" The overseer chose that moment to push through the crowd. Cursing, he grabbed at Olwen's body, causing her to tumble from Dafydd's grasp.

Servant and slave alike released a gasp at such disregard for the dead.

Dafydd blanched.

Enid reached for her child, sobbing.

The overseer blocked her way.

"If you please, Master. My child…Let me hold my child," Enid said, her voice eerily calm and strong.

"Silence, woman. Another word and you'll be at the post with your gown around your waist."

Dafydd, bless him, had gathered Olwen into his lap again. He smoothed her clothes and her hair as best he could with his hands. If he was aware of my presence, he did not show it. All his attention was fixed on the child he cradled with such love.

Yes, a man can be tender. At least a boy named Dafydd could. I admired my brother's infinite store of compassion. And I felt shamed for the accusations and anger I had thoughtlessly flung at him earlier.

I took a step backwards and bumped into Padrig.

We stood shoulder to shoulder in silence, the scene before us of far more import than our differences of last night.

The overseer had turned his attention to my brother. He grasped my Dafydd's collar and hauled him to his feet.

"The truth, boy. Now."

Dafydd never loosened his hold on Olwen. No matter what it might cost him, he would not let her fall again.

"I know not how it happened, Master. I found her thus."

"Found her? Where?"

"Here, at the well, Master."

"What, pray, were you doing at the well? Aren't you supposed to be shoveling shit?"

"Yes, Master. I was, Master. Someone commanded me to fetch water."

"Who?"

Incredibly, the overseer seemed not to believe my brother.

When had Dafydd ever lied?

"I do not know his name, Master, but I can point him out."

"Never mind. For now. Go on."

"There is not much else, Master. She was lying there on the step when I got here." He nodded, indicating the stains of blood on the stone. "I thought at first that she was badly hurt and needed help. But when I drew nigh, I saw that she… That she was… dead."

The overseer released Dafydd.

"This is beyond my ken," he said, scratching his crotch. "I cannot pass judgement on a death. Someone fetch Prince Agravain. Or Prince Modred."

I felt Padrig's hand on my shoulder.

"I am certain your brother will be well, Lin. But you might be wise to keep as far back as possible."

I shrugged his hand away. "I cannot abandon him, Padrig. He would never leave me. They cannot think Dafydd guilty of this. 'Tis mad. Someone has to make them believe he is innocent."

"They make the rules here. They can believe what they want."

Indeed, but—

"Donall, come take this." The overseer pointed to Olwen, still nestled at Dafydd's chest.

Enid fell to her knees and clutched the overseer's trews. Tears streaked her face.

"See, Master?" she said. "I beg. What harm in letting me hold my child one last time before you take her from me?"

The overseer kicked at Enid and a warrior stepped from the crowd. Niall, my former escort.

"Allow me," he said, yanking the woman to her feet and pinioning her arms.

The two men laughed at her struggles.

It was clear, we would not be permitted to mourn Olwen's passing. She was merely *cumal*. She had no value.

I shivered from the strong wind gusting from the north. The sky had darkened since I had stood in the kitchen yard, babbling rot about my own lack of value, Enid embracing me. It seemed a lifetime ago.

"Make way for the prince," someone shouted from behind me.

The crowd parted and I saw the crop of dark hair.

Of course it would be him. Not that the other one would have been any better.

Prince Modred strode into the clearing, steeped in arrogant authority. Performing a duty for Mummy. He surveyed the situation with a glance at Dafydd and the overseer. I could not see the prince's face, but he must have been surprised to discover that I was not directly involved.

"What is she worked up over," the prince asked Niall, sounding annoyed.

"Hell if I know, my lord."

"Well, woman. What is it? Speak."

Like commanding a dog. I half-expected him to snap his fingers.

And Enid obeyed.

"If you please, young Master. Your Highness. My child has been killed. Show us your justice in finding the fiend. At least, be merciful to a grieving mother and permit me to hold my Olwen and bid her farewell."

"Your Olwen? I think not. You and the brat belong to my mother. Besides, there is no time for your sentimental foolishness. The whelp is of no concern to me. You should be tending your duties, not wasting my time."

Enid bucked against the warrior restraining her.

"Bitch," she screamed, casting her gaze beyond the prince to the palace looming over us all. "I've given both of my daughters to the bitch Queen of Orkney. Both of my daughters, gone. May the Queen's next lover have leprosy."

Thunder grumbled as though in agreement.

The prince's fists clenched throughout. His lips drew tight across his teeth. An arm rose, as though to strike, then fell to his side.

"Sell the hysterical creature, she has wasted too much of my time," he said.

Niall began to obey, but before he could make more than a few steps, Custennin burst from the midst of the throng, and flung himself at the warrior, dragging his wife away.

Shouting curses, he wrestled Niall to the ground. In the initial impact, Enid was thrown against the well.

Before any of the other soldiers could react, I heard the sickening crunch of bones breaking. Then Niall moved no longer.

Not even winded, Custennin glowered at Prince Modred.

"You're next, boy," he said, pushing to his feet.

The prince fingered one of his rings, as though untouched by the threat. Surely he must sense his danger. Though no scrawny boy, the prince would be no match for Custennin's passion-fueled advantage.

Enid clutched her husband's leg.

"How touching," the prince said. A wave of his hand and guards dragged the couple apart. Two held their swords at Custennin's throat.

Another soldier knelt over Niall and listened at the fallen man's chest.

"My lord," he said, standing. "Niall's dead. His neck is broke. That slave murdered him. We all saw it." He stood at attention. "The Queen's warriors plead for justice."

"Aye!"

Justice? Oh, the world had gone mad. And I could merely stand on the fringe, watching the madness unfold. The soldiers demanded justice, while the slaves could not even beg a crumb of mercy or compassion for our loss. We would most likely never know the truth of Olwen's death. But I could guess.

"Hold the slave, I shall deal with him directly. Donall, dispose of…this. It will be starting to stink soon." He pointed at Olwen.

Dafydd was still clearly shocked by the recent events, so the one named Donall had no difficulty retrieving Olwen. The man had little regard, and much distaste for his charge.

He handled her more like a sack of grain than a child recently gone from the world.

It was too much. I could remain silent no longer. I—

"No," Dafydd said leaping to his feet. He grabbed at Donall's tunic. Defiance burned in the normally calm eyes. His sudden cry took everyone by surprise. "You cannot just toss her away like you did my mother. Olwen might have been destined for the collar, but she was a child of flesh and blood. Not waste. Let us bury her properly. Had you been decent about it in the first place, your warrior would still be alive."

The crowd agreed.

The overseer restrained Dafydd in the next instant, binding his hands at his back.

"So. You are like *her*," the prince said to my brother.

A cold numbness settled around my heart. *Dafydd, be careful. He is dangerous.*

I felt Padrig's hand on my shoulder, and this time allowed it to remain.

"Take the woman to the town slave pen. She has proved to be more trouble than she is worth. I want her gone."

The warrior who had taken Niall's place made short work of his task. One blow to Enid's head and she crumpled. He carried her away.

Prince Modred whirled to face Custennin.

"You killed one of my mother's warriors. Do you realise the penalty for that?"

Although at sword-point, Custennin tossed strands of hair from his face with the shake of his head.

"Who will pay for the death of my daughter, you heartless son of a whore? An innocent boy? I care not one whit for your mother's warrior."

"Spoken like a condemned man." The prince waved a jewelled hand. "Hang him."

"No," I whispered.

Padrig drew closer.

Again, I did not stop him. I dared not glance his way for fear he would see my helplessness.

The man who had once fought with the Pendragon did not resist when the guards moved. His face plainly showed his sorrow as he gazed at the remains of his daughter, slung in Donall's arms.

As they led him by my brother, he said, "Many thanks for minding Olwen for us, son."

Dafydd nodded.

What a calm dignity Custennin possessed. Here was a man worthy of the Pendragon. I felt honoured that our life paths had crossed.

They took him to the top of the defence wall, where his hands were bound and a noose slipped around his neck. The other end of the rope was secured to a stone that would serve as crossbeam.

How efficient the Irish were at dispensing their brand of justice. They heaved our companion over the side.

The crowd gasped.

Dafydd swayed in his place on the well step, then he sank to his knees, his chin drooping to his chest when Custennin's body finally came to rest.

My own legs wobbled and I felt an urge to vomit.

Padrig and others crossed themselves.

When would this sordid, wicked day end?

Prince Modred allowed several moments to pass for the example to drive its way into our souls.

Dafydd needed me more than ever now. I swallowed my vomit, willed my legs to bear my weight.

The prince no doubt saved my brother for last, to prolong the sport. For the first time since arriving, he scanned the throng.

I made things easy for him by stepping forward.

"I am here, prince."

He smirked. But I noticed a weariness in the blue eyes regarding me, as though the intensity of the last few moments had been more than he, or his mother, had anticipated.

How had the situation become out of control as it had? The death count was rising rapidly. To what purpose?

A grieving mother denied access to her child's body because the masters needed to exert their power over others? How senseless.

And the prince had Dafydd and me by the short hairs. Exactly as he wanted. He stood poised to destroy us both.

"Now to attend what I was summoned for in the first place. Then, perhaps we can get on with more important matters." He glanced at the stone-grey sky. "Before the rain. What is this one accused of?"

"Destruction of the Queen's property, my lord. I found him with the dead slave-girl in his arms. He said she was already dead."

"You do not believe him?"

"What's to believe, lord? He's but a slave. I thought it best to send for you, my lord."

"Indeed."

I watched, helpless, as the prince circled my kneeling brother like the carrion birds already hovering over Custennin's body, assessing him. Prince Modred stopped and cupped Dafydd's chin, tilting his face up and studied it.

"Mercy for Davy."

I could not see the man who spoke.

"Mercy for Davy."

This time from a woman.

Mercy for Davy, the words came from every direction of the gathering. Men. Women. I heard Padrig, Julia, Rhys. It soon became a chant, taken up by dozens of voices at once.

I could not resist my own smug grin at the prince. A single misstep and he would incite a riot. And I had done nothing to spark it. I'd had no need.

Mercy for Davy, I mouthed.

"Ach, this one is too pathetic to destroy a stalk of barley," he said. "The slave-girl's death was an accident. Flog the miserable creature for his outburst, and whatever other faults he might have."

My brother was led to the scourging post and everyone followed. We would play out the drama to its end. Even the prince was a puppet to the events now. He had as little control of the situation as I did.

Preferring to be back in the guard room, I again positioned myself where the prince could see me. Where I could watch my brother's ordeal.

The prince took his time testing the whip, plainly enjoying the moment, as Dafydd was prepared.

I am a stone, without emotion, I told myself.

The prince ran his fingers over Dafydd's bare back.

"How long have you been here, slave?"

"I was born here, Master."

"Born here? And your back has never been touched by the whip? How extraordinary."

The whip whistled and left a straight crimson line from Dafydd's shoulders to his waist. His body stiffened at the impact, but incredibly he made no sound.

Stop trying to be like me, Dafydd.

"Brave, boy. But for how long?" The prince taunted.

What would the others think of me if I did not do for my brother what I did for myself? What I had done for Olwen.

There are only two men here who matter.

And I will help my brother.

How, if you are beaten as well? Time to choose.

A painful choice. My brother or my pride.

I held my tongue.

Dafydd's silence did not hold beyond the first strokes. Quite soon his pain took over.

To the prince's pleasure. At that point he let the overseer finish, but he remained on the platform, watching me struggle with my pride and my heart.

I felt more exposed than when I was shackled to the post myself, stripped to the waist. I could never hide how I cared for my brother from the prince, or from anyone. But I could control my actions. I would witness my brother's scars as he did mine. I would hold the score in my heart.

At last the prince's bloodlust was slaked and he signalled a halt to the assault on my brother. He jumped from the platform to stand directly before me.

"Now his back is no longer perfect. It is scarred like yours. Next time, I might not have such mercy. There are always slavers in town wanting strong backs for the tin mines of Dumnonia. Or the salt mines of the midlands."

When he was gone, I scrambled onto the platform and knelt at Dafydd's side.

I bit my lips to silence my gasp when I saw his wounds at such close quarters. No wonder he was always so cross with me after my own encounters with the prince.

My brother moaned at my slight touch to his cheek.

"It's only me, Dafydd," I whispered.

CHAPTER 21

Life was cheap. Cheap and pointless. And my heart was sick from it. If not for Dafydd, I would have walked out the dunn's gates then, regardless of warriors. Regardless of the prince. And I would have kept on walking straight out into the North Sea.

But Dafydd was there, lying in a swoon, curled around the base of the scourging post. And when he awoke, he would be in the greatest pain he ever experienced. And I would do anything for my brother.

Even continue to survive in this nightmare life we'd been dealt.

First though, I had to move him to our quarters. They seemed miles distant. Yet the thought of requesting assistance never entered my mind. I would simply do what Dafydd always did for me. Somehow I would have the strength to carry him.

I managed to get him upright, as drops of rain began to splatter my head and arms. I would never make it to shelter before the deluge. I still had not figured out how to get him down the stairs.

Without warning, my burden lightened.

I had not expected any offers of aid either.

"Padrig?"

"Davy's too heavy for anyone to handle alone, fainted like he has," he said.

"Dafydd will…Thank you."

"It is well that he fainted though, this will be easier for him."

I nodded as we carefully balanced my brother's weight between us, although I suspected Padrig bore the brunt of the task.

We were drenched by the time we reached our quarters. Inside, we settled Dafydd near the cold hearth. Mercifully, he never stirred.

"I'll fetch you some water, Lin. And you'll need clean cloths. You can use my spare tunic." Padrig dashed off before I could argue.

Bone-weary, I stared at my brother. Where to begin? He was so vulnerable, so compleatly dependent upon me. And what did I know about tending wounds?

One thing I could not do was allow him to remain in his filthy tunic any longer. Already torn to his waist, a few tugs more and it gave way to the hem.

Padrig returned with a bucket and his tunic draped over his arm and sat beside me. He began ripping his shirt into strips.

"But—" I said.

"He needs it more. Besides, he would do the same."

"Padrig, there is no need for you to stay, endangering yourself." I glanced at the doorway, expecting the overseer or the prince to burst in. It would be typical of the prince's cruelty to gloat and taunt our suffering.

"I don't care about that."

"But Dafydd does. And I do, too," I added in a whisper. I might have been angered by our conversation from the night before, but I could never endure to see Padrig beaten.

He looked pleased by my words.

I felt my cheeks flush with warmth at the attention. I bent low over Dafydd, bathing his arms of the royal shit he had been shoveling before…

"I can manage this. He has done it for me often enough. Thank you for helping me though. I doubt I could have gotten him here alone."

"Davy's my friend. It is no great effort to help him in his need. When I arrived here, fresh from the slave market, Davy was the first to speak to me, not my collar. He was the first to offer kindness and friendship. I had thought those things were gone from my life forever when they closed the leather around my neck. Davy showed me different. I owe him much." Padrig stood. "You're certain you can manage?"

I nodded.

"I'll see you at dusk then."

He left me to my work.

It seemed even the gods favoured my brother over me. Dafydd did not stir until I had finished throwing out the bloodied water.

He groaned.

"Be still, Dafydd," I said, running to kneel beside him once more. "Stay flat on your belly, and try to keep your breathing even. It isn't much, but it does help some."

I moistened his lips with the clean water I had reserved.

"The overseer has given permission for you to stay here the rest of today." I tried to keep my voice even. But did not succeed.

Dafydd curled his fingers around my hand. I barely felt the pressure.

"They are gone." His whisper was as weak as his grasp, and yet contained a world of anguish.

"Yes." I had withheld my tears for as long as I could. I bowed my forehead to the floor where Dafydd barely touched my hand and released them at last, weeping hard heaving sobs for Olwen and Custennin and Enid and my brother.

* * *

The storm had spent the worst of its fury while I cleaned my brother's wounds. But the rain continued when I emerged to finish out my day. I reported to Brisen who immediately pointed to the two pails near the kitchen door. Slops for the pigs.

Once there had been a time when I had enjoyed that task. It took me near the practice yard where I could watch the princes at their training. I had admired their skills. A mere six years ago I had respected them and the house of Lot.

Life in Dunn na Carraice had returned to its usual routine. The courtyard showed no sign that anything untoward had occurred there so recently. The bodies near the well had been removed. The rain had washed their blood from the stones. Nothing remained.Wrong!

No. I would not look in that direction.

Except, the pig's pen was directly below…

I would not look up then.

The pigs grunted and shoved greedily against each other to get to their meal, as I emptied the first pail into their trough. They were indifferent to the world beyond their pen, right over their heads. I scraped the insides of the pail with my hand, and shivered as the wind picked up.

His rope creaked.

He had loved Dafydd like his own son. He had recently been one of us. To ignore him equaled betrayal.

I had to look.

The recent storm had worsened an already ugly death.

Clutching my stomach, I doubled over and vomited. A guard, high up on the rampart, laughed.

* * *

At eventide, as we shuffled into our quarters, no one spoke above a whisper. Dafydd lay where I had left him, either asleep or fainted once more. I could not tell. Not that it mattered. Anything to spare him pain. I used the chance to bathe his wounds again. This time I warmed the water on the hearth first.

"I could not help but notice you took no supper tonight, Lin," Padrig said. "I brought some bread. Eat. I'll finish this for you." He grasped the damp cloth.

But I was determined to repay my brother for everything he had ever done for me.

"No. This is my obligation. He has—"

"You'll be no help to him weak with exhaustion and hunger."

"I will eat when I am ready."

"Fair enough," Padrig said, setting the bread near me. "I just want to help him. And you. You don't make that very easy. May I at least join you?" He paused. "I promise not to kiss you."

That caught my attention. His eyes were playful and smiling. How did he dare while Dafydd lay…

Then I recalled how he had helped me to move Dafydd from the post. There had been only concern and care in his eyes while he had worked then.

"Stay. You are Dafydd's friend," I said, and redoubled my efforts.

Dafydd's prone form lay between us as my sole defence. I felt as clumsy as I had the night before when Padrig had his arm around my waist after dancing. Could he see my hands tremble as I wrung water from the cloth?

"After last night, you had the right to refuse me well come. Thank you for not doing so."

I shrugged.

"Lin, I did not come here just to enquire about Davy. I have a more selfish reason. I have something I must say, if you'll hear me."

What could he possibly have to say to me that I would want to hear?

My silence encouraged him.

"I would to God I could relive last night. It was never my intent to offend you, or hurt you in any way. And I apologise for having done so.

There is much I would do and say differently."

"Oh?"

He scratched his smooth chin.

"First off, I would say, *'Lin, I love you. Would you be my wife?'*"

A jolt shot straight through my heart. Love? What did love have to do with marriage? Or anything about my life beyond Dafydd? For me, love did not exist beyond us. Orkney showed that plainly. Everyday.

I stared at Padrig. He was quite serious now. No laughter in his eyes. No teasing.

I was constantly being reminded by someone that I was ripe for marriage. Other girls sought out the attention Padrig freely bestowed. Julia was not much older than me and she was already with child. So were a few others. Easy enough for them. They did not have the prince calling them whore.

Padrig waited. His broad hands rested in his lap. A farmer's hands. A slave's—

I set the bowl and cloth aside and sat back on my heels.

"What about my brother?" I said.

"He would simply have to accept your decision, as I would."

"No permission for my hand?"

He shook his head.

Had he spoken with Dafydd this morning?

"I accept your apology, Padrig."

"Thank you."

"You speak of love like a free man. Have you forgotten the prince?"

"I have taken him into full account. Perhaps it is because of the prince that you need so much more compassion and love than anyone else in the dunn.

"Your beauty caught my eye, Lin. I'll not insult you by lying. Your hair. Your eyes. I'm sorry I don't have the right words to explain. But your loyalty to Davy and your sheer determination against impossible odds captured my heart. You are remarkable. I admire your strength and courage. And I couldn't bear to know that my own stupidity lost you forever."

"I—"

"You needn't answer tonight. Not after all you've been through."

"Padrig, you are serious."

"I have never been more so in my life."

I detested the disarray within myself caused by the young man sitting with only my brother lying between us. My thoughts and emotions were a muddled turmoil. He spoke of love and beauty when no one else ever had, save my brother. I did not understand. I never believed it possible that anyone could care about me.

"I must think on this," I said.

"That's all I ask, Lin. Well, there is one thing more. May I fetch your supper now?"

"You are too much like Dafydd," I said, unable to stop my smile. "I will eat now."

*　　*　　*

The fire glowed nearly to coals when Padrig at last rose to take his leave.

"I thank you for your hospitality, Lin. I am grateful that you listened to what I had to say, and did not simply dismiss me. We've been dealt a cruel blow by the royals today. 'Tis but one reason more to cling to whatever happiness we can give each other. That's why I had to take this chance with you. I had to apologise and tell you my intentions are sincere. They were not simply brought on by the dancing and drink last night." He stretched and yawned. "But if I could relive last night, there is one thing I would not for the world change. I would still kiss you." His eyes smiled once more.

I pressed my fingers to my mouth, recalling his kiss, how warm and soft his lips had felt on mine. To be honest, I might have liked it had it not been such a surprise.

"And I would still not slap you for the kiss," I said.

"That would be well, Lin." He smiled so easily. It was just as easy for me to forget myself in it.

A multitude of feelings coursed through me as I watched him cross the room.

Wfft, but I had grown soft. Why did Padrig addle my brains whenever he was near?

I glanced at Dafydd. He was awake. For how long?

"Was that Padrig?"

"Yes. Would you like some broth? We kept it warm for you."

"Not now."

"Everyone has been asking about you. They are quite concerned."

"They miss their entertainment. I cannot talk to you lying on my stomach like this, Lin." He shifted his position and gasped with the effort.

"Are you sure you want to do this?" I asked, helping him to sit.

He took several moments to recover, struggling to contain his pain, looking very pale.

I feared he might faint again.

"I feel so wretched, Lin. I could not—cannot—endure once, what you have done several times over. I wanted so to be like you. Brave, taking whatever the prince had to give me. I am sorry I shamed you in front of everyone like that. In front of the prince."

"Dafydd, you can never shame me, so stop being impossible."

He grinned at the word he used so often for me.

"Still, I have often marvelled at your capacity for pain. When I look at you, I see my thin, frail sister, on the threshold of womanhood. And I marvel at the strength you possess. Which makes me feel all the worse for my weakness."

"My capacity for pain is fueled by my hatred for the prince. You have no room for hatred in your heart, Dafydd. I am glad it was you with Olwen those last ugly moments, lending her dignity. Your steadfast kindness made a mockery of today's cruelty. That is your strength."

"I miss them terribly." His voice broke.

"I know."

"Custennin was… Did you hear him call me son?"

"Aye."

"And now he is dead. And Olwen. Enid, too, for all we know." He struggled to contain his sobs.

"You need not put up a front for me, Dafydd."

"I shall never forget her face, Lin. As long as I live, I will always remember Olwen's sweet features twisted in fear and pain. Her soul shall never know peace."

He squeezed his eyes shut and tears slid down his cheeks.

"It was so senseless," I said.

"Aye. Thank you for all you did for me today."

"I did nothing today, save act a coward."

"You are never a coward."

"But—"

"Sometimes it is harder not to fight. Especially for you. I know you wanted to."

"And yet you risked a beating and spoke for Olwen."

My brother winced as he shifted his weight. "Not the wisest choice I ever made," he said.

"Is the heart ever wise?"

"Indeed. How in the world did you manage to get me here?"

"Padrig helped."

"He is a true friend."

I had no desire to speak of Padrig, for fear of betraying my emotions.

"You will need to tell me how to make one of Enid's poultices, Dafydd. I only cleaned your wounds with water. They need proper care. I do not know how."

"You made a good start, Lin. Thank you."

CHAPTER 22

A sennight later I had but one answer for Padrig's generous offer. As Dafydd began one of his stories for the others, I went to speak to our friend.

Padrig greeted me warmly and invited me to join him.

"Can we go outside? I wish a word with you and would prefer not to disturb my brother's efforts," I whispered.

Padrig stood and straightened his tunic. Then he smoothed his hair.

I paused at the door and waited for the guard to pass before stepping out.

"The sun never seems to set here, Lin. I doubt I shall ever grow accustomed to this."

"Wait until winter. The sun never seems to rise."

"Such a strange place, where the sun can defy God. Do you suppose it might be the Queen's sorcery?"

"I—" *Wfft*, but he was drawing me in again. I had called him outside for a purpose.

Stick to it, Lin.

"Shall we sit?" Padrig said.

"I would rather stand." I hugged my arms across my chest against the chill, damp wind.

It was not my intent to appear cold-hearted to the gentle lad beside me. But there is mercy in swiftness. For his sake, I had to do this.

"Thank you for waiting so patiently for my answer to your offer of marriage, Padrig. Kind as it was, I must decline."

Easiest? Why then did I feel hollow watching his expression change from hopeful expectancy to confusion? Why did my throat ache?

"Why, Lin? Why?"

I must be strong.

"I cannot." I stared at my arms. The stone wall of our hut. The nearly full moon in the pale sky. Anything but Padrig's pain.

"That is no reason. Am I so repulsive to you?"

I swallowed a lump.

Truth was, I found him far from repulsive. He had been taking his evening meals with Dafydd and me since the horrible day of Olwen's murder. I found Padrig's company as pleasant as my brother's.

This was proving more difficult than I had anticipated. What was the hold this youth had on me? More confused than ever, I only knew that if I took the time to figure it out, my heart would be ensnared. And I could not afford that. Family and friends paid too high a price for companionship with me.

I rubbed at my brand.

Padrig is a man, Lin. First a kiss, and then?

"No, Padrig. It isn't that. You deserve better than me. Find some other girl who won't bring you grief and pain. Once the prince realises—"

"Do you think you can save the entire world from him, Lin?"

"Only those I care about," I whispered, already crossing the threshold.

"The devil take him. He's poisoned you, Lin." Padrig's voice rose.

A young woman, giving suck to her child, glanced up at his outburst. Distracted from its meal, the babe tugged at its mother's collar.

"My apologies," Padrig said with a bow. So very like Dafydd.

The woman nodded, releasing the child's fist from the leather around her throat.

I took another step.

"Please, stay a moment, Lin," Padrig said more quietly, reaching for my hand.

Be strong, Lin. Go. Now. While you still can.

But his hand was warm. And his lips on mine had been one of the softest experiences of my life.

And he was speaking.

"I said I would respect your decision. I will not break my word. I only wish you would give yourself the chance to see how it should be between a man and a woman. The respect and sweetness like my mother and da had. Not the filth the prince has given you with his beatings and his lies and ugly words, trying to shame you. Lin, you make a grand effort against him, but… Think what we could achieve together. Let me help you."

If my gaze met his, if I stayed any longer, my resolve would melt. *'Tis better to leave him. For him. For you. Just pray you are not too late.*

For many heartbeats I stared at our entwined fingers. He wanted me to stay.

My heart, I realised, wanted me to stay, too.

I had to protect my foolish heart as well as Padrig.

"I dare not draw you in any deeper, Padrig. I must go." I pulled my hand from his clasp and walked away without a backwards glance. No regrets. No apologies. A clean severing.

The smoke-filled room was blurry and swam around me. And it seemed uncommonly large.

My brother was occupied with a story of Tir na Nog. Just as well for I had no desire to face his questions, to reexamine my decision.

You made the right one, I told myself yet again.

Why did right have to be so painful all the time? Why could it not be easy for once?

Soothed by my brother's voice as he wove his tales, I hugged my knees and watched the smoke curl from our fire. In my state, Dafydd's words mattered not, I simply clung to the music he spoke, proud to be the sister of the one who gave comfort to so many. Despite his own pain.

My sleep that night was fitful, fraught with the usual nightmares of auctions and beatings. Then a new scene formed. Prince Modred stood over Dafydd's limp body, triumphant, and laughing madly. When I screamed at him to leave my brother alone, he turned and extended his arm towards me. He held a small bloody lump. Instinct told me I did not wish to look closely enough to learn what he offered.

I woke abruptly, in a sweat, my chest heaving. The vision felt so real, it took several long moments of hard staring at Dafydd's sleeping form to convince me I had been dreaming.

* * *

"Why are you and Padrig ignoring each other?"

It was a rare time to be with my brother during the day. My duties were usually with the women. But there had been a new collaring that morning. Since floggings had not worked to silence my protests, the overseer decided a taste of true labour might. He sent me to the barley field with the boys to pull weeds and spread dung.

I found it no harder than scrubbing the royals' clothes at the stream. He had unwittingly given me a favour, to be with my brother the whole day.

"Padrig used to talk of nothing except you. Now it is anything but. And you have reverted to your old habit of seclusion, just when you were doing so well with others. Are you still upset with him for kissing you? Shall I give him a nudge to apologise?"

"I ended things with Padrig a few nights ago," I answered, intent on my work.

"You what?" Dafydd sat on his heels.

"You heard me. I do not wish to marry. Not Padrig. Not anyone."

"What do you have against marriage? People do it all the time."

"Why is everyone so obsessed with me getting married? Are you trying to rid yourself of me?"

"Never. How could you even think that, Lin? Why must you fight everyone? Not just our masters, but even those who try to be kind and give you a little happiness? That is all Padrig wishes."

"Happiness? Why should my happiness depend upon Padrig, or anyone? I find it arrogant of men to believe they have that sort of power over women. The cheek. Men know nothing beyond taking. What do men really care about a girl's happiness?"

"You speak of men, Lin. How many do you truly know? The prince? True, he has wounded you terribly. You've the right to your anger and distrust. None could deny that.

"But *he* is your standard for the rest of us? What about Custennin? Enid would say he knew a great deal about giving. Did you ever know him to have a harsh word for her or their daughters?"

My brother never had a harsh word either. Although still a youth—a boy—he would be a man someday, too. My words had been unfair.

"Kindness confuses me, Dafydd. It always has."

"Not always. When we were children, you had no such difficulty accepting love from Mother. Or forming friendships with the other children. You were a happy, care-free little girl."

"Then they had to put that collar around your neck and turn us into creatures of less value than this." I scooped a clot of dung from the basket and flung it to the ground.

"But if you truly believed that, Lin, why do you continue to resist

Prince Modred? Why did you protest this morning's collaring? If you do not know, I will tell you. It is because you have a heart that cares as deeply as my own. You are simply too stubborn to see your capacity to love and therefore your worthiness to be loved."

I heard a snap behind us. Saw Dafydd's body jerk. Heard his gasp.

My brother did not need a second warning to return to his labours.

"Think you this is a holiday?" the man wielding the whip said. It hissed again and landed across my shoulders.

I glared up at him a moment before returning to work.

After the guard moved on, I sat on my heels once more.

"When the prince raped me, Dafydd, he stole more than just my maidenhead. He stole my privacy. I did not realise how precious that was to me until it was forever gone. I know you try, but I doubt a man can truly know and understand that feeling of invasion.

"And because of that invasion, sweet as Padrig is, I doubt I could bear to have him touch me in those same places. Ever. I do not wish to speak of this any more, Dafydd."

Dafydd crushed a weed and held it out to me.

"This seems so trivial, does it not?" He tossed it away. "I know not what to say, Lin. Forgive me, for I had no idea. Please?"

"There is nothing to say, Dafydd. The damage can never be undone."

CHAPTER 23

Dafydd and I continued to pull weeds and spread dung as the summer sun beat upon on our backs. The wind, ever a constant of Orkney, tousled our hair, our clothes, and the barley plants around us.

It never took Dafydd long to turn to music, no matter the situation. He began a song I had never heard before.

I watched my brother work as he sang. His movements graceful and fluid. His voice true and clear. He belonged in the Queen's hall, studying with her bard, not wasted in a barley field. If only she could hear him, she would surely correct the injustice.

He noticed my regard and flashed his smile. Little wonder everyone thought of him so highly. How could there be such cruelty in Dunn na Carraice when Dafydd was there?

The song was easy enough and soon I lent my voice with the others in the answering refrains. Our bodies kept the beat. Dafydd's smile broadened.

I had pleased him.

I would strive to do so more often.

Near mid-day, we were allowed a brief time to rest and provided with ale and a crust of bread.

Dafydd winced as he eased to the ground. The wounds the prince had inflicted were healing, but I had little of Enid's herbs left with which to tend them.

"That cloud looks like a horse drawing Boudicca's chariot in a race with the wind," he said, his gaze skyward.

"Where?" My eyes followed the direction of his finger. "I see nothing that resembles a horse or a chariot up there. How is it you can see shapes in the clouds when I cannot?"

"Maybe because I use more than my eyes. To you they are merely clouds that will eventually block the sun. But to me…"

What nonsense was that?

I frowned.

He took his cup and drank.

"I do not expect you to understand now. But someday, I hope you will, like you did once before. Before this." He touched his collar.

Still trying to draw me into his dreams as when we were children. A time comes when dreams must end. Did Dafydd not realise that?

I set my own cup on the grass next to me and leaned on my arms, my legs stretched out before me. The other boys had broken into small groups and chattered, while the man in charge over us lounged near the supply cart.

Not far from Dafydd and I, Padrig sat on his own, his face sullen. I know he yearned to join us because of his friendship with Dafydd. But was reluctant because of me.

"Dafydd, you should go talk to Padrig," I said. "He is still your friend. At least he should be. I refuse to become a wedge between you. Despite what he might think, I do not hate him. I simply cannot wed him. I hope someday he will understand and not hate me either."

"Are you certain?"

"I insist."

Padrig's face brightened as my brother approached, but saddened as quickly when I remained seated.

'Twas because I cared and liked him that I resolved to hold fast to my decision.

On my back, I watched the clouds speed past. I tried squinting, but that produced no recognisable shapes either. Was there something wrong with me? My eyes?

"Julia would never survive this sort of work."

"I am not Julia, Rhys," I said, sitting up.

"Agreed." He knelt beside me. "Not just Julia, but most of the addle-pated chits she considers friends would have cringed at the thought of touching shit. It doesn't seem to trip you up at all. You pitched right in this morning to do your share."

"When have I ever been known to shirk a duty?"

"Never. What I meant was you did not complain about being

assigned men's work."

"I have handled royal shit before. Besides, this is easier labour than endlessly scrubbing cloths clean. So much for girl's work. I feel like I have been done a favour, more time with Dafydd."

"I regret insulting your brother. He was right to hit me."

"Back to work, dogs," our guard shouted.

Rhys walked away without an offer of regret for insulting me. Typical.

I reached the dung cart before Dafydd and began to fill our basket.

"Finally, we have found the proper task for my proud *cumal*."

The prince. Why could he not leave me be? He rode across the field from the road, holding his horse to a slow walk.

Everyone fell to his knees.

Everyone but me.

The prince drew rein beside me.

"I think this suits the slave so well, we shall keep her at it," he said.

"Brisen won't be liking the lack of hands, my lord," the overseer said, trotting on foot to catch up to the prince.

"She need not miss any hands. Send that one to Brisen in the firebrand's place." The prince pointed at my brother.

Dafydd bowed his head so I could not see his face.

I glared at the prince.

"One would think from all the lessons I have provided, you might have learned the smallest bit of humility by now. On your knees and address me properly, *cumal*." He nudged my shoulder with his foot.

I do not know from whence the idea came. The depths of my madness, I suppose. The chance presented itself. I was there. The prince was there. And his fucking boot was close enough.

I spat on it.

"My gratitude for your lessons, prince."

Before my next heartbeat, the prince slid off his horse and had me by the collar.

"You dare." He backhanded me across the mouth.

I tasted blood.

"Why do you not obey me? Why can you not be quelled? From whence does your defiance come?"

I had to tilt my head to gaze into his eyes.

"From you. You made me."

"Enough. Make her back bleed." The prince shoved me towards the overseer.

"Without delay, young master." The older man reached for my collar.

"Do it here. Do it now. Tie her to that cart and do not stop until I say."

My clothes were torn and I was bound with a coarse rope to the wheel of the dung cart. Its foul contents were directly beneath my nose. A restorative which prevented me from fainting.

Between the pain and the stench, my stomach revolted and I vomited what little I had eaten. Maddened. Dazed. I clung to the hope his passion would lead to my release.

Let me die.

If I let him win, will he stop?

No.

Then let me die.

I felt the prince cut the ropes binding me. I landed on the ground.

Is he finished?

He knelt above me.

My gown, bunched around my waist, pinioned my arms at my sides.

Our guard had moved closer. Peering over the prince's shoulder, he licked his lips.

I shuddered.

He is not important.

I had a prince to fend off.

"Who will rescue you, *cumal*? Your weakling brother? Those pathetic creatures you call friends?"

Rescue? I had seen that look before in those cold eyes. From the same position. We had the dung. The only thing missing was his brothers' giggling for the joke. I had not helped a boy in need that morning six years ago. By removing that wedged board blocking the privy door, I had released a monster. A monster who would not forgive me for witnessing his fear and helplessness. A monster who hated my existence.

Prince Modred yanked my skirt up.

No. The gods, not again, please?

The only fight I had left in me was to clench my legs together.

"Seems my whore is a wee bit shy," the prince said. With a raised hand, he declined an offer of assistance. To me, he said, "That is the best you can do?"

"Leave her be. Haven't you done enough?" Padrig shouted, running towards the prince. But the guard caught him.

My efforts to save Dafydd's friend had been in vain.

The prince dropped his hand from his trews and glanced behind him.

"Hold him," he said. "I will not be long in this."

Then the distraction was gone. I had missed my chance. I could not get me knee to where it might at least have postponed the inevitable.

Prince Modred released a mirthless chuckle. It chilled my blood.

"I regret that day, too, prince," I said. "I regret ever taking pity on you and showing you any kindness."

"Shut your gob."

With a fist, he struck my head and the world turned black.

* * *

Not a soul challenged me as I crossed the courtyard, drawn by my brother's voice. How curious for mid-morning. Dunn na Carraice should be teeming with warriors, the nobility, and other slaves. Yet I saw no one.

The familiar tune led me to the slaves' hut, then silence fell. I shivered, reluctant to enter. Sensing danger, I peered inside. The normal murk of our hovel had been replaced by an eerie brightness. Neither of the sun, nor of any earthly torch. Near the cold hearth, someone hunched over a prone figure.

Somehow, I knew 'twas my brother on the stones.

"Leave him be," I shouted, stepping forward.

My brother's attacker turned.

I froze.

Prince Modred.

But my gut had already warned me.

"Dafydd?" I said.

No reply.

My fists clenched.

"Murderer."

The prince chuckled and extended an arm in my direction.

"A gift," he said. "For my *cumal*."

Instinct told me to flee.

And abandon Dafydd? Leave him un-avenged? Never.

"Do you not wish to see the gift?" The prince grinned.

Gall burned my throat. I had no desire to learn what he offered. I shook my head.

"I shall make it easier." The prince strode in my direction.

I backed away until I met damp stone.

"Have a good look."

Cornered, with no other choice, I gazed into his hand. I recognised and understood his jest then. The gift. The reason for Dafydd's silence lay in the prince's open palm. He had cut out my brother's tongue.

Prince Modred's mad laughter blended with my screams.

*   *   *

"And no one knew where Myrddin took Uther Pendragon's infant son, Arthur. Whether the mage—"

My brother's voice. But how—if?

Cool water bathed my brow.

Oh, but I had a furious thirst. And I was drenched in sweat.

The cloth was withdrawn. I heard splashing.

"Some say Myrddin raised young Prince Arthur himself, teaching the future king the ways of the druid."

I knew my brother's touch. Was I dreaming?

What if it was a dream? Did I want it to end and revert to—

"Lin? You did move your hand. The gods be praised. I was scared I would lose you."

My arm was raised. My fingers stroked his cheek and were dampened by tears. His breath warmed my palm.

The wet cloth he held to my lips felt real enough as I tried to draw the moisture into my mouth.

"I know you are thirsty, Lin. But I dare not give you too much at once just yet, lest you become ill." He removed the cloth only long enough to resoak it. It was the sweetest water I had ever tasted. It had to be a dream.

I opened my eyes anyway.

"I am real, Lin."

Real. And he still had his tongue. A single tear slid over my nose.

CHAPTER 24

"Has she rallied any, Davy?"

"Yes, thank you, Rhys. Her fever broke this afternoon and her sleep has been restful ever since."

"That is happy news. Maybe you'll be getting some rest now yourself?"

"I promise I shall, Julia."

The straw rustled as they walked away.

Groggy, but awake—at least aware of the others in our quarters—I blinked open my eyes.

"Well come back, Lin." The most beloved of voices and smiles greeted me.

I tried a smile of my own, but only managed to crack my dry lips.

"I…" It hurt to talk. "Thirsty." I felt an immediate flood of shame. My steadfast brother deserved better than that selfish request.

"Of course, you are," Dafydd said, smiling all the broader. He raised me and held a cup to my mouth.

The simple act of swallowing was painful.

"Not too fast, you have been too many days without."

Days. I have never loved my brother's mild scolding more than at that moment.

The water tasted exquisite in spite of the cramp in my belly.

Dafydd noticed me clutching my stomach and withdrew the cup. Concern wrinkled his brow.

"I was right, you are sick. We shall try more later." He eased my head back to the pillow he had fashioned from his tunic.

"Thank…"

He tucked the blanket around me.

"How many days?"

"A sennight has past since…"

I beheld a black boot in my mind. A gobbet of spittle glistened near its toe. I did not want to recall the rest.

Dafydd fussed with my cover.

"Blackness is the last thing I recall."

"They carried you like a sack of grain to the guard room. Your back was torn and bleeding and they chained you with rats and more filth."

"I did not dream that then."

"Perhaps not, but you did have some rather nasty nightmares. You cried out more than once and thrashed about. I suppose your fever brought them on. Your wounds were so filthy, as hard as I laboured, I feared it would not be enough to save you. I am glad the overseer allowed me to stay with you."

"You have been here the whole time?"

"Yes."

"However did you manage that?" I marvelled at the feat.

"I asked."

"That was all it took? And he consented?"

Dafydd nodded.

"The prince was frantic for your release. I saw. I was there. You had only been locked up overnight, but…" My brother pushed hair from his eyes. "The latest rumour is the Queen struck Prince Modred," he whispered.

"No."

"Truly. Word is, she was furious by the incident."

"Why should she care?" I wondered aloud. I had been a mere curiosity for the Queen and her sister when we had met in the corridor.

"I only know," Dafydd was saying, "that the air in the dunn has been tense ever since. The overseer checks your progress every morning and evening, and at least once during the day. I think I would have been commanded to tend you had I not asked. They gave me nothing more with which to work in order to heal you, but the overseer made plain that he feared your death."

"How many lifetimes since Beltane and my twelfth natal day? How many lifetimes since being collared and claimed by Prince Modred?" I said, my throat raw.

"Too many for one person—one girl—to bear. You have been right to question things, Lin. Our treatment is not fair. I should have offered you aid. But I froze, unable to move or speak. Your own brother cowered. Like a slave. The image of what that monster did to you—in the mud!—will forever be in my heart. Branded there just as surely as the mark he burned into your arm. It sickened me and I did not even move."

I recalled the mid-day sun flaring in my eyes as I lay in the muck. And the barley plants waving overhead. Then the prince's shadow once more.

What could anyone have done?

"Where would you be if you had acted, Dafydd?"

Dafydd rested his elbows on his crossed legs, propped his chin in his hands.

I watched the smoke curl up and out the hole in the roof. The people we lived with spoke of their own troubles amongst themselves. Their murmurs seemed to merge with the wispy swirls and float with them.

"I do not know, Lin. But I shall never forgive the prince for what he did to you. I would to the gods I could make him pay."

The signs of Dafydd's anger went no deeper than the tightened muscles of his face and the shadow in his eyes. But I understood.

"I know, Dafydd," I said with a weak smile. "And I thank you. I also thank the gods you froze."

Dafydd dragged the back of his hand under his nose.

"How is your stomach, Lin? Ready for more water?"

Wincing, I rose on an elbow without his aid.

"Lin!"

After panting a moment or two to ease the pain and wait out the dizziness, I took the cup and drained it. Slowly.

"More," he asked.

The effort had taxed me and I sank to the floor.

"No, thank you," I whispered.

"I need to fetch more anyway," Dafydd said, getting to his feet. "I shan't be long."

My brother greeted his friends, answering enquiries about my well-being, and promising to convey well wishes as he crossed the room.

One voice was missing. He would have asked about me too, had he been there.

"Padrig is gone, isn't he?" I said when Dafydd returned.

He heaved a deep sigh before answering.

"Aye. It took two men to carry him away, the prince beat him that hard. Padrig is well on his way to the tin mines of his homeland."

I hid my face in the crook of my arm and allowed a sob to escape my lips.

I felt my brother's hand smooth my hair.

"Lin?"

"Why did you not just let me die, Dafydd?"

"Because a brother does not abandon his sister. A brother does not simply sit back and watch his sister die if there is anything at all he can do to prevent it. I might not have been able to protect you from the prince, but I can patch up the damage after."

The sheer hopelessness of our lives pressed upon me from every side. I was cursed. Everyone who came near me was doomed, from Mother through…

The rest did not bear thinking.

"If I'm dead, mayhap he'll leave you alone, Dafydd."

I shivered.

Dafydd tucked the blanket tighter around me, his lips drawn tight.

I clutched his trews.

"I am sorry, Dafydd. I owe you my life and—"

"You owe me nothing."

I was too weak to argue further.

"When was the last time you slept? I can see your weariness," I said.

Dafydd yawned, pushing strands of hair from his face once more. Had he lost his cord?

"Last night Julia came and insisted I have a lie down while she took up the vigil. She provided a clean shift for you. I did try, but found it impossible to rest while you were still so ill. My mind kept tormenting me with visions of you dying and me not being there in your last moments. I could not bear that.

"I have a gift for you, though. I made a new story to celebrate your recovery. Would you like to hear it?"

"Do you not wish to see the gift, slave?"

That was one nightmare I remembered too well. Its meaning was now clear as water. All of my brother's stories and songs—wonderful as they were—they were naught without the giver.

"You are my gift, Dafydd. I would love to hear your story, but it can wait until the morrow. You must be exhausted. Please. Come rest."

Before you are stolen from me, too.

Dafydd yawned, deeper this time and rubbed his eyes.

"Odd. I did not feel tired until just now. You needed me, so I kept pushing myself. Denying my own weariness."

He stretched out on the floor beside me.

"I know you believe I would have an easier time here without you. I never want to know if you are right or not."

I was at a loss for words, but not tears.

"Sleep soundly, Dafydd." I leaned over and kissed his brow.

He was already asleep.

* * *

Next morning I woke long after cockcrow. Our quarters were empty except for Dafydd and me. The door stood wide and sunlight streamed through it and the unshuttered windows.

Dafydd tossed a clump of peat into the fire.

Warmth and my brother. Luxury and comfort for a slave was uncommon within Dunn na Carraice. That Prince Modred showed concern over me was beyond my ken.

My stomach rumbled.

"That is a good sign, Lin," my brother said, grinning. He took a bowl from the hearth.

But when he slipped an arm beneath me to raise my head, I stopped him.

"Help me to sit, Dafydd," I said.

His grin faded.

"Please? I cannot bear having you feed me like I am an infant."

Dafydd sat on his heels looking as though I had slapped him.

"What?" I said.

"Will you ever allow me to forget that?"

"Forget? Oh!"

"Why do you insist on dredging up those careless words of mine seven years later to fling at me?"

"I never… Dafydd, I spoke in innocence just now because I am tired of being helpless."

To prove my point, I began the slow, agonising process of rising on my own.

He reached a hand towards me.

I would have swatted it away, had it been within my power.

"Do not touch me."

What was I thinking? I nearly swooned from the pain and dizziness. I needed his help. But to back down now? Never.

Once sitting, my appetite was gone.

"Lin? I am sorry. I thought—"

"I know what you thought. Why would I want to hurt you with something you said in pain after Mother died?"

My brother's hands trembled as he tucked strands of hair behind his ear.

"It has been a long sennight. My heart has been dragged through the mire and is still in tatters at the moment. But I spoke without thought. Forgive?"

I took the bowl he offered and swallowed some porridge. It was still warm.

"Forgiven."

"Our friends will be pleased to know of your progress, Lin," Dafydd said after I had finished eating and was lying once more on the stones.

"I cannot afford friends. I am cursed."

"Cursed?"

"I have the most dangerous enemy on Orkney, perhaps in all of Britain. And Padrig… Why did you not try to change his mind? I wish I had not waited so long to refuse his offer. I wish I had been stronger to fend him off from the beginning. I should have slapped him when he first kissed me and had done with the entire nonsense. He would have had a chance at survival then. I am sorry I waited so long. My weakness cost you a friend, Dafydd."

"At what cost to you?"

I found his ability to know my soul unnerving. I avoided his gaze.

"You truly did not want to refuse his marriage offer, did you?

I pushed stalks of straw into a pile. Then swept it down.

"What I said about not wanting a man's touch was true."

"I never doubted that. But you must care deeply for Padrig to have wanted to protect him."

Care? I felt the sharpness of Padrig's absence as keenly as though the prince had used a knife to sever the youth from my life.

"I feared his touch, yet—" I clutched my breast.

"Time might ease the ache you feel, Lin. A little. But I doubt it can ever be erased entirely. Meg has been gone for two years and still…" He squeezed his eyes shut.

No words of comfort came to me. My silence was a poor offering when my brother hurt and needed my aid.

After many long moments, I decided it might be a good thing to remind Dafydd that he was not alone. I touched one of his tightly clenched fists. My gesture was rewarded by his fingers relaxing.

"See what I mean?" The smile he gave was a shadow of his usual easy and cheerful demeanour.

"I wish I could understand. I believed he would be better off without me, but—"

"Love is a precious, mysterious gift for our hearts, Lin. I think it would lose its spell if it were ever understood."

"Love? How can anyone love me?"

My brother smoothed the blanket over my shoulders.

"You encased your heart in armour after Mother died. I think you lost some of your innocence that morning. Neither did I help, calling you a baby, forcing your thumb from your mouth. And you have held yourself distant from others ever since, believing yourself unworthy of love. But you are wrong. The ache in your heart is its way of telling you how wrong and unfair you are to yourself. What makes you think you can withstand that which everyone else cannot?"

"Do I hear one hundred in bronze for this fine, strapping youth?"

I gasped and thrust the vision from my mind.

Shuddering, I clutched the blanket.

"I must try anyway."

CHAPTER 25

"I would dearly love to wring that creature's neck," I said next morning. The cock had recently heralded yet another dawn in Dunn na Carraice.

"Indeed," Dafydd said. He pushed himself up from our bed of straw and stone. "Hungry, Lin?"

I had resolved to no longer argue over food with my brother. I would make whatever time we had left together peaceable.

I ate the porridge he offered.

"You are awfully quiet this morning, Dafydd. What are you thinking?"

I wanted him to feed me a dream. I was disappointed.

"Things nobody should ever have to contemplate. I nearly lost you and now…" Dafydd's words trailed off as the overseer entered.

"It begins once more," my brother said. He tied his hair back. "You have always been so strong, Lin. I had not realised how fragile you can be. With his bare hands, the prince could send your spirit to *Annwn* and the King of the Dead. With a word—"

"I shall try hard not to undo all your efforts too quickly. Dafydd," I said to stop him speaking the thought. Tears stung my eyes.

"I shall tend you and your wounds as many times as I am able. Give it no more thought. Do what you must, let me deal with the aftermath."

I threw my arms around my brother, as if clinging to him would keep him near me forever.

"Be strong, Noble One. I am proud to be your brother and nothing the prince does can ever change that. Not the greatest distance. Not even death."

"Well, well. Isn't this a scene to touch and warm the heart?" Laughing, the overseer squatted on his haunches and thrust the handle of his whip between Dafydd and me. "So, the Mistress of Dung has finally recovered from her scratches."

Across the fire-pit, Rhys leapt to his feet, shouting, "Scratches? You laid her back wide open."

"Silence, or yours will be next, boy." The overseer rose, fists on his hips, still clutching the whip.

Julia clasped Rhys' arm, begging with her eyes for him to be quiet.

The brash youth shrugged her off.

"You nearly killed Lin. If not for Dafydd, she'd be dead now. You should be thankful he saved you from the prince's wrath."

"Silence!" The overseer stepped around the fire-pit and struck Rhys to the ground.

Julia scrambled to hover over her husband.

"Been taking lessons in rebellion, I see," the overseer said.

Rhys held a hand to his bloodied mouth, watching me.

What was he doing? Why, when he never had a kind word for me? Why would he risk a beating for me now?

I rubbed the raw skin beneath my collar. I could not allow anyone else to be hurt because of me. Even Rhys.

"Leave it, Rhys. I am fine," I said.

Rhys shot a questioning look to Dafydd, who shook his head.

"Who's next?" The overseer stabbed the air over our heads with the handle of his whip.

No one moved.

"You, boy. Are you quite finished playing nursemaid?" The overseer pointed at Dafydd.

Dafydd bowed his head, eyes downcast. The perfect picture of subservience.

"Yes, Master. But my sister—"

"I'll be the judge of her. She looks well enough to work."

"Yes, Master." Dafydd drew his knees to his chest.

"Perhaps you might find the time to get on with your duties to the Queen, scullery maid."

"Yes, Master."

"And you, Mistress of Dung, To the peat bog."

The overseer walked out, assured he would be obeyed.

Dafydd stared at the man's wake, then turned his care-worn face to me. Tears streaked his cheeks.

"They wanted me to keep you alive so they can murder you?" he said. "You are not strong enough to cut peat. Your wounds will reopen and—"

"No worries, Davy. I'll help her," Rhys said. He brushed Julia's hand from his face. "Enough, woman. This is nothing. What about it, lads? If we all pitch in, Lin will have her share cut and stacked at eventide."

"Aye, leave it to us, Davy!"

So, the concern was for Dafydd, not me. I should have known.

My brother offered his thanks as the others filed out.

We should not tarry either and I nudged Dafydd.

"Will you walk with me, Lin?" Rhys said. He stood at a respectful distance from where I sat. "It would be my honour."

Curious to learn the motive for his strange behaviour, I agreed.

"I shall join you outside shortly."

He nodded then walked out, holding Julia's hand. Everyone seemed to sense the need Dafydd and I had for time together.

Once alone, I found I had no words for my brother. We might… Best not to think on the future. Better to cling to the now.

I bit my trembling lower lip.

Dafydd kissed my fingers. "Be strong, Noble One. Be brave. May the gods be kind to us."

I drew a deep breath and willed my voice to remain steady. "Until next we meet, Bard. Please the gods that time will be soon. Go now, our duties call." I kissed his cheek.

But my brother was not content with a kiss. He embraced me.

"I am so frightened, Lin. We may—"

"Do not say it, Dafydd. Please? The prince will no doubt prolong his decision in order to increase our torture. I am already mad with fear. But let us not tempt fate with the words."

"Agreed. We must hope it will not happen today, then. Hmm?" He wiped my face with his sleeve. "Just like a girl, you never could keep your cheeks dry."

"You used to do that whenever I fell and bumped my knee."

"Because you never could keep your balance."

On the verge of calamity and he still tried to bring me to smile.

"Fare you well, Dafydd."

"Until later, Lin."

Arm in arm, we walked out. My first in many days. The sky was its typical grey, promising rain. The air itself was heavy and damp. I shivered.

Dafydd joined Julia where she had waited for him. He turned and waved, then they headed for the kitchen.

I felt a hand on my shoulder. Startled, I spun to face Rhys.

No. It would not take long before I had been worn into a pitiful heap.

"Sorry, Lin. Ready?"

I glanced over my shoulder in time to see Dafydd disappear around the corner of our hut.

Will I ever see him again?

May it be so.

Staring at the palace, I nodded.

"Davy'll be all right, Lin."

But will I? Was the prince lingering in his bed, scheming how best to torture my brother and me?

Our single guard cracked his whip.

We began the trek to the peat bog. Rhys fell into step with me.

"Why did you challenge the overseer, Rhys?"

"Someone had to," he said with a shrug.

"Is that not my task?"

"Why should you be the hero all the time?"

"Hero? Heroes do brave deeds. They save kingdoms from dangers. They fight wickedness and slay giants and monsters. I have done none of that," I said.

"Ballocks, Lin. You are the only one here who has the stones to make a stand against the royals time after time. No matter what sort of shit they fling, you hurl it right back. Sometimes it even lands in their eye. If that is not a hero, then I don't know what one is."

Hero? The boy was daft. Heroes were never powerless.

"Dafydd is most vulnerable to the prince right now, yet I can do nothing. And I put my brother in that position. I am sorry I ever started this bungle."

"Don't be, Lin. We need our Pendragon, as surely as the rest of Britain needs theirs."

"Pendragon?"

"I mean you, silly girl. Did you think I meant King Arthur? They treat us like beasts here, Lin. But every time you spit on the prince's boot, I—we—remember we are human after all."

"I am only me, Rhys. Only Lin. Not a hero. Never a Pendragon."

"Like it or not, you are my hero."

We passed the footpath to the stream. I rubbed my brand, remembering Sir Lamorak. For all his fine words and court manners, he probably forgot me before he even reached the dunn that morning. I had been a fool to believe he might have cared and informed the Pendragon of Queen Morgause's slaves.

"Why the sudden change, Rhys?"

"Not so sudden. I have admired the way you stand your ground with Prince Modred for some time now. The two of you are true equals. He's a worthy foe for you. Orkney will never see the like of your rivalry again. Besides, I like you."

Considering the source, that was a large compliment. "I do not know what to say."

"No need. I was jealous that a mere girl made cowards of the rest of us. I have never seen anything as horrible as your rape, and yet you were so brave. Not a soul who witnessed that scene is the same, Lin. The prince could not have sent a more powerful message of our slavery and his mastery. But you have shown us that we do not need to accept this." Rhys fingered his collar. "I hope it isn't too late to set things right between us."

"You must be careful, Rhys. Friendship with me can prove dangerous."

I heard hoof-beats in the distance behind us. A pair of riders was coming from the dunn. We were commanded to halt and clear the road for the riders to pass.

The pair rode at leisure, in no great hurry to reach their destination, enjoying the companionship. One of the riders had the unmistakable flame-coloured hair of the royal house. Prince Agravain. The other's head was dark.

"Rhys, you would do well to stand away from me."

He did not move.

"You need no longer fight the prince alone. Say the word, and we are all behind you." With his eyes, he indicated our companions.

I shook my head. "The war, the hatred is between the prince and me. I cannot keep Dafydd from it, but I refuse to allow anyone else into the fray. So long as I am alive, I can handle the prince."

"My head, but that is truth." Rhys cuffed my shoulder, then stepped back.

"Show some respect for your betters, dogs!" Our guard threatened with his whip and boys knelt in the mud.

The two Irish princes were now abreast of us. Close enough to touch. A smug smile stretched Prince Modred's lips across his teeth.

His elder brother glanced in my direction. "Is that nae your girl, Modred?"

"Aye," Prince Modred said, with what sounded like pride. We glared at each other. He would be dismounting soon.

"You are right. Her brother does have a pretty mouth. My thanks for pointing him out."

What had they done to Dafydd? His mouth? His tongue? Oh, the gods. Had my nightmare come to pass?

My hand rose to clutch the prince's boot, to drag him down from his horse and demand answers. Then I remembered my promise to my brother. I would not reopen my wounds so soon. I dropped my arm.

Once the royal pair had gone by and the road was clear again, we were ordered to move. But our supply cart had stuck fast in the mire. It took all our strength under the whip to free it. I had no more time to worry over what the prince might have already done or planned for the future. There was only the cart, its wheels half-buried in muck, to free as my hero's claim to fame.

* * *

The boys were true to their word. Every time I sank my shovel into the soggy peat, someone would add a block he had already cut to my pile. Most came from Rhys. He had taken a place nearest me.

Our Irish guard did not seem to care, he sat perched on the cart, his feet dry.

"It would not take much to overpower the lazy Irish bastard," Rhys said.

"And then what," I asked.

"Think of it, Lin. We're outside the fortress walls. And we have weapons." He brandished his shovel. "Give us the word, and we'd be free. We could use his dagger, cut off our collars, slip into town."

How little he knew me.

"With Dafydd still up there, Rhys? I will not leave my brother. And how can you think to abandon Julia and your babe?"

My words doused the fire in my companion's eyes.

"I have never wanted to lead an uprising. That was never my purpose," I said.

"What of your defiance?"

I leaned on my shovel, breathing heavily. My shoulders and arms ached and what trickled down my back was probably a mixture of sweat and blood. I reworked the waist of my gown up and around the length of rope to keep the hem of my skirt clear of the wet bog. Next time I would borrow Dafydd's spare tunic.

Rhys awaited my answer.

"My defiance began as pure reaction to something I saw as unfair. They put a collar on *my* brother. They made him a slave."

"No one wears the collar with such dignity as your brother."

I tugged at my own. "I knew when my turn came, I could not be silent like Dafydd. Something inside me said to cling to who I am and never let go. Something, I know not what, told me that to accept the collar, to become a slave, I would lose the only possession a slave ever has."

"What is that, Lin?"

I pried the block of peat I had cut and hauled the dripping mass up and over to my stack.

"Myself, Rhys. I only want to be left in peace, to be Lin. And to be with my brother. But how long do you think the prince will allow Dafydd to remain in Dunn na Carraice now? You saw what happened to Padrig."

Rhys gripped my arm when I turned away. "All these years you have been staunch in your loyalty to others. Dafydd. Olwen. Custennin. Padrig. I wish to do the same turn for you. Why do you resist?"

"Think you this is easy for me, Rhys? To know that everyone I so much as speak to might be sold merely as a ploy to master me? Think you it is easy to hold myself beyond the pale so that others are not ensnared in my curse?"

I jerked my arm free and slogged through the bog, not giving him a chance to answer.

What Rhys had proposed was madness. No doubt we would have been successful against the lone Orkneyman. But where would we have gone? Who would have harboured runaway slaves? Of Queen Morgause? My brand would have betrayed us.

I straightened and noticed a newcomer speaking with our guard. He pointed in my direction. Curious, I moved closer and recognised the new man. Donall, who had carelessly taken Olwen from Dafydd. Then I saw another figure, mostly hidden by the Irishmen. What was this about?

I moved closer still and heard, "Are you sure, Donall?"

"My order was for that one there and the rebellious one. What other rebellious one have we got?"

"You, girl. Here." The guard shouted.

I had no reason not to obey. But the going was slow through the bog.

Just then Donall moved and revealed the slight figure standing near him. Sandy-haired head bowed. Wrists shackled. What felt like Prince Modred's hand seized my heart and stomach and bowels all at once and squeezed. The rest of the world faded from my awareness.

"Can't you move faster, girl? I'll make you regret me having to come out there to motivate you."

I stumbled forward, willing my legs not to buckle. It seemed to take days to reach the fringe and the supply cart.

I was pushed forward.

"There you are, Donall. One rebellious slave girl, delivered. Mind you, things will be dull around here without her."

Laughter.

"Sure you don't need help getting them to town, Donall?"

Town? That meant…

Where was the prince? He must be near, but I saw no sign of him.

"I think I can handle the docile one and this chit," Donall said, grabbing one of my wrists. "She seems tame enough now. I should have no trouble getting them to the slave pen, with time left to stop at the public house for a measure."

But the prince should be here gloating. Should he not?

Donall locked my wrists into the shackles. They were connected to Dafydd by a chain. Iron is so very cold. And so very hard and unyielding against warm flesh.

The warrior tapped my brand. "This will no longer protect you. For too long, you've hidden behind it. For too long, you thought yourself special. Well, *cumal*, special you have never been. Move."

I cannot panic.

CHAPTER 26

"Lin, who will lead us now?" Rhys shouted.

Before I could answer, the guard brought his whip down across Rhys' shoulders. My new friend never broke his gaze from me. Neither did his back buckle beneath the lash.

He had called me hero. Who was I to disappoint? Despite the numbness enshrouding my heart, I forced my own fears aside.

Squaring my own shoulders, I said, "You, Rhys! You are my successor. Dunn na Carraice's new Pendragon." Maybe he would lead them to the freedom he craved.

Donall cursed in Irish. "I haven't got all day," he shouted, jerking the lead chain.

Dafydd and I lurched forward.

I was as familiar with iron as I was of my brother's voice and gentle touch, and had thought I had grown accustomed to the weight. But this time, I was chained *to* my brother. And we were on our way to market. Like animals.

Dafydd slipped his hand into mine.

I squeezed it in return. I dared not look at him, however. I was not ready to see his pain. I stared instead at the mud-churned track we called a road.

I must be strong for Dafydd. He had asked it of me.

Too soon I saw our destination at the crossroads. A wooden-fenced enclosure, easily twice my brother's height, with a grated iron gate and no roof. The slave pen. Within the shadows, I could see the people it contained.

"Oh, Lin," Dafydd whispered.

I could not reply, for my mouth had long since gone dry.

Two men lounged under the shelter of a lean-to beside the enclosure's entrance. The shelter was furnished with table, bench, and a brazier, aglow with warmth. The remains of a meal littered the table.

Beyond the shelter rose a stone platform, much like the one in the fortress courtyard, with one exception. No post.

"Ho! I got two more for the next auction," Donall said. "Property of the Queen."

One of the slavers rose. Tall and lean, he looked as though he might have been carved from the same stone as the platform. He eyed us.

"Next one's tomorrow. Mid-morning," he said. "Still plenty o' room left. What have you got?" He folded well-muscled arms across his chest.

"One of each. The boy's fairly well behaved. Has a few manners. He'll give you no trouble." Donall gripped my collar. "But it is only fair to warn you o' this one. I doubt you'll get much for this ugly and ill-mannered creature." He released me, pushing me forward so that I landed on my hands and knees.

Dafydd helped me up amidst the guffaws. My stomach twisted into a knot.

"You'll see that the profits are sent up to the Queen's seneschal?" Donall said, unlocking our manacles.

"Wouldn't dream of holding back from Herself," the slaver said. He gave markers to Donall to take back to the dunn.

Donall draped the chains over his shoulder and disappeared into the crowd of townspeople, whistling.

"What we got, Fionn?" The second slave trader tossed a gnawed chicken leg on the table and joined his companion, smearing grease from his fingers onto his tunic.

"The boy's rather ordinary. A field slave, no doubt. Give him a number and lock him up, Ronan. But I want a closer inspection of the girl."

Ronan opened the gate to the pen. "Here, boy," he said.

My brother shook his hair from his eyes. "My name is Dafydd." He barely spoke above a whisper, but 'twas enough.

Dafydd held his head high as he walked to the gate, amidst the men's guffaws.

Ronan hung a wooden placard around my brother's neck. I doubted the scratches on it said "Dafydd."

"In ya go, *boy*," the paunchy slaver said, a hand on my brother's shoulder.

Dafydd paused, gazing back at me.

"Oh, she'll be joining you soon enough, *boy*."

The gate grated closed behind my brother.

"He's got number eighty-nine, Fionn."

Dafydd gripped the bars of the gate.

"Fetch some water, Ronan. I want to see what's beneath all this mud. What you been doing, girl? Wallowing with the pigs?" Fionn said.

I glowered at him.

"There's still too much fire in those eyes," he said. "It isn't often we get an unbroken one from the Queen. By the time she's finished using a slave, there isn't even so much as a spark left. I wonder why it is that you haven't been tamed."

His partner returned with a bucket in each hand.

"Strip," Fionn said.

In the street? I could not move.

Where was the prince? This must his doing.

Fionn grabbed a handful of my gown and drew me towards him. His breath stank.

"I said get those clothes off, girl. Do you not understand plain Irish? If I have to do it for you, there will be naught left o' this rag."

It was all I had. I could not let it be ripped. I pulled my gown over my head and draped it over my arm.

"I said strip. That means everything, you stupid wench. The shift too."

It was torn from me before I could react.

Dafydd turned away.

Ronan returned and tossed icy water at me. First over my head and then from the front. Shivering, I felt the eyes of the world gawking at me. And tried to cover myself.

"The little slut is modest," Fionn said.

Both men circled me, assessing me from crown to toe.

"Ho! Ho! This one isn't as bad as that chap made out, Ronan said. "Now the shit's gone. Just the sort that merchant we had last week liked to take to the East, for the kips of Rome and Constantinople. He preferred 'em young like this. He would have paid for the pair, to boot."

Fionn merely grunted.

"Have you a name? Or did your master call you 'girl'?" Fionn said. He had returned to the shelter and perched on the edge of the table.

I stared at him, trying to forget I wore naught but a band of leather around my neck and that two men leered at me.

Ronan slid his hands over my body, pinching the buds an unknown merchant would have paid dearly for. People walked by, casting curious glances in my direction.

I raised my chin. "I answer to Lin."

Ronan jammed a filthy finger into my mouth.

I gagged.

"Tooth missing," he said, withdrawing.

I coughed as he wiped his finger on my cheek.

My arms were pulled away from my body.

"Brand, inside left wrist."

I was spun around, my hair lifted.

"Back's been well marked by the whip. Recently."

"How long have you had your collar?" Fionn said. He filled a cup, drank, dried his mouth on his sleeve.

"I got it some few days after Beltane," I said.

"The Queen collars 'em at twelve, don't she? Coming of age gift, you could say. No other marks I can see."

"Have you begun your bleeding times yet?" Fionn said.

Affronted by the question, I gave him silence.

Ronan slapped me across the mouth. "Answer the question, girl."

"Yes." I dabbed blood from my chin.

"No manners at all. We could hold her up for the auction next week, Fionn and teach her some in the meanwhile."

"The Queen will be expecting her profit before then, Ronan. You willing to risk her wrath?"

Ronan shook his head.

"Are you still virgin, girl?"

"What?"

"You dare question, slave? We ask. You answer. Understand?" Ronan's second blow sent me to the ground.

Indifferent, Fionn rephrased his query as though I had not understood.

"Are you still a maiden, or have you been fucked?"

Dazed and curled into a ball on the ground at Ronan's feet, I never wanted to rise again.

Let me die. Please?

"Answer!" Ronan drew back his foot.

Kicked. Like a dog on the roadside. Stripped of clothing, dignity, and my name, I could not be degraded any lower. And Dafydd had to see it.

My name is Dafydd. My brother had the dignity. He was my strength.

I pushed myself to my knees and glowered at Fionn.

I found voice to say, "I am no longer virgin."

"Who? Your master? A fellow slave? That bloke you were brought with perhaps?" Fionn cast his gaze to the slave pen.

Enough. I had endured worse than this. I had survived the prince with spirit unbroken. I could survive these two. I heaved myself to my feet.

"Dafydd is my brother. What does it matter which thief stole my maidenhead? Prince or slave, one phallus is like any other."

I paid for the outburst with a lashing. It had only been a matter of time before Ronan resorted to his whip.

"What sort of work can you do, or do you only know how to whore?"

The questions resumed as Ronan recoiled his weapon.

Weakened with pain, weariness, fear, and confusion, I answered them.

"How many masters have you had? How many times have you been sold?"

"I was born up there."

"A virgin to the block?"

"As you say."

"By the powers. We'll be lucky to get a silver coin for all our labours."

"Perhaps," Fionn said, polishing his nails on his tunic.

The questions ended, they allowed me to retrieve my gown from where Ronan had trampled it. As soon as I had dressed, he placed placard around my neck. I was now number ninety.

I refused to have Ronan shove me into the enclosure. Distasteful as I found it, I walked through the gate with what little of my dignity remained.

Dafydd immediately tried to embrace me as I entered.

"Don't touch me! I never want another man to touch me! Ever!"

He shrank away.

"This is what you wanted me to give in to, Dafydd, but a month ago. To be treated like an animal. Why did you not let me die when I had the chance? Why did not you just let me die?"

Tears streamed down my brother's cheeks.

I bit back the rest of my tongue-lashing.

I turned from him and searched for a spot where I could nurse my tattered pride.

I found an empty corner, a few paces from the gate. The ground was pure mud, so I leaned a shoulder against the closely spaced slats of the fence. The fresh welts on my back and shoulders throbbed. Even my belly and breasts had not been spared this time.

My last hours with my brother and I had to lose my temper. How could I be so selfish? He had remained at the gate throughout my ordeal.

"I am so very sorry, Lin. Sorry I ever tried to change you. The gods—"

"There are no gods. There is no heaven. There is only Hell. There is only Orkney. The two are the same. And the prince is Satan—Hell's king," I said.

I released a sigh.

"I am sorry, too, Dafydd. I know you want to help. I lost control."

"Never mind, Impossible One. I understand."

"Thank you, Dafydd."

"For what?"

"For… For being you. For being my brother and my friend." A tear slid down my cheek and I turned my head away.

"After all we have been through, you still try to hide your tears from me? You are impossible." He cupped my chin in his hand and tilted my face upward. His eyes glistened and yet he greeted my gaze with a grin.

Weary, I rested my head on his shoulder, positioning my ear over his soothing, steadfast heart.

"I should thank you," he whispered, stroking my hair. "For being Lin. For being my hero. For coming into my life and being my dearest friend and sister."

He began to sing a hero's song I had never heard before. A song of a warrior with a heart of steel, who refused to yield or bend at the knee, save to one lord, the Pendragon. The only man proven worthy of such loyalty from her.

"Where did you learn that?" I said at the end.

"I made it for you. I spent all last night and this morning working on it. I feared you might never hear it. Especially—"

"I have heard none finer. My thanks, Bard."

"My pleasure, Noble One."

"I wish that just once I had something worthwhile to give you in return. But I have nothing that equals your gift."

"You are wrong. Dafydd, the Bard, would not exist without you, Lin. Without your warrior spirit to drive me, I would have no heart for stories or songs. Your bravery is my inspiration."

"How I have feared the prince removing your tongue, Dafydd."

"I remember, vividly, that nightmare from your fevered days."

"I saw him this morning, on the way to the bog. Prince Agravain was with him. They said you had a pretty mouth and I thought they meant…"

A shadow flitted across my brother's eyes.

"Dafydd?"

He shivered.

"I am certain they merely intended to threaten you with that, Lin," Dafydd said, at last. "The very thought of all my stories being locked inside me forever—"

"Is more than I can bear. Every time you speak, images of beauty and wonder flow from your lips. At those times, I think—how can the world be ugly, when it has Dafydd? My life is better because of you. But soon…"

We fell silent.

I rested against the fence, tired, knowing the worst was yet to come.

Studying the faces of the others in the enclosure with us, I saw despair and defeat in every pair of eyes that met mine. Not many did. Was this to be my fate? Had I survived Prince Modred's efforts to enslave me simply to become one of these creatures, devoid of hope? Is this how I would look on the morrow when Dafydd was gone?

Without the sun, I had no way of guessing how much time had passed since Donall had arrived at the bog and brought us to town. I was surprised by the lateness of the hour when Ronan and Fionn announced supper.

Slaves surged to the gate, bowls in hand. Dafydd and I had none. What we had used in the fortress belonged to the Queen. They would remain in Dunn na Carraice. I marvelled at her generosity that we still had clothes.

Prince Modred would claim them later, no doubt.

Dafydd joined the line and patiently waited his turn.

"Master?"

"What, boy?" Ronan said.

"Master, my sister and I were sent from the Queen with only the clothes we wear."

"Why should this concern me, boy?"

"Master, if it please you, we have nothing to eat with. Have you a spare you can suffer us to use? We can share the one."

"On your knees, boy. Beg, and I might," Ronan said.

Dafydd paused for a moment. And it seemed as though he was about to comply.

"I already have, Master. To ask *is* begging," Dafydd said.

The men laughed, but my brother's shoulders never sagged as he walked back to where I stood.

"I tried," he said, spreading his empty hands.

"You did grand, Dafydd. I am sorry you must go hungry though."

"Even I have my limits, Lin. I know you must think me weak because I use the word 'master.' Because I accept the collar. But I could not do that. I could not degrade myself and beg for those scraps of food. Not after your dignity this afternoon."

"I have never thought you weak. Only more gentle and kind. I would rather starve than have you beg."

Dafydd glanced at the grey sky, then the mud around our ankles.

"It is going to be a long night."

"Not nearly long enough, Dafydd."

"I know. Still, we cannot stand the entire time. We might as well sit, even if in the mud."

Neither of us relished the idea, but he was right.

"One would think they'd take better care of the property in their charge. If only to increase their profits." A young man stood before us with a bowl filled with steaming porridge in his hand. He spoke British.

"You are well come to use my bowl. My name is Llwch."

"Thank you, Llwch." Dafydd took the bowl and handed it to me. "I am Dafydd. This is my sister, Lin."

"Well met."

I had no appetite and would have been content going without, but I took a few mouthfuls before passing the bowl back to my brother.

He finished it readily enough. Dafydd never seemed to lack an appetite.

"Thank you again, Llwch. That was most kind." Dafydd tried to return the bowl.

"You're entitled to a portion each. No one would say you nay if you had it filled again. Besides, your sister hasn't had very much."

Dafydd returned to the gate and Ronan poured out a ladleful of the crowdy. I doubted he was happy at being thwarted his power.

I forced a few more mouthfuls down, in politeness and for my brother's sake. But again, Dafydd had the greater share of the portion.

"If you don't mind my asking, that song you sang earlier, I've never heard it before. Is it from your homeland?"

"You could say so," Dafydd said.

"You should not be so modest, Dafydd. He made it himself, Llwch."

"Truly? Did you have some bard's training before you were a slave?"

The colour in my brother's cheeks deepened. "No," he said. "I was born to a slave-woman in the Queen's fortress. 'Tis the only life Lin and I have ever known."

"You've a fine gift, Dafydd."

"I don't know about that. I only know when I have need of them, the words are there for my tongue. Where they come from, I cannot guess."

"Perhaps you might give us another song later," Llwch said.

"Perhaps."

"It would do much to hearten us all."

Llwch stayed for a few more moments then took his leave, promising we could use his bowl again in the morning.

From where I sat, I had a clear view of the fortress. The Queen and her family would be sitting down at table about now, in their chairs with soft cushions. Their servants hovering to ensure goblets were never empty and that more meat was always near to hand.

Rhys and Julia and the rest of our companions would be returning to the slaves' hut. How would they be taking the news that Dafydd was gone?

After holding back all day, the clouds opened and it began to rain, hard and steady. It quickly soaked through our thin clothing.

Why not? It only proved my point that there were no gods.

"If ever there was a time for song, this is it," Dafydd said, standing.

I knew my brother would sing. No matter how disheartened he might be, he always rose above his own sorrows to help others.

He began a familiar tune. A male voice joined his. Llwch? Then another and yet another.

My brother would get along well enough in the world. He was male and would never have to endure the humiliations I did as a girl. Like rape. Like unwelcome hands groping my body. I had a feeling all women went through Ronan's inspections simply because they were powerless females. I envied Dafydd having been born male.

Dafydd led a few other songs, peering at me frequently, trying to get me to join in.

But my heart and soul were beyond being soothed so easily.

He ended with my favourite tale, about how Arthur became Pendragon by drawing Excalibur from a stone, and then sat down.

"How different we are, Dafydd."

"Aye."

"Did you ever know my father?"

Dafydd shook his head. "I was too young. Does it matter so much now?"

I could not say why I had brought the subject up.

"I guess not. Whenever I look at you, I see Mummy. Soon, I might lose that last connection with her."

I allowed the tears to spill.

"No simple slave could have fathered you, Lin. Surely one of the Queen's warriors made you."

"I often wish I had gotten more from Mummy and less from my father."

"Impossible One, you are never content."

"No longer noble?" I said.

"You are always noble, Lin."

* * *

The rain continued for most of the night. We sat huddled close to each other, sharing our warmth. Neither of us slept.

By cockcrow the sky began to clear. The sun would grace our auction. Those who would part with their money would not experience undue discomfort while at market.

Fionn and Ronan enlisted several of the men from the pen to prepare the platform for the sale. They carried up the table. And the massive block itself.

"Maybe it is better not to watch, Lin."

"Nothing will help now. Nothing will make the least bit of difference," I answered my brother, still staring through the fence at the activity.

A crowd had gathered around the platform. Conversations were of the weather and business and the Queen. Daily, ordinary affairs. I gripped the fence tighter, my palms too calloused to feel the splinters in the rough wood. Did they not realise we could see them and hear their every word? Occasionally someone would break from the rest and come up to the fence and peer inside, then walk away.

Was the prince out there?

"This is how rape feels, Dafydd. Powerless. So you know."

His eyes told me he understood. His lower lip trembled and he bit it. No one in the enclosure paid us the least attention, yet I clung to my old habit and held my own tears in check.

Several men had arrived to aid Fionn and Ronan. All our placards were checked and the first group was herded from the pen.

"There is so much I want to say, Lin. Everything, for the rest of our lives must be said and done now, for there will be no more 'later, this afternoons.' There will be no more 'tomorrows' for us. I shall never have another chance. And it is ripping me apart. Why did I never see the cruelty like you did?"

I flinched when Fionn called out the first number. A male. It was begun. My stomach knotted.

"You are not to blame, Dafydd."

"Neither are you, Lin. Look at them out there, with their fine woollens and leather boots. Well fed, clean. Dry. And haggling over a copper or a bronze coin for their chattel. They are to blame. And the Queen to allow it. You were right to question. And resist."

A man checked the signs around our necks yet again, then left us alone for the moment.

How little time we had left. How precious little time.

Dafydd took up my hand and pressed the fingers to his lips. I felt his tears as well as his kiss.

"I would fail miserably, Lin, if I tried to express my heart now."

"I already know your heart, Dafydd. I would fail, too."

"There is not much we can keep from each other, is there? Never has been. Be strong, Noble One. Be brave."

"Never stop dreaming, Bard. Remember me in your songs."

"Always. Even Excalibur could not sever you from my soul."

He drew me into his arms.

I went readily and pressed myself as tightly as I could against his slender form. And wept.

"I love you, Lin," he said with a sob.

"And I you."

We were still clinging to each other when a man separated us, checked our numbers. He indicated it was our turn to wait near the platform. Our turn to become sheep.

A boy, as young as Olwen went for thirty copper coins. A woman fetched two silvers. Numbers. Fionn called out numbers and genders and hair colouring. Men and women called out numbers of coins. Numbers. Nameless numbers. Meaningless coins.

A hand fell on Dafydd's shoulder, spun him around, and began pushing him to the stage. I heard his gasp, saw the surprise in his eyes. I raised my fisted left hand high above my head, brand facing out. It was the only sign of strength I had left to offer my brother. I would spend it for him, for I would have no need of it later.

Dafydd did not resist, but went as gracefully as he performed his stories and songs. No one but us knew what truly lay behind his quiet demeanour as he mounted the steps and then the block. No one but me noticed his trembling. No one cared.

Dafydd stood meekly, with his head bowed. Ronan placed the whip's handle under Dafydd's chin and jerked it up. My brother's hair swung back, giving the crowd a clear view of his features.

"Male, lot eighty-nine. Aged fourteen. Blond hair, grey eyes. Docile, with a strong back and shoulders. Collared. Former owner, Queen Morgause. Easily worth fifty coppers."

Bids came from every direction. Some of the bidders used their fingers to indicate the number of coins they offered. Sixty. Seventy coins of copper. They changed to silver.

Throughout, I could not rip my gaze away. I was afraid to blink and miss that one last glimpse of my brother.

"I'm bid two silver coins. Any one else?" Fionn waited. Asked again. "Come now. Look at the potential before you. This boy is surely worth more than two silver coins."

"Three!"

"Are you all finished now?"

The crowd stood silent.

"Sold!"

The gavel cracked against the wooden table, driving home the last nail of my coffin. The sound echoed in my soul. No one but me saw Dafydd flinch.

It was done and over so quickly. One moment I had a brother. The next, he was being shackled and led away.

He was brought down the steps to his new owner, passing near me.

"Lin!"

That single utterance contained all of the world's suffering.

I caught his tunic.

A fist grabbed my collar and pulled me away, but not before Dafydd's fingers skimmed mine for the last time.

"Dafydd," I shouted as he disappeared into the crowd. I watched until I could no longer distinguish his sandy hair from the rest of the world.

My soul was dead. Why had my life been spared for this?

Above me, the auction progressed. The gavel fell, more coins changed hands and yet another mother, father, sister, brother, daughter, son vanished from the world.

Still dazed, I became aware of being shoved forward myself. I recall nothing of the steps. Before me jutted the block. My heart pounded in my breast as I stood in full view of the throng.

"Female, lot ninety. Aged twelve. Auburn hair. Hazel eyes. Tooth missing. Collared. Branded by former owner, Prince Modred. Hold your arm up, girl so they can see the mark. Who'll give me thirty coppers?"

Dafydd's worth began at fifty.

The prince must be out there somewhere, gloating. Dafydd would want me to be brave. I might feel defeated inside, but for my brother's sake, I would be brave. The prince would not win.

Those people would know they bid for a girl, not a beast.

"I gave an order, *cumal*." Ronan grabbed my arm.

Orkney's coffer would not swell with coins gained from me. I would not go easily. Or quietly. I jerked my arm away.

"Are you out there, prince?" I shouted, my eyes searching. "Do you hear me? Listen well. I am not your piece of meat, you fucking bastard."

I glared at the faces regarding me.

"Bitch!" I heard Fionn curse from where he sat at his table, behind me.

Ronan's whip hissed in the air before biting into my back. Dafydd was gone. Sold. I felt no pain from such a small effort.

A voice, far to the rear of the throng, offered ten bronze *folles*. A low bid I gathered from the laughter.

No further offers came. Who would pay more for a defiant slave?

"Damn you!" Fionn tried once more to coax a few more coins from the crowd, to no avail. “Sold, for ten bronze *folles*!”

“Buy yourself some bloody boots, prince,” I shouted in the gavel’s echo.

CHAPTER 27

More manacles. But I barely felt their weight this time. A man attached me to a common chain with several strangers of both sexes—various ages. Slaves, every one. Even me.

My heart and soul might as well have been trampled by a war-host.

"Move, dogs," the man said. He jerked the lead of our chain.

Get called dog often enough and you begin to believe.

I know not how, but my legs obeyed the command. Of the town we shuffled through, I saw but blurred shapes and colours from the corner of my eye. Easier to keep my attention fixed upon the dark hair of the slave directly before me.

Lin, the firebrand, was no more. Prince Modred had won the battle of our wills.

And I no longer cared.

Eventually the coffle reached a ship moored in the harbour. Men shouted orders to herd us on board amidst the activities of others loading supplies.

The vessel rocked beneath my feet.

I was leaving the only home I had ever known.

Without my brother.

The prince had condemned me to spend the rest of my days living with a hole in my heart from where Dafydd had always dwelt.

Below deck foul odours and gloom assaulted my battered senses. Misery hung in the air itself. I breathed it in. It clung to my skin. How fitting.

The widely spaced oil lamps created more shadows than they dispelled. Chains rattled in every direction. But I was beyond the compassion necessary to wonder how many bodies like my own filled the hold of the ship. One must have a heart to care. Mine was shattered.

I shivered as a wave of bitter cold washed through me. Dafydd had used similar words after Meg had been sold. He had recovered.

No. That was not quite right. Just a few days ago he had grieved for her loss. One never recovers. One simply patches the fragments one manages to find back together before moving on. Or gives in to despair.

"Move."

The command might have been for me, or any one of the others in front of, or behind me.

"Stop."

I did so.

"Sit."

My ankles were chained to a ring embedded in the floor.

The men moved to the next slave, and so on down the length of the ship.

When the last of their human cargo was in place, the slavers climbed up top, drawing the ladder behind them. Ironbound, how could we follow? Then they dropped the hatch, leaving us in darkness.

The vessel's wood and ropes creaked as the ship bobbed.

I hugged my knees.

Wfft, but I was weary. Weary of life and I wanted to be rid of it.

Someone across the way moaned as though in pain. Another wept. I heard whispering.

"Lin!" My brother's final scream of my name rose above the din of despair.

I tried covering my ears to blot out the sound. To no avail. I would never escape it.

I felt tears course down my cheeks. Cold coins would fill the Queen of Orkney's coffer while my warm tears slid into the icy sea.

I did naught to check them. Who would care?

Dafydd would. You know Dafydd would care.

Piss off. I no longer care.

You lie.

A plague on Prince Modred and the house of Orkney. I shall never forgive you, prince. Never.

Frustrated by my impotence, I yanked the chains with all my strength. The iron cut into my chafed flesh. The pain only served to fuel my passion. I tugged the more wildly until I exhausted myself.

Why had my life been spared?

Why had I not listened to my brother years ago and accepted the inevitable? We might still be together.

As slaves.

Wrapped in self-pity, I withdrew deeper into the shadows of the hold, just so much dung in the bowels of a ship.

Breathing became my sole task.

*   *   *

"You were wrong, Eoghain. This one isn't dead. See? You can tell by the recoil when you kick 'em."

The overseer spoke as though from a great distance. Was the prince finally releasing me? Would I find Dafydd awaiting me?

A boot nudged my leg.

I heard a moan.

"Wake up, lazy baggage. Your barge has docked."

Laughter. Much closer.

Wood creaked.

The guard room floor heaved beneath me.

"This one for Arbeia?"

"Nae. Anfri says he can do better with this lot in Ebrauc."

"I still think he wasted ten *folles*. You didn't see this hellion on the block."

Then I remembered. I must have been dreaming about the guard room and Orkney's overseer. And Dafydd would certainly not be waiting for me.

One of the men removed my fetters and hauled me to my feet.

How long since I last stood?

Fool. What is time to a beast?

I clung to a support beam until I heard the snap of a whip. A familiar straw to clutch and draw myself to the now again. Pain driven activity I knew and could respond to without thought. Familiarity, sweet kingdom of the lost.

I stumbled up the ladder with the others, shielding my eyes from the glare of daylight.

The girl in front of me tripped and fell to her knees.

I extended my hand like I would have to help Dafydd.

The girl stared at my hand for the briefest instant before clasping it and pulling herself to her feet.

We joined the queue of human sheep.

Easy enough to guess what would come next from the clang of metal ahead. The wait was not long. The smiths worked swiftly at their task, hobbling each slave with a short length of chain.

My chain dragged the ground, the weight pulling my soul to the dirt where the prince had always wanted it.

"Thank you for helping me," the girl beside whispered. She was about my age and I noticed she had no collar around her throat.

"It was nothing," I murmured. I wanted this contact with another human ended. I turned my gaze to the sea that had brought me to this new place without curiosity.

"My name is Tighan."

I watched the crew of the ship next to ours wheel crates and carts laden with parcels onto the pier. From their shouts I learned we were at a place called Arbeia. The name meant nothing to me.

"I tried to speak to you before—when you were ill."

I remembered retching and heaving. My stomach had refused not only gruel, but water as well throughout much of the journey. How many days? Years?

"I'm from the Out Islands."

Mayhap she was newly enslaved and frightened.

The sooner she learns the harsh reality of slavery, the better for her, then. I turned my back on her.

When the last slave stood on deck, sullen and hobbled, there were perhaps two score of ragged souls along with me. Every one of them looked as pale and infirm as I felt. I doubt a thread of faith in humanity existed among us.

Shuffling in single-file under the watchful eyes of the many slave traders and sailors, we crossed the wooden plank bridging ship and pier. How easily I could cast myself into the depths below. I even had the added weight of the irons to assist me. But I missed my chance.

And then at last I stepped on dry land once more. Well, mud. But I continued to feel the roll of the ship. And my stomach refused to calm.

Several men, mounted on horses, waited near a supply wagon. Two more men perched on the wagon's seat. The slavers on horseback snapped their whips, and our journey resumed.

The muddy road sliced through the harbour town. We passed row upon row of identical, long and narrow stone structures. For all I knew, we had simply sailed to the opposite side of Orkney. Except, the place had an air of efficiency and precision in spite of the fact that most of the buildings stood empty. And too many men spoke British.

Emerging from the southern gate, I beheld a sweeping expanse of green land. Dafydd would have pretty words to describe the sight. What was it the men had said on the boat? Ebrauc? I remembered Custennin mentioning it as headquarters for the Dux Britanniarum, the Pendragon's northern warlord. My first sight of Britain. Camelot and the Pendragon existed somewhere in this land. Mayhap—Nae, that dream was dead, murdered by Prince Modred when he offered Dafydd for sale.

Without pause, I trudged behind Tighan, my bundle shouldered in one arm, my other hand clutching my unsettled belly. I could ill afford to spare a thought for nonsense and pretty words about the land.

What was poetic about slogging through ankle-deep mire?

All the same, my head jerked up when my ears caught the familiar song, coming faintly from behind me, far back down the line.

What madness was this? Had my mind snapped once and for good? Now I had myself thinking I actually heard my brother singing.

I had to stop torturing myself like that.

Dafydd is gone.

But the well known tune continued, with some of my companions joining the chorus, so someone back there sang. No. Surely I must be mad. It must be my fanciful and wishful thinking playing the trickster.

CHAPTER 28

Wishful thinking or no, I held my breath anyway and listened harder. My soul stirred with anticipation. How could anyone else sound like him?

I had to know.

"Dafydd? Is it you?" I shouted over my shoulder.

The singing ceased and there was a grumble of disapproval.

Heedless of the consequences, I stopped, and the small bundle of supplies I carried slipped from my grasp. Let the slave traders do their best with their whips. I had already endured Hell and survived to tell the tale. If I was wrong in this, nothing would matter. I peered to where I had heard the singing, stretching my neck. I saw no sign of the sandy hair.

"Is there a youth named Dafydd? Coming from Orkney and Dunn na Carraice?"

I waited.

"Lin?" My name came back to me, questioning and full of hope. Vastly different from the last time I had heard it.

My legs turned to water and I sank to my knees in the muddy road.

Please, let this be real.

"Yes, it is me, Dafydd," I shouted.

"The gods be thanked! I have my sister once more!"

And I had my reason to live.

My brother was too far back in the queue for me to see, but that mattered not. The knowledge of his presence was all the comfort I needed to renew my spirit.

A shadow fell on me. One of the slavers had trotted his horse to where I knelt hugging myself. He neither asked for, nor waited for me to offer excuses. He flicked his whip across my shoulders. The lashes might have been the stings of insects for what I felt of them. I had not lost my brother.

Yet.

I shoved that thought from my mind.

How could I not have known Dafydd was so near?

Ach, stop questioning. Be grateful for the boon.

I retrieved my bundle, stood and slipped back into the coffle.

Dafydd renewed his song with a greater enthusiasm than I had ever heard from him. And I happily joined him. My heart and soul soared with the sea birds. The weight of the chains hobbling my ankles seemed to lighten and walking became less of a chore. My stomach even settled as the sun reached the point of mid-day.

The road followed the coast for some distance before curving toward the sunset. As we journeyed farther inland, the crashing of the surf grew fainter until it faded entirely. The world became strangely silent without it. And the air tasted bland, lacking the usual seasoning from the sea spray.

The slavers drove us until the sun hung low in the sky and we reached a crossroads. Two of the men spoke within earshot.

"Five miles in the saddle is long enough for one day, eh, Anfri?"

Anfri. I had heard the name before.

"Aye. We should have enough daylight left to set up camp. We'll take the road south at cockcrow."

He turned his head and I saw his features.

He had laid out ten coins for me.

"How long to Ebrauc?" the first man said.

"I've pushed a coffle from here to Ebrauc in a sennight. We time it right, we'll be there for market day."

The men rode down the line shouting orders.

Much later, after the slavers had eaten their fill, we were given leave to take our meal. My brother approached the cauldron and waited in the queue with a patience he alone possessed, while Tighan and I ladled out portions into bowl after bowl. My hands shook so hard, I marvelled I did not spill any of the pottage.

And then he was before me, the same blue-grey eyes, the same sandy hair, still barefoot. He had acquired a cloak of faded green, blue and red, which he had knotted under his chin. I always knew he would fare better than me in the world. He most likely got it for a song.

I left the ladle in the pot and we simply leaned into each other's arms. I felt the sting of tears as I held fast to my brother. Mindful of the eyes of so many strangers, I blinked my tears back.

"By the stars, Lin."

"How I missed you, Dafydd."

"And I you."

"When the gavel fell, I never thought—"

"Hush. Do not say it, Lin." He pressed a finger to my lips. Then he embraced me tighter than before.

I clung to Dafydd awhile longer, then I pulled away with reluctance.

"We are holding up the line," I said.

Tighan and the others stared at us.

"She is my sister," Dafydd announced, while I filled his bowl with the steaming pottage of vegetables. "Have you never seen a reunion before? I shall wait for you, Lin." He stood aside so the people behind him could be served.

"You have not seen each other in a long time, have you?' Tighan said.

"As long as it took to journey from Dunn na Carraice."

"I do not recognise that name. Is it in Eire?"

"Orkney. 'Tis the fortress of Queen Morgause."

"We had but little news of the world beyond our village. Go to your brother," Tighan said, taking the ladle from my hand.

"But we have not finished serving yet."

My companion surveyed the remaining line. "I can manage. He is your brother. Would that I had such a chance with my own brother. For all the pranks he played on me, I'd still be overjoyed to see him once more."

"Now it is my turn to thank you."

Tighan smiled and echoed my own words, spoken just that morning while still on the ship. "It is nothing."

I took my portion of food, then joined Dafydd. He had found a spot near the cooking-fire where we could sit side by side as always.

No words exist for such an unlikely gift. Even Dafydd, who usually had words for everything, sat in silence.

While I ate, I studied his face. What I saw disturbed me greatly. A residual of the auction?

"What have they done to you, Dafydd?"

"Have I changed so much? It is hardly a fortnight."

"Enough for me to notice."

Dafydd took several bites of his supper, chewing each with care. His collar bobbed when he swallowed.

"Never mind about me," he said. "It is past. Leave it."

"I will not. You would never accept such an answer from me. Do not expect me to either. You have changed. Something hurt you deeply. I can see it in your eyes. They never lie."

"There are some things too terrible for words, Lin. You know this. Things you have experienced and know all too well. Things no one should ever live through. Things better left in private."

His desire for privacy I understood and respected, for now.

"But where were you? Not in the hold. Surely I would have known. I would have sensed your presence."

Dafydd set his bowl aside. "I think you are right. The captain of the ship required a cabin boy. The man who bought me—that one over there." Dafydd pointed to the slaver who had lashed me earlier. "He heard me sing the night before the auction. He thought the captain might enjoy my talents. My duties were simple—keeping his cabin clean, his boots polished, serving his meals, a song now and then, amuse him, those sorts of tasks. The captain seemed pleased with my service. At least he rarely beat me and he allowed me to sleep on a pallet in his cabin where it was warm and dry. And he gave me this cloak to use as a blanket."

His fingers stroked the shiny, worn material. The cloak had been quite fine and costly when it had first been woven, many owners before. The colours had long since faded. Yet it was the first material possession of pure luxury either of us had ever owned and my brother was proud of it.

Something sinister lurked beneath his words that I could not quite place. An ugly truth within the outward innocence of his duties that felt painfully familiar. What was it?

"He rarely beat you, but there was something worse."

Dafydd sighed, pushing hair from his eyes. "Yes, there are things worse than a beating. Through it all, I always thought of you. In my mind, I would see your silent dignity as you endured the tortures the prince dealt you. And I would tell myself that no matter what indignity I might be suffering, it was nothing compared to yours."

I did not need to understand fully to see how his purity had been soiled. My body shook with my anger.

Dafydd put an arm around me and drew me close. "Please, Lin. It is past. Speaking of it will only stain this precious gift we have been given. How many people are allowed a second chance in life? How much more rare for those with collars?"

"Do you suppose this is merely some cruel jest of the gods? To be reunited only to face that dreadful moment of separation again?"

"I thought you no longer believed they existed, Lin."

"I know not what to believe any more. How is it you are no longer with the captain?"

"I was but on loan." Dafydd's face twisted in a grimace as though the words tasted bitter. "The captain never made an offer to purchase me and—"

"But he let you keep the cloak."

Dafydd nodded. "I had it easy compared to you from the looks of you. You are more thin and pale than ever. You have not been eating, have you?"

I shrugged. He knew me.

"You went the entire journey without food?"

"I was sick most of it. Times even water came back up. Life did not seem worth the effort without you."

Dafydd wagged his head. "You are incredible, Lin. Truly. A warrior's soul dwells within you. A lesser person would never have survived. I would not have."

"You are wrong. You have your stories, your songs, your dreams, and your great need to share them with the world. They are your protection from the despair I felt after the gavel fell and they led you away from me."

"I—"

"Do not apologise for being yourself, Dafydd. I envy you. I wish I could rise above my feelings and offer comfort as you do."

"The conditions below deck must have been beyond words. How cruel that I was given such privilege while you were chained like a beast."

I peered at the length of iron between his ankles.

"Privilege? You were on loan, Dafydd."

"I am glad you have not changed, Lin. You are as impossible as ever," he said, smiling. At least that part of him had remained the same. "I was worried for you. Worried that since you were alone, your fire might have been quenched. I am so very glad it was not. The world does not need more slaves. It needs more people like you."

CHAPTER 29

"Unwell again, Lin?" Dafydd whispered. He crouched beside me and rubbed my heaving shoulders.

"Get back in the line," I said, gulping air. "They will beat us both for lagging." Shuddering with my illness, I watched for signs of one of the slavers approaching. The nearest had already stopped.

"Let them." My brother made no move to rejoin the coffle limping by us. He draped a protective arm around me.

Where had he gained such defiance?

I wiped my mouth on my sleeve.

"My thanks, Dafydd, but I shall be fine. You know this rarely lasts beyond mid-morning." Indeed, the worst seemed over.

"Aye, but—"

"It is nothing," I said, standing to prove my point. "We will never catch up to Tighan now."

My brother grinned. "Impossible One. You think that matters?"

The slaver nudged his horse in our direction.

"Can you manage now?" Dafydd said.

I nodded and we slipped back into place.

At mid-day we had a brief rest and a dole of bread. The men driving us could not begrudge us water though. The brook we had paused beside did not belong to them. A pathetic sight. I am shamed to have been part of the surge of humanity sinking to its knees on the bank to press lips to the precious humours and gorge.

Prince Modred would have been proud to see me so reduced and humbled.

* * *

Later, our day's march ended, I felt the first cramp, much like from my monthly flow of woman's blood. How long since my last? It felt like years since I had left Dunn na Carraice, but knew that was not right. I tried to recall the phase of the moon at that time. Gave up as the cramp subsided and decided my courses must have begun. Or would soon.

Not far behind me my brother engaged Tighan in easy banter. The three of us and a few others had been assigned to gather wood. Dafydd said something that made Tighan giggle. I smiled, happy he could share his heart with someone besides me once more. He had always had a cache of friends in Dunn na Carraice. No surprise that he had already gathered more.

A second spasm of pain sent me to my knees, my armload of kindling scattered.

I felt Dafydd's presence at my side even before he spoke.

"Let me help you, Lin." He slipped an arm around my waist.

I did not resist his aid. Indeed, I leaned on him as I tried to rise, giving him assurances that he had naught to fret about.

"Did you trip?" He stopped abruptly, staring at my gown. "By the stars, you are bleeding."

"Of course I am, Dafydd," I said. "'Tis the flux."

He seemed on the verge of accepting when I doubled-over, gasping.

Too much blood. It had soaked through my gown and stained my fingers. My brother eased me to the ground as I wondered where and how I had been so sorely wounded.

He tore his cloak free of its knot and draped the rag over me just as the slaver on guard-duty reached us.

"Back to work, dogs." He cracked his whip in warning.

Dafydd shielded me from the lash.

I wanted to tell him to save himself, but— My head swam.

"Master, please. My sister needs help. She is bleeding."

I heard his pleas and tears as he spoke.

"What—"

"Help is here, Dafydd," Tighan said. She and an older woman hobbled towards us as fast as their chains would allow.

"My name is Morwen, child," the woman said, kneeling opposite my brother. Her fingers stroked my arm. "Tighan says you are called Lin?"

"Aye."

"Can the girl not have some privacy?" Morwen said over her shoulder to the hovering guard. "Where do you think she will go, bleeding the way she is? And in chains." She spoke without a trace of subservience.

I liked her.

"Privacy? For a slave? How amusing. Back to work."

Morwen knelt up and faced the man with the whip.

"You cannot sell a dead slave. I cannot promise you I'll be able to save her, but it's better than watching her bleed to death in this field."

That hit the mark, his purse. He left.

"How can I help?" Dafydd said.

"Keep yourself occupied with work in the camp. The time will pass easier for you. And send another girl back with a torch."

Dafydd began to rise, but I clutched a handful of his tunic. "Dafydd? Do something for me? Please?"

"You have only to ask, Lin. You know that."

"Sing for me?" If I was to die in that field, I wanted to give up the ghost hearing the only comfort I had ever gotten in life.

"It would be an honour. All will be well, Noble One. You shall see. You can conquer this easily." Forever the poet, my brother. He kissed my brow and managed a grin before leaving.

Morwen waited until the girl bearing the torch arrived. I never did learn her name. Tighan, her face ghostly, held my hand while Morwen eased the skirt of my gown over my hips.

The woman spoke calming words as she worked. Her hands were gentle in their probing of my most private places, trying to find the source of the bleeding.

From the direction of the camp I heard the hero's song Dafydd had made for me before our auction on Orkney. His voice sounded unsteady with his fears. I had not asked an easy favour from him. I clung to his gift.

Several moments later, Morwen withdrew her hands and sat on her heels.

"I'm sorry there is nothing I can do to help you, child. Your pains are coming too close together. Things are too far along for me to stop. You must ride out the pains. I have no herbs to ease them."

"Will I die, Morwen?"

"Only the gods know that, child. I can do no more than wait with you and then stanch the bleeding when the process has compleated its course."

The trio remained by my side, lending what little comfort they could by the light of a flickering torch. The pains seized my innards, twisting and squeezing, ripping them from their walls and expelling them into the dirt. Each ebbing barely long enough for me to draw breath before beginning anew.

Only cowards scream. And babies.

I also had my brother to think about. Cries of anguish would break his heart. I must be brave for Dafydd.

The pains ceased as abruptly as they began. Sweaty and exhausted from the exertion not to scream, I gasped for air. Allowed myself to relax.

"The worst is over, child. I am sorry I could not save your baby," Morwen said softly. Her hands kneaded the area of my belly where the pain had been most intense.

What was she saying?

"It was too soon for the little one to enter the world This babe simply wasn't meant to be. But there will be others. You are young. Perhaps too young to have carried a child the full term. Do you want me to tell the babe's father for you? Oft times such sorry news is easier coming from the midwife."

Midwife?

"Baby? Father? What do you mean?" I tried to sit up, but Tighan held my shoulders back.

"Did you not know you were with child?" Morwen said.

"With child?"

"I thought you knew by your morning sickness."

So. The prince had succeeded at putting his bastard into me and I had not even known. And Morwen assumed Dafydd was the father. I found the situation absurdly funny.

Morwen, Tighan, and the torchbearer stared at me while I laughed.

Thus the fate of Prince Modred's bastard. Fitting attendants and surroundings, I should say.

At last I dabbed my eyes dry, explaining that Dafydd was my brother.

"There is no need to tell him anything, Morwen. I can manage that."

After Morwen and Tighan bathed away the blood, Tighan went to fetch Dafydd.

"How is she," he asked, drawing near.

"I am fine, Dafydd."

"I thought you might be asleep, Lin. Sorry." He knelt beside me and took up my hand.

"Don't be. You must have been frantic."

"Indeed. Can she be moved, Morwen? She should be closer to the fire, I think."

"Aye, she should. She's out of danger. For now."

"Now?" Dafydd said.

"Don't fret, lad. Let's get her warm."

Dafydd carried me across the field.

Normally, our companions crowded selfishly around the small fire allotted us. But as Dafydd stepped into the ring of light, I could see they had cleared an area large enough for him to lay me down.

"Do you want me to stay?" Morwen said, mainly to Dafydd.

"I can manage." He tucked his cloak around me once more. It had gotten cast aside as Morwen began her ministrations.

"He has tended my wounds many times, Morwen."

"If you're certain. Watch for signs of fresh blood. See that she gets water, perhaps a little broth down."

"How can we thank you, Morwen?" Dafydd said.

"I wish I could have done more. I'll talk to our masters, try to get them to remain camped tomorrow. Your sister needs rest. I fear a full day's march so soon would—"

"Would kill her," Dafydd asked.

Morwen patted my brother's shoulder. "Send for me if you need me."

Tighan excused herself as well.

"See if you can find some moulding bread," Dafydd said to her. "The more green with the stuff, the better."

Our friend peered at him as though he had lost his reason.

"Yes, Tighan. Mould. 'Tis a trick for wound care I learned…from a friend."

"I'll try, Dafydd."

"Thank you."

"It was a baby," I said after she left. "I had not even realized I was with child. That is why I have been sick every morning."

"I am sorry. You must—"

"You are well come to your grief, Dafydd. I have none. That child was conceived in hatred. It is better off now."

"You cannot mean that, Lin."

"I can. And I do."

"Still… The poor tiny soul. And all the pain you had to suffer for it."

"I will kill any man who tries to touch me like that again, Dafydd."

"Please, do not speak of murder, Lin. You cannot cancel out a crime by committing one yourself."

"How do *I* heal, then? Shame stains my soul. How can I scrub it clean?"

Dafydd stroked my cheek. "My brave Noble One. I would sing it clean, if I could."

* * *

I received a purseful of compassion from the slavers. They allowed the extra day of rest on Morwen's suggestion, not wanting to lose any profit so close to their destination. But they drove us the harder the last three days of our journey to make up for the lost time.

The closer we drew to Ebrauc, the more crowded the road became with other travellers on their way to the great market. I did not know there could be so many people in all the world, let alone gathered in one place. Men and women pushed by us, more concerned with their own affairs to pay our ragged band the slightest attention.

And as for the city—the walled fortress was easily three and more times larger than Queen Morgause's dunn. Her palace was but a hovel compared to the Roman splendour rising before me. The stone walls touched the sky.

Along one wall a field had been allotted for travellers. It was a city unto itself with the tents and pavilions—tinted in every colour of the rainbow—already in place. Merchants had set up their wares amidst the campsites to make the best use of the remaining sun to sell everything imaginable and more besides. Musicians and storytellers roamed about in search of an audience. Farmers hawked produce. Beasts of all sizes brayed and neighed and bleated and squawked and barked. Legs of lamb and haunches of beef roasted on spits, their aromas mingling with frying fish and stewing chickens.

Children darted from camp to camp, free to laugh and play. Free of collars and chains. One stopped and watched our lurching procession. The girl's dress, face and hair were clean and tidy, her feet shod. Her gaze met mine for a moment before she turned away.

"Why are those people in chains, Mother?"

The woman's dress was of the same vivid green as her daughter's. Seated in a chair at the entrance of their pavilion, she glanced up from her needlework and surveyed us with a look of disgust.

"Cath." The sharp cry startled her child. "Come away at once, Cath. They are slaves."

"Foolish woman," I said to Dafydd. "She has no notion of how little it would take to turn the tables on her. She and her child could quite easily be in our place."

"Aye, Lin. We spend our lives balanced on a knife."

"And tomorrow—"

"Let us live for the now. We haven't much else."

We reached a clearing that suited the slavers and set to work. I watched my brother on the opposite side of the camp, as good-natured as ever. Quick with his smile, laughing at another boy's wit, lending assistance. What chance did we have of being together on the morrow's sunset?

Since the miscarriage, the others had been most kind to me, expressing sympathy for my loss and relieving some of my heavier burdens. I appreciated the latter. As to the sympathy? What did I have to mourn? The product of violence and hate? It was *his* child.

Why can I not be more like my brother? He seemed to shrug off the indignities of slavery and rise above them. His songs of heroes openly mocked our masters. Try as I might, I would never come close to his humanity.

"More meat, girl," the slaver named Anfri shouted.

By right of ten coins, I belonged to him. My back to the man, I spat into his bowl before ladling stew into it.

His partner, the one who had bought Dafydd and loaned him to the captain, drained his cup and belched. He thrust it in my path as I returned to Anfri.

I peered into his half-closed eyes.

"By the powers. You're a cold bitch," he said, his body swaying even though he was sitting. "I wager I could warm you with this." He patted his whip.

Two other girls shared the duty of serving the slave traders. I beckoned the one bearing the wine jug. She hastened to fill the man's cup.

Long after the sun set on what might very well be my last day with my brother, Anfri released me from duty. The other girls were older, prettier. They remained. I pitied them.

I found Dafydd and Tighan and sank to the ground beside them.

"I don't think I can take another step," I said.

"Did you eat, Lin?"

I nodded.

Dafydd stretched his arms over his head and yawned.

Tighan moved behind him and began to knead the muscles of his neck and shoulders.

"Hmmm… That is nice, Tighan. If I do not fall asleep, I shall return the favour."

"Don't you dare fall asleep, Dafydd *ap* Elen." She tried to sound stern, but her giggle came through.

Dafydd grinned at the mention of Mother. He grasped Tighan's hand as it boldly slid forward to his chest.

She squealed as he pressed her fingers to his lips.

"You make it impossible to remain angry with you, Dafydd." Tighan embraced him from behind. "Has he always been such a loveable rogue, Lin?"

"Girls have never held any hope against his charm," I said, but their play stabbed my heart. I felt more like an intruder than a sister. I rested my chin on my knees, staring at the fire. Memories of Padrig haunted my mind. His smile while we had danced. His soft, warm kiss.

His battered face after the prince finished beating him.

I rubbed my eyes, hoping to erase that last vision.

How could Dafydd and Tighan be so light-hearted? He now soothed her muscles under his gentle caresses.

"What's it like to be sold?" Tighan whispered the last word.

My brother gathered his friend into his arms, peering at me over her shoulder.

Neither of us had spoken of our experience on the block since reuniting.

Dafydd heaved a sigh, "Beastly," he said. "Standing on that block, warm from countless feet before mine ever touched it, I was no longer Dafydd *ap* Elen."

* * *

I stretched my legs before me, working the stiffness out as a cock crew somewhere amongst the campsites. Our fire had gone cold hours earlier. I had watched the red coals fade.

Soon now.

Too soon.

"You did not sleep last night, did you," Dafydd asked, sitting up.

Tighan, wrapped in my brother's cloak, did not stir.

"No," I said.

"Thinking about today?"

Tears had already begun to choke me. I doubt I could have uttered a simple "yes." I nodded.

"You'll be dead on your feet."

"Perhaps my price will go down for it."

Dafydd gave me a fierce hug, trying his best to hold tight rein of his own tears.

"Never let them break your spirit, Noble One."

I performed my morning duties through habit alone. Anfri accused me of being made of wood. He came close to the mark.

But I gave him no cause to beat me. Dafydd had no need for that additional heartache.

At mid-day, we stood in a pavilion within Ebrauc's walls and waited our turn for the block.

Again.

Tighan clung to my brother's arm.

He tried his best to soothe her fears.

I needed his comfort as well, yet held myself a step away, my back straight and my head held high.

"Are you not frightened, Lin?" Tighan said. "How can you be so calm?"

"Lin? Afraid?" Dafydd said. "Her skin is like chain mail."

The gavel.

"Sold."

Morwen was gone.

Inside, I flinched.

To the world, I held my face steady.

Calm? Silent witnesses, we watched as each of our companions got knocked down. One after another a fellow human enriched the purses of heartless men.

A mere handful of people remained before me in line. And one on the block.

"I call it dead, Tighan. You have only had to suffer separation from your brother once."

"Lin," Dafydd whispered.

I shook my head, unable to face him.

Coward.

Aye.

The gavel fell again. The girl who had borne the torch.

I will not live another day without my brother. Whoever buys me next will own a corpse by eventide. Do you hear me?

My brother's hand rested on my shoulder. He repeated my name.

I wanted to fling myself into his arms, hold him fast. Instead, I brushed his hand.

"How tender. Move, dogs."

I shuffled another step closer to the block.

"No farewell, Lin?" Dafydd's voice cracked.

"I cannot, Dafydd. Not twice." If I turned and saw his anguish, a mirror of my own, my strength would dissolve and they would need to drag me up there to the platform.

I could never allow that.

"Please?"

The bids for the boy on display grew lively. But they did not drown out my brother's plea.

Then I noticed a man enter the pavilion. People had been coming and going since the auction began, but this man had an air of importance in his bearing and a sword at his hip. A soldier? No common soldier, I'd wager. His eyes scanned the activities.

"Hold," he said, just loud enough to be heard above the bidding.

Silence fell and heads turned.

"By whose authority?" Anfri said from the platform.

"The Pendragon's."

The world stopped. Who was this man?

"You are breaking the Pendragon's law, selling slaves," he said, striding through the crowd. "You are nicked, boy-o. These children are no longer slaves."

Had I heard him correctly? Slaves no longer? My heart raced. Dafydd and I exchanged a brief questioning glance.

The Pendragon's man started at the far end of the line and cut the first collar with his meat knife.

Anfri leapt from the platform.

"Keep your hands off my property," he shouted.

"You have no property. These people are free subjects of the Pendragon."

Free?

"And just who might you be?" Anfri still stood undaunted.

The newcomer spun, drawing his sword. He levelled it at Anfri's throat.

"I am Cai, the Pendragon's seneschal. And foster-brother. Rest assured, I do hold his authority in this. Any other questions?"

Anfri stared at the naked blade, mere inches below his nose. He shook his head.

"Good." Sir Cai resheathed his weapon and returned to cutting collars.

What a proud moment to see my brother's collar fall away.

I could scarce believe this turn in my life.

Sir Cai's hand wavered when he reached for my collar. Surprise flared in his eyes and then vanished just as quickly. Without a word, he cut the leather from my neck and moved to the next person.

I was free.

CHAPTER 30

"If only Sir Cai could remove your brand as easily as he did your collars, Lin," Tighan said.

I nodded as though in a dream. Free? I savoured the word's taste. I touched the pale band of skin of Dafydd's neck that his collar had hidden from the sun for two years. Touched my own. Was this real?

"What is wrong, Lin? Are you not happy?" My brother gripped my shoulders, his smiling blue-grey eyes regarding me.

"Of course, I am happy, Dafydd. It's…"

A smith arrived to pry open our chains. That weight gone, my soul soared.

"Would that Prince Modred could see you now," Dafydd said, retrieving his collar from the damp earth.

I rubbed my brand. "The prince can rot."

"We can do whatever we want. Go anywhere. It is like we have been reborn. Ah, the endless possibilities."

"We need to find a way to live," I said.

"I shall sing my way to Camelot for you, Lin."

I smiled knowing things would not be so easy. But loving the offer.

My brother belted out a raucous tune, taking Tighan into his arms. They danced around the base of the platform.

How would we survive? We knew nothing of the world. What about my brand? Questions crowded my mind, threatening to choke my joy.

I watched Sir Cai, the noblest man in all of Britain for sparing me a second separation from my brother.

He worked with efficiency, directing a pair of warriors to take the slavers to the palace guard room in chains. Some of my companions in bondage spit at the men filing past. Others hurled their collars.

I scooped up a handful of soft muck and took aim at Anfri and hit him in the eye. My accuracy garnered applause. It also earned me a frown from Dafydd.

My moment of spite done, I approached the seneschal before he left to crow over his good deed to his friends.

"Many thanks for your kindness, my lord. But what will we do now?"

The seneschal surveyed our ragged band, frowning. The last of the chains had been removed. What was left for him here? He could go back to his business, forget about us.

A dozen newly free subjects of the Pendragon looked to him expectantly for guidance.

"Follow me," he said. "I can promise you a decent meal. Clean clothes."

A cheer rose from us. In eager anticipation of full bellies, we would have followed him to *Annwn*.

"Are you always so forward, lass?" Sir Cai said as we stepped from the pavilion.

Forward? Had I not—

"Forgive, my lord. I but—"

"How long have you been in slavery?"

"Since birth, my lord."

"You thought I would abandon you and the others? Leave you to fend for yourselves?"

"You are the Pendragon's seneschal. You must be very busy with his affairs and cannot be bothered with the likes of us, my lord."

"You are the Pendragon's... He will rejoice in your new freedom, for he does not abide slavery in his realm. Tell me, who was your master before this lot took you on?"

He asked me several other questions in the short distance to the palace.

The courtyard was a flurry of activity not unlike Dunn na Carraice. Filled with warriors, servants. Visitors? Not a collar in sight.

A red and gold standard flew beneath the heavens, fluttering in the breeze. Everyone knew and recognised the gold dragon of our high king. I had heard it described often enough. I paused to stare at the wondrous sight, my heart stirring.

"He is here, Dafydd," I whispered.

Sir Cai stopped a young man and gave him orders to provide us food. With a full belly, my mind would be clearer. Then we could formulate a plan—Dafydd, Tighan, and me.

"Come with me, lass," Sir Cai said, at my side once more. "You and your companions." He nodded at my brother and Tighan.

He did not spare us a moment.

We ran to catch up with the seneschal across the smoothly paved courtyard. At the top of a flight of stairs, we entered a small chamber. A closed door stood at its far end.

Sir Cai told us to wait.

"Arthur," he said as he opened the door without knocking. He did not close it behind him. "Arthur, this cannot wait." Sir Cai walked to the man seated at a desk, piled high with scrolls.

The Pendragon? My heart tripped. What a morning. Freedom and now the Pendragon?

"Cai. I am busy." The Pendragon, clearly not pleased with the interruption, directed Sir Cai's attention to the third man in the chamber.

"My apologies. But trust me. You know I would not disturb you were it not important."

The King studied his seneschal. What he saw must have satisfied him, for he nodded.

"Very well, Cai," he said. "We shall finish this later, Peredur."

The man he had been in audience with rose, saluted, then left. We stood aside for the nobleman to pass. He did not close the door either. Nor did he glance our way.

Sir Cai stepped around the desk to speak privately to the King.

I watched from the doorway, fascinated by the man who had inspired so many stories and invoked warriors to unite under his banner. My first impulse was to kneel, for surely I was in the presence of Lugh, god of the sun incarnate.

His features and spun-gold hair favoured Morgan rather than the Queen of Orkney.

"Bugger me, Dafydd. He's beautiful," I whispered.

"Let me have a look." Tighan wriggled between us. It wasn't every day that former slaves had such a close view of the Pendragon. We were not about to let the chance slip by us.

"He is handsome, isn't he," she asked.

The King's expression, annoyed at first, turned quickly to puzzlement as he listened to Sir Cai. At one point, the King said, "Where?"

He glanced up and saw us watching.

I did not cast my gaze aside. When would I ever have another opportunity such as this? I ignored Dafydd's hand tugging my sleeve. This was not Orkney. I was not dealing with Prince Modred. And I was merely looking.

"Come in, lass." The gentleness of his voice took me by surprise.

"Me?"

"Aye, lass."

I drew a deep breath and stepped over the threshold, into the presence of the Pendragon. For the first time in my life I felt humble. Here was a man who commanded armies. Defeated Saxons. Creator of the Round Table. The most powerful man in Britain. Maybe even the world. And I was covered in muck, ragged, barefoot, and bruised. Not at all presentable to anything above a gutter. My proud defiance against Prince Modred had fled. Should I bend my knee to this man? Should I bow?

I peered over my shoulder at my brother and Tighan hoping to regain a grain or two of courage.

"You have naught to fear, lass. I do not bite."

"The men would disagree, Arthur."

"That will be all, Cai."

The seneschal left, closing the door behind him.

The Pendragon was a much younger man than I had expected. A man with the worlds of experience he had and the lifetime of passing judgement upon other men surely required many more years than this man possessed.

It would never do to allow such a man to see me trembling. I crossed the room, my back arrow straight and my head held high. The tread of my bare feet made no sound on the wood floor. My heart pounded in my breast.

"That's right. Here, by my desk. Do you know who I am, lass?"

For a High King, I found him to be plainly dressed. He wore no crown, nor any other badge of rank as far as I could tell. Nor was there much in the room that signified the presence of a king. His desk and chair, a brazier, a sword and scabbard hanging from a hook on the wall—Excalibur?—had he drawn it from a stone?—a second chair facing the desk, a sideboard with pitcher, cups and a bowl of fruit were the entire furnishings. But there was no doubt as to who this man was.

"Yes, *tigernos*," I said, using the loftiest title I knew. "You are the Pendragon."

I now stood directly in front of his desk, hardly more than an arm's length away from Britain's champion.

"Well come to Ebrauc." His smile was a warm and genuine reenforcement to his words.

I had found true nobility. My head reeled, overwhelmed with the sensations and emotions the man evoked within me.

"My thanks, *tigernos*." I bowed my head in my first ever act of deference.

"You must be thirsty, lass." He walked to the sideboard and filled a cup. Returning, he offered it to me.

The Pendragon, serving me? This would be sight for Prince Modred.

I stared at the cup.

"'Tis but water, lass."

"I... My thanks, *tigernos*." I took the cup, surprised that my hands were steady, and drank.

"More?" He was at the sideboard refilling the cup before I could answer. "What's your name, lass," he asked.

"Lin, *tigernos*."

"Lin. I like that better than lass, don't you?"

"And many other things besides, *tigernos*."

"Oh?"

I drained the second cup as quickly as the first.

"I have been called many things, *tigernos*. None of them pleasant. And rarely by my name. Lass is a vast improvement."

"I see. Sit down, Lin." The King indicated the chair last occupied by a nobleman.

"But..."

"Something wrong?" He took the cup from me and set it aside.

"Only Dafydd has ever been so kind to me, *tigernos*."

"You are a guest of my household, Lin. Everyone who comes under my roof, rich or poor, is treated with courtesy, whether I am at Camelot or any of my holdings. Everyone is provided refreshment and lodgings as needed."

He brushed aside sheaves from his desktop. Several tumbled to the floor.

Without a thought, I knelt to gather them up, honoured to perform a duty for this man.

"You needn't do this, Lin. It was my fault." The Pendragon was on one knee beside me, close enough for me to notice the blue of his eyes. The shade of a cloudless summer sky and very nearly identical to—Prince Modred's. But with a great deal more of summer's warmth within them.

Disconcerted by the unexpected reminder of my nemesis, I diverted my attention to the work, hoping the King would not notice. Although I doubted there was much, if anything, he missed.

"I do not mind, *tigernos*. I have spent all of my life cleaning up after others."

Together, we gathered the fallen scrolls and maps and returned them to his desk.

"My thanks, Lin. Be at ease now and sit. Please."

I settled myself into the chair, sliding my hands over the smooth wood of the arms. I marvelled at the richness of such an ordinary experience.

"Cai told me he cut this from your neck recently." The Pendragon sat on the edge of his desk, clutching my collar.

My hand went to my throat, still feeling the leather's shadowy presence.

"Yes, *tigernos*."

"Where did you come from, Lin?"

"From Orkney, *tigernos*."

"Quite a distance. Were you born there?"

"Yes, *tigernos*."

"Are your parents still there?"

"Dafydd and I were orphaned many years ago when our mother passed over, *tigernos*. Neither of us ever knew our fathers, they were not the same man."

"I gather Dafydd is your brother?"

"Yes, *tigernos*. He is just outside."

"Indeed. Tell me about Orkney."

How much had his seneschal told him about what he had found in the pavilion?

"May I ask a question, *tigernos*?"

"Certainly."

"Do you know what that is you are holding, *tigernos*?"

"Tell me." The King leaned forward to listen, his arms folded across his chest. His face unreadable.

"It was a slave's collar, *tigernos*. Dafydd and I were born in slavery. I hated seeing it on my brother's neck. I hated the strangling feel of it on my own."

This time I raised both hands to touch my neck again. The sleeves of my gown slid down.

I heard the King's breath catch.

"That's a rather nasty scar. How did you come by it?"

"That, *tigernos*, is Prince Modred's handiwork. He marked me as his property with a horse brand. He wanted me to always remember my station. Dafydd calls it my hero's mark, because I did not cry out in pain when the glowing iron touched my flesh."

"Truly? Were you beaten often?"

"At every opportunity."

I saw the Pendragon's anger plainly in his blue eyes. A familiar sight and I felt myself cringe in fear for the first time in my life. The prince was nothing but a bastard. I hated the prince. The Pendragon was different. I did not wish to anger him. I had never wanted to please anyone except Dafydd until now. I wanted very much to please this man who was Pendragon.

Through the tangled veil of my hair, I saw his hand advance.

"Please, *tigernos*. I meant no disrespect. Beat me if you must, but please, do not send me away."

I gripped the arms of the chair and braced myself for the worst.

"Beat you? Certainly not. Nor do I have any intention of sending you away. You have not angered me, Lin. You were answering my questions. Commendably. This is what has angered me." He shook the fist still clutching my collar. "It angers me that a woman of my own blood would sanction branding at all, much less a child.

"I only want to see your face, Lin. It is important for a ruler to see to whom he is talking." He brushed my hair behind my ears and raised my chin. The anger that had so recently made me cower had softened with compassion for what I had suffered at the hands of his kin. "Much better. You are a lovely girl, Lin. As pretty as any at Camelot. How old are you?"

"Twelve at Beltane, *tigernos*."

"Then I should say you are a lovely young woman."

I felt the colour rise to my cheeks.

"You mean no boy has ever told you he thought you pretty?"

"No, *tigernos*. Not really. Padrig… Padrig was sold for showing an interest in me. Prince Modred always said I was ugly and stupid."

"Modred is wrong. You are neither. Were all the princes of Orkney equally cruel to as Modred?"

"Not all *tigernos*. Mainly Prince Modred. His mother had given me to him as a gift. The day I got my collar. As his property, he could do as he liked with me."

Were any of them in Ebrauc at the moment? Would they try to take me back?

"I see. How is it you are no longer in Dunn na Carraice?"

"I was sold, *tigernos*. To the men Sir Cai had arrested."

"Where are my manners?" the King said, turning aside. "You have had a gruelling journey and worse, and I interrogate you without offering what little I have on hand. You must be hungry, Lin."

I hugged my arms around myself and shivered. "I—"

"You are cold."

I nodded.

"These Roman rooms were designed for warmer climes than what we have here in Britain, especially this far north. Even in summer, we must have braziers lit."

He rose, went and swung his own chair around to face the brazier. He stoked the glowing embers and added a fresh log. Sparks swirled heavenward as it fell into place.

He returned and lifted me into his arms. His cream-coloured woollen tunic was soft against my cheek and clean smelling.

"Dear God. You are naught but skin and bones, child. And your gown is threadbare. No wonder you are cold. Is this all you had to wear in Dunn na Carraice?"

"I used to have a shift as well, *tigernos*. But it was torn by the men at Orkney's slave pen. They wanted to inspect their merchandise. So they stripped me. On the roadside. One of the men—"

"Speak no more, if this is too painful, Lin." He pressed me closer to his chest. It was a protective gesture. An act of compassion by a king looking out for one of his defenceless, homeless subjects. I could understand the love and respect the people and his warriors had for him. So even though his arms could easily have broken me, I had no fear.

His cloak was draped over the back and arms of his chair. He settled me into it and wrapped the luxurious folds of tightly woven scarlet wool around me.

"Warmer?"

The entire experience was beyond my reckoning. I could only nod.

"Cai is having a proper meal sent for you and your companions. I am afraid all I have is this to offer you."

He returned from the sideboard with an apple. Red and unblemished. He held it to me. The sight of it made my mouth water.

"Take it, Lin. It's yours."

My fingers closed around the apple and for an instant we both held the fruit.

"My thanks, *tigernos*."

Knowing it would do little to appease my hunger, I was none the less grateful. I tried not to devour the crisp, sweet delicacy too quickly, and strove for a bit of dignity while I ate.

The King waited for me to finish.

"If you please, *tigernos*. What will become of us?" I asked when I had licked the juice from my fingers.

"Who?" He tossed the core into the fire and the room soon filled with the sweet perfume.

"I mean Dafydd and me and the others. As slaves, our masters were obliged to feed and clothe and shelter us, begrudging as some of them might have been about it. We have no means to support ourselves now. We have no place to sleep. Will we be turned into the streets? Reduced to begging? *Tigernos*?"

"Reduced? From slavery?"

"Even in a collar, *tigernos*, I have never begged for anything. Now that I am free of the collar and the prince I do not intend to start."

"You will have no need to resort to begging, I promise."

"And Dafydd?"

"And Dafydd. Tell me more about Modred."

"What is to tell, *tigernos*? He considered me his property. When he tired of me, he sold me. He is also your kinsman, *tigernos*. Do I dare speak ill of him?"

"Speak the truth. No one has ever come to harm in my presence for honesty." There was a soft rap on the door. "Come," the King called.

Sir Cai entered. "Everything is arranged, Arthur," he said.

"Excellent. Lin, I have enjoyed our talk. I am glad Cai brought you to my attention so I could see for myself the blight still afflicting my lands. I would like to hear more of your story."

My time with the Pendragon was at an end. I peeled off his cloak and stood, staring up into his eyes. I cannot say what compelled me to do it, I just knew I had to kneel for this great man. He was unlike anyone I had ever known. Even Dafydd.

"My thanks, *tigernos*, for your generosity and the honour to speak to you. I shall never forget it."

"Nor shall I." With a hand he raised me to my feet. "Rest at ease, Lin. You will have no wants or needs while under my roof. No abuse. Later we can give thought to your future. For the now, be assured you'll be cared for and sheltered. Cai will show you to your quarters."

He smiled. Its warmth filled the room.

"If you'll come with me, lass," the seneschal said from the doorway.

I followed him to the outer chamber where Dafydd and Tighan still waited.

Dafydd leapt from his chair and rushed to my side.

"Well?"

"Not now, Dafydd. I just want to bask in what just occurred." My body tingled from the experience. "I do not want to pick it apart and ruin it."

We were shown to our quarters, which until that moment I had assumed would be in the hall with all the other staff and our travelling companions. But I was given a room with an antechamber to share with Tighan, and Dafydd had one to himself.

"Feel free to avail yourselves of the room's contents. You should have everything you require. Food is on its way." Sir Cai left before any of us had a chance to question.

Tighan and I explored the inner chamber, not sure what to expect. We found a bed with a thick straw stuffed mattress, large enough for at least four people, piled high with fur bed-robes and pillows. Someone had spread two sets of lady's garments, compleat from white linen shifts to matching hair ribbons, neatly on the bed. Beside the bed was a huge copper tub filled with steaming water.

We stared in wonder at the sumptuous provisions.

"Do you think he made a mistake, Lin?" Tighan whispered. I think, like me, she was afraid everything might vanish if she spoke aloud.

"I hope not." I stripped off my rags and tossed them to the floor.

Tighan paused only a heartbeat longer.

What a luxury to wash in warm water rather than an icy stream, and with soap. We assisted each other, scrubbing and rinsing our hair, then our backs. All the while, Tighan chattered about the turn of our fortunes. I listened and responded when necessary. Our fortunes certainly had turned. The pattern of my life was now unfamiliar to me. Freedom. Largess. Humility. In a matter of hours. But how long until we were homeless? We could not expect the Pendragon to support us very long. What would we do then?

Would I always be dependent upon someone else?

I pushed those cynical thoughts aside. I simply needed time to adjust to such an extraordinary day. And rest. After I ate, I promised myself a test of that bed.

I stepped out of the tub and dried off.

Tighan was already dressing. She had chosen the gown of woad blue. My gown was the colour of new grass. Then we went to the antechamber to brush and comb our hair. Tighan was just finishing tying a ribbon at the end of my braid when someone knocked. She answered it and a well-dressed young man entered.

"Dafydd, you look splendid," I said.

He had been as well provisioned as Tighan and me. Tunic, trews, belt, boots, no detail had been left out.

"And I have never laid eyes upon two more beautiful beings. You look like princesses."

"Oh, Dafydd." Tighan giggled at his flattery.

Before long, our meal arrived, consisting of two whole roasted chickens, several thick slices of ham and of beef, joints of lamb, a pitcher of milk and of water. And the bread. We could chew it without having to soften it in milk first. And there was honey and clotted cream. A veritable feast in our eyes and stomachs. We hardly knew where to start.

While we ate, Dafydd and Tighan questioned me about my audience with the Pendragon. My brother was speechless when I got to the end.

"You? Kneeling?"

"The Pendragon is everything Custennin said about him and more. Every fragment of gossip we heard of his glory is true. I do not regret the deference."

"What do you think will happen next?" Tighan asked. She wiped her fingers on a cloth.

"I don't know," I answered. "The King told me he wanted to hear more of Orkney. Queen Morgause is his sister. Naturally he would be curious. I guess we wait and see."

"If I eat another bite, I shall burst." Dafydd pushed himself from the table and walked to the brazier. "Will you help me, Lin?"

"Name it."

He pulled a dark slender shape from his sleeve. As he stared at it, I realised it was his collar.

"Here." He held it out to me. Dafydd must have used a meat knife to slice away the lock. "I would like you to have this honour, Lin. No one fought against it harder than you. No one deserves to destroy it more than you."

I joined him.

"The King kept mine," I said. It seemed a curious act for a king. I regretted not being able to burn it as well.

I tossed the collar into the flames.

"We're free, Dafydd," I said.

My brother slipped an arm around my waist as we watched the fire consume the despised leather band.

"Free. You asked earlier if I felt lighter. I feel human."

CHAPTER 31

"Lin, wake up."

Tighan said something about the Pendragon that made no sense. And I had not heard the cock crow either. It could not possibly be dawn. I rolled over and nestled deeper into the bed-coverings, wanting to prolong my dream of freedom and meeting the High King.

"Lin. Hurry. You mustn't make him wait." She shook my shoulder.

"Who?"

"The Pendragon. Have you not heard a word I've said? He is in the other room."

I bolted upright, fingering my neck. My collar was gone. I had not dreamed it. I stared about me. The shadows in the room had shifted.

"Did I sleep all night, Tighan?"

"The sun hasn't set yet, Lin. But you must hasten. It would be unseemly to make the High King wait overlong."

Unseemly? It would be right out impertinence. Conduct I wished to avoid for a change. It would never do to repay his generosity so rudely.

Tighan helped me dress and brush out my hair. We had no time to plait it, so I left it hanging loose around my shoulders and went into the antechamber.

The Pendragon stood near the table where we had consumed our feast earlier. Its remains had been cleared away. A flagon and cups were left.

My first impressions were confirmed. He was a beautiful man, lean and well-muscled from daily exercise and drills. Still dressed in the simple tunic and trews and boots I had seen earlier, he now wore his scarlet cloak as well with its folds thrown over his shoulders. At his left breast was a brooch of gold as large as my fist, fashioned into a dragon. It glistened in the uneven lantern-light. He embodied every hero's tale and song I had ever heard. The sight was enough to make a young girl's head spin.

"Greetings, *tigernos*," I said.

His gaze swept over me from head to foot and back.

I did not know what to do with my empty hands. A strange feeling, for I normally had them filled with some sort of heavy burden. I clasped them in front of me.

I felt my cheeks warm at his smile of apparent approval. Giving him one of my own was easy.

Tighan curtsied and excused herself to join Dafydd in his chamber.

"Cai did well in providing for you and your friends, I see. You had plenty to eat?"

"Oh yes, *tigernos*. More than was necessary. You are most generous. We are very grateful." Perhaps I should have curtsied like Tighan had.

"And you are rested from your journey?"

"Yes, *tigernos*."

"Good. You must have been very tired."

"Yes, *tigernos*."

"Come sit with me, Lin. No need to remain on our feet." He gestured to the chair opposite him. "I did not mean for your friend to awaken you. I could have returned later."

"You are the Pendragon. We must do your bidding."

"I am the Pendragon. I do as the people bid me."

I thought that a curious statement, but who was I?

"I know you must have questions as to why Cai singled you out this morning and brought you to me personally, when a simple report would have sufficed."

Questions crowded my head, but I forced myself to wait on the King's lead. I nodded.

"You must certainly have wondered about your quarters and provisions."

"Yes, *tigernos*. They are much finer than I deserve."

He frowned.

"I do not mean to sound ungrateful, *tigernos*. I thank you with all my heart for your kindness. It is just that I…I am unworthy."

"Cai had his reasons. He thought you resembled someone he knows, as well as someone else he once knew. Someone who had gone to Orkney a dozen years ago and would be about your age now. His suspicions were aroused when he heard you had belonged to Prince Modred. You were brought to me to be certain.

"Cai was right. Between us, we have no doubt you are the person he had in mind when he first saw you in the slavers' pavilion."

"But how can this be, *tigernos*? How can he know me? I have never been off Orkney until now. And I would remember a visit by so high a personage as Sir Cai."

"No doubt Orkney is all you remember. But you were not born in Dunn na Carraice, Lin. And certainly not in slavery."

"How can you know this, *tigernos*? If I might ask, who is it I resemble?"

"Your mother."

"My mother? She was at Camelot once and you knew her, *tigernos*?" I forgot for the moment that Dafydd looked like Mother, not me.

The Pendragon nodded, smiling with what I assumed was a fond, distant memory. Had Mother been a serving maid—perhaps even to the High Queen—before misfortune struck, sending her to Orkney and slavery and her death?

"I know your mother quite well, in fact."

What was he saying? He spoke as if she was still in this world.

"But surely, *tigernos*, my mother is dead."

"I assure you, she is not, Lin."

"But I saw them carry her out." The King spoke in riddles. Cruel riddles, at that. Or was he wrong about me? Yes, that must be the answer. I could not possibly be the person he believed me to be.

"I see you are distressed, Lin. You were born at Camelot."

"Camelot?" Even Dafydd never dreamed that. Then another thought struck me. "Do you know my father as well, *tigernos*? Was he… Is he an *eques*?"

The Pendragon chuckled softly.

"Of a sort. Lin." He leaned forward, resting his arms on the table and paused.

His gaze caught mine and I found it impossible to break free. Odd how the same shade of blue can possess such utterly opposite properties between two men. Here was the warmth and compassion that the prince's eyes had lacked. Words might not always speak true, but eyes never lie. This man, who was Pendragon, knew mercy and kindness.

"Lin. Your mother is my wife. *I* am your father."

Had I been standing, I doubt my legs would have supported me.

"Your wife, *tigernos*? The High Queen?"

"Gwenhwyfar."

But if… Oh.

"And you?"

"Aye."

"Then Dafydd is not…"

"I'm afraid not, Lin."

The revelation was like a blow to my chest that left me winded. Dafydd was not my brother. Not even my half-brother as we had always believed. Nothing else seemed to seep into my addled brain. All that mattered to me at the moment was my loss of a brother. I sat stunned, staring at the tabletop.

"Lin?" I heard the King's concern. Heard liquid spilling into a cup. Unable to form words, I looked up at the King. At my father.

At my father.

He pressed the cup into my hand. "Here. Drink. It's watered wine. It should take the edge off the shock. I wish I'd had some other way of telling you."

I swallowed the wine, then set the cup aside.

"My thanks, *tigernos*."

"Please, no more *'tigernos,'* Lin."

"What should I call you then, *tig*… I mean, sir?"

"I am your father. Sir will do, until… Sir will do."

Numb, I sat rigid in my chair.

"Lin, you know that Morgause is my sister by half?"

I nodded, afraid my voice would fail me if I tried to speak.

"Before you were born, your mother and I had plans to send our son to Lancelot's family in Armorica, to be trained as a warrior and statesman. And to keep him safe from enemies. I selfishly assumed I would be given a son. I had no plans for a daughter."

A shiver ran through me as I recalled the conversation with Dafydd and Meg about the Pendragon's daughter. How I had doubted her existence.

"Besides," the Pendragon said. "I had—"

"Other more pressing matters to consider?" My hand flew to my mouth.

"I deserved that, Lin. I want you to speak your mind. Especially about your life in Dunn na Carraice. But yes, the Saxons were pressing forward from their territory. More Irish were raiding our western shores. Local chieftains—by far the worst of the lot—required placating. It all took up more time than I had.

"Morgause was in Camelot at the time of your birth. I was away on campaign. Had I been home, I would have sent the scheming shrew back to Dunn na Carraice, for I did not trust her. She had betrayed me once already. But your mother believed Morgause harmless, helpful, and thought it would be best to send you to a kinswoman for fostering rather than a stranger. Morgause had managed to convince your mother I would hurt you when I learned you were not the son I had hoped for. So, mere days after your birth, Morgause took you to Orkney."

"But if you did not trust your sister in your own fortress, sir, why did you allow your child—me—to go with her? Why did you not—"

"By the time I learned, it was too late."

"Too late?"

"Morgause sent word that you never arrived in Orkney. The messenger reported that your ship had wrecked in the turbulent waters of her harbour without survivors. How convenient that Morgause and her sons were on another vessel."

His fist pounded the tabletop.

The force of his anger thrust me against the back of my chair. Again, I saw the familiarity of cold blue eyes staring me down, determined to quell me. But it was not the prince who sat across from me. This was my father. What was I to believe? Feel? Say?

"I shall never forgive Morgause this. Her quarrel is with me. That she would even think to bring an innocent into it is reprehensible. Her treatment of you is far, far worse even than that first wound she dealt me."

"How did she betray you, sir? Everyone in Dunn na Carraice knew how much she hated you. No one knew why. The compound was divided—those who shared the Queen's opinion and those who saw you as Britain's saviour against the Saxon horde."

"Indeed? I could not even keep my own daughter safe from harm by her own kin."

"What did cause the quarrel, sir?"

"I suppose you should know, Lin. I made the mistake of hiding the truth from your mother for too long, because I believed it was something I had to bear alone. It would have saved you, I think. Nothing I say now will change the past for you, I know, but it might help you understand.

"When I first became Pendragon, I did not know who my true parents were. I knew that Ector was not my father. He never hid that truth from me. Yet he treated me as well as he did Cai, his own son. I will always consider Cai my brother. But many of Britain's chieftains did not like the idea of a boy of questionable birth ruling over them. My earliest days on the throne were spent fighting civil insurgencies, not Saxons."

"The world knows that, sir."

If I had angered him by the interruption, the King did not show it.

"One day, a woman arrived at court with her sons. I was headquartered at Caerleon then, Camelot was still but a dream of mine. I had not even met your mother yet. The woman's name was Morgause, the widow of King Lot of Orkney, foremost of the chieftains who had opposed my appointment as Pendragon. She wanted her eldest son, Gawain, to remain with me as a hostage in a gesture to restore peace. I was young, barely seventeen. I knew plenty about war, but decidedly little about women. Her proposal was wise and I accepted. I also thought she was the most handsome woman I had ever seen and was flattered when she came to my chamber, and my bed, late in the night. It was not until after the damage was done, that I learned her mother was also mine and we had committed the unpardonable sin of incest."

I looked up in that moment and saw the deep suffering in his beautiful eyes. Incest. What a dreadful burden to bear and for so many years. I wished I had not asked.

"Imagine my horror when I learned the truth. And that she had known our relationship all along. Had mocked it. Imagine my horror when I learned she carried my child."

The eyes. *His* eyes.

Ice chilled my heart.

"Modred?" I whispered hoarsely, dreading the reply.

"Modred."

The room felt close and stifling of a sudden, darker and I found it hard to breathe. I gripped the table. Modred was my half-brother, not Dafydd. Modred the prince. Modred the—

A monster had not sired him after all.

"Lin?"

Tears smarted my eyes. "I can do better than imagine, sir." I struggled to keep my voice even. I would never forgive myself if I caved under to such blatant weakness now. "This is difficult."

The Pendragon waited with surprising forebearance.

I did not know at the time that his inner turmoil was as great as mine.

"He…The Prince…Modred…" I stammered, grasping for words. "My womb rejected his child mere days ago."

"Sweet *Jesu*. She wanted you for Modred."

I had been about to ask him if he thought Modred knew the truth of my identity. I had no need.

"Why? Why do they hate me, sir?"

"It is me she hates, not you. What Morgause did to you was to hurt me. I can well imagine her scheme to destroy you, short of murder, so that—"

"I would that they had killed me, sir. I wished it many times."

"No," he said. His smile softened the sharp lines from his anger. He reached across the table and took my hand in his. "I am glad they did not. I am glad that God saw fit to intervene and bring you home. Your mother will be overjoyed."

"Is the Queen… Is my mother in Ebrauc, sir?"

"No. Your mother remained at Camelot. Word will be sent to her to prepare for your arrival."

I drank some of my wine. Modred was not my only Orkney kinsman.

"What about the other princes of Orkney?"

"Gawain is here. Agravain should be on his return journey from Dunn na Carraice by now. Gaheris and Gareth are with your mother at Camelot. You will, of course, need to meet them eventually. But I see where we shall need to handle this with care. Earlier, you mentioned both Agravain and Modred abused you. I *must* know, Lin. Did Agravain rape you?"

I shook my head.

"Did the others *ever* touch you? Hurt you?"

Memories swirled in my head and I crossed my arms over my breast for self-protection.

"Nothing more than taunts, sir."

I noticed his fists were clenched once again.

"It is long past time I went to Orkney. I assure you, Morgause and Modred will pay dearly for their crimes against you."

And deny my own vengeance?

"I am pleased that you wish to avenge me, sir, but how will Gawain and the others react?"

The King studied me for several moments.

I could not allow myself to waver under his intense gaze. Even though my pulse quickened, I stared back.

At last, a small smile stretched his lips and he nodded.

"Well said. What would you have me do?"

"Me, sir?"

"You."

I touched my neck.

"Ever since Dafydd got his collar, when I understood the truth of slavery for the first time, I have wanted to be Lin, not a slave. Not an animal. I have that now and I am grateful. I shall always hold Sir Cai in high esteem."

My own smile grew as I thought of my father's question.

"Have Gawain return to Orkney, sir." Agravain would have been better for my plan, but… "Have Gawain demand payment of the penalty you impose for slavery."

"That paltry fine? A pittance compared to your suffering. I would do more."

"Have Gawain demand, in your name, that Modred free all of Dunn na Carraice's slaves. Demand that Modred remove all the collars."

The king laughed. "How apt," he said. "It shall be done just as you say." He poured out more wine for us and raised his goblet in toast. "To my daughter and her wisdom to divert civil war."

More selfish than wise. I sipped my wine.

"Camelot and Britain think you are dead, Lin. And Morgause no doubt believes that another slave has vanished into the world. We shall let them think that a while longer, until I decide how to announce your miraculous resurrection."

"Will you send Dafydd away, sir?"

"Certainly not."

"But if he is not my brother…" The words tasted bitter. "What of the court?"

"What of the court? I, too, have a foster brother. I am quite fond of him, enough to have appointed him my seneschal. We shall find a place for yours. You speak so highly of him, I look forward to getting to know the lad."

"And what of Tighan?"

"If she wishes, I shall see that she returns safely to her home. Or she can remain with you. You'll need a lady's maid after all. Naturally, the choice will be hers."

Choice? A maid? Me? It was as though he spoke of someone else.

"Lin, there is naught I can say or do that could remove the scars from your body or cancel the suffering you endured. I do not expect your forgiveness. I dare not ask it. But I am truly sorry for my part in your being sent to Orkney."

He rose.

"You need to recover from your shock. I'll leave you to your rest. We shall dine together, later. There's much we need to learn of each other. I want to hear everything. Cai will send for you."

"Sir? A last question?" He already had his hand on the door-latch.

"Yes, Lin?"

"What name was I given at my birth?"

"Helin. But I like Lin, as well."

He left, closing the door behind him.

I remained in the chair where the Pendragon… Where my father had left me, contemplating what I had just learned. My father. I had a father. And a mother. What was she like? What sort of mother would abandon her child at birth? Had she been so disappointed in my gender that she sent me away? To be rid of me? Why did she not just smother me then, as is often done to girl-children? She might as well have for what she sent me to.

Someone knocked on the chamber door. I lacked the strength to tell whoever it was to leave. The knock came again, more insistent. Perhaps he would give up and go away.

He did not. The door opened a moment later.

"Lin?" Dafydd's voice pierced the silence and my thoughts. "I was getting worried. We heard the Pendragon leave long ago."

He was not my brother. The thought kept stabbing my heart. The hurt was worse than from anything else the Pendragon had told me.

My father, he is my father.

And I had to tell Dafydd.

"You were with the Pendragon for quite some time." He crossed the room to stand near my chair.

"There was much to discuss, Dafydd."

"And you did most of it, no doubt," he teased. His face sobered when I looked up at him. "You have been weeping."

I had not realised it. I wiped my eyes with my hands.

"What *did* he say to you, Lin?"

"I do not know how to tell you this, Dafydd."

"Tell me what?"

Slowly, unable to meet Dafydd's gaze, I related what I had just learned.

Before all the words were out, Dafydd was on his knees before me.

"Your Highness," he said.

I froze at the homage.

"No," I cried. "Dafydd, please. Please, not this. I cannot bear to see you so." I got to my knees with him, tried to raise him, but he moved back slightly, but ever so noticeably, from my touch.

"But I must. You are the Pendragon's daughter. You are a princess. I always knew you were different. Special. I am only Dafydd mac *cumal*. Only Dafydd, the slave-girl's son."

What had happened? Was there no end to the assault on my heart? More than ever, I needed Dafydd. Only now a sea of rank divided us.

CHAPTER 32

"He is my grandfather," Bear said. Late afternoon shadows hid my son's face. He sat unusually still, had remained so throughout much of my discourse.

"Yes."

I sank back against the armoury's wall, exhausted. I had talked long and revealed more than I had intended. I would have preferred to have left most of those memories buried. But now that they were released, they could never be reinterred. And with the release, mixed with the exhaustion, I also gained a peace such as I had never known. I felt cleansed, as though I'd taken a refreshing plunge into the River Thamesis.

"Is that why you wear this, Mother?"

Bear laid his fingers on the silver wristband. They traced over the graceful, and intricate interlace pattern, of the sort that made British and Irish craftsmen famous throughout the world, which had been etched into the metal and then enamelled with bright colours. My father had commissioned his own silversmith to do the work. My father had wanted the bangle wrought of gold. I had insisted upon the silver, for I was unaccustomed to such finery at the time. I never regretted the choice. The bracelet had never once been removed since the day my father's own hands had placed it on my wrist. It was one of the few remaining possessions I had kept of my life as a princess, as an *eques*. A last remnant of Camelot.

My son had aged in the hours since we had entered Camelot

together. Whatever Bear thought or felt about the violence of my childhood, or being the Pendragon's grandson, he showed none of it at the moment.

"Yes," I answered at last.

I was grateful for the wineskin Dafydd had brought earlier. I took a long quaff and the wine's warmth spread through my body. I leaned back once more, relaxing my hold on the wineskin in my lap.

Bear took it up without a by-your-leave, and raised it to his lips. It was his first taste of wine. I did not gainsay his action. He drank as deeply as I had and did not grimace at the sweet-sour taste as I thought he might. When he finished, he wiped his mouth on his sleeve, then set the wineskin aside.

"I remember when we were in Aquae Sulis a few years ago, a thief tried to take that silver band from you. He had you against a wall, with a knife at your wrist. You killed him with your dagger before he had the chance to make so much as a nick. Before I had time to call for help."

"It is very dear to me, Bear, and I shall not be parted from it. And not simply for what it covers."

"Special enough to kill a man?"

"That man was prepared to kill your mother for the price of the metal. There was no time for you to call for help. I had to defend myself or die."

"You knew what you were doing when you sank your dagger into his gut. You knew where to place it for a swift kill. You did not act like a distressed mother slashing out in panicked self-defence. You did not learn that in Dunn na Carraice, did you?"

"No."

"You said you were not ashamed of your past. Why the secrecy? Why did you keep the truth of your parents from me and the girls?"

"The secrecy was never from shame, Bear. When I decided to go into exile, I had to give up everything of the life I'd had here. To protect us from the warlords scrambling for the crown, I had to keep silent. They could ill-afford to allow the rightful heir to remain at large. I had to hide, throw away my birthright. I could not tell you. Although I have wanted to for a long time."

Wfft, what had I done?

My calm vanished as the spectre of Modred's body on the battlefield materialised in my mind. Even in death, he had managed to haunt my life and nightmares. Mocking me as ever he did in life. But this time, a revelation shoved itself to the fore of my awareness at the same time. A truth of myself darker than the memories just related. Why had I not seen it twelve years ago? Dafydd had. Why had I been so blind?

"What is that, Mother?"

"Hmm?" I glanced at my son.

"You have been fingering it for quite some time." Bear indicated the gold in my hand. I hadn't been aware of pulling my father's ring from its hiding place. "Is it some sort of ring?"

"It is the Seal of Camelot. My father wanted me to succeed him as Pendragon." With the cord remaining around my neck, I held the ring out for my son to inspect.

My father had believed in my capabilities. The best judge of people I had ever known and I had failed to even try to live up to them. I did not deserve the ring.

Bear held it a moment, then said, "But you did not. Why?"

I felt as though my son saw my innermost thoughts.

"I was too busy wallowing in self-pity."

"You ran from duty?"

The truth can be keen as a sword at times. Especially coming from one so young. But the past twelve years made sense to me now. The nightmares. The urge to return to Camelot. The need to tell Bear about my years of slavery, fighting Modred every moment, before revealing the truth of my father. For twelve years, I had been fighting a ghost and my own mind.

"I saw it as hopeless. The whole battle of Camlann was hopeless and senseless to begin with. Everything Father had worked for was destroyed on that battlefield. Many of his allies refused to even lend us aid against Modred and his army, partly because they did not want to support a woman. The same sort of hard-headed nonsense Father faced in his early days on the throne.

"I had gained the acceptance of the Round Table and that strength behind me would have helped my cause as Pendragon. With that support, accepting my duty would have been easy and quite natural. But the Table was destroyed. At the end of Camlann, only five *equites* still lived. Your father. Dafydd. Bedwyr. Lancelot. And me. The brotherhood of the Round Table was the only hope Britain had of unity, and it was no more. I faced having to start where my father had. With nothing. An impossible challenge for a woman."

"You call Father 'Ris.'"

Time for the other half of the truth.

"Yes."

"Prince Gaheris?"

"Aye."

"I thought you hated them."

There was so much more for me to tell my son. So much more healing I had to do.

"After I met him at Camelot, we became friends. He and his brothers, Gawain and Gareth. Agravain was too far gone under the influence of Modred and their mother. From Gareth especially, I learned not to hate."

Ris would have to know now, of course. I could no longer keep my secret from him.

"Modred caused the Round Table to break and brought about Camlann, didn't he?"

"Things are never as simple as Dafydd's stories, Bear."

"What caused it then?"

"That is a story for another day."

Bear stretched his arms over his head, then stood. His boot heel smudged the map I had drawn in the dust earlier, obliterating Orkney.

"Where were you during the battle of Camlann? Here?"

"In the right flank, between your father and Dafydd."

"A warrior?"

"*Eques*."

"Oh." He sat down beside me once more.

"I shall tell you more of that another day, as well. It goes with the rest."

I stared at my father's ring for several minutes, feeling the weight of the gold and the responsibility that accompanied it. I offered a silent apology to my father's spirit.

"Bear, you asked the reasons for my actions after Camlann. The simple truth is, I failed. I was so consumed by self-pity and self-doubt, I let Modred win. After everything I had survived by him, I allowed Modred to defeat me at Camlann. At his death. He had presented me with the greatest challenge of my life, and by my refusing to accept it, he won. The son of a bitch got the best of me. And I let him." I beat my breast with my fist. "No wonder he has been laughing at me from Hell ever since."

It was not easy confessing such utter failure. But through the admission, I now had the answers I had been searching for by coming to Camelot. I knew what I had to do. I knew why I had returned. I looked forward to a peaceful night's sleep. I doubted my other brother's ghost would ever haunt me again.

"Come, Bear. We have been closeted for too long. Time we headed back to camp. You must be famished."

I began to rise, but Bear threw his arms around me and hugged me fiercely. My little "Bear Cub". I kissed the top of his head and returned his hug. When he looked up, his eyes were red-rimmed.

"What is this, Bear?" I wiped a tear from his cheek.

He sniffed and dragged a hand under his nose. After a few gulps of air, he sat up to his full height. "I am honoured you told me all those terrible things that happened to you and Uncle. But you won. I am especially glad of that."

"What do you mean, Bear?"

"You are my mother, Lin *ferch* Arthur, not a slave. And Prince Modred is dead and cannot hurt you ever again."

I smiled at my young son's wisdom. A child saw what I had not.

"Aye, I did win." I tousled my son's hair. "I have you and your sisters." The true heirs of the House of Pendragon. My children were my father's legacy, not a gold ring.

"I am proud to be your son and the Pendragon's grandson."

"You look very much like him, Bear."

"I do?" Bear grinned, puffing his chest. "Will you tell me more of him?"

"That is a promise."

We left the armoury side by side.

Bear's sisters attacked us with questions as soon as we emerged. I was surprised neither Ris nor Dafydd had returned with them to our camp. None of us had planned on staying quite so long.

My husband and brother joined us at a slower pace than the girls. I slipped an arm around Ris' waist, needing and wanting his strength and support.

He cast a questioning eye at my rare show of affection.

It made me hold him closer. I wanted things to be different for us.

After a moment's hesitation, he returned my embrace, wrapping his arms around me.

I revelled in his comfort.

"Bear knows that my father was Pendragon before me," I said aloud as announcement to our daughters.

Melora regarded me, holding her sister's hand.

"King Arthur was your father?" she said.

"You are the princess from Uncle's stories," Gernie said.

"Yes, my girls. And Camelot is our rightful home." I took my walking stick from my true brother.

"You named me for Grandfather, didn't you?" Bear said.

"Indeed," Ris answered our son.

"I should like to be called Arthur now, rather than Bear."

My heart swelled near to bursting.

"Of course, Arthur," I said, the first to comply with his request. "Shall we head back to camp? 'Tis past time for supper."

"Where will we go next, Mother," Arthur asked.

"Nowhere," I said. "We stay."

Ris and Dafydd stopped short.

"I, for one, am tired of roaming aimlessly about the country-side."

"My God. What *did* you tell Bear in there?" Ris said. Our habit of young Arthur's pet-name would be difficult to give up.

"The truth," I answered. "You were right, Dafydd, after Camlann. I had tossed away my identity. The one thing Modred wanted to strip from me. But if I had returned then, there most likely would have been another battle. Fresh after Camlann. I thought to spare Britain from more civil strife."

"There will be a battle now. And you with no army. Have you gone mad, wife? I said I'd follow you, but this?"

Our son was undeniably proud and pleased with my decision. Dafydd, I could not tell. We were going to be awake long into the night discussing this.

"I did not have an army then either, Ris. And even less heart to lead the fragment I had. There is much I must atone. That is the reason I am here. This should have been done twelve years ago, yes. But had I taken that path, I doubt that I would have had the children. They are much more important than this seal." I had left it outside my tunic. I held it aloft. "But now it is time for me to reclaim what I gave up."

At the gates, I let the others pass through before I turned to close them. I gave a different, more personal salute this time. I touched my fingers to the spot on my wristband just over my brand, then spread my arms out, palms open, announcing:

"Father. I have come home."

DEBRA A. KEMP

Ever since seeing the movie *Camelot* in the mid-70s, Debra A. Kemp has wanted to write her own version of the Arthurian legends. She could hardly disobey when King Arthur himself commanded: "Don't let it be forgot…" The idea of her main character was conceived that very night. She just wishes she could remember the specific date of that important moment in her life. But what started as an innocent evening at the cinema turned into Debra's obsession. She read everything she could find on the topic, slowly building her now-extensive Arthurian library and quirky collection of artwork, movies, toys and figurines.

Before Debra took up her fountain pen to write, however, she earned a nursing degree from Indiana University, married and raised two children. Originally from Highland, Indiana, Debra's husband's career in the United States Air Force sent the family to Louisiana, England, Michigan's Upper Peninsula, and finally the Black Hills of South Dakota. While in England, Debra felt a special connection with the land and especially a few of the sites that play key roles in her novels and stories. She would dearly love to return to England someday, perhaps to stay.

The nursing career long abandoned; Debra now balances her writing around her part-time hours at a local secondhand bookstore. There is no better job in the universe. She is also active in the Black Hills Writers Group and various critique groups. Debra's work has earned a variety of writing awards and has appeared in such literary journals as *Samsara*, *Mythic Circles*, and *Lost Worlds*. Earlier this year her short story, "A Passing Fair Lady" placed in the top ten of the Preditors and Editors reader's Poll. A sample of her second novel, currently in progress, can be read at bardsongpress.com.

Although no longer living in Northwest Indiana's Calumet Region, Debra is still a die-hard Cubs fan and will always enjoy an Indiana University Hoosiers basketball game when she can catch one on television.

As excited as Debra truly is about seeing her lifelong dream finally becoming reality with the publication *The House Of Pendragon, Book I: The Firebrand*, nothing will ever top the birth of her first grandchild, Victoria, in March of 2003. Her own children might be grown and married, but they are still very much a part of Debra's life—her personal cheering section.